IF I WERE BOSS

IF I WERE BOSS

The Early Business Stories of Sinclair Lewis

Edited and with an Introduction
by
Anthony Di Renzo

Southern Illinois University Press
Carbondale

Library of Congress Cataloging-in-Publication Data

Lewis, Sinclair, 1885–1951.
    If I were boss : the early business stories of Sinclair Lewis /
edited and with an introduction by Anthony Di Renzo.
        p.   cm.
    Includes bibliographical references.
        1. United States—Social life and customs—20th century—
Fiction. 2. Business enterprises—United States—Employees—
Fiction. 3. Businessmen—United States—Fiction. I. Di Renzo,
Anthony, 1960–   II. Title.
    PS3523.E94A6   1997
    813'.52—dc21   96-52565
    ISBN 0-8093-2138-6 (cloth : alk. paper).   CIP
    — ISBN 0-8093-2139-4 (paper : alk. paper)

The paper used in this publication meets the minimum requirements
of American National Standard for Information Sciences—Perma-
nence of Paper for Printed Library Materials, ANSI Z39.48-1984. ∞

To
ERIC GLOCKNER
Traveling Man

What is a salesman?

He's a lot of things, Billy. He's a front-office buck private . . . a general in the field.

He's a fellow that feeds a thousand stomachs every day in the year— stomachs that belong to those who make and distribute the things he sells. But he seldom finds time to feed his own face at home with Mom and the kids. . . . Whether it be chewing gum or tractors, he sells—sells those things that make Americans American.

Quotas to him are sales-convention handicaps that make the game fun. Others may work a forty-hour week. But the salesman kicks because there are not more hours in every day. He's the fellow that does while others don't. And he loves it! Let's hope he keeps on—for the sake of the life we enjoy in the U.S.A.!

—*George Horace Lorimer,* The Saturday Evening Post,
responding to a letter from a ten-year-old boy

[George and the boys] went profoundly into the science of business, and indicated that the purpose of manufacturing a plow or a brick was so that it might be sold. To them, the Romantic Hero was no longer the wandering poet, the cowpuncher, the aviator, nor the brave young district attorney, but the great sales manager, who had an Analysis of Merchandising Problems on his glass-topped desk, whose title of nobility was "Go-getter," and who devoted himself and his young samurai to the cosmic purpose of Selling—not of selling anything in particular, for or to anybody in particular, but pure selling.

—*Sinclair Lewis,* Babbitt

CONTENTS

PREFACE

Expecting Sinclair Lewis to conform to the rules of conventional grammar is like expecting brokers in a bull market to conform to the rules of etiquette. As Louis N. Fiepel, a Brooklyn pedant, discovered when he proofread the first edition of *Babbitt,* Lewis's "mistakes" are almost always intentional. They reflect his love for puns, dialect humor, and advertising slogans. Accordingly, I have left untouched Paul Manning's showroom malapropisms, Ray Moller's slight German accent, and William John Buckingham's drunken boosterese. However, I have updated and standardized Lewis's sometimes heterodox spelling and have punctuated for clarity without impeding the rhythm of Lewis's staccato prose. Otherwise these stories appear as they did in the popular magazines of Lewis's time, with all necessary corrections made—whenever possible—from Lewis's original manuscripts.

The fifteen stories in this collection were published between October 1915 and May 1921. For thematic reasons, I have reversed the order of the first two stories. Here, however, is an actual chronology:

"Nature, Inc." *Saturday Evening Post* 2 Oct. 1915.

"Commutation: $9.17." *Saturday Evening Post* 30 Oct. 1915.

"If I Were Boss." *Saturday Evening Post* 1 and 8 Jan. 1916.

"Honestly—If Possible." *Saturday Evening Post* 14 Oct. 1916.

"A Story with a Happy Ending." *Saturday Evening Post* 17 Mar. 1917.

"The Whisperer." *Saturday Evening Post* 11 Aug. 1917.

"Snappy Display." *Metropolitan Magazine* Aug. 1917.

"Slip It to 'Em." *Metropolitan Magazine* Mar. 1918.

"Getting His Bit." *Metropolitan Magazine* Sept. 1918.

"Jazz." *Metropolitan Magazine* Oct. 1918.

"Bronze Bars." *Saturday Evening Post* 13 Dec. 1919.

"Way I See It." *Saturday Evening Post* 29 May 1920.
"The Good Sport." *Saturday Evening Post* 11 Dec. 1920.
"A Matter of Business." *Harper's Magazine* Mar. 1921.
"Number Seven to Sagapoose." *American Magazine* May 1921.

I wish to thank the Beinecke Rare Book and Manuscript Library at Yale University and the George Arents Research Library at Syracuse University, for access to Sinclair Lewis's manuscripts; Paul Gitlin and the Lewis estate, for copyright permission; Dr. Thornton Parsons, for his mentoring and guidance; John Crowley, Sally Daniels, and Frederica Kaven, for their laughter and input; Carol Burns, Connie Fritsche, Tracey Sobol, and Southern Illinois University Press, for their enthusiasm and support; and my professional writing students at Ithaca College, both past and present, whose love for Lewis inspired this collection.

INTRODUCTION

Critic William Rose Benét recalls an important dinner with Sinclair Lewis in September 1915. After a grueling day at the office, he and Lewis had stopped at a midtown bistro before catching their train back to Port Washington, Long Island. Next-door neighbors, the two men had known each other since their more idealistic days at Yale and the Carmel Writers' Colony. As usual, Benét was spellbound by his colleague's outrageous anecdotes about New York publishing. Physically and temperamentally, Lewis resembled Loki, the Norse god of fire and deceit. A gangly, popeyed chain-smoker, nicknamed "Red" because of his flaming hair and radical politics, Lewis was all flash and sarcasm and manic equivocation. This renegade provincial from Sauk Centre, Minnesota, had transformed himself into a city slicker with a taste (if not an income) for House of Kuppenheimer business suits, and his wildly improvisational speeches about literature and salesmanship were a cross between a Pullman smoker monologue and the immolation scene from Wagner's *Götterdämmerung*.

But Lewis was more than a blowhard. His background in journalism, advertising, and public relations, his uncanny grasp of demographics, popular trends, and the mass media made him the shrewdest marketer at the George H. Doran Company. Nevertheless, he still smoldered with dissatisfaction. Burning to be a writer, he had published two Horatio Algeresque novels, *Our Mr. Wrenn: The Romantic Adventures of a Gentle Man* (1914) and, just recently, *The Trail of the Hawk: A Comedy of the Seriousness of Life* (1915)—the latter written during his commutes to and from Long Island. Though politely reviewed, these books had not been successful, and Lewis, who had turned thirty in February, hungered for fame and fortune.

As Lewis attacked his roast beef, a nattily dressed stranger, a traveling salesman with an over-eager smile, approached the table and introduced himself. Deliberately wedging himself between Lewis and Benét, he ordered a meal and began hawking his wares. Benét resented this intrusion, but Lewis seemed delighted and plunged into conversation with their new dinner companion. "Before he knew it," Benét reports, "the [sales]man was revealing all his characteristic ways of thinking and emoting, as well as giving us a good slice of life" (422). After exchanging business cards and shaking hands with the man, Lewis turned to Benét with a quizzical smile. Benét was flabbergasted. How could Lewis waste his time on, risk missing their train because of, such an obnoxious, shabby character? "That's the problem with you, Bill," Lewis replied. "You regard him as a hoi polloi. He doesn't even represent the cause of labor or anything dramatic. But I understand that man. By God, I love him!"

Seven years later, Lewis would more fully express his peculiar affection for the American salesman in *Babbitt* (1922), which celebrates its diamond (or is it zirconia?) jubilee in September 1997. Nevertheless, Lewis's chance encounter in the restaurant seems like a significant turning point in his creative life, the moment when he may have first discovered his material and identified his audience. Soon Lewis would find his stride and develop his style as a satirist, creating "the sharpest parodies of the lush, rococo, euphemistic sales-talk of American business life that we have" (Cantwell 111). However, although he would produce three more apprentice novels about the American Dream, *The Job: An American Novel* (1917), *The Innocents* (1917), and *Free Air* (1919), before his literary breakthrough in *Main Street* (1920), Lewis actually established his reputation as a writer in short fiction.

Beginning with "Nature, Inc." (1915), which deals with a crooked realtor and a fraudulent professor bilking the gullible at a Transcendentalist commune, Lewis published—between October 1915 and May 1921—over sixty short stories. These were mostly written for and about "the tired business man" and appeared in such popular slicks as the *Saturday Evening Post* and *American Magazine,* the periodicals we find in George and Myra Babbitt's living room (Dooley 17). Thanks to George Horace Lorimer, the influential editor of the *Post,* business fiction was in great demand in the magazine market of the teens and twenties, and Lewis specialized in this genre for practical as well as artistic reasons. As Clara Lee R. Moodie has shown, Lewis's success with these early stories not only enabled him to court a wide popular audience, something not possible with his early novels, "but also permitted him to explore various areas of American [commercial] life and to establish his attitudes toward them" (203). Even Mark Schorer, Lewis's biographer, who dismisses most of his apprentice work as trash, grudgingly admits the importance of his early business fiction:

> Here Lewis investigates the world of George F. Babbitt and Elmer Gantry, the world of high-pressure salesmanship, and he exploits his knowledge of New Thought, Chautauqua, quack religion, the dressmaking business, the automobile industry, patent medicine, trade publications, poetry for businessmen—the whole world of boosting and commercial razzmatazz and the fast buck, all presented in a raucous tone of satiric exposure. (239)

Despite their significance, however, these stories have been virtually ignored for the past eighty years. Previous collections of Lewis's short fiction, *Selected Short Stories of Sinclair Lewis* (1935, republished 1990) and *I'm a Stranger Here Myself* (1962), have focused respectively on the range and regionalism of Lewis's humor. Recent critical studies, however, have renewed interest in Lewis's early business satires. Christopher P. Wilson's *White Collar Fictions: Class and Social Representation in American Literature, 1885–1925* (1992) claims that Lewis's business stories articulate the anxiety and duplicity surrounding middle-class professionalism and argues that Lewis's own experience as a copywriter and publicist gives his fiction a special insight into modern capitalist culture. In fact, his early satire is the first anemometer measuring "the cold wind of absurdity blowing off the waste lands of our American commercial chaos" (Rorty 8). English business historian Anthony Sampson in *Company Man: The Rise and Fall of Corporate Life* (1995) calls Lewis one of the twentieth century's earliest and most perceptive critics of the alienating effects of white collar labor. Over the past five years, Lewis has re-emerged as America's premier satirist of the modern office, and such Lewis scholars as

Martin Bucco and James M. Hutchisson have called for a whole-sale reassessment of his early work. This collection hopes to satisfy this long neglected need.

If I Were Boss features fifteen of Lewis's funniest and most poignant early business stories. None of these have appeared in print since their original publication. Entertaining in its own right, this fiction provides us with a better understanding of the background of *Babbitt* and of American commercialism in the age of vaudeville and ragtime. For all their quaintness and formulaic crudities, their props and dialogue from a bygone era, these stories remain surprisingly fresh and contemporary—partly because the office is still a purgatorial sideshow; partly because Americans, even in this age of Dilbert and downsizing, maintain a dysfunctional romance with the values of big business.

Like *Babbitt,* Lewis's early satire graphically depicts the seductive power of the American sales pitch, its poetry, pervasiveness, and perversity, and it traces the madness of the American workplace—the paranoiac class anxiety of office managers like Whittier J. Small in "Commutation: $9.17" (1915); the face-saving double-think of sales representatives like Charley McClure in "If I Were Boss" (1916); the self-destructive chauvinism of corporate executives like Leonard Price in "A Story with a Happy Ending" (1917); the sexual infantilism of car dealers like Paul Banning in "The Good Sport" (1920), the sheer megalomania of advertising men like Lancelot Todd—back to a regimen of perpetual, self-defeating salesmanship.

The sociological insights in these stories anticipate C. Wright Mills's classic study, *White Collar* (1951). For Mills, the very nature of office work—its masochistic "service" component, its emphasis on personality and persuasion, its precarious negotiations between upper management and workers, institutions and the public—turns ordinary people into Dale Carnegies. Likewise, Lewis's white collar types—his clerks and secretaries, car salesmen and realtors, copywriters and novelty proprietors—can never escape the values and language of the salesroom, not even when, like Terry Ames and Miss Bratt in "Honestly—If Possible" (1916) or Leonard Price and Mrs. Arroford in "A Story with a Happy Ending," they try making love in their own homes. "Essentially" salespeople, these middle-class characters are compelled to develop "a salesman's style" in their private lives (Fussell 37). They devour self-help books, dress for success, and "talk a language of brand names" (Lundquist 12). Their naive faith in the American system, notes Christopher P. Wilson, is exploited by the cultural institutions created and sustained by their class: corporations and bureaucracies; banks and pharmaceuticals; automobile, advertising, and real estate agencies.

Before he drew his first map of Zenith, Lewis—like a realtor studying zoning patterns for a new housing development or an advertiser targeting a new test market—already had mapped out a terrain then unique in American letters. The landscape of his early fiction is less a concrete place, however, than a rhetorical topos, the emerging discourse of what James B. Twitchell calls Adcult, the "jabberwocky" of the American Dream (Rorty 71). The mass-produced dialect of Madison Avenue, not the homegrown dialect of the Midwest, is Lewis's true métier. Although such talented predecessors as W. D. Howells, Harold Frederic, Frank Norris, and Theodore Dreiser had also written about the marketplace, Lewis was the first American novelist to reproduce and adapt the forms and language of business and advertising for social and artistic purposes. Moreover, his personal obsession with American enterprise, his professional background in advertising and public relations, made him uniquely qualified to attack the absurdities of American capitalism. Like Professor Harold Hill, Lewis knew the territory, and *If I Were Boss* traces his complicated feelings about American business as he moves from bemused admiration to savage indignation to nostalgic regret. From whistle-stop to whistle-stop, these stories mine the collective hallucinations of the working middle class and form an archaeology of American salesmanship.

Sinclair Lewis was "born" to write *Babbitt,* said John O'Hara, because he himself "identified" with salesmen (qtd. in Schorer 351). As a lonely teenager, Lewis had worked as a night clerk at the Palmer House, a popular stop for traveling salesmen in Sauk Centre, and became intimately acquainted with their habits, manners, and speech patterns. After books, these drummers, as they were called, were the most important influence on his young imagination. Colorful, articulate, and relatively sophisticated, they broadened Lewis's horizons with their travelogues, satirical anecdotes, and sermons on progress and technology. In his novel about hotel-keeping, *Work of Art* (1934), Lewis later called these salesmen "pioneers in spats" (65). As Truman E. Moore states in *The Traveling Man: The True Story of the American Traveling Salesman* (1972), turn-of-the-century drummers paved the way for modern consumer culture, tempering the austerity of the hinterlands with modern conveniences and entertaining stories. Without them, Moore concludes, America as we know it would not exist. However, their day already was passing in Lewis's youth as corporatization, improved communications, and scientific training eliminated the need for free-spirited field agents. Lewis would dramatize this painful transition in such stories as "If I Were Boss," where Charley McClure solidifies his position as sales manager by defeating independent old timers like Little Thomas Snider.

Although Lewis himself never took to the road, the figure of the sharp-dressing, fast-talking hustler must have provided him with a way of rebelling against his stern and practical father, a successful country doctor. Moreover, as Tobin Simon has suggested, the salesman's Horatio Alger ethos goaded young Lewis to become a success. He began keeping a Gatsby-like notebook full of self-help maxims and entrepreneurial ideas, a habit he retained even after he became a famous novelist. Some of his proposed business ventures seem downright prophetic to us: plans to design and manufacture recreational vehicles, blueprints for theme-based hotel chains, a formula for mint-flavored toothpaste. Like William Wrenn, the clerkish hero of his first novel, Lewis came of age in the heyday of business colleges and Spencerian script, Sears Roebuck catalogs and Midwestern boosterism, Chautauqua lectures and YMCA pep talks. Hoosier Elbert Hubbard was touring the country, preaching the gospel of self-help and philistinism, and Michigan-born Claude C. Hopkins, star copywriter at Chicago's Lord & Thomas, was perfecting Reason Why advertising. Even though he later flirted with socialism and was influenced by H. G. Wells and Thorstein Veblen, Lewis, even as a mature satirist, remained something of a Progressive Era Republican.

"When I buy an Ingersoll watch or a Ford," declares attorney Seneca Doane, George Babbitt's liberal counterpart, "I get a better tool for less money, and I know precisely what I'm getting, and that leaves me more time and energy to be an individual in" (*Babbitt* 85). Doane's spirited defense of mass standardization reflects the side of Lewis that seriously argued that business should be the chief subject of twentieth-century American literature:

> Industrialism—more dramatic than the universities, more impressive and more terrible than an army with banners, a topic for Shakespeare and Zola combined, single organizations with 20,000 employees engaged in the most active and cunning war with a half a dozen like armies—who of our young people longing for Greenwich Village or Paris so that they may "find something to write about" has been able to, or has dared to attempt, this authentically epic theme? Is Waterloo a more gigantic spectacle than the Ford plant at River Rouge? Is the conquest of an Indian kingdom by an English proconsul more adventurous than the General Motors' invasion of the German motor world? He that hath eyes, let him see! (*Man from Main Street* 145)

As a young man, Lewis genuinely believed in the utopian vision of "Scientific Business," a capitalist efficiency "so broad that it can be kindly and sure" (Geismar 12). In fact, Lewis in his early twenties wrote inspirational office stories and essays on friendly service for Nautilus, a New Thought magazine whose beliefs he later mocked in "Nature, Inc." Even as his work became more critical of capitalism, part of Lewis still maintained that the modern office, for all its problems and absurdities, provided people with genuine opportunities. "If at times he suggests that there are other things in life besides the building of better mousetraps," says D. J. Dooley, "he has a businessman's affection for rugged enterprise and material progress" (55). This theme is central in such novels as *The Trail of the Hawk* and *The Job* but it also occurs in his early business stories, most of which are set in bustling midtown Manhattan. Like O. Henry and Edna Ferber, Lewis deliberately focuses on the little people, the aspiring white collar workers of a burgeoning service industry. Lewis knew that however much his middle-class readers might be interested in the fall and rebirth of a proud executive like Leonard Price, the prototype of Dodsworth in "A Story with a

Happy Ending," they were more likely to identify with the yearnings of a bank clerk like Valory in "Bronze Bars" (1919).

The positive dimension of Lewis's comedy celebrates perseverance, self-reliance, and transformation, and the typical Lewis character is either a provincial young man from the Midwest or Central New York (notice how Lewis cleverly uses geography to stress middle-class aspirations) or a genteel young woman abruptly thrown on her own resources. For both, office work becomes a crucible of positive change. Lewis's young men gain sophistication and subtlety. Lewis's young women—Susan Bratt in "Honestly—If Possible," Nancy Arroford in "A Story with a Happy Ending," and Emily Banning in "The Good Sport"—gain power and economic independence. All participate in what Lewis sincerely calls in *The Trail of the Hawk* "the Adventure of Business" (227). "How bully it is to be living," declares aviator-turned-salesman, Carl Ericson, "if you don't have to give up living in order to make a living" (408). Teddy Roosevelt, the namesake of Babbitt's son, Ted, could not have said it better.

This affirmative strain in Lewis's fiction perfectly suited the business milieu of the time and attracted the attention of the Great Cham of American popular fiction, George Horace Lorimer of *The Saturday Evening Post*. Nine of the fifteen stories in this collection first appeared in the *Post,* and with good reason. Beginning with its successful serializations of such classic business novels as Harold Frederic's *The Market-Place* (1899), Frank Norris's *The Octopus* (1900) and *The Pit* (1901), and Lorimer's own *Letters of a Self-Made Merchant to His Son* (1902), the *Post* single-handedly created the market for business fiction. Specifically tailored for the middle-class businessman, the magazine soon commanded a mass audience by stressing, in Lorimer's words, the "adventure" of American enterprise (qtd. in Halsey 26). As Jan Cohn demonstrates in *Creating America: George Horace Lorimer and the "Saturday Evening Post"* (1989), Lorimer articulated and shaped the entrepreneurial, middle-class values of Main Street America. In a sense, he was George F. Babbitt's other father:

> It is not too much to say, in fact, that Lorimer virtually created the idea of the businessman. By this term he did not mean "man of busi-

ness" or "man of affairs" in the nineteenth-century sense, but something a good deal more inclusive, embracing the established professions to include lawyers, doctors, and even clergymen, and reaching down to absorb drummers, clerks, and even men who raised chickens for sale in their own backyards. The term businessman was at once a great leveler, denying any European specter of classes, and a powerful incentive, for to be a businessman of even the most meager sort held out the promise of becoming a businessman who achieved great success. (Cohn 31)

"Every business day," Lorimer declared, "[is] full of comedy, tragedy, farce, romance—all the ingredients of successful fiction" (qtd. in Tebbel 28). *Post* fiction, however, served a powerful ideology. It masked "the contradiction between the old [nineteenth-century] values associated with production and the emerging new realities of consumption" by emphasizing "the shadowy middle ground of distribution" (Cohn 12). *Post* stories, therefore, particularly honored the salesman because he was the heroic "agent" of distribution (13). Lewis's business fiction suited perfectly Lorimer's aesthetic and ideological needs, and his go-getting sales reps and earnest office workers took their place beside Randolph Chester's eccentric broker, J. Rufus Wallingford; Montague Glass's cut-up retailers, Potash and Perlmutter; Ring Lardner's harried sportswriter, the Busher; and William Hazlett Upson's legendary tractor salesman, Alexander Butts. Lorimer appreciated Lewis's gift for blending satire, sentimentality, and straightforward business instruction in his fiction and promised to make his name "a byword" among *Post* readers (Moodie 203). He encouraged the young writer to submit frequently to the magazine and "paid magnificently" between $500 and $1,000 per story (Lewis, "Mr. Lorimer and Me" 81). Lewis, for his part, eagerly incorporated the conventions of *Post* fiction into his own business satires.

Lewis learned two important things from his *Post* apprenticeship. First, he fine-tuned his already formidable ear for popular speech by studying the works of his colleagues. The *Rashomon*-like "Way I See It" (1920), which successfully plays with different Midwestern dialects, including second-generation German American, is clearly modeled after Ring Lardner, right down to Lardner's trade-mark line, "You know me, Al." Second, Lewis experimented with form. *Post* humorists often included memos, sales letters, and re-ports to re-create the atmosphere of the office, sometimes narrating an entire story solely through business documents. As editor, Lorimer encouraged this practice because he wanted the magazine's fiction to blend with the editorials, business articles, and ads. Lewis needed only a hint. A former copywriter, he was a master of the business letter. His correspondence with his publisher, Alfred Harcourt, later published as *From Main Street to Stockholm: Letters of Sinclair Lewis, 1919–1930* (1952), is must reading for any professional writing class, and he frequently sent his wives and friends prank circulars from bogus companies and hotels. Taking his cue from Lorimer, Lewis stuffed his stories with inquiry letters, requisition orders, manual instructions, field trip reports, newsletters, and ads. Copywriter Terry Ames in "Honestly—If Possible" agonizes over every word as he attempts to write the perfect *Post* business letter.

Lorimer, amused by this moxie, responded by slyly using ad-vertising layout to highlight and comment on Lewis's humor. When the social-climbing Whittier J. Small gets his comeuppance in "Com-mutation: $9.17," a Stein-Bloch ad plays Greek chorus: "Style, like culture, abides most with those who are least frantic in their efforts to secure it, and least clamorous in their announcement that it has been attained" (32). Charley McClure's request for better commu-nication in the field in "If I Were Boss" is answered by an ad for "Backing Up Your Salesman," a free booklet from the Hampshire Paper Company about writing better prospect letters to and for sales representatives (39). Emily Banning's decision to remain a dental hygienist, over the objections of her sarcastic, garrulous hus-band, is supported by a toothy full-page ad for Pebeco Tooth Paste, which "counteracts Acid-Mouth" (99).

Contrariwise, Lewis used *Post* advertisements as material for his fiction. His eager beavers resemble the Pierce-Arrow Man, speak the language of self-help testimonials, and bear the names of prod-ucts and appliances, such as Packard, the realtor in "Nature, Inc.," who is named after a luxury sedan. Indeed, the biggest influence on Lewis's satire were automobile ads, which generated over 40 per-cent of the magazine's revenues. As Ashley Halsey comments, "the automotive industry and the *Post* prospered simultaneously as if geared together," and Lewis shrewdly responded by writing to this market (18). Three of the fifteen stories in this collection deal specifically with the auto industry. Motor-mouthed car salesmen like Paul Banning also appear as supporting characters in other stories. Lewis would perfect this ironic interplay between business forms, advertising, and satire in *Babbitt*. Babbitt not only spends most of his time composing sales letters and ads, but his very name is a multiple trademark, a brand of soap, frictionless bearing, and crankshaft.

Although Lorimer and Lewis seemed made for each other, they were bound to fall out. The autocratic Lorimer, speculates Tobin Simon, became a father figure to the incorrigible Lewis, a beloved tyrant whom he was compelled to overthrow; and Lewis's growing disillusionment with capitalism, his hatred of and resentment toward a system he helped sustain, further widened a yawning generation gap. "Shelley himself," declares William Rose Benét, "could never have been more deeply stirred by the injustices and tyrannies of the economic order, or disorder" (421). As a college student, Lewis had been exposed to radicalism during his stay at Helicon Hall, Upton Sinclair's retreat in Englewood, New Jersey, but the real source of his indignation was not *Das Kapital* but *Walden,* a copy of which he kept in his desk at work. His first glimpse of New York in 1903 was a Thoreauvian nightmare—faceless commuters leading lives of "quiet desperation" (111), browbeaten sales clerks "contracting" themselves into "nutshell[s] of civility" (110). Lewis later recalled:

> To me, they were out of [the] *Inferno* [illustrated] by Doré. In that smoky darkness, . . . pushed, elbowed, jammed by umbrellas, my suitcase banging my legs, I saw them as the charging army of Satan himself, their eyes hateful, their mouths distorted with fury, their skinny hands clutching at me. (*Man from Main Street* 56)

By the time Lewis began working in Manhattan, however, he had overcome his initial horror and had cultivated a cynical detachment. To his keen demographic eye, New York was less a monolithic metropolis than a consortium of competing villages; and for

all their supposed sophistication, midtown white collar workers—
restricting themselves to a familiar routine of apartment, office,
and half dozen restaurants—were as limited and provincial as the
Main Streeters back in Minnesota. The only difference was that
their hometown happened to be a firm or an agency. Lewis makes
further use of this insight in *Babbitt* when he describes the Reeves
Office Building as Babbitt's "village," but even in these early stories his city dwellers are "actually rustics," interested only in their
colleagues and their place of work (30). This imaginative empathy
allowed Lewis to enter a world

> whose noblest vista is composed of desks and typewriters, filing-cases
> and insurance calendars, telephones, and the bald heads of men who
> believe dreams to be idiotic, . . . whose crises you cannot fathom
> unless you have learned that the difference between a 2–A pencil and
> a 2–B pencil is at least equal to the contrast between London and
> Tibet. (*The Job* 42)

As Lewis knew, however, such dreariness served a sinister purpose—the imperialistic expansion of a capitalist economy at the
dawn of the American century. "[This] vast, competent, largely
useless cosmos of offices," he states in *The Job*,

> . . . spends much energy in causing advertisements of beer and chew-
> ing-gum and union suits and pot-cleansers to spread over the whole
> landscape. It marches out ponderous battalions to sell a brass pin.
> . . . It turns noble valleys into fields for pickles. It compels men whom
> it has never seen to toil in distant factories and produce wares, which
> are never actually brought into the office, but which it nevertheless
> sells to the heathens in the Solomon Islands in exchange for com-
> modities whose very names it does not know; and in order to per-
> form this miracle of transmutation it keeps stenographers so busy
> that they change from dewy girls into tight-lipped spinsters before
> they discover life. (43)

Lewis addressed these political issues in his short fiction. "Many
of his stories for the *Saturday Evening Post*," says James M. Hutchisson, "contain subversive subtexts; when read in opposition to

the surface narrative, they invert its social attitudes and parody its stereotypes" (ix). Christopher P. Wilson argues in *White Collar Fiction* that even Lewis's milder, more affirmative office comedies are actually cautionary tales with disturbing social implications. In a sense, says Hutchisson, "Lewis was practicing a type of covert satire that resembles the low-key career that Melville undertook in the 1850's when he published his remarkable tales in *Putnam's* and other 'family' magazines" (ix). Lewis never wrote anything as profound as "Bartleby the Scrivener," but he was deeply concerned about the impact of business writing on the psyche of the nation, and his mordant ironies and trick endings have a way of puncturing middle-class complacency.

Lewis's business stories uncovered the ideological contradictions that most *Post* fiction sought to conceal. Humbled when the Long Island Railroad revokes his discount commuter rate, Whittier J. Small becomes a better boss in "Commutation: $9.17"; but despite this Lorimeresque endorsement of "shrewder personnel management," the story's real "commutation" has been Small's hairbreadth escape from social ostracism and imprisonment (Wilson 232). Bill Packard's decision to start his own commune at the conclusion of "Nature, Inc." can be read as a conman's pathetic attempt to con himself. Charley McClure's final epiphany in "If I Were Boss," his mystical participation in a sacramental business efficiency that is making America stronger, is compromised by the fact that he has wasted his life selling stupid novelty games like Golluf and is on the verge of losing his job to a younger man. At the end of "Honestly—if Possible," Terry and Sue's shared resolve to live more authentically is predicated on their telling better lies at the office, while the fairy-tale marriage between Leonard Price and Nancy Arroford only accentuates the Dreiserian gender reversals that have undermined "A Story with a Happy Ending." Even Paul Banning's more convincing conversion to domesticity and good sense in "The Good Sport" cannot detract from the story's disturbing message that home is an extension of the salesroom, that a marriage vow is only a smooth line closing a deal.

Inevitably, Lewis's satire became more blatant and aggressive. "The Whisperer" (1917) openly attacks the pharmaceutical industry, a subject to which he would return with a vengeance in

Arrowsmith (1925). Dr. Chester Doremus, whose Napoleonic ambition to become the next Lydia Pinkham leads him to seize control of the Bowen Drug Company, prides himself on scientific marketing and modern advertising, but he is no better than a nineteenth-century medicine man. Although Doremus is ultimately foiled, he ruins the lives of a half dozen *Post*-style business men and completely wrecks the company. Lorimer, whose advertisers included Freezone Corn Remover and Mum Deodorant, had qualms about the story and asked Lewis to revise the ending. Lewis sardonically complied. When the rival Vanvick Pharmaceutical Company buys out Bowen, most of Doremus's victims are rehired and the doctor himself is blackballed from the industry. However, Lewis more than hints that Vanvick has used Doremus as a patsy in industrial sabotage.

Lewis's fiction has turned a corner. The office is no longer a harmless joke.

Lewis's increased hostility toward capitalism was both personal and political. His years hacking at Doran had begun to take their toll (like Carl Ericson, Lewis compared himself to a hawk trapped in a cage), and the outbreak of World War I had brought out the worst in American business. As America beefed up production to make the world safe for J. P. Morgan and Standard Oil, the workplace virtually became a recruitment office. Martyring oneself to the clock, meeting impossible deadlines, and breaking sales records were now a patriotic duty. As Wall Street profited from mutilation and murder and advertising became little more than state-sponsored propaganda, corporations created a shadow economy that implicated the middle-class readers of the *Saturday Evening Post*. Lewis knew it was time to take off the gloves, but where would he find a forum for this kind of bare-knuckled satire?

During the war, Lewis published a series of seven remarkable stories about Lancelot Todd, a maniacal advertising man, in *Metropolitan*. (An eighth story, "Gladvertising" (1918), appeared in *Popular Magazine*.) Sophisticated and irreverent, *Metropolitan* targeted the urban smart set and displayed a Menckenian contempt for the entrepreneurial, middle-class values of the *Post*. Lewis had gone over to the enemy, who relished his jugular humor and wicked caricature. The four Lancelot Todd stories in this collection, "Snappy Display" (1917), "Slip It to 'Em" (1918), "Getting His Bit" (1918), and "Jazz" (1918), show Lewis perfecting that cacophonous, free-wheeling style that makes *Babbitt* so delightful to read. They also reveal Lewis's intimate understanding of copywriting and, sometimes to an appalling degree, his own guilt and self-hatred about having worked as a publicist. Together they form a miniature *Dunciad* of early twentieth-century American advertising.

Lancelot Todd, whose name symbolizes both "the romantic excess" and death-dealing power of American commercialism, is not a human being but a mythical figure, the copywriter's copywriter (Wilson 239). Lecturer, consultant, and racketeer, Lancelot has a national reputation, and his colossal swindles—using a suffragist organization to infiltrate New York high society, designing and marketing a fake Italian sports car, posing as a war correspondent to distribute the Khaki Komfort Trench Bench on the black market, exploiting the faith of millions of grocery clerks to publish America's most successful house organ—have an epic grandeur. Like Colly Cibber, the antihero of Pope's *Dunciad,* Todd is the Poet Laureate of Dullness. At his word, billboards sprout like redwood forests, soda fountains spurt a Niagara of Coke, and locust clouds of flyers invade the Wheat Belt. Lancelot plunders Byzantium to sell Raw Gold Perfume, subjugates India to promote Orinoco Tires, and butchers plains of Texas longhorns for Fairy Tale Leather Belting. Constance Rourke rightly called Lewis a modern "fabulist" (30), but his best satire is less concerned with the tall tales of the Midwest than with the "fables of abundance" of American advertising (Lears 19). Advertising, Lewis recognized, was the new American folklore, and Lancelot is the Brer Fox of Madison Avenue, the overconfident trickster. His schemes often backfire, but he remains indestructible, a goblin of popular culture. He is also a personal demon, Sinclair Lewis's alter ego.

With his lanky frame, red hair, and taste for Kuppenheimer clothes, Lancelot is a self-portrait of the artist as a young hack. Tony Sarg's original illustrations for the Todd series "eerily" resemble Lewis himself (Wilson 236), and the first story, "Snappy Display," contains a photo of Lewis with the following caption: "This author is at his best when his stories center around his lurid past. Before he became a full-fledged novelist he was a reporter, advertising man and editor" (7). However scarring and humiliating, Lewis's "lurid past" as a copywriter was indispensable to his development as a satirist. As a cub reporter for the *San Francisco Bulletin*, Lewis proofread and rewrote countless display ads and concocted promotional hoaxes for advertisers. A story he wrote for a prominent hotel—about a dedicated bellhop who inherited a fortune from an eccentric guest—received national coverage. "I made [the bellhop] so tender to his elders," Lewis later remembered, "so given to brushing his teeth and combing his hair and saving of his electric bills and pieces of string, that he was a model for all future youth. Probably you can still see the influence of it, almost forty years later" (*Man from Main Street* 95).

Lewis eventually was fired for this chicanery, but his slimy initiation in advertising prepared him for what H. L. Mencken called "the Cloaca Maxima" of New York publishing (17). As his business letters show, Lewis was fiendishly good at designing ads and writing blurbs. "I am the George M. Cohan, the Billy Sunday, and the Mary Pickford of modern fiction," he once boasted (qtd. in Wilson 236–37). Not surprisingly, his formidable talents helped him in selling his own books. *From Main Street to Stockholm* contains some of his promotional ideas. To market *Free Air*, his improbable automobile romance between a Midwestern mechanic and an Eastern socialite, Lewis created an eye-catching display case for hundreds of service stations in his target market: Minnesota, North Dakota, Montana, and Washington, the setting for most of the novel's action. He then ran this ad in the appropriate papers:

> *Whenever you see the sign*
> FREE AIR
> *before a garage think of*
> *the one book that makes motoring romantic*
> FREE AIR (7)

As an ad man, Lewis—like most of the young men of his generation—was strongly influenced by Claude C. Hopkins, the Dean of American Copywriting. Hopkins himself was something of a Lewis character. A spectacled milquetoast, whom friends called

"Thee Thee" because of a pronounced lisp, Hopkins resembled a somewhat seedy Guy Pollock, the Prufrockian lawyer in *Main Street*. He had a passion for loafers and gardenias, and he wore his provincialism like a ceremonial sash. Nevertheless, Hopkins transformed American copywriting by blending the regional speech of the northern Midwest with the standardized mass speech of Eastern advertising. This new language—at once nostalgic and modern, folksy and surreal, natural and synthetic—used echoes of the farm and country store, Grange and Sunday school to sell such modern conveniences as Goodyear tires and Palmolive soap. It became the lingua franca of American popular culture. Needless to say, Lewis copied Hopkins's technique in *Babbitt,* only for satirical purposes, and Hopkins's syntax and style are a strong presence in Lewis's early fiction, especially the Lancelot Todd stories. In fact, Hopkins appears, barely disguised, as the boss in "Honestly—If Possible." The story even parodies Hopkins's famous campaign for Sunkist, "Drink an Orange."

If advertising was Lewis's finishing school for satire, the tuition was very high. Lewis not only detested the lies in which he trafficked but was sickened by the damage they did to his colleagues and himself. This malaise was widespread in the industry. James Rorty, advertising's first great historian and critic, also worked as a New York copywriter in the teens. Like Lewis, he hid literary ambitions and leftist politics behind a facade of smarmy efficiency and knee-jerk sarcasm. His description of the copywriter's dilemma explains the ferocity and despair behind the Lancelot Todd stories and portions of *Babbitt* and helps us understand both Lewis's state of mind in his early years and his subsequent decision to become a social critic:

> Your ad-man is merely the particular kind of eccentric cog which the machinery of competitive acquisitive society required at a particular moment of its evolution. He is, on the average, much more intelligent than the average business man, much more sophisticated, even much more socially minded. But in moving day after day the little cams and gears that he has to move, he inevitably empties himself of human qualities. His daily traffic in half-truths and outright deceptions is subtly and cumulatively degrading. No man can give his days

to barbarous frivolity and live. And ad-men don't live. They become dull, resigned, hopeless. Or they become daemonic fantasts and sadists. They are, in a sense, the intellectuals, the male hetaerae of our American commercial culture. Merciful nature makes some of them into hale, pink-fleshed, speech-making morons. Others become gray-faced cynics and are burned out at forty. Some "unlearn hope" and jump out of high windows. Others become extreme political and social radicals, either secretly while they are in the business, or openly, after they have left it. (19)

Despite the glowing editorials in *Printer's Ink,* Lewis knew that he and his fellow ad men were victims as well as perpetrators of a cruel practical joke—exploited by the very commercialism they so energetically promoted. Lewis would comment on this bitter irony in his unpublished introduction to *Babbitt:*

> Those farflung billboards, the banners of [a pickle company's] gallant crusade—their text was written by forty-a-week copywriters, their pictures—their very terrible pictures—painted by patient hacks, and the basic idea of having billboards, came not from the passionate brain of [the company president] but was cautiously worked out, on quite routine and unromantic lines, by hesitating persons in an advertising agency. (*Man from Main Street* 25)

For every spectacular success like Lancelot Todd, there were hundreds of failures like William John Buckingham, the alcoholic copywriter in "Jazz."

Buckingham is the creator of Uncle Jerry Ginger, the booster guru beloved by American grocery clerks. Todd, his boss, systematically denies Buckingham the credit he deserves and, to add insult to injury, instructs a mediocrity to pose as Uncle Jerry at public events. Although Buckingham regains his self-respect in a copywriting duel at an Atlantic City convention, his days are numbered. Fired by Todd, he embarks on one last spree and probably will be dead within months. Truth in advertising literally kills. Lewis's personal acquaintance with the real Buckinghams of advertising (alcoholism was one of the leading causes of death among copywriters in the teens and twenties) gives this farce a Gogolesque pathos. The same is true of all his Madison Avenue stories. Lewis's copywriters are "dead men." As James Rorty observes:

> Their bones are bakelite. Their blood is water, their flesh is pallid—yes, prick them and they do not bleed. Their eyes are veiled and sad or staring and a little mad. From them comes an acrid odor—they do not notice it, it may be only the ozone discharge of [their typewriter]. When you ask them to tell you what they are doing, they do not know, or at least they cannot tell you. They are voiceless, indeed, selfless—only the machine [of advertising] speaks through them. . . . Dead men tell no tales. (68–69)

Although the Lancelot Todd stories improved Lewis's satire and exorcised his demons, they damaged his relationship with George Horace Lorimer. Lewis had mocked Lorimer's advertisers and, worse, had implicitly criticized the war. Lancelot in "Getting His Bit" both prospers in the black market and impersonates J. L. Leydendecker's famous Doughboy, who appeared on the covers and in the pages of the *Saturday Evening Post*. Lorimer remained professional and courteous toward Lewis, but his stories appeared much less frequently in the *Post*. Significantly, after *Main Street* was published, rumors circulated that Lorimer had refused to serialize the novel, had privately advised Harcourt to shelve the manuscript, and had recommended that the Pulitzer Committee deny Lewis the prize. These charges proved insubstantial, but they point to an actual rift—a rift that became a chasm with the publication of *Babbitt*.

"The book," says Jan Cohn, "enraged Lorimer. He found in Babbitt a mockery of conventional values, a denigration of much that he prized in Americanism and especially in the American businessman," and he denounced the novel in a scathing article in *The Bookman* (193–94). It was the roar of a wounded lion. Lorimer's influence was beginning to set just as Lewis's was beginning to rise. The postwar boom of the twenties, with its frenzied consumption and flippant cynicism, obsoleted Lorimer's old-fashioned values of thrift and hard work. True, *Post* business fiction was still popular and successful, but many readers now found it quaint and nostalgic.

Ironically, Lewis himself contributed to, and profited from, this nostalgia. Just as Henry Ford created a successful museum for horse and buggies while mass producing Tin Lizzies, Lewis continued writing highly marketable *Post*-style fiction even while working on his iconoclastic novels of the early twenties. The final stories in this collection are a valedictory to the Lorimer era, tinged with irony and regret. "Bronze Bars" (1919), an O. Henry romance between a Broadway bank clerk and a destitute debutante, is set in New York, but the other stories mostly take place in Vernon, the friendly Midwestern city that redeems the Bannings in "The Good Sport" (1920). Combining the best elements of Gopher Prairie and Zenith, Vernon is a Lorimer "Utopia" where neighborliness, honesty, and hard work create the perfect business community ("Mr. Lorimer and Me" 81). Despite a serious falling out at the office, realtors Ray Moller and Homer Huff renew their friendship in "Way I See It" (1920), supporting each other when they are forced to relocate to New York. Jim Candee, the ethical stationer in "A Matter of Business" (1921) chooses to lose money on the handmade folk dolls of a French Canadian farmer rather than to cash in on the popular but shoddy kewpie manufactured by the Skillyooly Company.

Lewis's satire is gentler in these stories. He softens the caricature and allows his characters to savor their little victories. Lewis can afford to be generous because both he and the reader know that his characters, in the long run, will lose. Chivalrous Valory rescues Miss Page, but their impending marriage is doomed to fail because of the couple's class differences. As the story ends, Marcella berates Valory for his taste in collars. Ray and Homer, succumbing to Midwestern nostalgia, form a touching father and son bond in Manhattan; but both men probably will remain bachelors, and it is unlikely that a fifty-year-old provincial like Homer can compete against younger, city-trained realtors. Candee, for all his winsome independence, cannot continue defying corporate suppliers without losing his stationery shop.

Although Lewis in these stories seems to celebrate Lorimeresque business ethics, they actually demonstrate that such values have become untenable. His characters are doomed to fail because of their old-fashioned decency and work habits. "Lewis," says Alfred Kazin,

[saw] clearly enough the failure of the Horatio Alger tradition; the brand of economic individualism for which he yearns was, almost from the start of his career, more a vestigial than a vital force in society: even then, in the dawning age of the cartels, a myth and memory of the past. (137)

Its passing would haunt Lewis the rest of his life.

"Number Seven to Sagapoose" (1921), the last story in this collection, is Lewis's touching elegy to the hardworking drummers of his youth. Part tall tale, part wish fulfillment, the story deals with Joseph D. Rabbitt, a traveling salesman for the Excelsior Shoe Company. Though his name prefigures Babbitt's, Rabbitt is more saint than hustler. He sells people a belief in their own dreams. Through the course of his travels, Rabbitt convinces a short-order cook to become a surgeon, a political boss to nominate a reformer for state senator, the state senator to pass a child labor bill, and a runaway wife to return to her husband. After reviewing the accounts of his life, he presumably dies in his sleep in Chicago's Grancourt Hotel, but not before dreaming he has filled a big shoe order for the Excelsior Company.

Lewis's requiem for the traveling man would become his own, for he himself lived and died a salesman. His phenomenal success in the twenties can be attributed to his genius for marketing and publicity. Critics of his day, half admiringly, half contemptuously, compared him to an entrepreneur. "His impudent satires sell like bargain-counter silk stockings," quipped Vernon L. Parrington. "We pay handsomely to see ourselves unhandsomely depicted" (63). Walter Lippmann called Lewis a Ford plant that produced "a line of mechanical and completely standardized stereotypes as a practical convenience for daily use" (85). Lewis laughed all the way to the bank and deliberately shocked the literati by playing the brash operator in public. He talked about his novels the way car dealers "talk about their cars" (Farrar 59). He posed as a shoe salesman whenever traveling by train, pestering passengers for their shoe size and business cards. He substituted the toast at his wedding reception to Dorothy Thompson at the London Savoy with an improvised annual report on "the jute trade throughout the British Empire" (Sheean 96).

If the man was crazy, he was crazy like a fox. As this collection reflects, Lewis's training in advertising and publishing taught him to master the laws of supply and demand in popular fiction, and his best satirical novels, *Main Street* (1920), *Babbitt* (1922), *Arrowsmith* (1925), *Elmer Gantry* (1927), *The Man Who Knew Coolidge* (1928), and *Dodsworth* (1929), cashed in on the postwar disillusionment of the twenties just as his earlier fiction cashed in on the business ethos of the teens. Like a brilliant manufacturer, Lewis "prospered" by "inventing and marketing useful devices . . . by [which] millions of Americans perceived and expressed their new . . . sense of America" (Lippmann 85).

Even the best salesmen can play themselves out, though. Like Lorimer, Lewis's importance waned with the passing of his era. Although he remained a productive and fairly popular writer throughout the thirties and forties, he had lost touch with his customers—pushing the same product, repeating the same sales pitch. He coasted on his royalties, took to drink, and died in a Roman hospital in 1951, a Gideon Bible on his nightstand. For some critics, Lewis's Lomanesque life and death prevent him from being a great American novelist. Mark Schorer's famous biography depicts Lewis as a hack and a Rotarian who had too many business lunches with the bitch goddess, Success. Pointing to the two halves of Lewis's personality, the slick copywriter and the moralistic Nobel Prize winner, Martin Bucco asks, "Was ever a major writer in hot pursuit of the American Dream so divided as Sinclair Lewis?" (70).

That division, however, is not personal but cultural. The contradictions of salesmanship, which Lewis embodied in his life and illustrated in these stories, are the contradictions of modern America, the grotesque contrast between "the promise of America and the often unhealthy results of American life" (Douglas 661). Our first and perhaps best chronicler of consumerism and commodification, Lewis knew that "the ultimate disillusionment" of American capitalism is that "in the midst of seemingly infinite variety so many things are the same and carry the same price tag—loss of freedom" (Lundquist 128). His America is not a functioning democracy but a dysfunctional sales convention where business, medicine, and religion are all a scam.

This relentless billingsgate of slogans and gimmicks, however, goes beyond the real estate offices, car dealerships, and ad agencies of the teens and twenties. As George H. Douglas argues, Babbittry is still the dominant language of our most prestigious institutions— "from big government, to the techno-structure of the large corporation, to the research university" (662). Wherever they work, whatever they do, Americans are still condemned—like these early Lewis characters—to sell, sell out, and be sold. Even though the computer age has replaced the industrial age, Sinclair Lewis remains a disturbingly relevant writer. "Empty [business] discourse still qualifies as art," comments James M. Hutchisson, "and it has increased through the proliferation of hypermedia, as is witnessed by the daily parade of carnival pitchmen who appear on television talk shows, shopping clubs, and 'infomercials'" (xxviii).

Thanks to new technologies, the home—more than ever—is an extension of the office, and the office—more than ever—is a hothouse for the despairs and delusions of the American Dream. Lewis was the first American novelist to address these problems, hence his enduring importance. As long as Americans buy Franklin Planners and enroll in seminars to Awaken the Giant Within, as long as they daydream about starting a business with just a PC and natter like telemarketers even among their intimates, as long as they paper their cubicles with Emersonian catch phrases to wall out the horrors of the office, they will need the satire of American literature's Master Salesman, the man Sherwood Anderson called "the Babe Ruth of Boosters" (qtd. in Schorer 279).

WORKS CITED

Benét, William Rose. "The Earlier Lewis." *The Saturday Review of Literature* 20 Jan. 1934: 421–22.

Bucco, Martin. "The Serialized Novels of Sinclair Lewis." *Sinclair Lewis*. Ed. Harold Bloom. New York: Chelsea, 1987. 63–70.

Cantwell, Robert. "Sinclair Lewis." *Sinclair Lewis: A Collection of Critical Essays*. Ed. Mark Schorer. Englewood Cliffs: Prentice, 1962. 111–18.

Cohn, Jan. *Creating America: George Horace Lorimer and the "Saturday Evening Post"*. Pittsburgh: U of Pittsburgh P, 1989.

Dooley, D. J. *The Art of Sinclair Lewis*. Lincoln: U of Nebraska P, 1967.

Douglas, George H. "Babbitt at Fifty—The Truth Still Hurts." *Nation* 22 May 1972: 661–62.

Farrar, John. "The Literary Spotlight 12: Sinclair Lewis." *Bookman* Sept. 1922: 54–59.

Fussell, Paul. *Class*. New York: Ballantine, 1983.

Geismar, Maxwell. "Origins of a Dynasty." *Sinclair Lewis: A Collection of Critical Essays*. Ed. Mark Schorer. Englewood Cliffs: Prentice, 1962. 10–16.

Halsey, Ashley. *A Short History of the "Saturday Evening Post"*. Philadelphia: Curtis, 1953.

Hampshire Paper Company. Advertisement. *Saturday Evening Post* 8 Jan. 1916: 39.

Hutchisson, James M. Introduction. *Babbitt*. By Sinclair Lewis. New York: Penguin, 1996. vii–xxviii.

Kazin, Alfred. "The New Realism: Sherwood Anderson and Sinclair Lewis." *Sinclair Lewis: A Collection of Critical Essays*. Ed. Mark Schorer. Englewood Cliffs: Prentice, 1962. 119–38.

Lears, T. J. Jackson. *Fables of Abundance: A Cultural History of Advertising in America*. New York: Basic, 1994.

Lewis, Sinclair. *Babbitt.* 1922. Afterword by Mark Schorer. New York: Signet, 1961.

———. *From Main Street to Stockholm: Letters of Sinclair Lewis, 1919–1930*. Ed. Harrison Smith. New York: Harcourt, 1952.

———. *The Job: An American Novel*. 1917. Lincoln: Bison, 1994.

———. *The Man from Main Street: A Sinclair Lewis Reader*. Ed. Harry E. Maule and Melville Cane. New York: Random, 1953.

———. "Mr. Lorimer and Me." *Nation* 25 July 1928: 81.

———. *Our Mr. Wrenn: The Romantic Adventures of a Gentle Man*. New York: Harper, 1914.

———. "Snappy Display." *Metropolitan* Aug. 1917: 7–8, 68, 71.

———. *The Trail of the Hawk: A Comedy of the Seriousness of Life*. New York: Harper, 1915.

———. *Work of Art*. Garden City: Doubleday, 1934.

Lippmann, Walter. "Sinclair Lewis." *Sinclair Lewis: A Collection of Critical Essays*. Ed. Mark Schorer. Englewood Cliffs: Prentice, 1962. 84–94.

Lundquist, James. *Sinclair Lewis*. New York: Frederick Ungar, 1973.

Mencken, H. L. "Consolation." *Sinclair Lewis: A Collection of Critical Essays*. Ed. Mark Schorer. Englewood Cliffs: Prentice, 1962. 17–19.

Mills, C. Wright. *White Collar*. New York: Oxford UP, 1951.

Moodie, Clara Lee R. "The Book that Has Never Been Published." *Sinclair Lewis at 100*. Ed. Michael Connaughton. St. Cloud: St. Cloud State UP, 1985. 201–12.

Moore, Truman E. *The Traveling Man: The True Story of the American Traveling Salesman*. Garden City: Doubleday, 1972.

Parrington, Vernon L. "Sinclair Lewis: Our Diogenes." *Sinclair Lewis: A Collec-*

tion of Critical Essays. Ed. Mark Schorer. Englewood Cliffs: Prentice, 1962. 62–70.

Pebeco Tooth Paste. Advertisement. *Saturday Evening Post* 11 Dec. 1920: 99.

Rorty, James. *Our Master's Voice: Advertising*. New York: John Day, 1934.

Rourke, Constance. "Round Up." *Sinclair Lewis: A Collection of Critical Essays*. Ed. Mark Schorer. Englewood Cliffs: Prentice, 1962. 29–31.

Sampson, Anthony. *Company Man: The Rise and Fall of Corporate Life*. New York: Random, 1995.

Schorer, Mark. *Sinclair Lewis: An American Life*. New York: McGraw, 1961.

Sheean, Vincent. *Dorothy and Red*. Boston: Houghton, 1963.

Simon, Tobin. "The Short Stories of Sinclair Lewis." Diss. New York U, 1972.

Stein-Bloch Smart Clothes. Advertisement. *Saturday Evening Post* 30 Oct. 1915: 32.

Tebbel, John William. George Horace Lorimer and the "Saturday Evening Post": *The Biography of a Great Editor*. Garden City: Doubleday, 1948.

Thoreau, Henry David. "Economy." *Walden and Other Writings*. 1854. Ed. and introd. Joseph Wood Krutch. New York: Bantam, 1981. 107–63.

Twitchell, James B. *Adcult USA: The Triumph of Advertising in American Culture*. New York: Columbia UP, 1995.

Wilson, Christopher P. *White Collar Fictions: Class and Social Representation in American Literature, 1885–1925*. Athens: U of Georgia P, 1992.

IF I WERE BOSS

COMMUTATION: $9.17

Mr. Whittier J. Small wasn't popular, either at Crosshampton Harbor, where he haughtily had a restricted suburban residence, or at Woodley & Duncan's, where he was office manager. Yet neither was he disagreeable enough to be notorious. Wait! That wasn't his fault; he was as mean-minded as he knew how to be; but he hadn't much imagination. He was able to annoy his neighbors and the office force only by the ordinary old-fashioned methods which everyone knows and doesn't mind.

He did all he could. He would talk about efficiency to a five-dollar-a-week addressing girl; and in the mind of Mr. Small efficiency had nothing to do with increasing profits or saving time. It meant making clerks unhappy. He crawked at the girls whenever they stopped to take a drink of water and interrupted the work they should have loved so well, such as copying a form letter six hundred times or hunting hours for a letter that was on Mr. Small's desk all the while. He had the generous habit of discovering at four-fifty almost every day that there was some work which simply had to be done that evening—if it was quite convenient could Miss Rosenbaum stay and finish it?

He also did his modest best at Crosshampton Harbor. He kept a guinea hen that gave an imitation of a sawmill at three, five and six-thirty A.M. daily. But the poor man never became a professional irritator until that glorious combat of which the suburbs still speak on stormy nights, when families gather round the hot-air registry and father tells his real opinion of the neighbors.

The curious thing about Mr. Whittier J. Small—if it was the poet Whittier his parents meant when they christened him, they must have been thinking of "Snow-Bound"—was that he had a passion for popularity. He didn't know that he was mean. He resented meanness. He spoke as feelingly of other people's howling dogs as did they of his guinea hen. Or, take his office girls: Why did they try to put things over on his trusting kindness? He thirsted for local fame. He wanted to be asked to join the Harbor Yacht Club. He wanted people to call him up in the evening and invite him over for a game of five hundred. His life was one of rectitude and baths. He read the proper newspapers and wore the proper clothes. He spoke harshly of sports shirts and hated progress. He never offended people by such eccentricities. He wore pyjamas and smoked ten-cent cigars, and hated office boys who snapped their fingers. He was a normal and solid citizen.

Yes, Crosshampton Harbor was far less interested in him than in the iceman, whom if courted and flattered and asked about his offspring's educational progress, could sometimes be persuaded to bring the ice before the meat spoiled.

If you have ever come into the city on the seven-fifty-four you have undoubtedly seen Mr. Small—only you probably did not notice him. He was neither meek and meeching nor tall and pompous. He was neither young nor old, bearded nor clean-shaven. Even other commuters remarked that he looked like a commuter. Everyone who was introduced to him said confusedly: "I think we've met before." He wore clothes—oh, clothes of a gray that was rather brown, and he had a moustache—you could never remember whether it was brown or black, or colored like hairbrush bristles. His face was medium looking. He was medium sized. He was medium.

Except in meanness. Whittier J. Small had potentialities of meanness that had never been discovered.

He had recently moved away from Cosmos Villas because the benighted people paid no attention to him. They had spoken to him pleasantly, and even borrowed his lawn mower, at Cosmos Villas; but he had never met with any social recognition except election to the Matthew Arnold Culture Circle at a time when the circle had to get some new members or go under. For this lack of recognition he blamed Mrs. Small—a worthy woman who was always to be found in the parlor, gently sighing and knitting something that never got beyond the stage of resembling an earmuff. But mostly he blamed Cosmos Villas itself, and after five years he decided to move to Crosshampton Harbor.

Mr. Small started out brilliantly in Crosshampton Harbor—or the Harbor, as its inhabitants called it in their jolly fashion. Mr. Litchfeld, the real-estate man who leased him a house, was such a breezy, lovable chap. He assured Mr. Small that the Harbor needed just such a substantial citizen and would make him welcome to their neighborly social life; so Mr. Small applied for membership in the Harbor Yacht Club. The membership committee once invited him to a club smoker and once called on him. He gave them cigars and homemade root beer that he guaranteed equal to vintage champagne for exhilaration and cod-liver oil for benefit. He entertained them in the sunniest manner with stories about the unfriendliness of his former neighbors in Cosmos Villas, and the cleverness of his two children, and the incompetence of his wife, and the inefficiency of the girls who worked under him and the chief who worked over him, and the complete undesirability of a mysterious phonograph that disturbed his slumber—the phonograph belonged to one of the committee. He pressed them to call again, and spent several days in expecting not only to be elected to the club but to run for commodore on an opposition ticket. He rehearsed an inauguration speech. After four weeks he received a courteous note from the committee informing him that the club membership list was full for the year and that they must regretfully request him to go to the devil!

Mr. Small was not hurt. He spoke of plots. There were those on the membership committee, he said, who were afraid to admit a man who would be so formidable a rival in club politics. He said it a great many times to his wife, who listened patiently and replied, "Yes, Whittier; that's so!" in a voice like that of a toy terrier with influenza.

Then it was that Mr. Small remembered with a wistful unhappiness the evenings he had spent at the Cosmos Villas Matthew

Arnold Culture Circle, getting all sorts of thrilling encyclopedia information about Java and fish glue, and carburetors and Henry VIII, and Felicia Hemans and the technic of writing essays. He decided to show his lavish public spirit and start in this pitiable Crosshampton Harbor another Matthew Arnold Culture Club.

On the street he met Mr. Litchfeld, the real-estate man, who promised to herd his acquaintances to Mr. Small's the coming Thursday for the formation of the Culture Circle.

An amazing epidemic of assorted ills struck Crosshampton Harbor that week. Some Harborites had colds and some had headaches, and some were just sick; so only six people gathered at Mr. Small's residence on Thursday evening. Mr. Small's residence wasn't really a residence. It was simply a house; about as houselike a house as ever was first carpentered and then architected. It had a low turret and a couple of bay windows precariously pasted on one side. It was made of shingles and clapboards and rubblestone and scrollwork in patterns like the lace paper in a candy box. Even the chimneys had little tin inverted pants. The exterior hinted of furnace heat and semi-hardwood floors and one servant. A swing couch, a perambulator and a doormat, strangely lettered EMOCLEW, bedecked the porch.

In the parlor, Mr. Small frequently sat in a red-plush easy-chair with dragon-carved arms and acquired culture by the page. Most of the culture he dug from seven sets of books two feet and seven inches in combined width, containing nine books of selections from Persian poetry, three books of Greek orations, one of Early Victorian geology, and one of the history of Spanish literature. There were fifty-six hundred and thirty-two pages in the set; and by reading—as he incredibly did—two pages every evening, Mr. Small would be a gentleman of learning in seven years and two hundred and sixty-one days.

In this refined abode, facing the determined volumes, the six applicants for wisdom gathered. There were Mr. Litchfeld, his wife, his daughter with the repressed teeth, his stenographer, and two unclaimed ladies with riprapped false fronts. Mrs. Small deprecatingly joined them.

Mr. Small stood before them—that's all he did at first—just stood before them like a district attorney, or Billy Sunday, or General Joffe reviewing troops. When he had awed them to such perfect silence that they wanted to yelp and run, he began:

"To show you how interesting and valuable Mrs. Small and I found the Matthew Arnold Culture Circle at Cosmos Villas, I will read you a paper on the Humor of Mark Twain which I read at the circle. I trust you will find it worth some serious attention."

It was obvious that he hoped no one would take this composition on humor lightly. They didn't. He paused to permit them to express pleased gratification, which they did not express, and announced:

"Now we will proceed to the adoption of the constitution and a program, and finally to the election of officers. The following is the constitution."

He had the constitution already made out. Possibly the Harbor never realized it, but he was wonderful at constitutions. He could easily have created a Mexican constitution that would have united all parties; though what the parties would have done to him after they had united the historian does not presume to know. When he was but a studious lad of eighteen he had drafted the whole constitution for the Young Men's Friendly Society of Ogden Center.

The Culture Circle constitution provided for every contingency and invented a number of new contingencies for which to provide.

No member of the circle was to have a single evening free for anything but culture. When they weren't preparing papers they would be reading up for debates or watching the Trend of Affairs as revealed in Current Events, which last seemed to be a study of the tariff schedules on phosphates plus chess news and a close examination of the census returns from Peru. The constitution sounded like Mr. Small's office rules.

The program was still more definitive. There were to be sixteen meetings for the remainder of the year: three evening were to be devoted to Persian poetry, two to Greek orations, one to geology, one to the history of Spanish literature, and the rest to short-story writing, movie-scenario writing, American industries, and the grand finale with an amateur play by the least intelligible Swedish dramatist who could be discovered.

Mr. Small astounded them by promising to let them try to elect officers all by themselves. Incredulously, as though he might withdraw the privilege at any moment, they distributed ballots to one another while Mr. Small sat in a corner and looked pleased with himself.

As president of the C.H.M.A.C.C. he would be a prominent figure in the most select sets of the Harbor. Dear old Harbor! Here, at last, they did appreciate him as the middle-class lowbrows of Cosmos Villas had never done. . . . The real-estate stenographer was whispering violently to the others—except Mrs. Small. In response they grinned and filled out their ballots.

Mr. Small collected the ragged slips that were to elevate him to fame. For an instant he held them in his fat white hand—a hand like veal—and beamed on the friends and neighbors who were forcing this honor on him. Then he counted the vote. His smile skidded and turned turtle. Hastily:

"Eight present and voting. For president—Mr. Litchfeld, six; Mr. Small, two. Vice president—Mrs. Litchfeld, six; Mr. Litchfeld, two. Secretary and treasurer—Miss Zenia Litchfeld, eight votes— unanimous. Constitution and program adopted unanimously."

Mr. Small stopped. Triumph overspread his face.

"We shall, therefore, meet here each Thursday evening and carry on the program as arranged. Miss Litchfeld, you will please read us a paper on Omar Khayyam a week from tonight, and Mr. Litchfeld will give us this week's Current Events. Motion t' 'journ 'n order."

He glared at the real-estate man. He was challenging Mr. Litchfeld to reverse this order, whether or not he had by some election fraud obtained the presidency. Mr. Small resembled a motion picture of the Honest Young Reformer Defying the Boss. Evidently he impressed Mr. Litchfeld who rose and said:

"Move t' 'journ. . . . We've had a vurry, vurry pleasan' evenin', Brother Small. Come, my dear; we must be going."

Mr. Litchfeld stopped to give Mr. Small a chance to surprise them with refreshments, as one who from afar scents the chocolate wafers; but Mr. Small had no such desire to surprise them, either with refreshments or with anything else. Refreshments were all very well, but they didn't bring him any four percent in the savings bank. Besides, what had he got out of it the time he'd simply crammed the Harbor Club membership committee with the choicest refreshments? No, no! This evening, he had decided, should be devoted to culture, pure and unrefreshed. So he said nothing but "S' sorry y'ave to go"; while Mrs. Small echoed, "Sorry y'ave to go!" And Mr. Litchfeld and Mrs. Litchfeld and Miss Zenia Litchfeld and Mr. Litchfeld's stenographer and Mr. Litchfeld's two maiden-lady neighbors chorused: "Sush pleasan' even'!" and filed abjectly into the entrance hall.

After all, Mr. Small grimly decided, as he lay awake and worried—while Mrs. Small made indelicate sounds of slumber—he had shown that fool Litchfeld just who was really running the Culture Circle; and when Mr. Litchfeld resigned we'd see what we'd see! Then, as President Small of the C.H.M.A.C.C. at last, he would come into his rightful rank.

The two maiden ladies separately telephoned their tearful but resolute regrets at being unable to attend the next meeting of the Culture Circle; but Mr. Litchfeld's flock didn't take so much trouble— they merely did not come. There were no more meetings of the circle.

Mr. Whittier J. Small sank into a social position in the Harbor which resembled that of a highly respected caterpillar in an extensive forest. He could not understand it. He blamed the girls at his office for having worried their good, kind manager. He blamed Mr. Litchfeld for not having introduced him to the right people. He blamed the right people for being right. But he never blamed Mr. Whittier J. Small.

He sat whole evenings through, paying no attention to his wife's jerky efforts to entertain him and trying to ascertain why the Harbor did not value a man of his caliber. He gave it up.

He was left with but one acquaintance in the Harbor—Mr. Percy Weather, a neighbor who was also a social error, and who gratefully shared Mr. Small's seat in the smoker of the commuters' train and listened to his discourses on politics, baseball, shoes, the disgraceful ways in which modern parents bring up their children, and Mrs. Small's incurable vice of not always having dinner ready at seven P.M. on the dot. Mr. Weather was not, like Mr. Small, a man you thought you had met before. He was a man you could never remember having met.

Mr. Small and he became as companionable as a sophomore and pipe. To everybody he met Mr. Small defiantly piped:

"Percy Weather is a fine fellow, sir—a fine fellow! It's a pity this fool town hasn't enough sense to appreciate a fine, quiet, sensible fellow like him, when some fellows—— Now take that fellow Litchfeld—he's always blowing his own horn. Percy Weather isn't that kind, let me tell you! . . ." Though to Mrs. Small he sometimes remarked that, while Weather wasn't a bad sort, it was a pity the man didn't have a little backbone. He, Whittier J. Small, would never have climbed to office managership if he hadn't ever shown any more gumption that Percy Weather.

"Yes, Whittier, that's so!" said Mrs. Small in a manner which betrayed the fact that she was thinking of the maid's indecent treatment of the white sauce.

Then—— At a time when peace and social inactivity seemed to brood on the land, the world turned upside down, to the enormous astonishment of any number of people.

Splendid was the beginning of the Great Commutation Ticket Row! It flashed into full-armed magnificence. The railroad changed the seven-fifty-four from an express to a local. To Crosshampton Harbor, whose whole religion and philosophy were the seven-fifty-four, the heavens were darkened. Committees of Crosshampton Harborites and overdressed contingents from Crosshampton Gardens and East Northwest went to protest to the general manager, the general traffic manager, the general passenger agent, the divisions superintendent, the auditor, the auditor's office boy, the gatekeeper at the city station, the bootblack-stand proprietor, and Mike Kolowski, who swept the city station steps—all of whom assured the committees that they would see what could be done—and then did not do it.

The seven minutes' increase in the trip was not the only grievance. Now the train stopped at several stations between Westborough Junction and the city, the passengers had to show their commutations twice—once when the tickets were punched and once between the junction and the city. The tumult and the shouting rose. What! Dared the railroad demand that twice on one trip they reach into their waistcoat pockets and hoist the weighty tickets a full inch in the air?

The task would take them ten seconds at least. So the commuter spent ten minutes daily for each man in argument with the conductor. The favorite termination of the argument was to shout:

"No; I won't show my ticket! And, what's more, you can't put me off the rain neither. Go ahead; try it—try to put me off! Maybe you think I won't sue the railroad!"

Meantime everybody knew perfectly well that the conductor had no power to put them off, and day after day the more valiant souls, the free and adventurous spirits who played tennis at the Harbor Club, defied the trainmen.

The conductor on the seven-fifty-four who collected the tickets in the forward two cars was old Barton, twenty-three years in the service, large and kindly, with the diplomacy of a fashionable physician and the memory of a club hallman and a moustache like a white-fox muff. He never lost his temper; he discussed the question patiently; and he spent in peaceful gardening the five-day layoffs the office was known to impose on him when he did not insist that the passengers reëxhibit their tickets. Conductor Barton was accustomed the simultaneous abuse by passengers who believed he owned and mismanaged the railroad, and superintendents who believed he owned and mismanaged the passengers.

Like the other Harborites, Whittier J. Small was accustomed to cheating the railroad when he could. He rather enjoyed slipping his commutation ticket to Percy Weather when Percy had left his own at home in that other suit; and he expected return courtesies. Therefore, he felt a peculiarly sacred wrath at the railroad and was granted his inspiration.

The morning of the inspiration seemed outwardly like any other morning. Mr. Small had finished his paper, including the obituaries and personal ads, and was conversing agreeably with Mr. Weather, Mr. Small himself doing most of the talking part of the conversing. Said he:

"Well, sir—funny thing this morning! I always take just one cuppa coffee—say, Weather, have you tried this new brand their advertising in the cars?—but somehow this morning I said to my wife: 'Emma,' I said, 'it's funny but I feel just like taking another cuppa coffee this morning,' I said; and she said to me: 'Why,' she said, 'you don't ever take but one!' You know it takes a woman not

to understand a business man; she can't understand that if he's going to go on slaving and wearing himself out providing luxury for
her he's gotta have what he wants when he wants it. And then,
here's these old hens—they wouldn't do it if they were married—all
running around wanting the vote! Let me tell you there wouldn't
be any of all this industrial unrest and wars and things if it wasn't
for all this suffrage and them destructive theories. A woman's place
is in t' home, and she ought to stay there and look out for my
comfort; and when I want another cuppa coffee she ought to have
another cuppa coffee ready for me.

"Yes, sir; it was funny! I just felt like I wanted another cuppa
coffee and I told her so; and you know, before she could get it for
me—she hasn't no—more—sense of managing a kitchen, just like
all the rest of these women; if I ran my office that way Lord knows
what'd happen!—and before I could get just one more cuppa coffee it was seven-fifty! And you know I always allow four minutes
to catch my train from the front gate, and maybe even from the big
box elder—you know the one—right in front of the next place to
mine, and I had to hurry so that——— Oh, say, speaking of the
place next to mine, will you kindly tell me one single, solitary reason why that confounded snobbish bunch down there at the Harbor Club should try to keep my body off their beach when———"

"No, sir; I won't show my ticket!"

The voice came from the seat across from them. It was the mighty
commodore of the Harbor Yacht Club speaking, and beside him
sat the equally mighty vice president of the Crosshampton Club,
who knew personally a man that had once played McLoughlin.
They were defying Conductor Barton; they wouldn't show their
ticket a second time—no, not if they were hanged, drawn, quar-
tered, eighthed and put off the train! The conductor sighed and
passed on to Mr. Small and Mr. Weather.

Then exploded the inspiration that was to make Mr. Whittier J.
Small a man not like other men, but one to sit in great places and
converse with the great. He turned his head slowly from Mr. Weather
and to the conductor he shouted in a heroic voice:

"No! I won't show my ticket! Go on! Put me off! I dare you to!
I guess you fellows just want to see how much the passengers will
stand and now you're finding out."

His voice carried through the car and he had invented a new argument. He had the tremorous joy of hearing three men echo: "Guess you fellows want to see how much the passengers will stand!" Percy Weather was beginning to congratulate him in that stammering bleat which now, for the first time, irritated Mr. Small. Mr. Small paid no attention to Percy. He swung round and boldly entered into discourse with the man in the seat behind him. He was aware that the man behind him was none other than Commodore Berry, of the ancient Berry family, a man so accepted by smart society that he had once spent a weekend at Narragansett Pier—where the tide rises only seventeen minutes later than at Newport. Mr. Small had fondly dreamed of a day when he should know Mr. Berry; when Mr. Berry should address him on the station platform, "Good morning, Mr. Small!"—like that, politely. Here he was, talking to him, a comrade in resistance to oppression.

Heretofore a railroad had been to Mr. Small an insignificant means of getting to the office in time to catch that cheeky young man, the salesclerk, coming in late. Now he studied affectionately every detail of the travel, from the air brakes to the bobbing heads as the crowd surged upstairs in the city station.

He was at Harbor station early next morning, and as the train came in he leaped aboard and got a seat as far forward as possible from in the first smoking car. From that strategic position he defied Conductor Barton even more loudly than on the preceding morning and unmasked the phrases on which he had been working for an hour:

"You know perfectly well you can't do anything. Say, who do you think you are? Do you think we want to argue with you clear into the city? Maybe you think we haven't any papers to read! Now get it over quick!"

All down the car echoes rose: "Think you're paid to argue with passengers?" "Get 't over quick!"

This morning it was Cornelius Berry, young Squire Berry, who first addressed Mr. Small as they debouched on the platform at the city station. He commended Mr. Small on his stand for righteousness and civic purity. With Mr. Berry was the commodore, smiling in the best manner of the Harbor Club.

"Makes me tired to have these scoundrels take up a business

man's time," said Mr. Small. "I suppose that conductor thinks I haven't got a paper. I don't want to be hard on him, Mr. Berry, but let me tell you if I was a conductor I'd be a little respectful to my betters. But I suppose it turns his head to associate with us."

"Indeed you're right, Mr. Small. Hope shall see 'gain soon. *Good* morning, Mr. Small!"

"Good *morning*, Mr. Small!" said the commodore—both in the heartiest manner.

It was of this that Mr. Small had dreamed—prophetically. This was the polished sort of social amenity for which he could never depend on his jellyfish of a wife. He, Mr. Small, had to look out for it as he did for everything else. He felt so victorious that he rebuked the salesclerk with extra piousness that morning, and gave him advice about How a Young Man Should Succeed. The salesclerk was a stubborn young man and, as usual, he answered impudently; but Mr. Small, the friend of Cornelius Berry, treated him with contempt.

From that morning the social gates were open for our hero. Daily he led his faithful, fearless band of thirty or forty in defying Conductor Barton—who never answered back and thus proved that Mr. Small had roused him to some sense of shame. All sorts of people spoke to Mr. Small, introduced themselves, asked after the health of Mrs. Small—a subject in which they had hitherto been profoundly uninterested—invited the Smalls to sit in at whist, to call, to go motoring—not, perhaps, to go motoring at any definite time, but just as soon as the car should be out of the repair shop. He no longer had to sit with Percy Weather; which was as well, for he perceived the Weather person was of a flabby dullness that no gentleman could endure.

Finally, to state an epochal fact with plain and honest directness, Mr. Small was elected to the Harbor Club.

For almost a week he was so proud of the fact that three of the girls in his office resigned and the salesclerk threatened to punch his head; at which Mr. Small merely smiled, for he knew the salesclerk was going to be married, come the Fourth of July, and then he'd have the young upstart where he wanted him. Maybe he'd not be so flippant about office discipline once he had a wife to support! It was only with the chief himself, Mr. Woodley, of the firm, that

Mr. Small spoke in a little and delicate voice. To his wife he discoursed about social conventions from six-forty-nine to eleven-twenty-three without a break one evening.

Yet by the end of the week Mr. Small was dissatisfied. He began to realize that a man of his personality was buried in the second-rate grubbiness of the Harbor Club. He ought to belong to the Crosshampton Club, where there were gold links and a bar—where a gentleman could meet the right set. His time was valuable; he was not one to waste it with the wrong set. As well foozle with—oh, for example, with that rim of a zero called Percy Weather.

The sets in Crosshampton Harbor are of a subtlety. There is the Harbor Club set, consisting of an undertaker who wears suspenders, a fuzzy-faced lawyer, the real-estate person named Litchfeld, the chief plumber in town, and a collection of easygoing commuters and town merchants who play five-hundred until midnight every Saturday and attend the smaller wooden churches on Sunday. In the Crosshampton Club there are two sets, distinct but both good—the set that attends the stone church, and the set that never attends church but spends every Sunday morning in recovering from a swell Saturday evening dance. There is a town-merchant set that does not belong to clubs, and a social-uplift set, and a literary set, and the Old Inhabitant set whose families date back to 1700, long since which date, apparently, most of our families have been self-generated.

Now that he belonged to the Harbor Club, Mr. Small had an opportunity to study the real social structure of the town. He saw clearly that his was a nature too fine for any but the stone-church and Old Inhabitant sets. He redoubled his efforts at dismaying Conductor Barton. He spoke to the conductor with what he believed to be the manner of an old English squire—and in the next car men jumped and murmured uneasily of bomb explosions.

The annual election of the Harbor Club was approaching—and, as commodore, Mr. Small would be eligible to anything. He was being affable to quantities of people. He was sure that one should be optimistic in this best of all possible worlds and bring a little gift of sunshine to all influential members of the Harbor Club; but he was vexed this particular morning on the train. One Percy Weather had made as though to sit down beside him, and only by turning round and shouting at a member of the Harbor Club, "Looking for a seat?" had Mr. Small got rid of the fellow.

He chatted with his seatmate about the coming club election, giving him every reasonable chance to suggest that Mr. Small run for office. Then, on a hunch—"I always trust a hunch," he often told Mrs. Small—he left his seat and went four cars back to speak to the vice commodore of the Harbor Club about the vice commodore's beautiful wife, beautiful children, beautiful newspaper, beautiful tie, beautiful sunburn. . . . Mr. Small was still lauding the vice-commodorial virtues when the train passed Westborough Junction and the trainmen demanded a second glimpse of the tickets.

Still bearing his message of optimism to the vice commodore, Mr. Small merely mumbled: "No; I won't show my ticket."

"Yes, you will!" said an unfamiliar voice.

Mr. Small stared up with the hauteur of a hat boy. Then he remembered—Conductor Barton inspected tickets only in the forward two cars. It was an ordinary collector who dared address him—a surly youth with black brows and no forehead.

"Show your ticket, I said. You can't work none o' them games on me!"

The vice commodore hastily reached for his commutation. For that reason, Mr. Small was the more stubborn. He'd show people he wasn't a coward like the vice commodore—the present vice commodore!

"My ticket was punched up forward by the conductor," he said—"Crosshampton Harbor."

"Well, lemme take a look at it."

"I told you it's been punched. I don't have to show it again, and—I won't."

"You'll show me that ticket or I'll put you off the train. You may 'a' showed it to the conductor and you may not. You never showed it to me anyway."

The collector was young. He spoke with none of the weary suavity of Conductor Barton.

"Oh! You'll put me off the train! You'll put me off the train! You'll put me off the train!"

"You got it right the first time. I'll put you off, I'll put you off,

I'll put you off the train. Whathell do you think this is? Think we're speaking a piece together? Show me that ticket!"

Through all the car, surging with the wrath of a superman, brave with defiance to the collector, to the conductor, to the railroad, to the state, to the nation, and to the united armies and navies and revenue services of the entire world, rolled Mr. Small's voice:

"I've showed my ticket once. I won't show it again. That's the end of it! Gwan—put me off! Gwan! Put me off the train!"

Mr. Small was conscious that the vice commodore was leaning back in his seat corner, trying to look as though he did not know Mr. Small; that passengers were rising and staring at him; that the collector was making gripping motions with his grease-blackened hands. But it was his moment of glory. Now, for all time, he would stand out as the most prominent citizen of Crosshampton Harbor— defender of its liberties. He bawled on:

"I've had about enough of your lip, my man. I'll report you to the—to your—to the railroad; and I'll see to it that you'll lose your job. You ain't fit to be allowed to talk to passengers."

"Oh, gee!" said the collector. A curious expression wrinkled his face. "Would you do that now? I've got a woman and three kids."

"Can't help it." Mr. Small settled into his seat with finality. "You ought to have thought of that before."

"Well, then, all right, bo! Show me your ticket!"

"W-h-a-t?" Mr. Small was aghast. "Say! You fellows just want to see how much us passengers will stand. Well, you've found out now. I tell you for the last time"—his voice rose and rose—"that I will not show you my ticket, not even if I have to lick you. Putting a passenger—inconvenience—unnecessary—see how much stand! Why, if you want to—why don't you put me off the train? Go ahead; just try it!"

"All right," said the collector. "Been waiting here till we reached Martinsbridge. And here we are, brother."

Like a steam crane yanking a bale out of a ship's hold, the collector's arm whirled down, caught Mr. Small's collar, jerked him out of the seat, ran him stumbling and breathless along the aisle and down the vestibule steps. To the railroad policeman who guarded the repair material at Martinsbridge the collector chuckled:

"Here, Billy, pinch this guy for————"

"You can't arrest me for not showing————" from Mr. Small.

"————disorderly conduct and disturbing the peace and resisting an officer in the discharge of his duty, or whatever it is, and using gosh-awful language and the rest of it—will you?" the collector finished.

"All right, Tim!" said the railroad policeman.

Already the train was pulling out. Mr. Small was aware that faces once near and dear were staring with shocked horror; that fingers which had once signed lemonade checks for him were pointing in scorn; that every window and vestibule door was jammed with gaping people.

The train was gone round a curve and Mr. Small was left alone on a quiet, shabby, unfamiliar plank platform, surrounded by the hovels of a meaningless 'tween-stations town—that is, alone except for a railroad policeman who was advancing on him.

"You can't arrest me," said Mr. Small with severe gentility.

"No; but I'm going to."

"Why, you haven't got a single witness————"

"Oh, that's all right, Jack," said the policeman, taking Mr. Small's arm with smelly familiarity. "If there's any trouble, the collector will have plenty of witnesses when the trial comes up. Come along now, Jack, and don't try any funny business."

Again the art of the historian falters before the fact itself. Mr. Small was fined fifteen dollars and costs in the police court for disorderly conduct and several allied offenses.

The newspapers of the city, of Crosshampton Harbor, of Cosmos Villas and of Mr. Small's home town all reported the affair fully. A certain irreverent paper in the city sent one of its bright young men to interview him. Mr. Small talked at length about his rights as a citizen, a passenger, a clubman, a business man, a father. The reporter did not write a humorous account; he did something worse—he quoted Mr. Small's indignations word for word, so that Mr. Small thought he had been grossly misrepresented.

He threatened to sue for libel. But before he could undertake the suit he was otherwise interested.

Going inconspicuously into the city he saw Mr. Cornelius Berry, the various commodores, and everybody else he knew, reading the newspaper interview with him. They did not seem to see him. He silently showed his ticket a second time after the junction. He heard a snicker. When he reached the office Mr. Woodley, of the firm, called him in and gave him two weeks' notice.

"You've terminated your usefulness here, Small," said the chief. "You can't expect to keep office discipline when the whole office is laughing itself sick at your escapades. You'll instruct the salesclerk how to take up your duties. By the way, I've been looking into your work a little. Let me suggest that on your next job you don't try to make all the girls hate you. It may please you a lot, but we didn't hire you to have fun. . . . You want to learn something about efficiency, man!"

For the first time in his Whittier J. Small life our hero doubted his greatness. That evening as he slid into the train he saw Percy Weather—good old Percy, the one man in Crosshampton Harbor who was worth knowing. . . . For some curious reason he had hardly seen the dear chap for a month. . . . He murmured:

"Sitting here, old man?"

Mr. Weather stopped and foolishly stroked his straw-colored cheeks.

"Why!" he said—then: "No, by gosh, I'm not." And he marched on.

Mr. Small was in a rage when he reached home. "We will go down to the club tonight," he stated to Mrs. Small.

"Do you think—had we better?" she ventured.

"And why not?—if I may be allowed to venture a question about your high and mighty way of deciding where I can go."

"Oh, I just—I just wondered!"

"Then you can just-wondered about—can't you keep those children quiet for one moment?—you can just-wondered about something more profitable; about this boot-sole of a steak, for instance. Do you think that when I come home all worn out I want to look at a steak, or try and eat it? I suppose this is a suffrage steak. By the way, I got fired today, you'll be pleased to hear."

At first Mr. Small wondered why a woman tried to get round him by weeping. Then, as she sobbed on and could not get the courage to try to stop, he felt something break inside himself. He knew that all the time had been blackguarding her he had been wistfully glad that she, at least, would stand by him—not laugh at his arrest. . . . He stroked her hair as though he had not done it for years. His wife wept harder than ever; but in the end they went to the club together, arm cuddling arm.

He feared that he would be received in silence. Not at all! The club wag insisted on reading the libelous interview aloud, after trying to persuade Mr. Small to read it. The Smalls left early. This time it was Mrs. Small who was volubly indignant and Mr. Small who depended on her.

The next day was the end of the month—time to get commutation. He shoved his $9.17 under the wicket at the city ticket office and demanded, "Crosshampton Harbor; W. J. Small," with the peremptory manner necessary for keeping employees in their places.

The ticket man scratched his head, looked as though he was trying to remember something, reached up for a little book, and turned in it to S.

"Sorry, Mr. Small, but you can't buy commutation," he said.

"What do you mean?"

"What I said. Orders."

"Orders that I can't buy————"

"Yump. Don't block up the window. I've got my orders—that's all. Commutation is a reduced fare. The railroad doesn't have to sell it—and it doesn't to people who misuse it."

"Why, I can make you sell————"

"Yes; you can make us sell you first-class fare. You'll find first-class round-trip tickets at the window on the right—Crosshampton Harbor fare, ninety-four cents a round trip. Don't block up the window any more, please."

Mr. Small stormed into the general offices to find out whence came the order that he, Whittier J. Small, could not buy commutation. He did not find out. Apparently the order was self-made—but it was there on the books all right, he was suavely informed by the secretary of the general passenger agent. He stared quietly out of the car window all the way home. That evening he called Mrs. Small "Honey" for the first time in a decade. And he did not entertain her with his theories of how he should manage the kitchen. He listened to her account of the Dorcas Society meeting and even smiled—twice.

The girls in the office of which Mr. Whittier J. Small is now manager say that he is kind and considerate—comparatively.

The Smalls are moving away from Crosshampton Harbor next month. There is too much malaria for the children.

NATURE, INC.

This is not the history of the bland Professor Tonson, but of a man who became flamboyantly ridiculous and then became human, and along the way learned something of love, the intensive culture of the string bean, and Mystic Powers; and in the end discovered that if he was not afraid of being completely unreasonable he could make life glorious.

Professor Tonson was not a professor of anything or at anywhere, but he made a specialty of knowing everything. His prize subjects were Hindu metaphysics, and the food value of the humble but earnest peanut, and the most expeditious methods of extracting fortunes from elderly ladies of high moral tendencies. He looked a good deal like an English major with a white horseshoe mustache and a weakness for mixing drinks. Whereas Mr. William Packard, of the Cape Realty Development Company, knew nothing at all about dietetics or theosophy—though he was one hundred percent efficient at the methods for getting elderly ladies' fortunes back into circulation.

Mr. Packard was built like Mr. Jess Willard, the distinguished autobiographer and physical culturist, and wore his five-dollar hat at an impertinent angle on his mighty and baldish head.

He had symptoms of tobacco heart, coffee heart, motor heart, cocktail heart, poker heart and musical-comedy heart. He kept six different physicians expectant of his becoming violently ill with six or more ailments, though he always felt well after ten A.M.

He met the professor when the later pussyfooted into Packard's real-estate office with a preposterous offer for two hundred acres on Cape Cod for the establishment of an enlarged plant of the Nature and Guidance Colony—Inc. The professor teetered and Packard pounded on the desk, and the scene looked stormily tragic; and then they quite amiably agreed on a price and went out to lunch together.

The professor took a Black and White Lunch—he called it that; the waiter called it a crime—consisting of asparagus without dressing, ripe olives, and modicum of Bar-le-Duc—he called it a modicum. Packard took a beefsteak and kidney pudding, a baked potato, plum pudding, two pots of coffee and a cigar. The professor gently, stickily tried to persuade Packard that he ought to give up meat, tobacco, coffee, and most of the other things for which that well-to-do bachelor lived.

"Yes," said Packard; "but canning all that back-to-Nature dope, what plans have you got for the erection of your buildings? I'm president of the Barnstable County Construction Company; I've put up most of the hotels and the real classy houses that have gone up on the Cape in the last five years; and I'll make you an attractive proposition."

The professor took the attractive proposition; and five months later Packard motored up to Nauset Harbor to examine progress on the buildings of the Nature and Guidance Colony.

Though he made most of his money out of Cape Cod, Packard knew it only by motor car. He had never met a native who said "Twa'n't!" and he had the simple-hearted rule of staying only at hotels whose rates were six dollars a day or more.

He did not know a sand dune from a Swampscott dory, unless he saw one in a blueprint. He regarded the shellbacks and the kindly summerites, together, as one vast hog of cranberries, which he plucked, but with which he did not associate.

Consequently he was bored when he entered a tract of barren uplands, the grass dried to a wheat-gray and mulberry color, beyond which was a steel-blue inlet and a barricade of gray dunes.

His car staggered on a sandy road and he beheld a line of cottages like bathhouses, without even a boardwalk and a shower bath in front of them.

Professor Tonson met him with bouncing enthusiasms. Every time he said "Wonnnnnnderful!" or "Llll-Lovely!" it sounded like a hand drawn over the bottom of a whisk broom. The professor, who had worn a frock coat and a white waistcoat in the city, was neatly clad in a straight linen robe like the old-fashioned night-gowns that respectable gentlemen who parted their whiskers used to wear. He also had sandals and carried a book about the size of a tombstone. But Packard paid small to attention him, because in the professor's wake was a girl of twenty-four or twenty-five, like a silver image, with bobbed hair of shining ash-blond. She wore a garment like a gunny sack; but she had the grace of girlhood ivory-skinned, eternal.

The raising of Packard's hat was a study in sprightly gracious-ness. It was a perfect thing, like Matty's pitching or a Futurist cut-out puzzle by Matisse. He skipped from the car and was introduced to the professor's lieutenant, Miss Beulah Atkinson.

While the professor returned to his class in Upstirrings Toward the Infinite, which had already begun in the half-finished Taber-nacle—a wooden Greek temple of the First National Bank order of architecture—Packard was conducted about the grounds by Miss Beulah. Packard slid, in his nine-dollar tan oxfords, down the baking side of the dune; he kicked his way through long beach grass and thick cranberry patches; but he was oblivious of his martyrdom.

He had had a shock that turned all his briskness into exalted humbleness, for Miss Beulah's light-swimming eyes were raised to the clouds with worshipping exaltation; her low voice was intense with the happiness of the Colony's finding a place where they could be free and "real." Her hands, smooth-finished as enamel, touched his arm to herald the sea vista of silver-and-blue water, edged with gold-green downs. He finally got it through his head that this girl, whom he took very seriously, actually believed in the Colony, which he had despised.

As suddenly as though the touch of her fingers were a charm, he found the Colony—peanuts and linen gowns and all—a highly important and interesting discovery. He had been quizzing her about the small meanness of the colonists' cottages and the grandeur of the professor's new home; he had cynically learned that the Colony members gave one-tenth of their fortunes to the Colony. But now he stopped, threw back his head, expanded his huge chest, and drew in all the exhilaration of the sea breeze, while he volunteered:

"Well, it really is a beautiful place here—by golly! I'm more used to Washington Street; but there is something to————"

"Something won-derful!"

"Yuh! Wonderful! Sea and landscape———— Say, is there any good fishing here?".

"I really don't know; but————" Miss Beulah flung out both her arms. Her baggy sleeves fell away and her arms shone bare and exquisite. "We are fishing for human souls!" she cried. "Don't you know the city transforms the people into machines—into machines for digesting meat and doing silly, useless work? We want to make them free."

Packard trembled "Y-yes!" like an awed small boy. He wanted to kiss her hand. His regular rule for handling women customers— "Kid every chicken you meet"—seemed unutterably sordid in her presence. He stammered and drew in a full breath again.

"Don't you feel tired and useless first thing in the morning?" she demanded.

"Why, yes; don't you?"

"Never!"

"Wish you'd show me the trick."

"Nature has shown you the trick. It has given us the sea and the air and the nourishing vegetables."

"I wish it'd given me you to show me how."

"Perhaps it has."

"Would you show me the trick if I stayed down here?"

She flushed. Uneasily: "Why—why, if I could. But it's—it's Professor Tonson who shows us all."

"Oh! Him! I'd rather have your version."

"I'm only a silly child compared with him. It's he who has the Guidance, in Revelations that tell us what the Colony shall do— the Natural Food, and all."

"Yes," said Packard meekly—two hundred and six pounds of meekness that moved its feet carefully and tried to look like a gentle lover of Natural Food who preferred a bunch of Brussels sprouts to roast beef any day.

They sat on a dune looking to sea. Sometimes she was a very mature person who awed him by scraps of knowledge about metaphysics. Sometimes she was an eager girl who whispered "Look! Oh, look!" when a plover ran along the shore. The wind blew her grotesque garment into delicate lines and her bobbed hair fluttered constantly. She cried:

"Have you a bathing suit? No? Wouldn't you like a swim? It would give me an excuse! I'll get the professor to lend you one."

She herself changed to a coquettish garment of silk with a flounced skirt and a quite un-Natural bow of coral-hued satin. She led him plunging out into the surf, her white shoulder muscles flowing like ripples on an inland stream. As they breasted a breaker together he suddenly—and apropos of everything—knew that he was in love with her. And that love stood the test of her taking him to the professor's last class in the Hydraulics of Natural Food— and to the Colony supper, an original combination of old string beans and new corn mush.

An hour afterward, as he sat down to an English mutton chop and other things not included in Natural Food, at the Santequisset Inn, he kept shaking his head and muttering: "Well, I'll be darned!" And when his calm was so shaken that he was diverted from his fascinated interest in food and expectant of being darned during meals, then he was stirred indeed.

Mr. Packard, broker and constructor, builder of castles in Spain, in the air, on sand and on tidal flats, had ideals. They were mostly filed away under "I" in back files covered with dust; but the thought of Beulah, his vision of the flame of life as it flickered in her eyes, represented to him those ideals. He saw her as a victim of the professor's Revelations; but, for the first time in his years of selling shacks to people who wanted to get near to the primitive, he was willing to admit that there really might be something interesting in the life of barren shores—and more barren suppers.

More and more the decorative ladies who had cheered his city bachelor life seemed shoddy beside Beulah, after that day. He motored to the Colony once a week or oftener. The life there came to seem almost reasonable. He even felt satisfaction when the Colony membership grew to thirty—thirty lean gentlemen and agitated old ladies—and he did not protest very violently when the professor broke Beulah's heart by making her change her silk bathing suit for a garment that looked like a holland summer covering for a large chair. He had caught from Beulah her faith in the Colony.

She, the daughter of a dreamy New Thought clergyman, had all her life been accustomed to take cobwebby theories seriously, and on her father's death had become the lieutenant of Professor Tonson. Emotions, enthusiasms, theories, trust, were to her real things. She never grinned when she read in New Thought magazines the advertisements of gentlemen who offer for an insignificant sum to cure baldness by Thought Power, or to initiate you into recently discovered mysteries of the Tibetans that will increase your bank account and keep your cook from leaving. She could not convert William Packard to her theories, but she did convert him to a belief in herself.

On an October day, when the line of silver poplars and cottonwoods that shouldered across the hills back of the Colony was high-colored, when the sea breeze had an entrancing nip, and ducks hurried across the sky, and the course tide roared on the bars of Gosnold's Rip, Packard sat beside her on the dove-gray sands. His tie was gay as of old, but he wore black sneakers and khaki trousers smeared in crosshatchings with motor-boat grease.

His voice was not flippant, but quiet with friendship and a deep affection more genuine than any feeling he had known before in his bustling life. "Well," he said, "I guess our party's all over now. Buildings are done."

"Yes."

"And I'll have to go back to the city."

"Yes."

"Well, Beulah, it'll be kind of too bad to leave———"

"Yes; when you are coming to understand our simplicity here ———"

"Yes; but I wish you could see Boston. Be fine! Art galleries and opera and music and stuff—and, say, it wouldn't hurt you to be comfortable for a while! You'd enjoy it here all the more when you get back."

"Yes; but the sea————"

"Yes; but the streets————"

"Yes; but———— Oh, Billy you aren't going back and stay, and lose all the simplicity here, and lose—lose————"

"Lose you?" He stopped fencing. "No, no; I won't! Why, you absurd littleness, I could hold you in one hand and I could put one finger round your neck, and yet already you've become my boss. Will you marry me if I come here and live? I————"

"Yes."

He picked her up and cradled her in his arms. For an instant their lips blurred together as the waves met and blurred with the sands. Holding him off, she said, lucidly and quaintly as a child talking to a beloved uncle:

"Come, then; we'll get Professor Tonson to marry us this afternoon according to the rites, and then we'll drive right down to Orleans and be married again—to make it legal."

"T-this afternoon! Why, little girl, don't you want to be engaged for a while? Why, gee, I've never heard————"

"Oh, no, Billy. You see, I've had a course in Conversion of the Worldly-Minded to Higher Thought; and the professor taught us that when a man yields to the Natural Force of Love he'll be willing to follow the Clearer Feminine Light of the Woman—at first. But then he'll get old-minded, and want to go back to his worldly Spirit Habits and still try to keep his love; so he must be shown the way while there is yet light."

"Well, gee, honey, I thought a business man would be able to put it all over this Higher Thought bunch; but you win."

"Oh, yes, dear," she said serenely. "I expect to manage you, as a humble aid to the professor, until you get trained in the Higher Life. Come, child!"

She sprang from his lap. Her spring was like the swallow's darting flight along the sedge grass. She took his hand and led him toward the Colony. . . . They crossed the long flat sickle of beach; they stumbled up through loose sand and the tangled brown selvage of grass roots to a dunetop; they were outlined against the angry sky—her hair blowing out like the delicate filaments of mist that were flicked with the storm clouds. They turned back to face the sea and his arm was about her, his chin was high. Then she took his hand again. He followed her like a meek but enormously over-grown boy and they disappeared beyond the dunes.

Two pearly-breasted terns, flying in from sea, preened themselves on the sand and watched the vanishing lovers.

"Haw!" laughed one raucously, hoarse-noted as the surf. "There go two fools! Doesn't it make you landsick to see a fifteen-foot horse mackerel trying to play with a herring—like that?"

"You're a fool—and a young fool!" said the elder tern. "All you know yet is food. Don't you understand that everyone laughs at lovers because a laugh is the tenderest thing in the world? Come on! The sperling are running."

It was not only that his simple taste preferred a steak sprinkled with mushrooms to a tulip-bulb salad, but, furthermore, Packard considered it an insult that Professor Tonson should lecture him on the merits of the beans that he himself had raised. Oh, Packard—Brother Packard—had raised the beans, all right! For seven months now he had been a tremendously married member of the Nature and Guidance Colony, and he had brought those beans up by hand, according to the Montessori method.

He had fed them and watered them and called them religious-sounding pet names, and almost dandled them on this knee and taught them "Chopsticks" on the piano. He had weeded them daily—he knew nothing about botany and he could not have told you the Latin name of a single weed, but he had little names of his own for every one of them. There was a bunch of casual grass that stuck to the ground like your last stamp to a misdirected envelope. There was the flat, sneaky weed that sprawled like a fawning dog, with a lying and treacherous smile on its shiny leaves, and had to be yanked by hand.

Clad in a straight linen robe and sandals, and a Peter the Hermit haircut, with his poor patient desk-trained back contorted to a stoop, his tender neck slowly broiling to one red smear of unhappiness, Packard had weeded, and weeded, and weeded—he, the immaculate, whose diagonally striped ties, and club-barber haircuts, and manicured nails, and suits with a faintly distinctive pattern, once had made him as sleek as a newly groomed race horse! Now he had actually got used to is incredible linen Colony robe, which flapped with a sneaky sheepishness about his plump ankles.

He had been so wistfully good. He had not made once sign of wanting to beat the professor; he had not quarreled with him—well, had scarcely quarreled with him at all. But now, when the professor came nickering round at Colony supper, suave among the workhouse-gray benches and bare tables; when he praised the succulent beans as though Packard had never even heard of a bean before, Packard growled: "Y' ought to weed them!" And under the shelter of the table he bent a fork double. The professor merely smiled and flowed away.

After supper the colonists were instructed to retire to their cottages for Instructive Reading. Though he had not become particularly instructed, Packard had obediently read several pounds of books about Spirit Impulses and about sages who lived a long while ago and wore beards. The books all sounded so much alike that Packard would unintentionally skip from Yogi Trance, on page 223, to Navajo Concentration, on page 226, without knowing he had missed anything in between. And he had kept himself from smoking, though every ten minutes during the evening a bright realization would come to him that he wanted something new and exciting, and wanted it right now—and that something new would always prove to be the same old thing, a smoke.

The women sat across from the men in the Hall. Packard hastened across to where Beulah's silken hair and the lovely little curve of her chin were brilliant amid the discreet gray or earnest old women. As he approached her, as she looked up like a white verbena blossom tilted by a breeze, the resentment that he belonged to this ridiculous colony left him, and his smile was radiant when he whispered:

"I'm going out to try and meditate on the dunes. Be right home."

His whisper was a vocal caress; but he was lying, passionately, devotedly, for Packard was not as yet in such a state of Natural Grace that he really cared much for sitting on a damp dune and meditating on the *Bhagavad-Gita*. He was not going to go out and try to get into any such state of grace, either. He was going to have a smoke. And he concealed his vile object from his wife partly because he did not want to hurt her feelings and partly because—oh, any married man will understand!

He carted his huge form out among the dark dunes as delicately as a lone fern frond, lest he be discovered by the chronic Meditators and be invited to join in a real Meditation bee. He stole into a clump of pines and laurel and scrub oak—and luxuriant poison ivy, which gratefully parted to make it easy for him to get right into the midst of it—and after cursory fumbling reached his new hiding place for a box of one thousand cigarettes and two thousand matches, his last thoughtful purchase before taking a year's leave of Boston and his business. He felt in a nonexistent trousers pocket for a match safe he no longer carried. He took a match from the box, and as he scratched it on his shiny linen robe he mourned:

"This is a hell of a pair of pants for a Pride's Crossing Club man to wear! Gee, the prof might let us wear pyjamas, anyway!"

He clumped toward the cubicle they called home, with its sparse furniture and the Futurist paintings that appealed to Colony taste. But he forgot his troubles when he found Beulah in the golden silk kimono which was her only remaining vanity; when they curled together in the armchair.

Everything has a symbol—at least if you live in a Nature and Guidance Colony. If beans were the symbol of the day that the historian has just chronicled, then of the following day twain were the symbols—fog and a cow rampant on a field slippery.

At five-thirty A.M., the hour at which the well-to-do Mr. Packard, of Boston, had been wont to turn over in bed for three more hours of conscientious slumber, the Colony always rose and had a unanimous, though not necessarily enthusiastic, swim before breakfast— call it breakfast. This morning of fate a fog like a snowstorm hid the world, presaged vague dangers Out There, crept through clothing, and chilled the colonists until they shivered and moaned as they hesitated out of warm beds. A foghorn down on the Point moaned like an orphaned calf at such regular intervals that Packard kept listening for its recurrence as he put on his damply stiff robe instead of his bathing suit. The robe felt like a new towel used as a washcloth, but it was divinely preferable to a bathing suit this morning.

"Thank the Lord, we don't have to go swimming anyway!" he sighed to the nose-tip of Beulah—the only part of her that had as yet dared to slip out of the pillow on which her head had snuggled.

"Yes!" she said devoutly, and burrowed again.

Packard went to stand on their doorstep. He wrapped a table covering about his shoulders. He felt like a man catching a three A.M. train for the first time in his life as he stared at the bleary fields and the blanket of mist. He wanted to smoke. He wanted to devour beefsteak and coffee. And, with a longing that passeth understanding, he wanted to go back to bed.

A suspicion of abominations and treachery chilled him still more. Down the row of cottages came Professor Tonson in a bathing suit, his lanky shanks of a gristly bareness beyond any ordinary white and rounded nudity. And the colonists were falling in behind him. Packard tried to present an impersonation of an influential and cheerful broker as he called:

"Guess it's too foggy for a swim this morning—eh, professor?"

The professor retorted:

"Certainly not! I have a Revelation that, no matter what the weather is, we must not give up our communion with the strength of the sea. Quit ye like men; be strong! Into your bathing suit at once, brother!"

The stringy-necked men and women who followed the professor, like a string of broken-down horses with the springhalt, all sniffed at William Packard's towering beef as though they did not really care very much for quitting them like men, but, anyway, they were stronger than this. The flapping scarecrows disappeared into the fog like a fantastic chorus recruited from soggy November corn-fields.

The fog hid the shore, hid even the dunes; but Packard could fairly feel the sea. He was sure that it had never been so wet as it was that morning. He turned back into his house, looking for sympathy from Beulah. He was going to encourage her to stay in her comfortable nest and defy the professor; but he found her already struggling with the canonical bathing robe for women—her ivory shoulders, like those of a priceless statue, partly covered with snuff-colored denim.

"Why, Billy, you must hurry! Didn't you hear the professor?" she said wonderingly.

Finally, his bathing suit had not dried properly overnight. It was probably the clammiest thing in the fog-swathed unhappy universe.

On shore, gray, weary waves rolled from under the gloomy curtain of fog, and nearer now was the foghorn's yawping warning that perils innumerous were lurking out there.

He plunged into the breakers like a whale and splashed a good deal to show that he was not afraid; but he was afraid, and when he came dripping out his heart was no longer God's little garden, but weedy with resentment against Beulah and hatred for the professor.

It was as he sat at a breakfast of corn chips, milk of faint lavender hue, oat cakes, and nice sugared hot water to take off the chill of the swim, that Packard realized he almost hated Beulah, too, as she absorbed the long droning observations on the Symbolism of Mist with which the professor made breakfast jolly and gay. Her devotion to the professor threatened to destroy the sacred tenderness and respect for her that was his religion. He had to get her away from here if love was to survive. . . . And incidentally he wanted a breakfast table with a silver coffeepot and fatly sentimental buttery muffins, and a Beulah who, just risen, would praise her big brave boy for having dared to go out and swim in the fog.

Clearly though Packard saw the danger to their love, he forgot it in the early afternoon, during the affair of the cow.

He was sent to fetch a cow, which had been grazing in an upland pasture. As he crossed the rolling moors; as he saw the colored hillsides with their patches of lichen-green and rose, and a yellow like the essence of sun; as he gazed over a sea that was clear of fog now and shone in dark blue waves, with a schooner on the far sky line—Packard was happy. He trotted uphill without a trace of the smoker's feeble panting. He felt as strong as a locomotive; his blood ran gloriously; he laughed with well-being.

Then he realized that a curious itching between his fingers had been bothering him more and more all day. He stopped and spread his fingers wide, his massive face puckering with childish discontent. He was poisoned with poison ivy.

Occasionally scratching one hand with the other, he trudged up the next hill. In his eyes the ocean now shone no more than a pile of musty hay. His trusting heart had been deceived again. So he came like sulky Achilles to where the cow grazed; and, flourishing a rope halter, he growled at the animal:

"Come here, you son of a mush-faced rabbit!"

The cow turned and slumped gently away. It seemed to suppose it was a colt in a pasture. It stopped now and then, and with its ludicrous hoofs coyly patted the earth before humping itself on again. Packard was too much engaged in paddling after it, in shaking his big red fist and bellowing illimitable curses, to see a silent-running motor car stop on the State Road, at the farther side of the field.

His name was called. He stopped. In the car were two brokers he had known in Boston. They were smoking large cigars; they were wearing hats like chorus men in a Palm Beach musical comedy; they looked insultingly well-fed; and they were accompanied by two girls of the sort who had always sighed "Oh, Mr. Packard!" at him.

He turned away in dignity. He paid no attention to their shouts. He—William Packard, who had stalked Tremont Street looking every man in the face—hid in a patch of weeds until the motor car had driven away. And for hours he fancied he could still smell the incense of those large Olympian cigars, still catch some aroma of the biggest steaks in the world, simply wallowing in onions.

And he still had a cow to catch; in fact, any time during the next half hour it might truthfully have been noted that he still had a cow to catch.

When he reached home, expecting Beulah to comfort him, she was in tears. . . . A female neighbor, a lady of more ideals than bosom, had complained to Professor Tonson that Buelah's pet vice, the silken robe she wore for Packard, was a Stumblingblock; and the professor had a Revelation that Beulah must give it to be sold for the Nature Gospel Fund.

Packard began:

"Why, the rotten old scoundrel! I'll make him give back your pretty. I'll make him eat———"

Buelah interrupted in a manner of horror:

"Bill! You're sacrilegious!"

He went to sit on a miserable pine doorstep and brood of a future in which his beloved would drive him away by her childish faith in Predigested Nature. The fog again was creeping over dune and sea.

It was an hour before their supper, and it was Thursday. Thursday supper always consisted of lentil chops, chicory salad, and lukewarm coffee substitute, a repast that could scarcely be trusted to make him leap like the young roe or the dancing doe, with Optimism Invincible, or any of the other standard brands of optimism in which the professor dealt.

He could not stand it, he felt. And he would not stand it! But the awe of love was on him; he was afraid to kick Beulah's idol. He would never be able to revolt if he hesitated for one single minute. He made himself lumber up from the front step like a great brown bear unwillingly rising from a blueberry bush. He trotted through the sneaking fog, his linen robe rustling against his legs.

As he ran he had a joyous vision of finding Professor Tonson secretly enjoying a steak or a smoke; of exposing him; of breaking up the Nature Colony; of returning to Boston with Beulah; of eating all the chops between Brockton and Portland in one enormous gorge, during which he would laugh at the professor—but he found the professor beautifully meditative and reading Bergson's *Creative Evolution*. His mustache shone with silver. He was a saintly sight. His poise was so perfect that Packard felt like an iceman.

"Say, I want to see you!" he said.

"And you do, brother," beamed the professor.

"Say, you! Look here! Whatyuhmean by————"

"Ah! The little matter of Sister Beulah's vain gauds?"

"I don't know anything about her gods, and don't spring that mystic dope on me again. D'yuh hear?"

The professor and Packard were equally aghast at the snarl with which the last words came out. It was as though the old Bill Packard, the unredeemed, had come stamping in, seized the conversation and shaken it by its ratty neck. Packard expected to be answered with a flood of the professor's contempt. He would bluff it out. He tried to remember how much stronger than the professor he was. He stood big and red and fist-clenched—feeling like a fool.

But the professor answered timidly:

"Very well; I'll r-r-r-return the robe at once, B-Brother Packard."

"Oh, you will, eh? Say, do you know what you're going to do

next? You're going to have a Revelation that Beulah and me are to return to Boston and eat meat and smoke our—smoke my head off! You're going to have one of the overpoweringest Revelations you ever had that what Beulah needs is—oh, music and all that highbrow stuff—or darn near everything else that she can't find outside the city. Get me, Tonson? If you don't feel symptoms of that Revelation coming on pretty quick sudden, I'm going to beat you till your right ear and left foot change places!"

Packard banged his fist on the professor's light reading table as once he had banged it on desks and things in office. The table split in twain. The professor put his hand to his breast. Again Packard roared:

"I've been getting into very decent ringside shape, and if—you—don't—have—that—Revelation————"

"But if I do?" piped the professor with the voice of a much smaller and less dignified man than himself.

"It'll be worth five hundred dollars to you!"

"I'll take you!" said the professor. "If it wouldn't be too much trouble for you to make out just a little memo of that agreement? Of course, my dear friend, if the Revelation isn't granted to me the agreement's off; but if it does come————"

"D'you find you feel any Telepathic Premonitions of its coming, heh?"

"Why, seriously, I think I do," said the professor with quiet gravity.

Packard scribbled the agreement and handed it over with a curt:

"Here y'are!"

"Thanks! . . . Say, Packard, what the devil made you take so long in coming down to business?"

"D'you mean to say I could have bought out Beulah and me any time?"

"Why, sure!"

The two men grinned at each other.

"Have a cigar?" said the professor.

As they both lighted up the professor continued:

"By the way, of course I know you're planning to do me out of the five hundred dollars you've agreed to, and probably you could do it. And I'll tear it up if you'll put three thousand dollars into stock in my plant here. Paid eighteen percent last year. See the books if you want to."

"You're on!" said Packard. "Give you a check any time—after the Revelation. Say, make the Revelation so it won't hurt Beulah's feelings, you know—so the poor kid'll be really glad to go to Boston, you know."

"Oh, sure!"

"Say, prof, when you come up to town, how about a little dinner, eh? Like dinner at the Victorian?"

"A'right! Glad to. And I'm due in town pretty soon, Packard. I'm about at my limit on vegetables."

"Say, old hoss, I got a hunch! Wouldn't we make a little on the side if we opened a sort of summer Chautauqua here?"

"Not a bad idea," blandly considered the professor. "Be willing to go in on it?"

"Sure!"

"We'll talk it over. Anything I can do for you after I get the Revelation?"

"Yes, by gum, there is! You can give me a pair of pants."

When he first returned to Boston Packard started to make up for lost time in all his pet ways of poisoning himself. He slept until nine and he had two cocktails for lunch, and the only exercise he took was lighting cigarettes. He wore yellow chamois gloves, and he could not have been pushed in the vicinity of a cold bath by anything less powerful than hydrostatic press.

He delighted in all aspects of business, from files to telephone calls. He managed to get so much pleasure out of worrying about office details which, from the distant Colony, had seemed negligible that his work was as much of a poison as his dissipations.

But he no longer telephoned to ornate young ladies and he no longer ran races with himself to see how late he could stay up nights. He was always tenderly conscious of Beulah; eager to blunder out with her to concerts, picture exhibitions, lectures; considerably more eager to take her to restaurants where the head waiters knew his sleek portliness; content just to stay home and listen to her enthusiasms—though the enthusiasms grew vaguer and vaguer, now that she was no longer under Guidance.

For a month the excitement of resuming his old life continued. Then it seemed to him as though he had never been away, as though he had always, without break, been going along Washington Street to the Imperial Grill for his heavy lunches.

Within two weeks after his return he was again accustomed to waking up with a taste like quinine in his mouth. Within three weeks he had to have a cigarette before he got the energy to dress in the morning. And by the time he was quite accustomed to being back he was beginning to feel dissatisfied with everything except Beulah.

His great tenderness for her played about the fact that she was still under the sway of Professor Tonson. Though she had no more communications from him, no Revelations, she was to be found unhappily reading his books—books in black covers, apparently printed by the office boy and bound by the porter; books with titles like *Soul-Breathing* and *The Occultism of Optimism*. Packard was so pitiful toward her unchanged faith that it became horrible to him that he should be in partnership with the professor to make money out of the virtue of fools. He broke off the partnership abruptly in a short dictated letter.

Tonson came up to Boston to protest. Packard told him—you know, of course, where the simple-hearted Packard told him to go; and he said:

"I'm going to have my hands as clean as I can now, Tonson. And don't smile that hyena smile of yours, or it'll cost me a ten-dollar police-court fine—and money's tight just now."

Packard went home and told Beulah the full truth about Tonson and himself.

She heard him out dumbly, her eyes averted. Then, "Thank you for telling me," was all she said; and she went to her room. . . . For the first time since, as a child, she had begun to potter about theories with her pervasively credulous father, she had no prophet. And she was convinced of Tonson's frauds. She was keen enough, once she had the clew.

Packard's life with her had been easy enough hitherto. He had merely to agree with her enthusiasms. Now she had no enthusiasms and he could not create them for her. While she patiently and changelessly smiled, he tried to interest her in motoring, in the theatre of the Tired Business Men. Sometimes she seemed aroused by his suggestions. Then he was happy. Betweenwhiles he hammered at his office work. There, at least, he could get results.

But when spring came even this last comfort departed. Packard constantly pictured the shore lines and dunes at the Nature Colony; he imagined the stimulus of a plunge in the surf; he hated the stale air of the city.

So at last, though he still wore the uniform of Mr. William Packard, captain of business, he envied the ridiculous Brother Packard and almost cried for the impossible return of the happy days of the Colony.

And his humble attitude toward Beulah changed. A small thing began it—though for weeks he had been saying: "I've got to do something for the little girl."

When he came home to their apartment on an April evening with a smell of spring creeping through the musty city as a lavender bag scents a bureau drawer, he found Beulah at a closed window, pressing her temples with both hands.

"Why, honey bird," he said, "why don't you open the window? You that are so crazy about fresh air! And shure an' a foine large avening it is!"

"Oh! . . . So much bother," she said.

"But, gee, don't you care for fresh air now?"

"Oh! . . . Yes. . . . I must go dress now."

"No; but straight! Don't you?"

"Oh, yes, yes; I suppose so. I was too lazy—just looking out—dusk." She sighed as she trailed away.

At dinner he insisted again, with the boyish whining of a man hungry for simpler and surer love:

"But say—about the window: I was just thinking——— Don't you really like outdoor sports and all that, like you used to?"

"No—yes—oh! I don't know. . . . Oh, don't worry about me, you old angel! I'm tired tonight."

Nothing more—but all the evening, while they played at coon-can, which they detested and kept returning to, and all the next day, while part of his brain was busy in the office, he was absorbed in thinking: "The kiddy needs to go back to plain grub and cold swims, and a belief in somebody." As he was going home he meditated: "Why, by golly, that's what I need too! Think of Billy Packard wanting to do the primitive, like a fifty-dollar-a-season renter on the Cape! . . . Gee! Wonder if Beulah will want to go back now! Well, I guess I'll have to make her."

When he entered the apartment she was again standing list-lessly by the window. He blurted:

"Honey, we're going back to the Cape; and we're going to live in a shack, and swim, and eat every dern thing that's good for us—except maybe beans. . . . We'll stay there four or five months, and then we'll turn farmers and stay for good. How does that sound to you? Pretty good, eh? Pretty fine?"

"Oh, I——— Oh, I don't know! . . . I don't think I care to go back now."

"Sure you do, old honey! You'll feel fine after you've got a little tan on. Come on; let's start to plan our packing. Where's my big old trunk? In the basement?"

"No, no; really Billy! I'm sorry, but I couldn't go now. I hate the city, but I'd hate the shore or the country worse. I—I haven't any prophet now that'll guide me. Perhaps you don't understand what I mean, though."

"Yump; I understand. I'm going to be our household prophet from now on, and I'm giving a lecture on How to Take Life Easy this evening. Come on; we'll look up that trunk."

He picked her up from the chair and replied to her indignant "Well, really!" with a kiss.

When sundown turned the low-tide flats into plates of polished copper two children in scanty bathing suits—two brown, deep-breathing, bright-eyed children—dug for clams and skipped across the flats—Packard and Beulah.

"We'll have the chicken tonight," he said. "I'm hungry."

"Gee!" she said, quite unself-consciously. "So'm I."

"Now sit down on a nice soft pool and we'll have my evening lecture. No; let's have naturalization examination for your second papers, first: Who's the greatest living naturist?"

"Professor Bill Packard," she said meekly.

"And who's going to teach Professor Bill Packard to become a farmer next spring?"

"Mrs. Beulah Foolish Packard."

"And who's going to be Professor Bill Packard's successor as head of the Packard Nature Colony, Incorporated and darn Limited?"

She answered shyly, as she always did at this point in their game: "Billy Packard, Junior—unless Billy turns out to be Beulah."

IF I WERE BOSS

I. YOUTH CAN

Charley McClure had been a traveling salesman long enough to know how to get the goods on the shelves, but not long enough to know how the office helped the merchant to get them off again, and he was sure the whole office force was in a conspiracy against him.

To Charley McClure business was an adventure, and a salesman following up new prospects was more inspiring than all those old crusaders put together. So he told his best girl, Agnes, in the quick-talking confidence of youth, when he was in from the road, and they sat on the high stoop of Agnes's home on a side street in Brooklyn, planning to conquer the world. He told her that he'd rather be a hustler than a belted earl. Agnes giggled and said: "So would I, if the earl's papa belted him often." Then they laughed very much and kissed each other and went for a walk. This was back in 1890, when there were no movies for them to attend.

Charley McClure had always been in the ranks—messenger boy before the day of telephones, clerk, city salesman for a glassware importing company, traveling salesman for an art-novelty company, and now, at the age of thirty, salesman for The Greebe & Slosson Book Company. His territory was all the Middle West—that is, all of it except the towns where there were any accounts worth getting. He was used to the dollar-and-a-half commercial hotels, where you wiped the knives and forks on your napkins before using them. He made an average of two towns a day, and most of the towns consisted of red grain elevators, saloons, churches, and farm-machinery agencies. He traveled by smoker, caboose, buggy and even by handcar.

The Greene & Slosson Book Company's line consisted of blood-and-thunder juveniles, the Cutey Series for young children, the Sweetix and Sue Series for girls, and a rather ragged line of games and paper dolls. The Greene-Slosson paper doll, with three costumes printed in four colors, retailed at five cents.

The chin-whisker contingent in country stores "guessed" and "reckoned" that "they wa'n't no demand for them paper things, and if they was, they'd get them from the jobber next time they wrote him." But Charley McClure labored with them like a music teacher, and on his second trip he increased sales seventeen percent. Then in the middle of the trip the office took away from him the only fat towns in the territory—Madison, Eau Claire, Des Moines, Davenport, Duluth and Winona—and gave all of them to the wily second salesman, Tom Snider, usually known as Little Thomas.

Consequently Charley McClure arrived in New York with a desire to tell everybody, from the porters at the Grand Central Station to the firm themselves, that he had been given a raw deal. He thought seriously of getting someone to write up this injustice for a trade paper. Let the firm writhe, and realize what a wrong they had done the best young salesman in the business! Who, he pugnaciously asked himself, had taken up the Greene-Slosson game Gollywolly when everybody had said it would be a failure, and started its popularity? Why, he had!

Charley's plans for revenge by publicity, which had seemed highly feasible while he sat grouching on the train from Chicago to New York, suddenly became ridiculous when he caught a surface car at the Grand Central and, hanging by a strap, glanced about and realized how many other abused young men there are in New York. When he reported back at the office he compromised by looking savagely at Little Thomas Snider.

"Hello, Charley, you been making a record," said Little Thomas, apparently under the impression that Charley's savage look was a chatty greeting.

There was something about the office that robbed Charley of his fine youthful frenzy. All of them, even Little Thomas, who was just back from Cleveland, acted as though nobody in the world did anything but poke down to the office at eight-thirty, glue his face to a desk and sit there all day. Facing the bored calm of old S. R. Rice, the sales manager—who sold only to the biggest stores in New York, Philadelphia and Boston—and the placid immobility of the clerks and office women and bookkeepers, it was impossible for Charley to keep up his dynamic fury. Sitting in the salesmen's room, with its six stodgy desks, and the familiar tattered calendar over Rice's desk, and the sample room unchanging beyond, he could not believe that he had been hiking from one-story, false-front stores to red frame stations just a few days before.

He fled over to Brooklyn and kissed Agnes, his sweetheart, violently on her straight, anxious lips and her high, prim forehead, and told her all his troubles. She agreed with him that the firm and the sales manager and the other salesmen were all jealous of him. But Agnes' patient eyes grew teary and she begged him not to risk losing his job. She was already making curtains for the little house they hoped to have in Jersey.

He promised that he would not antagonize the office. "But," he declared, "if I ever got to be boss I'd chum up to the young fellows and find out what they wanted. I wouldn't do all this big-brass-hat business about discipline and all that stuff, the way the firm and Simmy Rice do. I'd just lay my cards down on the table, and be one of the boys, and work with them. I suppose Simmy rice thinks I'd take advantage of him if he acted like a regular human being instead of a sales manager. I'd trust a fellow if I was a sales manager."

"I'm sure you would—or if you were in the firm, dear!" Agnes thrilled. "Oh, it will be wonderful when you're the boss!" she cried. She took his cheeks in her two hands and in his eyes read glory. Her angular body throbbed with happiness.

Next day, when Charley was getting ready to make the rounds of some of the smaller city shops which he sold while he was in New York, Little Thomas Snider remarked: "Say, son, what seems to be the trouble? Strikes me I behold a little peevishness on the rosy young cheeks. Let's go out and have a drink."

"Oh, I got to get up to Goldfarb's and show 'em Gollywolly."

"Well, listen to our prize scholar! Rats; you've got time for a drink."

Little Thomas, who was as round and cheerful as a child's painted rubber ball, took him to the bar of the Magnificent and told him several stories about lady buyers. While they leaned against the marble bar and Charley thought about seizing his sample case and hustling up to Goldfarb's, Little Thomas demanded: "Now tell us what's the trouble, Charley?"

"Well, gosh, you ought to know—grabbing Des Moines and all the real cities I had in my territory! Look here, I was just nine miles from Des Moines, covering towns by buggy, and you sail into Des Moines and pick up all the fat orders and light your cigar and skip on to Omaha. Nice chance I got to make a record! I'll tell you right now"—Charley was getting excited—"there's got to be a change in routing. If you fellows think I'm going to get stuck with all the rube towns and not have any velvet at all, you're mistaken. I won't stand it, even if I am a junior salesman."

"Tut, tut, whoa-up, hold your horses, son! You've got the wrong view entirely. Look here, you've been with us long enough now so's it's time you got on to office politics. You want to get out with us fellows more and learn the inside dope. Simmy Rice is the meanest sales manager in the business. If the firm knew how he just deliberately goes out of his way to prevent our making sales he'd last about two minutes. I could have sold more Gollywolly and I could have sold the new Cutey book—why, I could have sold ten thousand Gollywolly to the jobbers in Chicago, and hundreds and five-hundreds all along the line, this last trip—but how could I sell any without samples? That's what I says to Rice when I gets back. 'Of course,' I says, 'if you're too busy to get me advance samples, two weeks after the manufacturing department gets 'em for you,' I says, 'why, you can't expect me to sell more than ten billion of 'em, can you? If you'd send me something to show I'd show it all right,' I says, 'but I can't just go to sleep and dream what the darn things are like, can I?' Then Simmy Rice claimed he'd sent me advance descriptive matter. 'Aw, descriptive matter me eye!' I says—oh, I talked right up to him. 'They won't buy descriptions,' I says. Then he said he'd sold 'em to New York and Boston and Philadelphia on descriptions, 'Well,' I says, 'if you can work miracles, all right,' I says, 'but don't expect me to. I ain't a faith healer; I'm a drummer,' I says."

Every selling concern has a salesman who is debonair, well-dressed, noisy, and a devil with the ladies; clever and convincing, but also lazy and careless, and full of fine, new plausible excuses for his failures. Such was Little Thomas. And most offices have salesmen who are serious and conscientious, more easily taken in, but making up for it by driving industry. Such was Charley McClure. Charley had heard other salesmen curse S. R. Rice, the sales manager, but not till now, when he had a grievance, had he taken part in their conspiracy against the rules, the fault-finding, the unfriendliness, the slackness of Rice. Little Thomas explained to him—while they had another drink, and the Goldfarb store's pressing need of that highly educational game, Gollywolly, was forgotten—that Rice had been selling personally only to New York; but that, in his wild conceit, he had taken on the jobbers and department stores and chief shops of Boston and Philadelphia for his personal territory. This had cut out the best territory of Little Thomas, and a general readjustment had been necessary, in which Charley had lost his chief cities.

"I tell you," Little Thomas made oration, partly to Charley and partly to a cynical bartender with a banneret of hair plastered on his red skull, "if I were sales manager, I'd be satisfied to stick in the office and give the young fellow a chance. But we'll fix right yet, you bet! Let me tell you, once Slosson gets on to what Simmy Rice is putting over on him, Simmy will last about long enough to pick out his own gallows in a nice sunny spot. Greene is an old dreamer, but Slosson—yeah, he's sleepy like a fox in a chicken yard. I was saying to Slosson just the other day—oh, I talked right up to him—and I said————"

Little Thomas had, it seemed, said a great many wise things to an impressive number of people, and most of his saying had been frightfully satiric descriptions of S. R. Rice. Charley and he had another drink, and gleefully described that Gollywolly was much too good a game to let Goldfarb see at all; so they had dinner together and went to a show without reporting back to the office.

Next morning Rice was severe to both of them. It was the first time Charley had been blamed for drinking, and a personal hatred for Rice harrowed him as the sales manager's acrid voice, carrying over the glass-and-wood semipartition, heralded to the entire office: "About one more of this sort of caper from you two, and you get hauled up on the carpet, and not by me neither, but by the firm, see? Now I mean it!" The office girls giggled at Charley all day, and with every giggle he hated Rice the more. He, who normally did not take a drink oftener than once a month, to be blamed by Rice, who had his nip of Scotch regularly at four P.M.!

While Little Thomas went roundly and cheerfully and colorfully on his way, drinking and eating and singing and dancing and talking violently about the sales manager—and never getting beyond mere talking—Charley McClure worked and brooded. It seemed hard that Rice should have three thousand dollars for merely sitting at his desk and reading reports, while he had only twelve hundred dollars, and the patient Agnes was still deprived of the cottage for which she yearned. Little Thomas' talking seemed to relieve his grievance; Charley turned his grievance into energy.

Charley hadn't much imagination or diplomacy, but he could do three things—walk, and pull goods out of his sample case, and be honest. So shop after shop in Brooklyn and Harlem and the newly developing district of the Bronx saw the light in regard to the Greene-Slosson games and books and paper dolls. Thus Charley expended much of the force of his hatred. But he did talk, too. One does in offices. As he became more and more an insider in office intrigues, he found it satisfying to join in the impromptu indignation meetings that were always assembling in the sample room or in the safe privacy of the packing room. Because S. R. Rice was unpopular, whatever he did was regarded as bad-tempered or foolish or unnecessary.

Little Thomas, having submitted a plan to get the Cutey Series moving by sending them out on consignment more widely, a plan which he regarded as touched with original genius, and having been received by Rice with sarcastic remarks on dealers' credit, came bouncing into the sample room where Charley McClure was arranging stock, and muttered cautiously:

"Now what do you think the old yahoo's latest is? I tell you I ain't going to stand it much longer. I've taken just about all I'm going to off Simmy Rice. Here I go to him with a plan that would boom the Cuteys, and do I get thanked? I do not. I get kicked—because Rice didn't think of it himself! I tell you what this office needs is a new sales manager. If I ever get to be boss you can bet your bottom dollar if a man comes to me with an original plan I'll take him out and buy him a drink and listen to him—that's what I'll do. Don't tell anybody—this is a dead secret—but the Kansas City Novelty Den are crazy to get me to manage their retail department, and one more slap from Simmy and I'll take them up."

At such conferences several salesmen would gather, and each would say impressively: "The trouble with this office is————" And each would, as though he were revealing a revolutionary secret, announce that he was thinking of taking a new job directly. You really wouldn't have expected to find anybody left in the office except Greene, Slosson and Rice next morning. But they differed radically as to what was "the trouble with the office"; and somehow they never took those jobs. By and by they cheerfully packed their sample cases and started out on the road for The Greene & Slosson Company.

Charley felt that he, and he only, really knew what was the trouble with the office. It needed new routing, so that a bright young man might have chance. But he enjoyed the conferences enormously, and he studied every aspect of Rice, from his religion and his ready-made ties to his unwilling manner of saying "Good morning." Charley was learning an important role in human affairs—that hatred of the same person unites people more than does love. He would not normally have felt any vast fellowship with that cheerful liar, Mr. Little Thomas Snider, but when they went out to lunch, and Little Thomas sympathized with Charley's statement that he would be chummy with the boys if he were boss, then Charley's heart swelled with glad pride at knowing such a cultured, handsome, understanding personage as Little Thomas.

During the evening talks of Charley and Agnes, on the high stoop or over a game of Gollywolly in her father's sitting room, the rebellion against the sales manager gave them an exciting new topic of conversation, just when the various brands of weather had been pretty thoroughly discussed, and even the plans for the cottage in Jersey had assumed a certain sameness. When Agnes was petulant, when her high, pale, gentle forehead was wrinkled and she doubted whether S. R. Rice was veritably the only and original Father of Evil, then Charlie triumphantly quoted to her the opinion of other salesmen.

Charley was no great thinker. He never realized that he and his fellow rebels were merely echoing millions of underdogs everywhere; that lieutenants discussing their colonel, interns berating the chief surgeon, and section gangs cursing the boss were all complaining: "Don't tell anybody I said, but what we need————" and "If I were boss————" But he did learn, during the time he was back from New York, that the salesmen's conspiracy was not the only one in the office.

The stenographers and the clerks talked constantly about the office manager, a jolly gentleman as unlike Rice as possible. And Charley learned that Rice had his own little private conspiracy. He ran into Rice dining alone, and they both put on cordial out-of-office manners. It was hard for Charley to identify this kindly, worried, tired man with Simmy the Fiend. After a drink, possibly two drinks, Rice burst out and talked about Slosson exactly as Little Thomas talked about Rice.

Slosson was the junior member of the firm, a youngish man, very busy, not very cordial: Said Rice: "If I were Slosson, I'd try to act as though somebody besides myself was a human being." Rice evidently believed that, with his mistaken theories of quick business expansion, Slosson was going to ruin his partner, who belonged to the old school, Rice shook his large, grizzled head and growled: "I tell you, McClure, you young fellows want to stick to Greene's methods. What our office needs is to keep away from Slosson's smart-aleck notions. It's either him or me some day, I can see that. Or I might say, it's either him or Greene."

Charley afterward thought of Rice as an old watchdog, a little bewildered, gruffly staunch, guarding Greene's interests; and he felt for himself a pitying fondness. But next morning in the office Rice acted as though he were afraid that he had talked too much at dinner. He was more glum than ever; and the result was that Charley hated him anew. He was outraged that Rice expected him to take an advantage.

Two weeks later Charley went out on the road again. While he was on the trip several good towns were given back to him without explanation. He worked them thoroughly, but he had never been so discontented. He watched every communication from the office for mistakes, and once when samples of new stock from the office were overdue he went round saying to himself: "Rice has got to go!"

To the gripmen who made the grocery stores in a small district every fortnight or thirty days, when they complained of the tedium of their constant rounds, he growled: "Yes, but you ought to try working so far from the office that you've got to depend on a double-distilled jackass of a sales manager for your samples, and then you don't get 'em and the office calls you down for not showing what you haven't got. You fellows are lucky, even if you do keep making the same burgs all the time. You can get into the office every seven minutes and scrap it out with the old man. Besides, you can get home and see—your folks. Gosh, I wonder how my little girl's getting on back in little old N.Y."

Every night, at golden-oak hotel writing desks ornate with glass-covered mosaic advertisements of the local bus line and El Slicko cigars, Charley wrote to Agnes that he was struggling against Rice's envy, but needed her dear help to keep going.

Sometimes he was sorry for Rice. "Poor old boy," he said; "trying to stop the wheels of progress!"

When he got back to New York, he found the office interested in a new game, Golluf, a form of parlor golf. Charley learned to play golf from Agnes' Scotch father. He saw in Golluf the possibilities of a new ping-pong or crokinole craze, and he became its loudest advocate in the office.

Old Rice, with worried lines on his bull-pup face, told him that he was a fool, that golf was a sport for the wealthy few and that a game related to it would never succeed. Charley retorted that the aristocratic reputation of golf made it all the more tempting to good democrats, and that anyway—"all that aside"—Golluf was going to be a world-beater.

The Golluf war was fought over desks, but it was as full of bitterness and threats as a battle. Charley took a Golluf set over to Agnes' house, and all evening they played it, with shrieks that filled the sitting room, while occasionally Charley remarked sarcastically: "And that's the game Simmy Rice says won't succeed!"

Whenever he tried to stir up Rice and Little Thomas to enthusiasm like his own, they turned on him like big boys shutting up a small brother. They ridiculed him and kidded him and twisted what he said and dismissed the subject.

Charley was so righteously angry that when he met Slosson of the firm in the elevator he burst out: "Say, Mr. Slosson, some of the—some people don't seem to think much of Golluf, but, by heck! I think I can make it go. D—d—do the firm think it will go?"

The Harvard eyebrows of Slosson lifted and seemed to remark: "We wouldn't have taken it on if we hadn't thought it was a good commercial proposition." Mr. Ellery J. Slosson had often been heard to say that, and his beautifully trained eyebrows seemed to express the sentiment heartily. But now he merely stared at Charley over the heads of the messenger boys and buyers from other floors, all packed in the slow old elevator of 1891. As they left the elevator, however, Slosson said quickly:

"Go ahead, McClure; I'm back of you. If anybody fails to give you any help you need, just let me know. And say, McClure, you've been doing good work. Keep it up. I won't forget it. G'-day."

That encouragement bolstered up Charley in the Golluf fight—which meant the fight against the conservatism of S. R. Rice. He was like a flame eating into kindling. If he was not very tolerant, not very kindly, it must yet be granted that he was chronically overworking; while the minute the whistle blew Rice forgot all about his job, murmured: "Well, call it a day's work," put on his fedora and went home. Charley hustled all day showing Golluf to city buyers, stayed at the office till six-thirty to write up his orders, and arrived at Agnes' house so cryingly tired that he would lay his cheek on the fresh coolness of her linen skirt and wail: "Girly, I'm done up! You got to read to me tonight. I wish we had the little house so I could just gallop round the floor and bawl like I was a small boy. Oh, I've got to buck up. Here, let's—let's have a game of Golluf!"

Charley caught himself waking in his furnished room at five in the morning, and lying awake to worry—sure sign of overwork. He visualized the office, the stores, the buyers, his order lists, saw the word "Golluf" written in darkness, tossed and sighed in his narrow wooden cot. He couldn't stay abed after six, and he was first man at the office, first out on his rounds.

It is not overwhelmingly surprising that he was uncharitable to S. R. Rice. Every day he was less respectful, more frankly hostile. He insisted that Rice ought to learn how to play Golluf. "Poo-poo!" grunted the sales manager. "You run along and play your little games with Thomas or the office boys. Golluf is never going to go, my boy. Be better for you—and a whole lot better for this firm—if you had sense enough to put all this energy into one of our staple lines! Learn to proportion your energy right."

Rice even declared that the name "Golluf" was too much like "Gollywolly," the leading Greene-Slosson game.

"Did you ever make that objection when the firm was first considering taking on Golluf?" demanded Charley, angrily hitching his chair nearer to the sales manager's desk in the corner of the salesmen's room.

"No, I didn't. What's the use? They had their minds all made up," said Rice, and he examined a letter on his desk and tried to look as busy as possible, evidently wishing that this pest would go away. "Anything else?" he demanded.

"Yes, there is. You got to get Slosson to advertise Golluf—and not just in the trade papers either. A real advertising campaign. I tell you advertising is going to be the biggest selling factor in every line more and more now." Apparently Charley McClure was beginning to learn how the office moves goods off shelves. He went on: "You got to get Slosson to use ad space in the newspapers and magazines and everywhere."

"Advertising! What next! You're going crazy! Why don't you ask me to ask Slosson to go out and throw his money in the East River! It might be worthwhile to advertise the Cutey books—but Golluf! You better give Golluf a rest. If you'd like to know, I'll tell you a good doctor for folks that go bughouse on fads. Golluf! Son, if you'd stick to Gollywolly————"

"Oh, drop the joshing! Will you ask Slosson about the ads or shall I?"

"Oh, I'll ask him, but it's all darn foolishness."

Charley rose, puffed out his chest, looked down triumphantly on the sales manager's bald head. He was young. And he was winning.

For Golluf was really going. Though it was very late on the market for the coming holiday season, and though Greene and Rice and Little Thomas agreed that Golluf was no better a selling proposition than Umtawawa or Squeetizzy—and tried to prove their contention by that safe, sane, time-hallowed method of remarking that Charley McClure was young and enthusiastic—yet Golluf was succeeding. People in general shouldn't have done so, according to Rice, but they really did take to Golluf. In October there had been a Golluf party in Flatbush, as reported in the Flatbush social notes in the Brooklyn papers.

Charley went on the road again, a passionate warrior, with a sample of that great game Golluf instead of a sword. And trouble began immediately. Rice had mixed up his route badly. Still worse was the fact that when they did advertise Golluf, just as an experiment, in the Iowa-Wisconsin-Illinois-Indiana-Ohio territory, Rice failed to let Charley know that the advertising would appear, and it was too late for him to use it as a talking point with his customers. Yet, Charley furiously reminded himself, it was he who had made the firm advertise.

His sorrows were forgotten in the big Plate-Glass Drugstores deal. Charley had for years known the Iowa salesman of the Great Lakes Wholesale Drug Company, an ingenious, energetic, thoroughly honest genius. He learned in a chance conversation with a Chicago-registered pharmacist-chemist and a North Dakota capitalist, was opening a chain of fifty drugstores, the Plate-Glass stores, in one grand splurge on November first. On the hunch he skipped three towns, hurried to their office in Davenport, and made himself as much a part of their establishment as the supplies cupboard. From his own experience as messenger boy he suggested improvements in their delivery system. While his own office was telegraphing to find his whereabouts, he nonchalantly loafed and, though he had just time enough to get them into the drugstores for Christmas, he got an order for one hundred thousand sets of Golluf, at a wholesale price of ten cents a set, the clear profit for his firm being nearly four thousand dollars. The drug people promised to write confirmation of the order that same night, and Charley telegraphed the office to O.K. the discount, make quick credit investigation of the new firm, and pack and ship immediately. Then he want gamboling on his way, and in the smoker looked pityingly at the drummers who boasted of large orders.

But he felt in a gamboling frame of mind for exactly four days. At the end of that time a telegram, chasing him from town to town, caught him at St. Hilary, Minnesota, one evening just after he had spread out his goods in the smelly, cement-walled basement sample room. He was hustling about in his shirtsleeves, despite the damp coldness, when a telegram was brought in. He opened it cheerfully. Surely it contained congratulations from the office.

It was from the Plate-Glass Drug Company, and read:

> Your office says cannot have credit as arranged on golluf can
> you fix this see good business in it holidays, little time, wire.

The time was seven-thirty. At eight Charley was on a train to Minneapolis. Forty-three hours afterwards—forty-three hours when he did not sleep, but stared grimly at the plush of the car seats in front of him or at the swaying dark of his berth—he landed at the Grand Central in New York. He was no longer the ardent young crusader. He had aged. His youth was dried out of him as blotting paper dries ink. And he was merciless.

Quietly, matter-of-factly, he tramped to a car through the gray cloudy light, with slush underfoot from an early flurry of snow. He paid no attention to the city, which he had always rediscovered upon each return. He stalked through the Greene-Slosson office and into the private room of the firm.

There, in the cloud-colored early twilight that sifted into the room till he could scarcely see the polished surfaces of two desks or make out Slosson's suave, shrewd face and the gray side-whiskers of old Greene, Charley fought out his battle for credit—for money credit as a symbol of the spiritual credit which his youth frenziedly demanded. All shyness of the firm, all feeling that these were the chiefs, sacred, different from ordinary men, was gone. He talked quietly but demandingly.

Greene admitted that Rice had told the bookkeeper, who was also credit man for the firm, to examine with extra care the credit of the Plate-Glass Drug Company. During Slosson's absence, Rice had consulted Greene about the whole affair, for this order of Golluf was the largest single order the firm had ever received, except one or two orders from the jobbers. The mercantile agencies had reported that, though the Plate-Glass people were doubtless very worthy young men, and though they were hypnotizing the pharmaceutical and toilet-article firms into granting big credit, yet their rating, based on actual visible assets, would be about zero, with six ciphers and a bankruptcy declaration after the zero.

While outside the window yellow lights slowly began to give golden tones to the unutterable sadness of the gray twilight, and Greene nervously lighted a gas bracket lamp, Charley fought the old fight of salesman versus credit, which is also the fight of faith versus research—a contest ancient long before a selling system was invented.

"These credit men make me sick," Charley snarled. "The traveler is right there on the ground; he sees just what a store is and who's running it. And then he decides it's safe and works his head off selling 'em a good bill. And the credit man sticks here in New York and looks into a darn big black book and thinks he knows all about it."

"Yes, yes, but you must remember any number of occasions when the credit man's word wasn't taken and concerns failed. We made special inquiry of the mercantile agencies, and even wired the Plate-Glass people to give them a chance to make their own report," said Greene wearily, glancing at Slosson for approval.

"Oh, the deuce!" Charley snapped. "I tell you there's some things you can't put down in a rating—nerve and hustle and ideas—and I know the Plate-Glass boys. All the time Rice was sitting here being a John J. Wisenheimer I was getting acquainted with 'em. I know what they can do. It's as safe to let 'em have credit as to buy Government bonds." While Greene shakily protested and Charley charged on him, the young Slosson silently tilted back in his chair and frowned. Gravely he listened to Charley's impassioned personal attack on S. R. Rice.

"It's Golluf he's fighting, not the Plate-Glass credit," Charley declared. "He's been against Golluf from the first. He said it wouldn't succeed and now—I hate to say it, but I do believe the old devil is willing to stop the sale of Golluf to save his own face and prove he was right. Now just take the question of these ads———"

When all of Charley's troubles were told Slosson said abruptly:

"Greene, I've been looking into Plate-Glass credit a little myself. We'll give them all the credit they want, and we might thank McClure for opening up the account. McClure, we'll give you a bonus on this order. Now get back on your route and hustle. You did right to come in, and good luck! As you go out, would you mind asking Mr. Rice to step in, if it's convenient—if he's still there—it's after closing time. Thank you very much, McClure."

Charley went into the main office. It was dark, mysterious, startlingly quiet in contrast to the agitated life that had filled it all day. Over the semipartition of the salesmen's room shone one light. Charley went slowly into that room. Rice wouldn't be there, he hoped; surely he couldn't be there. Ordinarily he left at five.

But Rice was there. He looked up nervously. He did not comment on Charley's presence in New York, except to say: "Oh, hello! Saw you coming into the office———"

"Mr. Slosson wants to see you," hesitated Charley.

"All right."

Before he rose Rice looked curiously about his desk and up at the tattered calendar above it. It had been a gorgeous calendar once, presented to Rice with the obsequious compliments of the Antismash Truck Company. It was like a glance of farewell. Rice seemed old under the single gaslight. He rose heavily. His thick shoulders drooped. His face was outlined against the darkness. He went painfully out of the salesmen's room into the silence and creeping shadows beyond.

Charley rang the bell at Agnes' house two months later, and waited for her so impatiently that he danced a jig all over the small stoop. When she opened the door he seized her shoulders and whirled her round till she was panting and her hair flew out in little tufts. Her pale face flushed and her eyes grew excited.

"Oh, what is it—have you got a raise?" she kept crying.

"Come and sit on my knee and I'll tell you."

"Oh, that's so common!"

"All right, if you won't sit on my knee I won't tell you."

"All right, then I won't marry you."

"All right, then I'll marry your cousin."

She was sure he was joking, but still you could never tell, and her pretty little cousin was perniciously attractive to men, though she was such a fool and——— And Agnes meekly perched on

Charlie's knee, while he grinned in masculine triumph and said blandly:

"Well, it's nothing much except that you're now sitting on the knee of the sales manager of the Greene-Slosson Company, and I go to work February first at two thousand per for a starter!"

"Oh, darling, then we can have the little house———"

"Yessir, everything from the kitchen stove to the perambulator. Now see the girl blush! Oh, I'm just as excited as you are. I got to joke about it or I'd blubber like a kid! We'll have a real front yard with trees and grass and everything, and we'll sit there evenings, and there'll never be any troubles. And when I'm in the firm——— Oh, I'm just crazy, thinking of all the wonderful things we've got coming! Let me kiss you right there on that funny little place beside your temple. Oh, say, forgot to tell you—Slosson warned me to keep up discipline. Can you beat that! I guess I know what I want. I'm going to give the boys a square deal, lay my cards right down on the table, let 'em call me by my first name and work with them. If I were Slosson I'd do the same thing even then. Gosh, isn't it wonderful!"

II. AGE KNOWS

When, on the Monday after Rice's leaving, Slosson had come to the conference of salesmen and announced that Mr. Charles McClure was herewith made sales manager, the other—and older—salesmen had looked amazed and hurt. Little Thomas had muttered: "Well, I'll be compoundedly gol-darned!" deliberately winked at the others, and slapped his knee with his cupped hand, making a peculiarly annoying sound. But little Thomas Snider was a gentleman of great astuteness, and instantly he began to welcome an appointment that would enable him to loaf on the job. He arranged a congratulation lunch for the following Saturday noon.

The lunch was at the Magnificent, which was the unofficial headquarters of salesmen in the novelty, toy and juvenile-book business. The news that young Charley McClure had been made sales manager for Greene & Slosson had spread, and apparently every salesman on earth was there to grin at him when he took his seat at the head of the table reserved for the Greene-Slosson salesmen.

His first great discovery was that by becoming sales manager he had not ceased to be young Charley McClure, whom it was fairly easy to "kid." Little Thomas said gravely to Charley: "Read about that poor old deaf-and-dumb man going to court, in the papers this morning?"

"No," said Charley. "How was that?"

"Yump, he went to court to get his hearing," answered Little Thomas.

You may agree with Charley McClure that this humor was not world-shaking, but the whole table roared, people at other tables looked over, and Charley felt that the entire world was sizing him up as a butt and a failure.

Later during the lunch Charley became conscious that Little Thomas and the Southern salesman were discussing the question of why Negroes always seem to have whiter teeth than Caucasians. It was such a dull argument that it fairly hurt. Charley couldn't stand it. He finally interrupted with: "I don't suppose Negroes' teeth really are any whiter. They just seem so by contrast." Then all the lunchers banged their several fists on the table, and pounded with their several spoons, and made a noise like the zoo at feeding time, and declaimed all together: "Don't you suppose we knew— that—before? We were waiting for you to say it!"

Charley was not, perhaps, the first young man to be thoroughly and conscientiously badgered by five older men, but he felt as though he were the one perfect idiot in history. He kept embarrassedly moving things—knife one inch to the right, coffee cup round and round in its saucer.

Yet he had the dignity of man who could do his job. When they lighted large cigars and the air became a good, firm, dependable solid that you could chew, Charley turned from cub into boss without in the least planning how to do so. He rapped on the table, and with a youthful but effective stiffness announced his policy as manager. He expected to make mistakes, he told them; but one thing he would try to do—not take himself too seriously. He would be as chummy with them as they permitted——— From the other end of the table a faint, ironic cheer from Little Thomas.

Charley stopped full-tilt. "I see that Little Thomas feels that I'm too confiding. Now, Thomas, you tell us what you'd do if you were boss."

The truth was not in Little Thomas, and his ways were the ways of falseness. He spoke up with an ingenuous smile, protesting: "Oh, you got me wrong, Chollie; I didn't mean you were too confiding." He looked innocent, and Charley looked suspicious, while the other salesmen nodded their heads as though the new sales manager had won the first scrimmage.

For the first time the mist of embarrassment cleared from Charley's eyes and he was able to look casually about the restaurant. He noted the pompous head waiter, the bus boys with pudgy rolls, the salesmen from other firms. They were no longer an intimidating mob of geniuses, but just plain folks like himself. And he could handle them! Perhaps some day he could even handle Little Thomas.

And, again, perhaps he couldn't! For one disagreeable fact remained after the luncheon—Little Thomas insisted on calling him "Chollie." and the other salesmen followed Thomas' example. Monday morning following, Little Thomas' exquisite, subtle, almost vorticist sense of humor moved him to keep shouting "Chollie" so mightily that all the office beyond the semipartition could hear. Charley, sitting self-consciously at the sales manager's conspicuous corner desk, pretended not to hear. He was sending Little Thomas out on a short trip to show a new summer game and to encourage pick-up orders on Golluf. With Little Thomas away his task would be easy.

It was. By the time Little Thomas returned, Charley had learned to act as though he knew everything, and to give arbitrary reasons, like a real boss. And he had been married, and in the little house in Jersey was still reverently discovering how happy life could be. Agnes had immediately become adorably matronly in manner, and delighted Charley by her solemn way of discussing the cleaning of the refrigerator as if she had been married twenty years.

His first struggle was the absurdly petty one of changing his name. The whole office seemed to have found merit in the assertion of Little Thomas—such a wit, that Thomas!—that Charley was a Chollie-boy. Charley found it impossible to command respect with that handicap. For the first time in his earnest and simple-hearted career he made himself learn the acting, the Machiavellian craft, that is part of the equipment of every manager of men.

He tackled the big, broad-shouldered Southern salesman, who was a red-headed cross between a Scotchman and a Yankee and hailed from Nova Scotia—hailed loudly and firmly at that. He lured the Nova Scotian into calling him "Chollie," then sprang from his desk and said very loudly: "See here. Mr. Benner, do you mean to insult me by calling me 'Chollie' or are you merely ignorant?"

He was young, and his joints moved with rather formidable ease. He looked as fierce as he could, as though he were hungering and thirsting for a terrific fight, a knock-'em-down-and-stomp-on-'em-and-gouge-their-eyes-out fight. He wasn't really. He was frightened almost to death.

The Nova Scotian was puzzled. It had been his theory that he could beat Charley McClure with one hand tied behind him; but the youngster looked very aggressive and, like most reasonable men, the Nova Scotian was willing to revise his theories in accordance with new scientific discoveries. He evaded.

"Thought you were going to be so chummy and all," he growled.

"Oh, cut out the sparring! Just why do you insist on insulting me?"

"Ah, thunder, I didn't mean to insult you, McClure! Gosh, you take a fellow up so!"

After that the force didn't call him "Chollie"—usually.

They were not bad chaps, the Greene-Slosson salesmen, and Charley intended to avoid Rice's error—of expecting them to do more than was humanly possible. But Charley had never known how often Rice had been called in by Slosson and urged to make the salesmen do a whole lot more than was humanly possible.

The Sweetix and Sue series was slowing down. Buyers were not interested in reorders. Slosson demanded the reason. Well—Charley hesitated, tapping his fingers on Slosson's desk and carefully clearing his throat—there wasn't any special reason why the books weren't selling, except that they weren't selling.

"Then what have we got salesmen for?" snapped Slosson. "Mr. McClure, if the salesmen round this establishment don't happen to like Sweetix and Sue books enough for their own personal perusal, or to steal them and present them to their relatives, that's very sad; very, very sad indeed. But I really think I must ask you to beg these gentlemen to sell them nevertheless. How they are going to sell them is up to you and to them. Poke them up a little and see if you can't get some business. Too much overhead, McClure, too much overhead! If you find that they are too busy holding up bars to sell goods I wish you'd just let me know."

So Charley went out into the salesmen's room and started a small Central American revolution—with the uneasy feeling that Slosson was there just behind him. He, in turn, was very sarcastic about their holding up bars. And the salesmen didn't like it. But it was Charley they resented, not Slosson.

"What's all the fevered special rush about these Sweetix books? They're going well enough," said the Southern salesman, who was preparing for a Baltimore and Washington trip.

"I don't know that you need any special reason. What I want you to do is not to reason, but to make the buyers think about Sweetix and Sue."

"Yeah, and you that were going to be so chummy, and let us understand all this star-chamber business. What's the special hunch on Sweetix?"

"The special hunch is that if you don't sell a bigger bill on all the juveniles I'll have to know why," said Charley, and, turning his back on the Southern salesman, he pretended to be very busy with correspondence.

Charley found that some of the salesmen were beginning to make certain towns in their territory over-Sunday picnics, skipping other towns to reach them by Saturday night. He remembers how pleasant it had been to spend Sunday with friends, and for a few hours to forget the hotel smell of oyster crackers and roast veal. But still, that wasn't any excuse for scanting intervening towns; and he changed the territories round, after spending three evenings at home with a new map, with a wet towel round his head and the gentle Agnes bringing him small cups of coffee.

Now, the general subject of routing is about as safe to introduce among salesmen as dynamite in a stove. Once the office knew that it was on the carpet every salesman who was in town immediately had bright ideas with which to help Charley. They came round and said: "If I were making out the routes———" They sneaked in and spoke furtively at all hours of the day, and were very solicitous about getting Charley out to lunch. All their ideas were concerned with getting better territory and easier connections for themselves. And they all desired short, lucid explanations for every single change he made—or didn't make.

"Why, the best territory I've got is Northern Michigan," complained Charley's successor in the Middle West. "Why don't you give me the South Dakota bad lands and the Arizona desert? It's as easy to sell to a butte or a cactus as to a mine storekeeper."

Charley knew how they felt. It was a battle, and what you won you won. He himself had tried to abstract good towns from other salesmen. He sympathized, but he couldn't satisfy everybody, and if he attended to all they said he wouldn't satisfy anybody. So he became arbitrary. Then, looking from his desk into the sample room, he saw three salesmen conferring quietly, glancing at him as they talked. He had joined in just such discussions so short a time before. He knew that they were saying: "What this office needs is a sales manager with some training! The poor yahoo expects me to cover Seattle and Key West on the same day, so far as I can make out. I tell you, if I were boss I'd arrange the routing so that the fellows would be satisfied with their territory. Yessir, that's the very first thing I'd do!"

He refused to change his map, once he had completed it; but he tried desperately to regain their friendship. To the men out on the road he did his best to get credit information, samples and price changes as soon as the material came to him. For men who were in town he bought various discreet drinks. He tried to keep himself from growing into the habit of hasty blaming which bosses so easily and unconsciously acquire—some bosses, not you or I, of course. And Charley tried not to be vexed by his subordinates' habit of denying all faults which, equally, most employees acquire—though never you or I, of course.

He succeeded fairly well in impressing the salesmen with his justice. Even the subject of routing—which belongs with religion and politics and the psychology of women, as a subject that is always good for a furious argument—did not come up so often that it kept them from working together. Charley liked authority, liked the chance to put through firsthand his ambitious plans for increasing sales, liked the salesmen under him, and in the new life of going home every night to Agnes and her wistful care he was imaginatively happy. He tried sincerely to be the little office sunbeam.

But he knew, and they all knew, that the truce in the battle would last only until the great Little Thomas Snider came back from the road with his reserves and artillery of "kidding." Charley knew that he had yet to match awkward youth and serious effort with the suave cynicism and experience of Little Thomas, and that, if he lost, the other salesmen would not grieve; because it is a safe general rule that another boss is always a better boss.

Charley had learned two military principles from this early border fighting. The first was one that every probationer policeman has to discover: If you wear the uniform or badge of office, and look as though you expect people to obey you, they will do so. The badge and a brazen visage will do the trick, no matter how much you are quaking down in your plain, ordinary, unofficial insides. The second trick that Charley learned was that it is better to start the fight and get it over. To Agnes, in their long evening talks about everybody in the office, he wailed:

"Oh, honey, I don't want to be hard, but if Tom Snider thinks I'll stand for anything when he gets back, he'll find out." Agnes sat and knitted and rocked and warmly agreed with him.

It was a day on which Fate had decided to do a day's work and show the world just how vicious he could be. When Charley arrived at the office his own office boy was sick, and a salesman was blithely and publicly considering resigning because he had a better offer. Charley felt it was a peculiarly nasty trick of the salesman to leave him in the lurch. While he was still worrying and carrying his own messages out to the packing room in the absence of the office boy, Charley's suburban landlord dropped in.

The landlord required very tactful handling because he was thinking, but not thinking hard enough to get a headache, about making certain repairs which Charley had demanded. Suburban householders will understand—that little matter of the broken rainpipe which was discoloring a ceiling. Apparently the landlord's decision as to what he would do depended on how much he should like Charley's conversation and office and cigars. He was willing to take the whole day off and discuss the history of repairs, from the first broken gate in the Garden of Eden to the millennium, when ceilings will never be discolored because the International Government will pass a law against it. He sat on the edge of Charley's desk and talked—and talked—and talked, while Charley's correspondence was untouched, and only the thought that Agnes had commanded him to be diplomatic as a pair of velvet breeches kept him from telling the landlord to take his rainpipe and go to the deuce with it.

When the landlord had brought the general subject of repairs, the kindness of landlords and the carelessness of tenants down to about the age of Julius Caesar, in came the buyer from the New England jobbers, an unimportant-looking man with a moustache like a well-used back-porch broom, but so powerful that he never let salesmen buy him dinners. He wanted, he announced, to see McClure himself. He also wanted to make a protest against the fact that the cover of the latest Cutey book was in two colors, not three. While Charley was paying royal court to him and trying to slip in some pleasant words about Golluf, one of the office girls came into the sample room and whispered:

"Mr. Slosson wants to see you, Mr. McClure, and I guess he's got an awful mad on this morning. You better hurry! Gee, you ought to seen him call me and Mamie down because we was laughing, gee, just a weeny bit when he come by!"

"Well, he'll have to wait," Charley whispered.

But while he was giving flattering heed to the remarks of the Boston buyer, he, who had once been so simple-hearted a salesman, was learning something of a boss's worries. One half of his brain was busy with Slosson and Agnes and the landlord and the repairs and the salesman who might quick and the sick office boy. Just as the Boston buyer was taking leave lingeringly, as though he might think of another joke for this appreciative listener, the office girl announced that two men were waiting to see Charley, and added in a stage whisper that Slosson had a headache and was getting nastier and nastier.

Charley was impatient to introduce the two waiting men to each other. He started them discussing that immortal topic, "Is business picking up your way?" while he himself fled into Slosson's room.

It was a short interview, but potent. If poor S.R. Rice had ever been so cranky Charley would have resigned instantly. But he couldn't afford to give up so good a job as sales manager, especially with Agnes dependent on him.

"McClure," Slosson grated, "I'm not very fond of being kept waiting. Of course I don't expect you to show up till it's convenient—oh, quite convenient—but sometimes I'd be glad if you could make it convenient for me too."

In the corner old Greene bent over his desk, more gray and futile and afraid of his partner every day.

"Had to see three buyers, sir."

"Well—look here, McClure: Tom Snider is due back today."

"Why, no, sir, not till tomorrow."

"I tell you he's coming today. Now, look here: There's one thing that you may have never given any attention to, but it's highly important. There's a rule in this office that no smoking is allowed except here in our private room. But you and Rice between you have simply let the rule become a dead letter. The salesmen all smoke; all of them sit round puffing like factory chimneys. I do wish we could get managers that would make some slight effort to carry out the bare rules of this establishment, even if nothing else. Smoking makes a very bad impression on everybody who comes into the office, to say nothing of the effects on the throats of the girls that work here. If necessary Mr. Greene and I will give up our own smoking in here, because smoking in the outer office simply must and will stop. And I expect you to see to it that the salesmen do their part. Now, Snider is the worst offender, and I expect you to start right in with him to see to it that he toes the mark. That's all."

Charley felt that it was enough. The picture of himself trying to keep the glib Little Thomas from smoking lacked all color and charm.

He remarked crossly:

"All right, then. Say, the Boston jobbers won't take the Big Gun Gang remainders. And Caruthers is thinking of getting through— better offer. I guess we'll have to raise him."

"Those things are up to you, McClure. I can't be bothered with them. But we won't raise Caruthers. Too much overhead as it is. You can rush out and get another man in his place."

As he left the firm's private room Charley was less simple-hearted than ever. The following were the things he pondered over:

Where was he to "rush out" to and find a man to replace Caruthers? Caruthers ought to be raised anyway. Slosson was the most unreasonable man living. If the salesmen knew how Manager McClure stood between them and that fiend Slosson they'd worship him instead of bucking him. Slosson was a fool to think that Little Thomas would be in today. Thank heaven, that trouble was postponed anyway! Poor Agnes—she never would get those repairs.

Charley had to do all his brooding about these wrongs between the firm's room and the sample room, where the two men were waiting for him. He had to show advance samples to one and talk to the other about the establishment of a hotel news and cigar stand. In the midst of which perspiring double role he heard, from the salesmen's room beyond, a noise something like a Weber and Fields revival and something like the return of the troops. He looked out and saw that Little Thomas, who couldn't possible return today, had returned—a picturesque mingling of a new, light gray overcoat and a tan derby and pointed shoes and round, shining face and boisterous greetings and sarcastic inquiries about Boss McClure and a big, long, fat, odorous cigar that was tilted 45° NNW and was simply cremating the office rule against smoking.

Charley finished his business and stalked into salesmen's room like a cat after a sparrow. Little Thomas, sitting on one desk with his feet across the aisle on another desk, greeted him:

"Hello, Chollie! How's it going with the big boss? Still love Papa Slosson?"

One salesman whispered to another, rather like a bad boy in school, though he was forty-five and grave and a prominent joiner. Charley fancied that he was saying; "Little Thomas ought to be boss."

Little Thomas's patronizing smile said much the same thing. Charley looked among the line of desks. Every detail of the room, of the men, he saw sharply. The whole office seemed expectant.

He noticed with irritation that Caruthers had left untouched a bunch of imported toy books he had given him to look over. Then:

"Tom," said Charley, "you call me either Charley or Mr. McClure. Next time you feel your sense of humor overpowering you and you call me 'Chollie,' I'll take it as a signal you want to start something, see? Now come here to my desk; I want to have a little talk with you. Caruthers, if you find yourself too busy getting ready for your new job to look over those importations, I'll hire you an assistant. Just let me know if you feel you're becoming much more important than us poor Greene-Slosson yahoos. Marcus, whenever you get time to go out and see the Harlem stores, I'm sure they'll be glad to see you—you have such a cheery smile today. And listen to this, all of you: There's to be no more smoking in this office, Mr. Slosson says, and the first fellow I catch doing it will be fired, even if I have to sell his territory myself. Come here now, Tom."

Charley didn't know it, but his voice had all the contemptuous, mastering ring that had infuriated him in the voice of S. R. Rice. He saw the men settle down to work; saw Little Thomas follow him to the corner desk, still smoking. Within him, again like the probationer policeman handling his first crowd, Charley wondered whether he could make Little Thomas think he looked like a real boss. He listened anxiously to his own voice as he demanded:

"Put out that cigar, Tom."

"Huh? That cigar, Chol—Charley? Why, that's a two-bits cigar."

"Thomas, my son, you've got the wrong hunch. This isn't going to be a kidding fest. It's going to be a real scrap. Get the idea quick; I'm going to make an issue of this."

"You mean to say you wouldn't overlook a little thing like a man smoking one cigar when he's just in from the road?"

"I mean to say I won't overlook a single thing. You know that sign they have in some offices: 'If you want to find out who's the boss, start something'? Well, you've come back all ready to start all sorts of things. You've been having a fine time on the train planning how you'd make young Charley McClure crawl. Well, you're not going to do it. You're not going to have me explaining. I'll make the rules perfectly definite, and if you don't like them go and kick to Slosson. Now put out that cigar, see?"

They sat glaring, eye holding eye. Charley answered defiance with a cold stare.

"Well, if you're so set on it———" grumbled Little Thomas crushing out the light of his cigar and looking down at the desk.

Charley exulted. Perhaps he really was contriving to look like a real boss.

Little Thomas went on: "Of course you'd run and tattle to Slosson if I didn't."

"No, my son, there's just one thing I'd tattle to Slosson about— that you think so little of me that you believe I'd be capable of running and tattling. That I certainly will take up with him, if you feel that way, because it would indicate that I'm too weak to be boss—and then we'd need some strong, noble character like Little Thomas Snider for boss. Do you want to come in and take that up with Slosson, heh? Let's get that settled right now."

"No, no, you know I don't think that. Gee, don't be so plumb savage!"

"All right. Now I want to know what the devil you mean by not following up the ads we put in the Central New York territory with better sales on Golluf? Did you show it at all?"

"Well, whatcha think I did?" wailed Little Thomas.

"Now cut out the injured innocent. That used to be one of your very best tricks to work on Rice. Get a new one."

"Well, thunder, what's the use of ads anyway? Let me tell you that most ads are simply useless. What do they do? They simply add to the expense of the goods and make 'em harder to sell. Do you know what you ought to do? Just add one half—just half—the cost of the ads on my salary, and I'll sell more goods than all the ads in ten counties, and the trade wouldn't have to pay so much—"

"You certainly are slow, Tom. You don't get the idea a-tall. I'm not going to discuss theories with you—aside from the fact that I've heard you spiel about advertising so often that I'm tired of it. I want to know by what right you presume to decide for this firm what we will sell and what we won't sell. And let me tell you that next time you don't key up to the ads I'll know the reason why."

Little Thomas flared up.

"Say, are you hinting round my resignation, McClure? Because you'll get it so——"

"No, I'm not looking for it, but I'm ready for it any time you feel it's beneath your dignity to work for a young fool like me."

Again their hostile eyes held each other, and while the slightly bewildered Mr. Little Tom Snider was trying to decide just how he did feel, Charley attacked again:

"And what do you mean by not itemizing your expense account? For instance, what did you spend fourteen dollars in a rube town like Mashemachee for?"

"Well, I had to take a cab to make the train."

"Cab? Oh, you—had—to—take—a—cab!"

"Yes, I did."

"Well, well, how Mashemachee is coming along! They must have a grand Chamber of Commerce. I've made that town five times, and the only cab I ever saw is the carryall that the old fellow with the whiskers drives. And your hotel is right across the street from the depot."

"Well, I don't remember exactly—it was a cab or something."

"Let's see, wasn't it Mashemachee where that lady-buyer friend of yours lived?"

"Well, gosh, I don't get any too much allowance. Say, do you know that Congressmen get twenty cents a mile mileage? That shows how much it costs to travel like a gentleman."

Little Thomas gave this his very best manner as office jester, kicking his right foot, crossing his right leg over his left, hooking his thumbs in his armholes, tilting back in his chair and raising his voice so that all the boys might have the benefit. Charley looked him all over, slowly, carefully, from his Fourteenth Street shoes to his La Salle Street haircut, and remarked slowly, carefully, and very coldly:

"The effect would be better if you had a cigar stuck up in the corner of your mouth, Tom. Now if you've got any more information about traveling like a gentleman, let's have it—only I'd like to know what gentleman you got it from. I note that Mr. Caruthers is especially interested in the subject. Let's have some more about it. Otherwise you might explain why you charged forty dollars railroad fare in Delaware."

"Well, gosh, the way you balled up my routing I had to crisscross my own tracks all the time like a kitten chasing its tail, and used twice as much fare as normal. Why, the plan of my route looks like a map of downtown Boston."

"That so? Say, speaking of Boston, I'm going to sell Boston hereafter instead of you."

"But that's my best town."

"Yes, but you see I can cover it cheaper. I don't have to travel like a gentleman."

Little Thomas sprang up, furious. With a leisurely sureness Charley got up and remarked:

"Now have you got any more bluffs to throw? Do you have to make another trip just as a vacation, or are you ready to work for that young fool Charley McClure?" His voice changed to a wistful friendliness which, as it was sincere and not merely a trick, carried conviction. "Drop it, Tom. I'm boss. We've had some pretty good times together, and I hope we can go on. All I want is a square deal."

The anger dimmed in Thomas's cheerful, protruding eyes. The little man could be roundly tearful quite as easily as he could be chubbily gay.

"Gee," he mourned, "I thought you were going to be so friendly, and here you are accusing me of everything but arson!"

Charley merely held out his hand. Little Thomas disconsolately took it. Absent-mindedly he drew a cigar from his pocket. With that bored cheerfulness of a schoolteacher Charley called out:

"Nix on the smoking, Tom."

"All right—boss," answered Little Thomas, and he saluted.

Charley McClure wasn't old—only fifty-four in 1914, and a better salesman than ever. He said that he had his job trained to sit up and beg. He was sales manager of The Slosson Book & Game Company, formerly the Greene & Slosson Company, and he knew personally all the bigger buyers from Sandy Hook to San Diego. What he didn't know personally was that he had become entirely mechanical in work, because his real interest was home with his wife Agnes, his golf score and his son Robert, who was eagerly beginning his career as real-estate salesman.

Twenty-three years before, Charley had been a road salesman, and as yearningly ambitious as his son was now at twenty. At this time Charley had believed that bosses were a race of congenital fiends organized to keep young men from getting jobs in the first place, and making good on them in the second. Now he was equally sure that the flighty young men of this generation were organized to teach one another new ways of being unreliable and generally worthless. He and his chief, Slosson, were glad to give youngsters every possible opportunity to develop themselves; but where could they find the men who combined energy with reasonableness in regard to pay? When they turned out well they took other jobs.

In the years that he had been sales manager Charley had seen every single person in the office drift away or die—all but himself, and Slosson the chief, and Tom Snider the office manager, now an obese little man of sixty-five, disinclined to get out of his chair, but once a laugher, a dancer, a roly-poly whom they had called Little Thomas. The others—gone, and replaced by nobodies.

One of the young salesmen whom Charley had tried to train was suddenly leaving for a job with slightly better pay, but nothing like so good a chance for permanent advancement, as Charley had gruffly pointed out. He had selfishly given such short notice that the entire selling system was disarranged.

In the days when Charley had been Young Charley, and he had wistfully gone about looking for any sort of chance to make good, he had never been so hard-driven, so worried as now, when he tried to find something resembling a real human being to fill Smith's place. There were plenty of men who came in to apply the minute the news of a vacancy ran like scandal through salesmen's circles. But mostly they were of that curious type known to all employers—the men who appear to make a living by going the rounds asking for positions they can't possibly fill, and offering as references the men who have discharged them for consistent incompetence. Usually they wear expensive hats and have charming smiles and a great deal of leisure in which to sketch their remarkable power of creating ideas to put punch in the business. The applicants who did have good records knew nothing about books or about any game except auction pinochle, which Slosson couldn't very well patent and sell. All the desirable men seemed just then to be so tightly tacked down to other jobs that they could be ripped off only by an offer of about fifty-one percent of stock and expenses, including cigars.

Slosson called in Charley and wanted to know why he didn't find the new salesman. Charley asserted that the stock was exhausted and the samples lost. The new generation, he stated, was too much interested in motors and tango teas to produce good salesmen. They could all be discounted at one hundred percent. Slosson made noises of boredom, and Charley flared up: "Why don't you find one yourself?"

Slosson smiled a long, chin-stroking, secret, apparently chewable smile and announced: "I will!"

That was all he said, and for several days the subject was not resurrected publicly. But it was thoroughly studied at lunch by Charley and his closest friend, his oldest crony, Tom Snider. They agreed—as they had been agreeing at lunches for perhaps fifteen years—that Slosson was a poor fool whose interests they kept from being wrecked. They wondered what Slosson had been planning when he had smiled that secret smile, which Charley described at length. They weren't exactly afraid of anyone who might be brought into the office; but they had fought through several revolutions which had threatened them and their 1900 ways of doing business. They had seen times when for a month together the news "The Old Man's got a grouch" had seeped through the office every morning and they had expected to lose their jobs.

Now, when they were unconsciously dreading the big chief's next move, they were grinningly relieved to have Slosson come in one afternoon and push forward a lightweight, eyeglassed, high-browed, shy youth with expensive tailor-made clothes and thin mouse-gray hair. Slosson remarked: "Mr. McClure, this is George Lanston, the son of my old friend Lanston of the B. & Q. Clock Company. He has just graduated from college, and we'll let him try his hand at selling."

Young Lanston didn't know an order list from a bill of lading. Charley McClure was kind to him; he explained the system of showing wares, and gave him all the printed material on the Slosson line. But as he watched the highbrow worrying papers at a desk in the corner, holding his forehead with a delicate-fingered hand and trying to look businesslike, Charley smiled rather sadly and compared this specimen of the new generation with the good, hearty chaps with whom he had once sold and who were holding big positions now, or gone—poor devils! He was sure that George Lanston would go back to his school books, where he belonged, but he tried to give him every chance. At lunch with Tom Snider, however, he indulged in a burlesque description of what would happen when Slosson's lily-handed pet encountered the buyers.

"Pleathe, thir, I want to show you thuch a pitty game," he mimicked. "Gosh, Tom, I bet the next time Slosson will spring a college professor on me. College! We'll have to have a college yell in the office, first thing you know—'Slosson, Slosson, siss, boom, bah!'"

Charley was wrong. George Lanston didn't lisp. He spoke with a Harvard accent, but when he spoke he said something. That same afternoon Lanston came up to Charley's desk and observed abruptly:

"There must be a mistake in this new material on the indoor polo game, sir. The prices don't agree with the general list."

"Um, yes, yes. Why, so it is, so it is."

That set him pondering on the bookworm, and to his delight Lanston showed possibilities. He went at the problem of learning salesmanship as though he intended to speak the language of commerce, not just read it. In his modest, too brusque way he tried to get generally acquainted, and the Western salesman reported to Charley that Lanston had joined a bunch of them at dinner, and in a pleasant *fiesta* afterward had won four dollars in certain games of chance and expended the same in suitable refreshments. Alas, it is a material world! This prowess at poker did more to make the office force forgive Lanston for looking like a Greek scholar than his rapid acquirement of the idea of business. In a month Lanston was awarded that greatest sign of approbation—the men "kidded" him.

Lanston went out on his first road trip. He made all the mistakes that good, respectable, normal youngsters are expected to make. He was too economical about hotels and Pullmans. If he had been a star instead of a cub he would have established a precedent that would have ruined the game. But older salesmen took him in hand. He was dining with a bunch, and to save expenses took crackers and milk and rice pudding, while the others had everything from clams to cheese. Then he discovered that he had to pay a full share of the check—after which he was less addicted to rice pudding. He wasn't persistent enough with gruff old-timer buyers and he was too persistent with others—wouldn't take "No" for an answer when good-natured customers explained that they were overstocked.

And, as Charley learned from letters, Lanston got his full share of practical jokes. Stones, quite large, unexplained stones, kept appearing in his sample cases. He was told that milliners of fabulous beauty were mad to meet him—and found that they were exemplary and indignant ladies of about sixty-five. All the way from Bridgeport he quaked over stories told to him regarding the Portsmouth Bonanza Store buyer, who was described by ever so many fellow salesmen as a large, strong quite unpleasant old gentleman who hated college men so much that he always threw them out of his store, preferably on their ears. Lanston sat for a whole evening in the Quaker House at Providence listening to a serious group of drummers tell stories about the crazy violence of the Portsmouth buyer—who proved to be a youngster of about Lanston's own age and an enthusiastic college graduate.

Nevertheless, Lanston got the business. Half a dozen buyers, writing in to confirm orders, took the trouble to inform Charley McClure that Lanston's earnestness, his studious knowledge of his line and his glib college tongue had made a real impression. So he was received in New York with open arms, taken out to lunch by Charley and Tom Snider, and given several big shops to handle while he was in town.

Only—Slosson also took Lanston out to lunch; Slosson, who had announced it as a policy that since he couldn't discriminate he wouldn't ordinarily lunch with any of his employees. In twenty-three years he had lunched with Charley McClure perhaps twenty-three times. Charley and Tom Snider attributed this favor to the fact that Slosson knew Lanston's father. They kept reassuring each other on this point.

Slosson took Lanston off selling for three weeks, and sent him on the rounds of the various factories and printshops supplying the Slosson goods. This totally disarranged Charley's plans for covering the city, and he himself had to waste time by going out to hole-and-corner shops. It wasn't that Charley was afraid to work, but for ten years or so he hadn't been passionate about it, and he grunted a good deal as he got out of his chair with its cushion of frayed newspaper. When Lanston returned he asked Charley a number of questions regarding things that had puzzled him in the manufacturing processes. Most of them Charley could not answer. He hadn't been near the factories for years; he depended on the Slosson manufacturing department to supply him with goods in proper condition and to inform him of any improvements in processes or materials that could be used as talking points in selling. When he didn't get these details he didn't worry. After a score of years of handling the same line, the most conscientious salesman finds it hard to run round shrieking for selling points that aren't really necessary.

Lanston was just a bit impudent when he found that Charley couldn't inform him, and Charley called him down with promptness and skill. When the youngster had returned to his desk, Charley sat rubbing the hair that grew in grizzled miniature burnsides beside his ears, and compressing his lips in a worried way. His glance after Lanston's back was regretful. But an hour later he merely smiled when he suddenly entered the sample room and found Lanston standing cockily, his thumbs in his lower waistcoat pockets and his hat on the back of his head, confiding to another salesman: "Yes, McClure sure has an awful grouch. By Jove, if I were boss————"

In late summer George Lanston made another trip, to the smaller New England cities, and he came back with a large, juicy, rosy idea. Charley pooh-poohed it. The idea, he informed Lanston, was a green crab apple; but Lanston, with the ignorance of youth, especially college-bred youth, insisted on prizing it.

The idea was for the Slosson Company to handle the gift-shop novelties that were beginning to be found in shops along Fifth Avenue, and more and more in the tea-and-souvenir rooms spreading from Maine to California. Lanston had noted that one single town in Cape Cod had half a dozen of these boudoirs of business handling wicker cages for celluloid birds, gayly painted wooden butterflies on sticks to be stuck in gardens, vases striped in black and white, bookends carved with fish and Phoenician gods, doorstops and doorknockers that pretended to be something else, gigantic match boxes with safety matches three feet long, and other fantastic fairyland wares, besides the tea and cake and beach-plum preserves which motorists from New York ate under the supposition that this was the native Cape Cod fare. The artistic novelties were all of them the outcome of the Arts and Crafts movement, which had started with simplicity as a keynote and was proceeding to a tune of Victorian bric-a-brac.

The Slosson Company needed a new line to replace gradually their children's books, which could not meet the competition of the importations of other firms, though it was true that the Slosson games held their own, and Golluf sold its thirty or forty thousand every year as regularly and sweetly as money in the bank. In the gift-shop novelties, declared young Lanston, was the needed substitute for the juveniles.

The other salesmen and Tom Snider agreed with Charley McClure that the idea was ridiculous; that, to quote Tom: "All this junk has about as much relation to our line as a dachshund to a shoe button."

Always during his career as manager Charley had tried to sympathize with ambition, though he had often antagonized cubs by the gruff bluffness which had been regarded as managerial manners in his younger days. He was like an old mastiff alternately growling and wagging his tail at a frisking kitten. Now, especially with the Great European War on the horizon, it seemed to him ridiculous that Lanston should suggest a pink-tea fad to the company. He did not know that the thing he said to Lanston echoed what S. R. Rice, his predecessor, had said to a young Charley McClure about boosting the game of Golluf. Why, Rice had been a turtle in a particularly thick shell, whereas he himself watched Lanston's career with a mingling of proprietorship and disapproval. He went out of his way to help him. Yet somehow the youngster answered curtly Charley's careful explanations of why the big idea was about as sensible as suicide by drowning in January. Regretfully Charley saw Lanston get more and more into the habit of whispering with the other youngsters in the sample room, glancing out at Charley with a cautiousness that betrayed them.

Meanwhile he was increasingly conscious of the intimacy between Slosson and Lanston. He once saw them together, in Slosson's new car, apparently driving home in the Ramapo Hills. Nevertheless, he growled to himself and to Tom Snider, he was going to bring Lanston up right whether Lanston was in personally with the big chief or not. Yet he wasn't entirely surprised when the thunderbolt struck.

Slosson walked up to his desk and curtly announced that they would try a few experimental items of gift-shop novelties.

"Well," growled Charley, "you're the boss, but you know as well as I do that they'll be flivvers."

He was there to guard Slosson's interests, but not to preach to him. He tried to be cheerful after this defeat, and courteous to Lanston, though he felt that it was good for the boy to continue joshing him about college ideas in business and to remark, perhaps one day: "Like to have tea served in the office, sir?"

But one evening when they were both working late—which Lanston often did and Charley rarely did, since he had his work trained—Charley discussed the men in the office, and Lanston opened up like an unfolding flower. He told of his voyages of discovery in the gift-shop world, and of a girl, head of Ye Arts Shoppe, who was helping him. Suddenly Lanston flushed and said good night abruptly. He left his boss unhappy.

The trip on which Lanston and the other salesmen first carried out the gift-shop goods, and searched for new outlets for business, ended in the spring of 1915. Lanston must have worked twenty-six hours a day and eight days a week. His record was easily equal to that of the second salesman, and in respect to the gift-shop items proportionately ahead of Charley McClure's sales in New York, Boston, and Philadelphia. For Charley admitted to his old friends among the buyers that he hadn't much confidence in the new line.

It was a new and older and far more arrogant George Lanston who returned to the office, and he even had the assurance to take up with Charley every bit of office correspondence that he had received, and to hint that Charley had given him no assistance from headquarters. Charley hotly defended himself and spoke of the matter to Slosson, who stroked his chin and gave no answer. It was an exciting topic at the lunches of Charley and Tom Snider; but after a couple of days Charley recovered his poise and declared:

"All this nonsense will blow over."

Then the second thunderbolt struck.

Slosson had for years been accustomed to call in Charley for conferences. With Slosson a conference meant inviting someone to give him additional reasons for doing what he had already made up his mind to do. Occasionally Tom Snider was present, but usually it was with Charley alone that Slosson smoked and grew friendly and commented on the failings of the other men in the office and finally "talked over plans." But on a May afternoon Charley was called in for a conference, and found Lanston settled back in a chair, smoking a Stock Exchange cigar, as though he had been there all day.

Said Slosson: "Mr. McClure, as you know, I'm never particularly anxious to waste a lot of money on fool schemes; but I should like to keep up to date, and since your profits are 'way below last year this time————"

"The war————"

"I'm tired of that line of talk," Slosson said sharply, while Charley was indignant at "getting a call" at the presence of his own underling, Lanston. "Just for that very reason we've got to make some changes. All this overhead going on, and less revenue ———— Lanston, will you outline our talk again?"

Calmly Lanston proposed: First, that they make an entirely independent gift-shop department, starting with two specializing salesmen. Second, a new type of advertisement, less garish, more quiet, to conform with present artistic tendencies. Third, plans for a new office uptown and for general office efficiency. Fourth, an advertising man and, for a time, an efficiency engineer.

At the word efficiency Charley visualized his own littered desk and his own way of handling memos, which was to leave them on the left side of his desk till they had been attended to. He thought of that because in the brief talk of Lanston there was such complete revolution that Charley was in a maze, didn't dare to admit what it meant. He stared glazedly at Slosson, whose left elbow was on his desk, while his right hand nervously jabbed with a blue pencil at a bowl of paper fasteners, which gave out a faint, disagreeable rattling. Charley was silent. He was trying to look nonchalant when Slosson demanded:

"Well, what do you think of the suggestions, McClure?"

Charley muttered: "Why, they're certainly worth thinking over, I guess."

Slosson snapped: "Thank you both. I'll consider them. McClure, may I see you a moment? I think that's all, Lanston."

The youngster who was dismissed marched out with a swagger, while the semiboss who was invited to stay slumped unhappily in his chair.

Slosson turned to him with a spurious brightness. "Keen boy that, McClure! What do you think of the idea of making him assistant sales manager to—uh—take some of the details off your shoulders and—uh—leave you free for the larger aspects of the business? Save you the trouble of monkeying with this gift-shop stuff."

Charley pulled himself together. He demanded: "Why do you ask me, Slosson? You've made up your mind already. Certainly Lanston's a good boy. He's young and he's too brash and too know-it-all, but at the same time he's a comer. But, good Lord, don't ask me to do a fox trot when you suggest my giving him about half my job! That's what it amounts to. I'm playing with my cards on the table, without any miffle-business. You know what I think about the gift-shop stuff—it's all right for these long-haired artists and hobohemians, but it's a good thing for us to let alone. Of course, if you want to turn the firm over to it, and let Lanston run you and me and all the rest of us, why———"

Never before had he spoken so frankly to Slosson, for the habit of respect to the chief was one of more than twenty years. Slosson interrupted him in an entirely friendly way:

"No, no, you've got it all wrong, Charley! I haven't made up my mind at all. But if I do, you've got to remember that you and I and Tom Snider aren't as young as we were, and the business is growing. Needs young blood. So if I do decide to make George—Lanston—your assistant, I'll need your help to get the boy started right, Charley. Of course, he's young and pretty fresh, but he'll learn."

"All right. I'll do what I can to help him, of course."

Slosson waited for him to go, and Charley fled for refuge to his desk. Not much of a refuge did it appear to the casual eye, merely an unfenced desk in a semipartitioned room with seven other desks; but here he had thrashed out his problems for a quarter of a century; here he was king and seer; and to the slow tune of a fingernail tapping this inkwell he had worked out his philosophy.

"I wonder," he fretted, "if that old fiend could be just planning to have Lanston pump out all I know about practical selling, and then let me go? I wouldn't put it past him."

With a brain that was not accustomed to think of psychology, except the psychology of selling, he unraveled the problem and decided that he would trust Slosson. He realized that he was worrying about the boss Slosson as the salesmen worried about the boss McClure. Nevertheless, he was as stolidly fearful as a man on a vessel entering the war zone. There was a curious uneasy feeling at the pit of his stomach; his spine was icy; he was restless—couldn't sit still; kept parading down to Tom Snider's department, ostensibly to ask business questions, really to get assurance from the plump complacence of Tom. Restlessness was in the air. Slosson, who usually sat tight in his room, kept coming out, wandering round, peering at everybody. It seemed to Charley that each time he bent over Tom's desk Slosson suddenly appeared somewhere near at hand, watching them. The office changed from its ordinary routine dullness and became sinister, filled with plots. Whenever Slosson stopped during his prowlings and spoke to George Lanston, Charley had a dread-filled desire to spy on them, to sneak up and listen. Lanston became suddenly a formidable rival, with dangerous secret plans, capable of any shocking surprise.

Tom Snider seemed to feel the tension. While he talked with Charley about shipments Tom's fat hands, with their peculiar, deep-embedded nails, rattled papers nervously; and he limped in speech, breaking off what he was saying to watch Slosson's appearances. Finally, staring straight ahead, not looking at Charley, he growled out of the side of his mouth:

"Come out and have a drink with me after office, Charley. Things look bad."

Like a conspirator, while he pretended to be very much interested in testing a sheet of paper by intelligently rubbing it between thumb and finger, Charley answered:

"They sure do. I'm with you."

A hundred times, these past years, they had agreed that "things looked bad—likely to be some changes in the office." But mostly they had been playing at fear; they had enjoyed their plots with that small-boy capacity for making drama out of our own lives which we all retain. Now they were quiet, direct, shaky. They stood at the bar of the Magnificent—which wasn't magnificent any longer—and Tom sighed:

"Going to be a bust in the office, Charley. Looks to me as if Slosson was bit by this young-blood-in-the-business bug. Well, I'm going to get out."

"Go on!"

"Yump. Straight. I've been dickering for a year, off and on, with Thayer, you know, Newark Art and Novelty Store, and this afternoon when I saw Slosson peerading round I sort of smelled a rat, and made up my mind to git while the gitting's good. I can take over Thayer's business on share—won't have to put up much money of my own. I'm not a kid any longer, Charley, but I guess I can show the retail trade a trick or two. Thayer wants to skip out to California—got a daughter living out at Pasadena, and I guess his missus don't like the climate here in the East any too well. Look, son, you better come in with me. I can't offer you anything to speak of at first——— Just between you and I, what's Slosson paying you now? I never did know."

"Forty-one hundred."

"Well, Lord, I couldn't even begin to touch that! Still I could give you an interest, with a guarantee of eighteen hundred or so."

"Oh, gosh, Tom, I'm so used to the Slosson office now that I'd be like an old cab-horse—put me out in the pasture and the trees would scare me and I'd starve for dry hay."

"Well, think it over. Look here, Newark is going———"

Charley only half listened to Tom's enthusiasms. He wanted to flee home to Agnes.

Agnes McClure was a woman of fifty, perhaps fifty-one now, thin-lipped, anxious, given to wearing bottle-green bodices and small black hats. Her neighbors in their suburb all said that she was a nice woman, but never said much more about her. To Charley she was the one woman in the world who had common sense. She agreed with him in fearing Slosson, hating spinach, and adoring the movies and their son Robert. For months at a time they were as unsentimental as two partners; but every so often, when things went wrong, Charley would run to her and be silent with her, and it would be all right. And always, after those silent confidences of theirs, she would manage to have prune-whip for dessert.

This May evening Charley came grumpily up the walk. He eyed his house, but he did not go in to find Agnes. He commanded himself: "Oh, don't go whining round. You're as bad as a kid!" He picked seven leaves off the lawn, pulled up a weed that had sneaked into the grass at the edge of the drive, and tried again to turn off a watertap that was always dripping. He proudly inspected the house, their new home, paid for a year before. It was square, of cement, with dormer windows and a large screened porch. The lawn in front was as trim as a boulevard parkway.

He was realizing that he might not be able to keep up this home if things went wrong at the office. He stared abstractedly at a cement hitching-block, and in his meditations he must for a moment have passed into the mystic state of a hermit brooding in the desert. He forgot all his own troubles; he sorrowed only because Agnes might lose this new house, which was her pride. He glided into a strange vision, of which he wasn't even conscious. Standing motionless, his hands prosaically in his trouser pockets, he felt that he had lost all individuality as Charley McClure; that he was only an indistinguishable part of the unknown force that drives business as it drives pilgrimages; that Slosson and S. R. Rice and Tom Snider and George Lanston and Charley McClure and Robert McClure were all one person, confusedly carrying on some vast work that was to make a greater world in which Agnes would have

———

"Charley!"

Agnes was calling to him from the porch. He did not hear her. She came down the steps, took his arm, rubbed her hair against his sleeve. She looked up at him, then "What is it, my little boy?" she whispered.

"Nothing, honey," he declared, but he gripped her arm, nor did he let it go as they stood together, silent.

He talked volubly through dinner—about Robert and the neighbors. Robert was away, working late on his job as local agent for a Jersey real-estate development. Agnes suggested that—oh, she didn't care a single bit herself, really she didn't, but if Charley was still thinking that they ought to buy an automobile, she had just heard of a used car that could be bought for almost nothing from a neighbor.

While she talked Charley swore to himself that, instead of being conquered by the young blood in the office, he had merely begun to fight. And he would carry on the fight. He'd put young Lanston where he belonged. Agnes should have forty cars if she wanted them. His first duty was to her, not to the firm, the boss, the job. While he smiled and accused her of wanting the car for himself, and she denied it, and they both laughed and had a great many helpings of the prune-whip which had suddenly appeared by household magic, Charley was wildly planning a combat that would put the office back in the security it had enjoyed before Lanston's intrusion.

He said that he felt like taking a walk and thinking over some business details. His wife let him go alone; she understood. He whistled to his English setter and in the spring twilight started down the suburban street with its pleasant maples, then took to the railroad track and walked the ties. He was not a dramatic figure. His back had a slight stoop; his thirty-five-dollar suit was neither smart nor shabby; his collar was of the kind advertised in the street cars, but it had a tiny crack at the fold in front. You knew that he was a capable office man, and that he played cards once a week with the neighbors.

He seemed not to be worried. As he plodded along he glanced appraisingly at the fields opening up beside the track; he whistled repeatedly to his dog, and leaned over to pat him.

Yet Charley was fighting furiously with all the devils of approaching sixty. He was pitilessly informing himself that either he or Lanston would have to go; that the same office couldn't hold them; that Slosson was favoring Lanston, was probably saying this very minute: "Oh, I like McClure, but Lord, I'm not running a charity institution; he's either got to get waked up or else get out."

Yet he knew how easy it was to flatter Slosson into giving up a plan. And he knew Lanston's vulnerable faults. Charley could increase these faults or cure them. Lanston wasn't popular with the men in the office. And he had two huge faults in selling. He oversold; talked a buyer into interest, and then, if his information held out, talked him into a state of exhausted boredom. Furthermore, he felt that he was called upon to tell the retailers how to run their business. Charley believed that if he passed the word to certain friends in the retail line Slosson would get such reports about Lanston that—oh, no, Charley reassured his conscience, Slosson wouldn't fire the youngster, but still he'd put him in his place.

"And that's what ought to happen," Charley insisted. "I had to fight for my job—fine lot old Rice ever helped me!—and now let Lanston fight for his. Why should I go down on my knees and beg him to take my job away from me? It's all right for a boss to help a young fellow; that's part of the game. But I don't see where it's part of the game to go round looking for somebody to cut your throat— yes, and probably have to buy him the knife! It's me or Lanston, and we'll fight to the limit—let him watch out for himself."

At home Charley found his son Robert, a clean-looking boy of twenty, whose appearance hinted of baseball and sailing. Robert was walking up and down the front porch, viciously swishing a tennis racket.

"What's the matter, son?"

"Oh, it's the boss again. Honestly, dad, you can say all you want to, but I believe the old hound is just deliberately trying to keep me from climbing. Talk about injustice————"

"Come off, Rob. What's the specific trouble?"

"Oh, it's that deal on plot seventy again. I know I could get the doctor to buy it—I just know it; but the boss wouldn't even let me show it to him. Says he's going to sell him something else, and then he keeps putting it off and putting it off. The firm's going to lose the prospect—that's what's going to happen. And all because the boss is afraid us younger fellows will show some real initiative and maybe get to be his rivals. That's justice, isn't it! And loyalty to the firm! Oh, fine! Honest, dad, if I were boss————"

Charley tut-tutted like the fathers in every generation, and de-clared:

"Why, son, I don't believe that any boss is going to be so delib-erately unfair as to keep youngsters from making good if they earn the chance. You'll be all right when the time comes. We always feel the way we do when we're young, but—b-but—you just trust your boss. He'll give you a square deal. If you can beat him, why, you win; he won't stack the cards on you—any m-more than I w-would if I were your boss. I wouldn't keep you back, would I? No matter what it cost me I'd—know that—progress has to go on progress-ing, whether it got me or anybody else."

"Yes, I know you would, dad."

"Um, yes—though of course I admit there aren't many like me!"

Charley said it very dryly, and did not explain. He stood watch-ing the passing motor cars. He was thinking: "When I go in with Tom on the Newark store I must arrange so I have time to work with Rob. Maybe Rob and I can turn a trick or two together. Going to be wonderful to watch the boy progress! Let's see, I must fix it so they don't neglect the Golluf sales when I'm out. Rob! How'd you like to play your mother and me a little game of Golluf?"

HONESTLY—IF POSSIBLE

I

Terry Ames didn't own evening clothes, and there was no running water in his furnished room, but every Saturday evening he paid a dollar and a half for dinner, which he always ate alone. He was one of the three thousand solitary and industrious young men in New York. He knew no one except the office force, his dentist and two insignificant "fellows from back home."

This gray-eyed youngster with the waist and shoulders of a half-miler, the thin, firm jaw of a surgeon, and the eager, awkward step of a young poet, this frequenter of offices and movies and beef-stew joints, was facing the blankness of life as somberly as an anchorite in a parching desert cell. If he could only be heroic or tragic or criminal or anything that would make him feel things! Any sorrow rather than row on row of unchanging gray days. He wanted to do the high, vague, generous things, and the city told him to strictly attend to his desk.

He was neither a success nor a failure. He was making thirty-two dollars and a half a week with the mail order real-estate firm of Hopkins & Gato. He wrote advertising copy, dictated correspondence, and occasionally was sent out to close up a prospect. He did not have the facts of his job: he knew the difference between a blueprint and a second mortgage; but he simply couldn't get the philosophy of the job to hang right. You would have been amused—or touched or impatient or morally edified—to see Terry trying to find out what a good, clean life really meant in the case of a young man whose boss pompously encouraged him to write advertisements that were deliberate, careful, scientific lies. He would have been discharged as dishonest if he smuggled the truth into a single advertisement of the Terrace Valley Development. Did goodness consist in lying, then? he wailed.

When he had first come to New York Terry had solemnly attended institute lectures that told him to be good and he would be happy, or to work hard and he would be rich, or to study shorthand and he would be famous. But most of the lecturers weren't happy or rich or famous—or interesting. And they always rushed down and shook hands with him. Terry hated damp handshakes.

He saved up his money and bought a large, gilt-edged book called *Punch the Buzzer on Yourself*, which claimed to give all of the latest and best brands of practical wisdom. It was a chatty book. It sneaked up behind you and yelled in your ear in fourteen-point italics. Yet all that it said was to be good and work hard and buy other books by the same author.

At last Terry took to asking the men in his office what this business world was up to anyway. He had chosen a peculiarly dangerous field for truth hunting, for the Hopkins & Gato office was a cranky one, boisterous and fearful and full of plots. Offices differ as much as bosses, and in about the same way. There are quiet, assured offices filled with pride and achievement. There are offices like Hopkins & Gato, where everybody gibes and is nervous about the gibes of others.

Old Hopkins had the habit of damning all your officemates when he was talking to you in order to make you feel that you were on the inside with the boss, as his most trusted adviser. That was his jolly little way of influencing you to confide all the scandal you knew. If you were aware of the trick and tried to defend Harry or Mac or J. J., Mr. Hopkins would comment on Harry's shambling feet, or Mac's sporty wife, or J. J.'s shiftlessness, with a thin, acrid smile that made you feel naive and absurd, and, first thing you knew, you were trying to prove your shrewdness by giving away every below-stairs secret. The men in the office were good fellows at heart, but they were spoiled by the bitter flavor of Hopkins.

They went the rounds of one another's desks, making beastly little jests. And they played jokes, hid hats and arranged humiliating fake telephone calls. After a few years in Hopkins & Gato's fine, solid, prosperous office you were qualified to go right out to the trenches and join the poison squad.

This was the font of wisdom where eager, fresh-colored, wistful, hard-working Terry Ames fished for the truth about his honesty, which sounds so simple in the books and works so jaggedly in ordinary life. He was always going out to lunch with J. J., with Mac, shrewdest of the salesmen, and with ancient Harry, the bookkeeper, who had detachable cuffs and a preternatural shrewdness in collections. While they all got on a mild coffee drunk, as is the way of business lunches, Terry persistently tried to bring the conversation round to the problem of commercial honesty.

The wild elders shrieked at him:

"Oh, give your conscience a rest!"

They gave their consciences a good, permanent rest and fed them soothing syrup if they waked and cried.

Sometimes Terry would get oracles out of old Harry, who defended the Hopkins system of exaggerating in advertisements, using much retouched half tones, hypnotizing old-lady customers, and selling jerrybuilt houses from which the concrete peeled off during the first winter.

Harry asserted:

"It's all right to talk, but you aren't in business for your health, are you? Besides, everybody does it."

The others would nod approval of Harry's pellucid philosophy and drop into Terry's truth-begging palms such pearls as these:

"This bull about building homes for the future and making suburbs beautiful listens well in high-school recitation, but how are you going to support the business meanwhile?"

"Why, we're regular angels compared with most of 'em. Look at this free-if-you-pay-for-the-abstract scheme."

"Why, if you did tell the people the truth they wouldn't be satisfied."

"I guess we're as honest as the next fellow."

"Yes, sure, honestly—if possible."

"When you're as old as I am————"

"Get the dough first————"

When Terry declared that other firms—big, reputable, national concerns—must surely have a higher standard of honesty than Hopkins & Gato, the men didn't take the trouble to argue: they merely smiled and made him feel schoolboyishly credulous. By his constant inquiring he was in danger of becoming the office pest; but in nauseated horror he realized that fact, and tried to conceal his restless fumbling for understanding.

In the city's somber corridor of brooding gods, gigantic graven idols with hands on their brutal knees and granite eyes insolently blank above this clerkly questioning, he prayed for guidance, but only an echo answered him, and over the temple brooded the shadow of Pilatus, still asking "What is truth?"

You—philosophers and poets and iron-jawed statesmen, foreign observers of America, and clever ladies of the literary tables d'hôtes and soldiers who demand that we take your military training—you know what our offices are—just desks and cigars and rubber bands, and derby hats over a slight baldness. Yes, you know there isn't any grave and quiet nobility or glorious struggle of youth among us who are dollar chasers.

Oh! Oh, you do, do you? Then listen.

II

Hopkins & Gato were on the jump, booming a new development. They had sold most of their Long Island suburb to unfortunates who had never seen New York State; and now, lest they seem to neglect the suckers in New York, they were taking on Tangerine Springs, "the citrus city, the best orange district in Florida," for mail and direct selling. Mr. Hopkins had a whole pamphlet of affable government figures about the yield in orange groves not more than ten miles from Tangerine Springs, figures so convincing that the Hopkins copywriter, Terry Ames, wondered where the flaw really was as he turned out notices about: "Golden fruit and a golden bank account; the way out for the city man who is tired of offices and Northern cold. Own your own bungalow among the palms and hibiscus; easy work and big returns."

"That's me. 'Tired of offices and cold.' Wonder if there's a single darn palm in Florida. Can't be if a Hopkins ad says there is," he grumbled as he viciously jabbed at his typewriter with two thin fingers.

Terry had grown accustomed to lying about the Long Island property, but he couldn't get up much enthusiasm about this new fraud. He wanted to believe in Tangerine Springs as long as he could. But he discovered the facts soon enough.

A Brooklyn man wrote that he knew Florida, that Tangerine Springs might perhaps be all right for trucking, but certainly was too wet and low for citrus fruits. His letter closed:

> "Tell the bright young man who is guilty of your ads that he might catch more fools if he said less about sunshine and bungalows and more about kumquats and mandarins. There's just one thing that saves the public from liars like you people—that is, you don't know how to run your own business. I bet you don't know flatwoods from hammock."

Did Mr. Clyde Hopkins blush at this letter? No, Mr. Clyde Hopkins did not blush. He called in Terry Ames and snapped:

"If you can't put a little more pep and novelty in your Tangerine copy, you better quit. Here, read this letter!"

Terry marveled, as he read, that Mr. Hopkins was willing to show this exposure of his own crime. He stammered:

"But, uh, how—how about this 'all right for trucking, bum for citrus fruit,' Mr. Hopkins?"

"Rats; always got to have a few kicks. How does he know it ain't good for oranges till he tries it? Now, get a good line about all the different kinds of oranges into your copy. And you might even want to write this boob, thanking him for the tip. Don't let him think we're sore."

Terry wanted to resign. But, if he did, Hopkins would merely laugh and go on selling Tangerine lots. As he gloomed back to his desk Terry sketched a moving picture of himself as the young hero who could convert the office to truth, single-handed. He saw Hopkins trembling before his denunciations, and even the old cynic Harry weeping down his alpaca coat sleeves and selling his agate scarfpin to get money to refund Hopkins' victims.

But—Terry wasn't a Galahad; he was about like the rest of us;

he wanted to be honest and also to get that little envelope next Saturday. So he studied a bulletin on orange growing till he had an artistic inspiration and was lost in composing a blurb which began:

"Do you know that the orange industry has just started? Do you know what a kumquat is? Do you know that the whole world is begging for the chance to give you money for the kumquats you could grow at Tangerine Springs?"

When the advertisement was glowingly finished, however, Terry gravitated to Mac's desk and complained:

"Say, hang it, I don't like this Tangerine project. Land's no good for citrus fruits. Why not sell it for truck———"

"Say, Ames, don't you ever give your conscience an hour off? Do you know what's the matter with it? You smoke too many cigarettes."

Then Mac laughed for four minutes and hustled round the office, revealing his new joke to everybody: "So I says to him, 'Do you know what's the matter with you? Why,' I says, 'you're getting smoker's heart in the conscience!'"

When J. J. sent Terry an office "memo" next morning he headed it:

"To the man with the ingrowing conscience and the outsticking cigarette."

Watkins asked Terry why he didn't smoke cigars, like a man, and Peter had some light, elephantine pleasantries about a pipe. In fact, Terry's general childishness was the office joke, till they had a new topic in the expected arrival of a woman to try to do a man's work.

This gave an almost perfect opportunity for them to dig out all the good shady jokes about women's foibles. Hopkins was, it seemed, going to get one Susan Bratt to manage the follow-up and circularizing systems—check up the lists, tabulate the returns, get out form letters, direct twelve girl assistants. She was out to replace Peter. Whenever Peter was out of hearing, everybody insinuated that he was a loafer, a borrower of small sums till Monday; but, even so, Peter was preferable to this Susan Bratt.

Terry pictured her as fat, forty, faded, dumpily industrious and wheezily sniffling, staring dully from behind thick glasses and making a bad precedent by staying late. He joined the others in referring to her as "the brat." The forlorn and lonely seeker of honesty was preparing to make it difficult as he could for the forlorn and lonely interloper.

On Monday morning Terry woke with the usual Monday-morning shock of discovering that the holiday was over, and groaned:

"Back to the mine! Oh, I can't stand any more rotten chirping little fifty-line ads about kumquats—but I will."

Every day in his life would be one more dinky page in an endless desk calendar.

He entered the office with Mac, who was the local ladykiller, and who stopped just inside the door to chuckle:

"Hey, Ames, the little Bratt has came. Some dame, kid, some chicken! Me for it! My lit-tle Sue, I could love you-oo."

At Peter's desk was the new office woman. She looked up. Terry caught the flash of her eyes. "Gee!" said he.

A slender, curly-haired girl of twenty three or four, with the untroubled brown eyes of a gallant boy, yet with curving shoulders in a blouse of white silk that looked as though it could never be anything but fresh. A quick-moving, self-possessed girl. Mac turned, as they separated, and winked at Terry, who hated the suggestive wink and the troublesome new girl about equally. He had, at least, grown used to his round of boredom. He had invented ways of pulling through the day—sneaking out for a cup of coffee round the corner, talking to old Harry, standing out in the hall at the mail chute and warning himself to work as though he did like it. Now, this satin-cheeked young Susan Bratt would inspire new jealousies and make the office intolerable.

All day long he watched Miss Bratt smile gratefully at the men who straightened their ties and went to introduce themselves to her. He saw Gato himself call for office supplies for her—even to blue and red pencils and a letter opener, tools for which the rest of them had to steal from one another. He saw the bunch maneuvering to find things to explain to her, advice to give her. And she was pleasant to all of them. Terry had to admire her modulating voice, though he hated to hear it responding to the smirking, much married Mac, who leaned over her desk and flashed his diamond ring at her. Terry found that he, too, had the most surprising number of errands that took him up to her end of the office. But he wouldn't introduce himself to her—no, not for anything!

When he left at five-thirty she was putting on a blue linen jacket with impudent white cuffs and collar, and a small toque which sat cockily on her brown, shining hair. All the Sir Walter Raleighs in the shop galloped up to help her, while the old dependables, the stenographers who had been with the firm since Hopkins was a yearling, somehow managed to struggle with their sateen-lined, tabby black jackets without assistance.

"Good Lord, look at them, everyone but old Harry and me and the firm! With J. J. holding her bag! Well, I know one person that isn't going to fall for the Queen of the Rancho stuff," Terry grumbled as he clumped out.

He walked down the Bowery and had dinner in Chinatown. He peered into pawnshop windows, he watched the bums, he chose the noisiest chop-suey den in town, he made much of ordering almond and omelet, and "sweet and pungent." He wouldn't admit it, but he was trying to flee from loneliness, the loneliness that usually was merely drab boredom but tonight was a tangible, pursuing presence. Fear was creeping into him, fear of himself, fear of the cryptic city. He rushed out of the restaurant. Through the streets deserted and foreboding he swung down to the Battery, listening to his own footsteps. Among the derelicts, dark, shoddy figures writhing on the benches, he sat, neat and efficient and—a derelict. Beside him sat Fear.

A barge load of immigrants was bound for Ellis Island. One of them struck up on his accordion a wailing folk song, full of the melancholy of brown moors, and Terry's frantic restlessness changed to a softer unhappiness in which every memory was tender and hopelessly sad. Then he knew that all the while he had been subconsciously reviewing Susan Bratt. Her harsh name changed to a sound of music. In the mist rising from the river he saw her face. He felt himself kiss her smiling lips.

He sprang up, amazed at the force of his fancy. He exclaimed:

"Why, I've never seen her but just one day—flirt that tries to work everybody. Why, I haven't even met her yet . . . But, by Jiminy, I will tomorrow! No, I won't either. All this kitten stuff!"

Her luminous eyes went home with him, and he could scarce sleep for longing to see her. Then it was morning again—same old prosaic awakening to the same old raucous alarm clock in the same old room, with the same old office details ahead. He plodded uptown. He already knew that his overnight fervor about Miss Bratt was a dream; that she was merely a business female, not a princess of romance. He glanced at her.

"Yup. Nothing but a pretty girl. Woods are full of 'em."

She had no relation to the lighted passionate face that had looked at him from the fog of the harbor.

Not till ten or eleven o'clock did he fall in love with her again!

J. J.'s desk was near Miss Bratt's. With J. J. late that morning, Terry had to work out a new form letter to galvanize installment payments. When he was really on the job Terry tried to be crisp, alert, practical, and in such a mood of justice he wondered if Miss Bratt really was looking for flirtations.

She seemed very busy, crosschecking two lists of alfalfa-land inquiries to be used for the Tangerine Springs circularizing.

J. J. and Terry were sitting in one of those familiar poetic abstractions, trying to think of a better phrase to close the letter which they were planning—tilted back, tapping their teeth with their pencils, heads on one side, one eye closed, the other eyes screwed up and anxiously regarding the ceiling, looking tremendously wise, and both of them passing the buck and plaintively hoping that the other fellow was going to hurry up and think of the phrase. Perhaps you've done it yourself.

Through the trance Terry heard Mac's voice, honeyed but slightly hoarse:

"Well, little one, things going better today? Sorry I been out this morning. Meant to stick around and slip you some more pointers."

Terry's tilted chair came down sharply and he stared. Mac was beside Miss Bratt's desk, in his very best lady-killing attitude, as used successfully with waitresses, telephone girls, and young ladies at hotel newsstands—hat on one side, both hands in his pockets, his trim feet doing a little private dance by themselves, all very gay and intimate.

Terry was groaning:

"Good Lord, what a simp I am, mooning over this girl, and she standing for Mac. Urgh!" Mac took his hands from his pockets, leaned over his desk, picked up her pastepot and fondled it. To the absurdly squeamish Terry it seemed as though Mac would take her hand next. Mac murmured, like a cooing jackass:

"Well, did the girlie get her hooky-wookies into the job pretty good today?"

Miss Bratt laid down her list of names, put a paper weight exactly in the center of the desk, straightened the nest of pencils and pens in front of her inkwell, and said with startling clearness:

"Mr. Mac—MacDervish, isn't it?—I'm very busy. I'm obliged to you for your pointers of yesterday, but I didn't really need them. I'm afraid I'm horribly competent. So if you would—how would you say it in your language?—if you would ring off you'd save me lots and lots of trouble. I think that's all."

And she did not smile with a sugary prissy sanctity; she did not look about for applause. She rose rather quickly and stood straight, her fingers on the edge of the desk, while for a second she seemed to look far away, sadly. Then, eyes down, she passed Mac and quietly began to flip through a file of names. As Mac shuffled away she ignored him.

Terry was glowingly happy—that is, till J. J. grated:

"Cranky little hen. . . . Well, have you got that phrase yet?"

During the several million hours that had still to drag themselves past before twelve-thirty, when he would be free to go out to lunch, Terry found the needed phrase, dictated some correspondence, and came back to study the big map of Florida that hung near Miss Bratt's desk. He had convinced himself that he needed to examine that map immediately—so immediately that he left his draft of the big Tangerine circular in the middle of a sentence. As he went up the central aisle of the office he felt kindly toward his fellow workers, toward Harry and J. J. and Gato and Watkins and this new Miss Bratt. What a good, knowable bunch of human beings they all were—all except Mac. And except Hopkins, of course. Then the office changed to a hideous tangle of dead, gaunt trees, a wilderness filled with ambushes that threatened the unconscious Sue Bratt. Mac was talking to Watkins, Mac's rival as office masher. The two men glanced at Miss Bratt and snickered.

While Terry was examining the map near her, Watkins came forward and oozily said:

"Uh, have you, uh, a date for lunch, Miss Bratt? Be glad tuh ———"

"I have!" said Miss Bratt.

This time she didn't flee to the files. She sat still, a slight droop to her shoulders that were so smooth and rosy under her silk waist, and she looked Watkins up and down, quiet, a little perplexed, very cool.

"Well, uh," he went on, "some day, if you could, uh, grace the feast with your charms———"

"No. Afraid not." Her right hand picked up a list of names. But behind the list, as Terry could see from his station at the map, her left arm pressed anxiously against her bosom, while her eyes somberly kept Watkins in view.

Terry broke in:

"Say, Watkins, come here a second. Where's the head of navigation on the Saint John's River? Let's see how much you know about Florida, old fathead."

Watkins unwillingly came over. Terry generously accompanied him back to his desk. As they passed Mac, Watkins tittered:

"I buy!"

At twelve-thirty, to the second, Terry grabbed his hat and hastened out to Henrico's Chop House to meet J. J. and Harry and Mac and Watkins—and large, solid food with too much coffee. He was rather keen for doing something spectacular and heroic if Mac or Watkins so much as mentioned Miss Bratt. He pictured himself slapping Mac, and he was so exalted with newborn devotion that he might actually have done something of the kind, although office lunches are not commonly the scenes of anything more melodramatic than spearing a toasted roll across the table. He waited, panting, inspired—though not fasting. But the only word of her was Mac's growl at Watkins:

"Stung, all right. Pretty standoffish. Pass us the chutney, will yuh, Wat?"

Thus they dismissed the tale of the weeping fair one and the secret knight.

Terry Ames wasn't always secret-knighting around the office.

He really did get out copy and correspondence, you understand. But he contrived to see how, within less than three days, Miss Bratt made a place for herself. She was pleasant to old Harry, who chewed tobacco and collected from widows but did not try to flirt with babes. She was sturdily independent in an argument with Gato. In the murkiness of this cranky, distrustful office she was a clear light that shone into the dark carelessness of former attempts at system. Tenderly he watched her march on.

Terry wasn't trying to pick acquaintance with her. He didn't dare! However, he was careful to be on hand when she took the elevator down, a little after five-thirty, a couple of days later. Just to ride with her, be near her, perhaps feel a casual touch of her magic arm that was of a more silken substance than the busy arms of the stenographers! She seemed unaware of him as she rang the elevator bell and waited. Her face was as serenely gallant as that of a boy crusader—fresh, smooth, rather round. She was so untiring, so incisively interested in her work. She would go far. . . . But wasn't she, he wondered in dismay, almost too inhumanly efficient? It wasn't quite decent to look fresh and competent after five-thirty!

Her hand, which had remained on the iron box of the elevator signal, suddenly slumped to her side. She wiped her other hand across her eyes, which remained closed for a minute, the lids bunchy and trembling with weariness. No, she wasn't too efficient!

It seemed to him, brooding beside her on the elevator, that her little, white, soft linen collar, the blue linen of her jacket sleeve, the line of her cheek, everything relating to her, was enchantment, set off from all the commonplace feminine things in the world, standing out as peculiar and perfect.

Next morning Terry was drawing water at the cooler that served the office as *patio*, garden, village green and memorial fountain when he became agitatedly aware that Miss Susan Bratt was waiting beside him. He heard himself blurting out:

"G'morning, Miss Bratt."

She didn't repulse him. Easily:

"Good morning, Mr. Ames."

"W-w-why, I didn't kn-know you even knew my name."

"I didn't, till you took Mr. Watkins away from me. I was very grateful to you. Then I knew that you must be Mr. Ames—I could see what you were."

"Yes, b-but———" desperately. "But what am I?"

"Mr. MacDervish had given me a chart of the office, and he told me that Mr. Ames wasn't practical; he said you 'seemed to think we were in business for our health—always yelping about honesty.' And it was so very much for my health to lose Mr. Watkins that I knew my Good Samaritan must be you."

"I wonder if maybe you and I don't belong to the same race of people."

"The———"

"Yes, the cranks, the people that aren't content with just galumphing along and making a living, but have to fuss round and take all the joy out of life by wanting people to be honest or efficient or original or some darn thing they don't want to take the trouble to be."

She hesitated a little over his youthful confidences. She inspected him—his flush, his lips open with eagerness. Then she nodded.

"Yes," she said: "though I guess I'm a frightful outsider in the race of people—just a hyphenated citizen. But I do like to fight for—oh, I don't know what to call it—sincerity, I guess. Hard to call it anything without getting into some kind of cant."

"Yes, and it's hard to know what the deuce it is. Take me! Oh, I'm a fine, walloping social reformer. I am! All day long I write lies to make poor devils buy swamp land."

"And I send out the lies for you."

"Let's go dig ditches."

"Let's—only we won't."

Miss Bratt was beginning to glance over his shoulder. He realized that he was keeping her out in the middle of the office floor, to the vast interest of Mac, Watkins, and the battery of stenographers. He sighed:

"Prob'ly be a scandal if we go on holding the Society for the Promulgation of Ethics among the Heathen Bosses any longer. I— it's——— Please let me welcome you to this punk office."

She did not answer in words, yet her smile, as she turned away, took him into her friendship.

The babes in the woods, lost in a thicket of industry, had recognized each other, and Terry had an impulse to take her hand, to run away with her who had, over two paper cups of water, become his playmate. But with Miss Rheinstein, the boss' stenographer, watching you, you don't take hands and run away. No, you parade back to your desk, you go over every word you have said to Sue, and worry lest you have started out by making a bad impression.

They met again and again. And they didn't talk of office honesty more than reasonably often. Indeed, though Terry invariably took away the impression that they had been conferring on subjects of great intellectual value, their discussions were often limited to a couple of smiles, a couple of nods and "Tired?" "Yes, rather." "Must be a perfectly corking day out in the country." "Yes, it must be."

Lingering needlessly over letter files, laughing while he helped her to dig out old lists from the document safe, O.K.ing the proof of a form letter, they came to depend on each other for fire that would kindle the dry wood of routine. He knew her square dimpled hands that hovered accurately over papers; she knew his thin, stained fingers that made amusing manikins out of wire paper fasteners.

III

The Tangerine Springs circular was out, its glossy envelope adorned with a sketch of an orange tree and a legend which in ten words conveyed two lies, a financial misstatement and a botanical error. Now, Miss Susan Bratt's corner of the office was filled with scrubby girls rented from an agency. They sat at long tables and blew their noses and chewed gum and addressed envelopes in elegant script all day long. Miss Bratt was mother and drill sergeant and police officer to them. She had to keep them till six-thirty and had to fight Hopkins to get overtime pay for them.

It was six-thirty-one now, and every single addressing girl had already piled into the elevator. Sue was among the long tables messily piled with circulars and lists.

There was no one else in the office except Terry, who was finishing an advertisement. The yoke of the job was on him. Till he sat back, his work finished, he was not Terry Ames, a person to desire and have dreams but a little shaggy dog in a treadmill of advertisements. Then, because he had smoked too furiously all day, and the good old family remedy for that is to groan "Oh, I oughtn't to smoke so much," and light another cigarette, he tried that remedy, slouching in his chair, ruefully wiggling his tired fingers. Slowly, as humanness began to flow again into his fingers and blurred eyes and beaten-out brain, he became aware that the person straightening up the addressing tables was not executive Miss Bratt, but golden Sue.

He loafed down the office, too conscious of the stiffness of his knees, which had been rigidly crossed all day while he was typing, to be a secret knight. And Sue showed in her crinkling brow the signs of that persistent, sneaking, office headache which pinches the back of your eyeballs every time you move. Her marvelously trim hair was beginning to be disheveled; her normally unerring movements were slow and pitifully fumbling. With her superiority was gone something of her self-dependence. She looked at Terry with a smile that was worn at the edges, forlornly welcoming his presence.

"All in?" he said.

"Yes."

"Both of us are, I guess."

He sat on the edge of a desk, his feet in a chair.

"Got a good bunch of girls to help you?"

"Punk."

"Yup. Mostly are."

"Poor darlings, we'd be as bad as they are if we worked just one week in a place, addressing circulars to Bazooza, Oklahoma and Winnepowunkus, Maine."

"Yup. Always said that if I were a day laborer I'd get drunk every Saturday evening to try to forget it. Say, as man to man, Miss Superior Bratt, does this cigarette make your head ache?"

"As man to man, nothing could make it ache more than it does now. If you'll give me one, I think I'll try one myself."

In the muted hours after the office closed, time ceases to register. There is nothing that must be done for Mr. Hopkins in fifteen minutes. Miss Bratt, who usually went straight home, sighed into a chair. She took a cigarette, lighted it unskillfully, smoked it very badly, with rapid, shallow little puffs.

She crushed it out and grumbled:

"Hang it, now you see why offices wear out women and scrap 'em. They simply can't do some things, though they bluff that they can. I'd be almost a good office man if I didn't wear skirts and if I could learn to smoke. I can't. I detest smoking. Yet whenever I get as tired as this I think I want to smoke. That's how big a little fool your superior Miss Bratt is."

"Poor kid! Guess we're both done up with this office grind, and no fresh air. And the object of it all . . . I ask you, why should we contribute our youth to getting out these cursed lies about Tangerine?"

"The old worry about honesty?"

"Yes. Always have it. And go on writing the lies. Ain't husky enough to dig ditches. Course, if I were a noble fiction hero I'd beat it to the open and lead a free, untrammeled life; but bein' just folks and not liking to roll my cigarettes, I suppose I'll stick here and go on kicking. But I'll worry, allee sameee."

"So shall I, I guess," she said. "Poor tired Terry Ames and Sue Bratt what want to run and play in the meadows!"

"We are just kids, aren't we, dear?"

"Yes, and the worst of it is, we can't complain. We aren't picturesque and heroic and romantic, like raggedy vagabonds. Nobody would want to let us play mandolins and things in nice rose gardens—we're too clean and well paid. Yup. We're just impractical, and any good business man would tell us we don't know when we're well off."

They fell silent, and round Terry was the sweetest spell, the most delicate incantation of his life. Her soft shoulders drooped so pitifully and so near him. He was enveloped by her fragrance, here in the office that usually smelled of paper and typewriter oil and eraser dust. The building seemed incredibly still—the only noises were the jarring of the night elevator and the rustle of distant sweeping. Through the windows they saw a pink glow from the lights of Broadway, the Broadway of theaters and restaurants that had so little to do with the workers who in the silence were letting the wonder of life infuse their drained hearts.

The charm was broken by the rrrrr-ram-slam of the elevator stopping at their floor and voices passing the door.

Nervously prowling about, Terry talked office gossip, and while she put her own desk in order and reached for her hat and coat, she answered him, quietly, frankly—his office mate. The wonder of being man and woman, which had begun to steal over them, was broken. But the comfort of being understanding friends endured.

"Why, it's almost seven!" she exclaimed as she headed for the elevator.

"And I've kept you," he said regretfully. "Terribly sorry—didn't know how late——"

"Oh, I'm glad we did stay and talk. I feel like a human being again!"

Then the elevator was waiting for them, and the bored, noncommittal face of the old watchman who ran the elevator after six-thirty forbade any more youthful confidences. They were silent in the cage, and at the street door they parted.

And then for five months he didn't get any nearer to her than he had that evening!

So long as he saw Sue in the office he could never know her much better. She had never invited him to call on her, and though she seemed to have formed an alliance with him against the rest of the office, yet he knew no more of her private life than he did of Mac's or J. J.'s or Gato's—rather less, for these men talked of "the wife" with startling frankness.

One evening he had suggested that he might walk with her to the subway or the elevated. She had refused rather abruptly. After that he had not dared to try again.

IV

A September day of almost midsummer heat. The office force had perspired all afternoon and secretly had tried to pull down garments which kept stickily and vulgarly crawling up their backs. They had no energy for work. Even Terry, who was becoming ambitious, guiltily put off every possible task. J. J. and Watkins stopped at his desk now and then to gasp, always in the same words:

"Hot enough for you today? Going to rain. That'll cool it off."

All day the sky had been a dirty, even gray.

Just before closing time the sky—and seemingly all the air itself—suddenly turned to a terrifying greenish black. Gusts of wind scattered papers. Everyone leaped to close the windows. The roar of the blast was muffled as the windows went bang-bang-bang. They all stood looking out at the storm. It was night dark. A feeling of awe and terror held them.

Terry saw Sue staring out uneasily. He also saw Mac, the irrepressible, moving toward her. He ranged down and joined her, while Mac pretended that he had been heading for another window.

"I'm scared," Sue said.

The air seemed to boil. But no rain came yet. The world was taut, waiting for it.

The city had warded off Nature, but here was Nature trying to recapture her domain. It seemed as though the walls must be beaten flat, and the wilderness creep back among the ruins. Angry supernal hands shook the windows. Fear was abroad, and turned the busily insignificant office folk into a more heroic race, more primeval and tragic.

Terry boldly laid his hand over hers as they faced the storm. He pretended that they were in the open together. They stood motionless, their hands stirringly warm to each other, unconscious of the fact that the rest of the office were muttering "Gosh, going to rain fierce," or "Got an umbrella, Mac? Left mine home, doggone it," or "Wonder how I'll get to the L," or, very often, "Ames and Miss Bratt seem quite chummy."

Mr. Hopkins stalked out of his office and stared about, whereupon they all guiltily left the windows and got to work—all but Terry and Sue, oblivious, shoulders comfortingly close together at the window. They did not move till the office had returned to its ordinary indifference to mere Nature, with typewriters chattering and desk lights snapped on to combat the abnormal darkness.

The cheerful yellow glow through the office made them all inattentive to the moment when the rain finally smashed down.

Terry's leaving time came fifteen minutes later. But he waited at a window, watching the rain change from a black torrent to a sheet of gray nastiness. The disappearance of the terror of the storm let him down. . . . Tonight he couldn't even have a walk. Too wet. And he was inexpressibly tired of movies and of his musty room. The prospect of another evening of boredom palsied him.

She passed him. She did not speak, but her smile was confiding. He heard himself urging:

"Gee, it's going to be dreary. Please let me come to your house and see you. Tonight."

She pressed her throat. "Why————"

"Please!"

"Oh, not—not now. Terry, I'm———— I don't like myself at home. Really! I prefer the Miss Bratt of the office. I'd rather have you know her."

"Some time?"

"Oh, perhaps."

She flickered past him, her cheeks colored.

Terry grouchily turned up his coat collar and left. From the lower hall he saw the whole street filled with flashes of rain. Gutters were full and pouring out fanwise at corners of the street. The street doorway was packed with a constantly growing crowd of sweatshop workers, anxious girls, and men without umbrellas. They were pitiful. And Terry didn't feel in the least superior to them as he was jammed in among them. He was muttering with inexpressible longing.

"If I could only see Sue tonight. There's nothing to do, if I can't see her. I'm going back to the office and ask her again. No, I can't do that." He gazed out, moon-eyed.

A voice at his ear, a gay voice:

"Why, you poor baby!"

She was beside him.

"Festive city!" he growled. "Munition millionaires. Crowded cabarets. Fine! I'll go home and play solitaire—if I can get anybody to play it with."

"You round-eyed little bunny rabbit sulking by yourself! Do you really————"

"Do I want to come up to your house? It scares me to think of how much I want to."

Her eyes turned from his. Her voice, which had always been so clear, was uncertain:

"Oh, do come up then. Oughtn't to let you, ought to leave office behind but—come. Blank East Eighty-seventh Street."

She hastily pushed him into the crowd.

The secret silver knight sat on a high stool at a lunch counter. He was so excited that he slopped too much catchup on his beans.

Also he let the trolley car carry him past the right street, in his perturbed worry as to what he should wear, what sort of menage he would find. Was Miss Susan Bratt of a family poor or well-to-do? Did she have a wholesale family or a spinster flat? Should he wear evening clothes or be cheerful and democratic in a clean shave and just clothes? Incidentally, he didn't own evening clothes. Of course he could hire them, but what was all this stuff about black and white ties, black and white waistcoats? In short, he had a perfectly tremendous and youthful time worrying, then put on the other suit, decided that his umbrella was no good, took said umbrella, and started for Eighty-seventh Street.

He found that she lived on cliffs above the East River, in a model tenement house of tapestry brick and many windows, a hygienic but stern cranny for his flower. He forgot clothes. He was the secret knight again, and he had found her castle. He trudged up several miles of steps, deciding, on alternate landings, that she would let him kiss her at the door, and that she would be icily stately. Then he changed from a romantic lover into a realistic and abashed young man calling on an ordinary girl. The Sue Bratt, in a white frock coat with a broad blue ribbon filleting her hair, who met him at the door, was not the keen and self-dependent comrade of the office, nor was she any sort of a lady of dreams. She was just a young lady, who was not so very different from the young ladies he had known back home. She murmured:

"So glad you could come. My mother will be pleased to meet you. And Mr. Meehan. He comes from our town—Wiletta."

"Uh———"

"It's almost stopped raining, hasn't it?" she droned as she led him down the hall to a living room that was filled with patent rockers and niceness.

Terry felt smothered as he ducked his head before Mrs. Bratt's creaking inquiries about his respectable health, as he grasped the flabby hand of Mr. Samuel Meehan, a thin, indigestive, baldish business grinder of thirty-eight. . . . "Gee, but I'd like to smoke; nothing doing here though," he groaned. He was piloted to a red plush chair flanked by a large Chinese case of the department-store dynasty, and they all began to converse. How they conversed! They took up, methodically and thoroughly, the topics of the weather, the church back in Wiletta, the movies, the wave of prohibition, what Mr. Meehan's boss thought about saving money, what Mr. Meehan thought about his boss, what Mr. Meehan thought about Mr. Meehan, vacuum cleaners, Sousa's band, and the nutritious quality of Brussels sprouts.

Sue seemed somewhat absent-minded about it all, but she responded readily—and dully—enough. She carefully divided her smiles between Mr. Meehan and Terry. At first Terry hoped that she was bored, but he gave up the hope. She showed considerable interest in the burning questions of sauce hollandaise and the passing of the tango. He became sulky, and was almost rude in thwarting Mrs. Bratt's desire to know all about his origin, income, habits and church affiliations.

Mr. Meehan was kind enough to go at nine-thirty, after dabbling at Sue's hand and, with a watery smile, bidding her: "Be our nice little Sue now, and don't let the suffering cats make you lose your sweet womanliness—back in Wiletta we don't believe in this shrieking suffrage sisterhood, Mr. Ames. Good-night, Susie, and good-night, Lady Bratt. Pleased metcha, Mr. Ames." Mr. Meehan kept up his chirping for at least five minutes more before he flowed out of the door.

Mrs. Bratt rather unwillingly made excuses to disappear, and the golden children were left alone.

Terry rushed to open a window. He drew a deep breath. He looked to her for an intimate grin that would banish all Meehan's to the old ladies' home and make this strange alien room happily familiar. But Sue was at the small piano and was flapping the leaves of thin musical-comedy pieces. She chose "The Nagasaki-saki Rag," and started to play it brilliantly. Terry tried to look edified. She struck two false notes, stopped, tried again, then slammed down the lid and faced him.

"I'm too tired to play tonight," she said complacently.

The outward Terry made a polite noise like a kitten sneeze, but a somber inward Terry complained:

"Why the deuce can't she be frank, the way she is in the office, and admit she can't play the thing, no more'n a rabbit."

"Don't you just love music?" she said.

"Why, why, uh, yes—gee, I don't know whether I do nor not."

Now, she was becoming as strange to him as was the room. He was uncomfortable.

"You ought to. It's so—uh, well, cultured," she went on. "I always thought Mr. Gato would make a good pianist, he has such sensitive fingers."

"He's a sensitive crook."

"Terry Ames, if you're going to be disagreeable you can go right home. It's almost time anyway."

"Oh, gee, Sue. I didn't mean to be grouchy!" wailed the metropolitan philosopher, very much like a young man back home. "It's just——— Honestly now, you know he's a crook. Sensitive fingers! For picking pockets! Oh, say, speaking of Gato, I just learned yesterday why poor old Harry is going to be fired. Struck the firm for a raise. J. J. told me———"

"I don't think it's nice of you to talk shop when we've both had so much of it."

"Why, you brought it on yourself—about Gato———"

"Well—well, I just mentioned Mr. Gato's artistic fingers, and I don't think it's very nice of you to call them pickpocket fingers, when you're always complaining about people in the office knocking. And I do think he has the strongest chin, he must be quite athletic."

"Oh, I s'pose he's husky enough." Terry gloomily thrust both of his unathletic hands into his coat pockets.

Without providing him with the smallest conversational bridge she leaped to:

"But anyway . . . Oh, you ought to see the Russian Ballet and ———"

"Uh, yes—yes—I must go see———"

"Though I'd almost as soon stay home and read. Oh, Terry, have you read any of Jessica Brentwood Pipp's Southern stories? They're so sweet and optimistic! Oh, I would like to see the Southland and the old plantations! Mrs. Pipp makes them so real, and the old darkies must be funny."

"Why, uh, no, I haven't read her books."

Terry was stunned by this conversation cabaret. He wanted to be frank, but what could he be frank about in all this flood? He was outraged at the empty talk of his goddess. And the amazing thing was that he didn't love her any the less. So he meditated, as she opened the piano again and struck occasional chords while pattering on: "Of course I don't mean Mrs. Pipp is a great writer, but she's so, so optimistic. . . . Oh, Terry, do you play tennis? Don't you love Maury McLoughlin?"

She had touched on one topic regarding which he did have enthusiasms, and he brightened up enough to carry them over the questions of golf, the subway, Lakewood, and the charms of Ethel Barrymore.

He bobbed up from his chair, pretending to look at a colored photograph of scrubby woods reflected in a second-rate lake, played with the dangles on an idiotic lamp shade, broke one, apologized perspiringly; straightened a sofa cushion; stalked up to her and, snatching her hand from the piano keys, dared to lay a finger on her pulse. He could feel her blood suddenly race, her hand tremble. They were silent. They stared at each other, frightened.

She uneasily withdrew her hand. The hot room was electrically charged with fear, hope, timid understanding. He was again, as in the office months before, conscious of her peculiar magic, which seemed to grow and glow in the spellbound room. It wasn't true; she hadn't chattered like a parrot; surely she hadn't! No, she was perfect, the true goddess, and, like a worshiper, he touched her hand.

Then she jumped up from the piano stool, dragged a photograph album from the table and began:

"Oh, I must show you the pictures we got on our vacation at Long Branch last summer. See, here's where we stayed. Isn't it the duckiest house! And here's the bunch on the beach."

They were off again.

The minutes were becoming terrible now. It was growing late. Already he ought to be going. Would he ever be allowed to come again, ever conjure up that spell of silence and love's tense wonder?

"I do adore Nature," she was saying. "I hate to be shut up in this horrid old city. It isn't like Wiletta; there are such pretty maples there and the———"

"Is that were our friend Meehan comes from?"

"Yes. He's always been such a good friend of the family. So kind to my mother."

"Huh! It's mother's daughter that Brer Meehan is interested in."

She moved to the dingy brocade settee and hugged a sofa cushion, hid her lips with it, and looked over it with tempting bright eyes as she insisted:

"Well, perhaps I'm interested in him too. I've known him ever since———"

"Oh, sure. You sat on his knees. I know. And he taught you Sunday school."

"You shan't make fun of him. Perhaps I'll marry him someday."

"Sue!"

He was stern, somber, no longer boyishly jealous.

"You couldn't do that, Sue! You do want to be big. And you do care, because I want you to be big, not—oh, not, Meehan. You make believe you don't know how much I honor you, dear, but you do know, you do!"

She tried to keep up the coquetry. She brushed the silken cord of the cushion with her lips and murmured:

"Well, Mr. Meehan never contradicts me, as you do. I must think about him seriously. He'd be———"

She stopped. Terry came and stood over her, his eyes hot. A flush came up in her cheeks, slow, painful. He sat down beside her, took the cushion away from her, took her hand and pressed it against his cheek till her fingers curved and clung there. The spell of silence began to fill the room again. Then the window shades rattled like spiteful laughter and the room seemed close, sordid.

He cried: "Oh, come up on the roof in the mist, where there's air and sky! I don't care if it's time for me to go! I don't care if it's raining! Oh, Sue, Sue darling, we're letting life get dusty. You—you who can't fight the whole office alone—you aren't going to go on pretending about love, are you?"

She hesitated, but he put an arm about her, lifted her up, drew her to the door, down the hall, up a flight of stairs to the roof. Below them was the East River, fantastically lighted from the barges; and in the distant fog the huge electric signs of a factory were a throne of fire. Above them the pale, rosy sky; about them a misty breeze that blew away pettiness. He put his coat about her, stood holding it close to her shoulders, then kissed her hair, in which the dampness brought out all the fragrance.

"Oh, Terry, you mustn't!" she sobbed.

"I will! I won't go through all this giggling and candy toting and love making and pretending. Leave that for Meehan and Watkins and people that can't make up their minds about love—or honesty, or anything. We've worked together, not just gone to parties. We buck the office together. We'll buck life that way. We will! Come out of Wiletta!"

He cupped her wet cheeks with his two nervous fine hands. He kissed her eyes.

"You frighten me," she quavered.

"Dear, listen! We agree that in the office we'll be honest—if possible. I don't know how I know you love me; it's just the feeling that when we're together here, there's something so intimate between us. And you hide it from yourself by talking of books and vacations and Wiletta! You, the worker————"

"Oh, Terry, how you talk and talk and talk! I do love you! But I'm afraid you'll talk me out of it again. When I just want to rest!" She pillowed her cheek against his shoulder, his damp, warm shoulder.

Not for many minutes did she say:

"I was honest—as possible. I knew I was talking rot about Jessica Silly Brentwood Pipp and all, but I couldn't think of anything else. I was so excited at having you with me, there in that quiet room. And when I tried to express it, I was so embarrassed that all I could think of was Mrs. Pipp. Only I really do like her piffle. I can have that one fault, can't I, my perfect man?"

"Gee, the way I try to make poor Sue into a little tin god! Gato's right about my being a crank."

"Gato?" She grated out the name savagely. "If he ever dared to tell me you were a crank! My Terry, my boy that wants to be honest!"

"Say! Why shouldn't I leave Hopkins & Gato and start in new, some place else? I've always wanted to, but before you came—just got to drifting————"

"No. That would be running away. Do you know, I'm going to hang onto my job for a while, even after we're married—I suppose you're going to be so kind and condescend to ask the milkmaid to marry you, sir, when you happen to think of it. And so, my little man, you won't have me depending on you, and you can put on your Boy Scout uniform and go tell Mr. Hopkins to change Tangerine from an orange development to truck farming. Do that! Do it tomorrow!"

"Um. Maybe I'd dare to buck him now with you backing me. But—suppose he fired me? Now? When I need the job for—for us?"

"Let him! That's why I'm going to keep my job. Oh, you won't be like the others—get cautious when you fall in love! You started me wanting to be honest, and I'm afraid you can't stop that sort of thing, once it's really started. You will fight it out with him! If you don't, I will!"

"Yes. I'll see him tomorrow. Maybe he'd do it now. Tangerine isn't selling anything extra. Might actually go better as a truck proposition. But what a rotten, petty victory—to persuade a boss to be honest because there's money in it for him."

"I guess there's nothing but petty victories in life, that and the real big thing of going on fighting——— Oh, Terry, Terry, we're talking again! Tomorrow you can fight with Hopkins, but now—I'm cold and tired. I'm just a bedraggled little girl, and I want to creep into your arms. Is that honest and frank enough for you, crusader of my soul?"

Great tatters of fog shut in the city children on the smug tenement, as though they stood solitary upon the roof of the world, mountain lovers, mates and fellow builders rolling boulders to make an enduring home.

A STORY WITH A HAPPY ENDING

I

Mr. Leonard Price was a colonel of business. Offices have grades as definite as the army—generals, who own things; colonels, who manage them; smart young lieutenants, who will be senior officers some day; and the ranks of the nameless. Price believed that all of these differences were entirely due to innate ability. He liked to talk about "natural born executives"; and he secretly—though modestly—believed that such was his case.

But he did not rub it in. He was pleasant to work for. He was a good-looking, ruddy professional bachelor, with a gray mustache. He was the general manager of the Motor Accessories Department of the Magnus Machining and Electric Company, of New York; and under him the department had grown from a machine shop located in a tin shed and manufacturing a few shock absorbers, to the most significant of the Magnus concerns. Price admitted that most of this growth had been due to the boom in automobiles; but he did congratulate himself that much of it was the result of his ability as chief.

He had been his own sales manager at first—yes, and salesman and accountant. He had taken the first shock absorbers out on the road and sold two hundred of them to a man in overalls who was building "horseless carriages" that looked like startled pullets and ran like perambulators. Nowadays he was a colonel, and had a crack regiment.

Just when the regiment was maneuvering at its best he had to stop and fill water bottles and polish buttons for a cub subaltern, who was not only ignorant of drill but was also—a woman!

II

Magnus came to him—rabbity, capable Old Magnus, the president—and implored:

"Mr. Price, I have a great favor to ask."

Magnus tapped on the tablet of Price's desk and looked humble, so that Price knew he was about to make an unusually unfair demand.

"My wife's second cousin," said Magnus, "has just lost her husband. She is a bright little woman, bright as a dollar, and the wife wants us to give her a job."

"She had any business training?" asked Price.

"Well, no—uh—but she's very capable."

"Um! You see, Mr. Magnus, way I feel is, office is no place for women. Trouble with them is, they can't create. Just imitative. And they're natural born intriguers and flirts. Instead of taking a job and carrying it, like a man, they try to shift it onto some goat of a man. Office is no place for any woman above the grade of stenographer; and, honestly, even the female stenogs are bad enough— shystering and making the same mistake over and over————"

"Yes, yes," purred Magnus; "of course, as a crusty old bachelor—hee! hee!—you have to knock women. But—uh—well, Mrs. Magnus has wished this lady onto us—Mrs. Arroford, her name is, wife's second cousin—and I'm afraid we'll have to take care of her till—hee! hee!—some other man marries her. She's a pretty, plump little widdy, by jinks, and young; and————"

"Couldn't you try her out in your own department?"

"Mrs. Magnus thought that castings and drills would be kind of heavy wares for the little woman to handle; and Mrs. Magnus said she was sure you would be kind to her————"

"Oh; all right! And you say she's young and pretty? If she were only an old hex!"

Before Mrs. Arroford presented herself at his office Price worked himself up into a beautiful frenzy about her. He received sympathy from his sales manager at lunch, and both of them snortled about bosses' wives' second cousins and "pull." They rather disregarded the fact that about forty percent of people get their jobs through pull, though afterwards most of them hold the jobs only by real work; in fact, they weren't philosophical at all, but glared into their mixed grills and consigned women to different places—none of these places in offices.

In a few days Mrs. Arroford's card was sent to Price—an engraved card, in delicate script.

She was a gray squirrel of a young woman, with black interested eyes, with furs, and a charming roundness. Her hat and boots and gloves were expensively smart; her cheeks were flushed; she bounced slightly in the dull office chair—and she didn't know a single solitary thing of any value to the Motor Accessories Department. "I have never been trained in business," she said; "but I was quite successful in managing a church fair in Mt. Vernon."

Price groaned.

"How old are you?"

"Twenty-nine."

"Do you want a real job or do you want a way to pass the time?"

"I have to support myself—or I shall have to when the insurance money is gone."

She was quiet and simple about it. She didn't shed tears or act as though she went the rounds being "brave about her troubles."

"Will you do what I tell you to do?"

"Oh, yes!"

"Um! Well, I suppose for a while I can keep you halfway busy correcting our list of supplies. You compare the proofs with the annotated typewritten schedules. But, you know, I'll scalp you if you let a single error slip through!"

He smiled.

He tried to make it a chill November smile, but he couldn't feel very bleak, with her so soft and eager. And she replied, with the earnestness of a good child:

"Oh, yes; please do."

"Meantime I want you to study stenography and typewriting as though you were an ambitious cash girl. I want you to learn it, and learn it right—study all evening and every Sunday—either take classes or get private instruction, or buy your books and grind by yourself. There isn't—of course you understand I'm just speaking generally—there isn't much place for women in business, even with all this suffrage and Lord knows what folderols; and it's up to a woman who wants a career to learn to serve in every possible way."

"Oh, yes; I know. I can see that if I'm ever going to be an executive I must first———"

"A what? Well, I'm afraid we'll have to wait a while to see about that. Executives are—well, born."

"Yes," she said so obediently that it sounded like "Oh, yes, sir."

"Huh!" considered Price when she had gone. "Not a bad little woman at all! Seems willing and well bred. But women in an office! Stuff and nonsense! Here I'll give her the benefits of a lifetime's experience, and she'll say 'Yes!' And then she'll get married again just as she begins to be useful. Well, we'll watch the good ship Flivver, with its lady pilot, wreck itself on the rocks of good intentions; in fact, I think I'll take Billy out and make him buy me a drink."

III

Mrs. Arroford, of Mt. Vernon, undoubtedly had good intentions; but they did not seem to be rocks in her way. She must have studied stenography during all of her spare time, for after two months, when Price's secretary became ill, she offered to take his dictation— and took it. She spelled accessories with an adequate number of c's and s's, and she didn't fidget when he was pawing the air for words; and she found the addresses of motor manufacturers in the files without bothering him about them. So she became his secretary permanently.

He discovered that she had moved into a furnished room in town, and that she was taking evening courses in applied electricity, metal forging, accountancy and cost-finding. And every Saturday afternoon she spent in the Magnus shops, till she knew almost as much about the actual manufacture of Magnus accessories as did Price himself. She became paler and less round of cheek, and her voice was more nervous; but when Price told her that she was doing excellent work and ought to take more time to play, she said that, in moving into town, she had deliberately got out of touch with all the neighborhood friends of her Mt. Vernon days. For relaxation, she said, she went to the Y.W.C.A. for a swim.

Ten years ago, this was; and even today women are accidents in business, except for certain classes—stenographers, store buyers, nurses, teachers. Mrs. Arroford had no standard, as has the young male, who can in half a city block find a dozen business men after whom he can, wisely or foolishly, model himself. She was enormously alone. And before she could work at all she had to learn what work itself was, for she had been brought up to regard work as the elegant supervision of a Lithuanian maid.

Picture her walking home after two hours of work at a forge, in the evening, less wearied by the toil than by the shrinking from the noisy young men who had been working beside her and dutifully seeking whether she would let them make love to her; walking home tired in arms and brain, yet plowing sturdily along, keeping her eyes away from shop windows so that she might not be interrupted in her reflection upon the modifications that might some day be necessary in the Magnus carburetor for the use of distillate.

At a time when Price had never thought of distillate as a substitute for gasoline she had read about it in some dusty chemical journal or other, and had talked about its possible use—and he pooh-poohed her; told her:

"You mustn't pay any attention to these freak enthusiasms."

She was walking home while Mr. Price was playing a last game of bezique at the club and fondly looked forward to bed.

She neither went out to lunch, nor did she eat her apple and sandwich with the gossiping, man-discussing stenographers. She lunched alone, with a newspaper propped up behind the bag that held her lunch, on the tablet of her desk; then she walked for a quarter of an hour and got acquainted with motor salesmen in a sexless, enthusiastic, friendly way that made them respect her.

There was a danger in this severe, clean application of hers, but it was exactly the opposite danger of what Price had feared; she was not disrupting the office by kittenish flirtations, but, rather, she was in peril of losing all her soft, adorable kitten quality; of becoming hard and driving and priggish; of hating too much the grace and affection to which she had been reared.

Two little incidents marked her climb to a control of the situation.

There was a certain Mac, a slender, impudent young man with a tilted Alpine hat and a cocked cigar, who used to come in to see Price. He would lean against railings and make love to the office girls. He said to Mrs. Arroford, after repeated attempts to impress his Apollolike charm on her:

"Say, little girl, it always strikes me as funny, the way you women that think that you're business women are afraid to go to dinner and a show, like I asked you to. You think that's being strong-minded. Why, you're simply afraid! Can't trust yourselves! Now a business man knows that if he can keep on the job only by showing he's so weak that he's scared————"

Mrs. Arroford replied in a high, clear voice that reached the telephone girl: "Why, Mr. MacLafferty, I quite agree with you. That isn't why I refuse your invitations. I'd be delighted to play with anybody I liked. But I don't like you. You bore me. Now go make love to somebody else till Mr. Price can see you."

Mac heard a good deal of that incident.

The other indication of Mrs. Arroford's progress was her illegal and inexcusable taking charge of the entire department for a week.

Price had a kind of an assistant general manager, a nice, strong young man who was about as original as a train announcer; and with this lamb and the sales manager he was motoring on the Boston Post Road, trying a new-model spark plug—and some new-model gin drinks—when a joy rider smashed into them; and all the visible heads of the Motor Accessories Department were taken home to their several beds. None of them was seriously injured, but they were away for a week, and just at this time the assistant sales manager came to Mrs. Arroford for an O.K. on a sale of ten thousand of the new spark plugs.

She refused. Nor would she call up Price; he had sent in word that he was not to be bothered. She had understood Price to say that he wanted to hold up these plugs—not let them out on the market for two months. The assistant sales manager snarled at her that he would make the sale, anyway; he had had no such orders. Mrs. Arroford went to Magnus and demanded—she did not ask, but, with her eyes vehement, like a cornered squirrel, she absolutely demanded—that Magnus order the sale held up.

"But who's running the department, Cousin Nancy?" inquired Magnus.

"I am! I know more about it than anybody else!"

"Well! . . . Well, I guess you are, then."

When Price came back he praised her decision and raised her salary,

After this triumph Mrs. Arroford settled back into obscurity— apparently. Really, she had become an unofficial assistant manager of the department. There are many such unofficial officials in the bureaus of our business government: men who have risen from office boy or packer, and still retain a shabby shyness, but know so much more about the business than most of the decorative heads that they run the concern. But they get neither kudos nor cash. They are not executives; they merely execute.

So it was with Mrs. Arroford. To the eye she was a pretty woman, tired and subdued. But she was left to handle important visitors, and she did not falter: "I don't know—I'll have to ask Mr. Price." She did know!

Unconsciously, still believing that she was only a feeble feminine makeshift of an aide, Price had come to depend on her as his eyes and ears and memory.

He had been kind to her. He had not nagged; he had taken her version of events; he had not slighted her in the presence of big outside visitors; he had guided her in her study of mechanics and office procedure. And he had never tried to hold her hand! He was still rather paternal and quizzical when she was excited over a new idea; but he was courteous always.

In return, she worshiped him—no, she did more than that; she really liked to take his dictation! She wasn't crotchety when he wanted her to stay after hours, and she personally mailed his late letters. When he slacked she covered up his errors and put them down in her mind to the strain of his position. Even when she had to keep after him to dictate a letter that should have been sent out two days before, it never occurred to her that she was anything other than the colonel's striker.

So she followed him zealously into the battles of the second great period of the motor war: the time when people ceased to regard the motor car as a luxury or an experiment, and saw it as a daily necessity.

IV

When the discerning historian of 3000 A.D. writes of this century he will give less space to the Great European War than to the development of gas motors. Already, incredibly, the motor vehicle has changed the face of the earth. It sends the most stodgy city dweller into places where he can find wisdom and fresh air; it has solved the ancient problem of the desolation of the farm. It has transformed the ways of pleasure—it has even changed the life-old ways of love-making! Though poets still call our attention to roses, a poetry more magnificent is being sung about us by popping—or sliding—valves.

Something of this romantic miracle was realized in the humdrum offices of the Magnus Machining Company. Till now people had—most of them—taken motor cars as they came. You bought a car, and it was hung all over with accessories; and you never thought of changing it. You didn't know how. But now ordinary motorists began to be discriminating about spark plugs, radiators, shock absorbers, speedometers, oil gauges; and to add them or change them to suit themselves. Magnus and Price, between them—possibly with some slight assistance from certain workmen and people like Mrs. Arroford—made good accessories, and got them out on time. So their business boomed enormously.

Price rose from colonel to brigadier general of business; his salary rose from nine thousand to fifteen thousand—almost painlessly—and promised to go higher. He was constantly in conference with the sales manager; jobbers and special dealers in accessories had come into existence, and their accounts were as important as those of the smaller manufacturers. Price was growing.

But it seems probable to the historian that he wasn't growing in the right direction. He was too contemptuous of detail.

You hear of executives who are geniuses at delegating details;

who keep themselves for the big decisions. But every decision is a synthesis of many details, and there is yet to be found even an executive who can walk up a long, a very long flight of stairs without touching some of the steps.

Price was, for example, bored by the question of whether the new Macklin & Macklin Company should be allowed to open an account. He was rather tart with the accountant who consulted him on the question at a time when he was planning a campaign to get the Viviere people to adopt the Magnus carburetor as a stock feature. Only—the Macklin account was opened, and it nettled Magus a dead loss of seven thousand dollars before it was caught; while the Viviere negotiations gave one revolution, sputtered, and went dead. . . . An executive isn't one who neglects details. He is a man who knows which details are significant. And usually Price did know; but———

Perhaps he was getting a little tired of year on year of grind. While Mrs. Arroford every day was more exultant in her power to steer the job.

This growing tiredness on the part of Price was indicated by his increasing love of expansive ease; of all the things that go with a well-to-do middle-aged bachelorhood—long lunches, with long cigars; hotel bars, with leathery chairs and carved-oak grills; club card rooms; taxis; recognition by head waiters. But he really did know motor accessories. And perhaps his very habit of being about with costly, large-waistcoated, throaty-voiced gentlemen helped him, for at dinner he met and unconsciously made an impression upon Vorhees, the gun manufacturer, and so came to be chosen for the Big Job.

Vorhees offered him the general managership of the new Pistoflash Company, with the entire Voorhees Rifle Corporation behind it; offered him a free rein in the business, a salary of twenty thousand a year on a two-year contract, and a ten percent share of stock after the two years if he made good.

The Pistoflash was a combination of revolver and flashlight. It was, Voorhees asserted, the one perfect weapon for the touring motorist—Price's special quarry—as well as for policemen and alarmed householders.

"I think," said Voorhees, "you ought to be able to sell one to practically every motorist in the country; and we use a special long-life battery, and get follow-up business on that."

"You're on!" said Price.

To work for his own share in the company; to work for himself—not just for rabbity old Magnus! He said good-bye to the Magus offices somewhat grandiloquently; much like a popular preacher "called to a wider field of usefulness."

He was buoyant with his friend, Billy Turner, the sales manager, who was to be his successor as general manager. He was polite but not too regretful with Magnus. He was noble-minded with the stenographers, the foremen. Then, in his office, with his personal letters cleared out of his desk, and his private fountain pen recovered from behind the files, where it had been marooned and practically useless these three months, and with his deerstalker hat and bachelor's tan overcoat and new yellow chamois gloves ready to put on, he started to be advisory and kindly with Mrs. Arroford.

Now that he was no longer to have her deft care, he realized how dear to him was the daily office companionship of this woman. She stood before him, eyes downcast, hands nervously straightening a wire basket on his desk. Her foreshortened face was pale but clear; her lips were the fresh lips of a girl. He was saying:

"Well, I'll be leaving you in good hands, Mrs. Arroford. Billy Turner will make a good chief. No reason why you shouldn't rise above this secretaryship. I don't believe that offices are just the place for women; but there must be some exceptions, of course, and I don't see why you shouldn't become a sort of assistant manager some day. Got lots of faith in you, child. The one thing you want to watch out for is getting too wildly enthusiastic over novelties—new customers and patents, and so on. Thing's got to have a good, sound practical basis, first of all. Well——"

"I'm sorry you're going," she said dully.

She was leaning against the desk. Her hand was trembling a little; the wire basket she was fingering clattered faintly on the oak top.

Then it was that he saw her not just as a tool, a rather intelligent notebook or pencil, but as a woman, with dear eyes and a smile that had made of the office a place of contented work. He visualized her woman ways; knew that he would miss her trick of sitting, waiting with brooding eyes and with cheek resting on inward-arched fingers, when they were interrupted during dictation.

He leaped up.

"You look tired. Sit down—please do! I'm a brute to let you go on standing there. Didn't mean to be rude. Got so used to depending on you as an aide that I suppose I forgot you're a mighty fine girl too."

"No; I'm not tired," she sighed. "Good-bye!"

She turned resolutely away and opened the door of his office. He might not see her again; not ever see that sturdy retreating back, at which he had looked a thousand times as she had gone off with his dictation, and which had, therefore, meant to him a thankfulness that some beastly pile of work was done and now in her competent hands.

"Don't—don't go yet!" he begged.

She looked back; he was startled by the glow in her eyes, then equally startled by the suddenness with which a mask of office impersonality covered the glow, so that she seemed merely to be awaiting orders.

"Will you miss me?" he said.

He was essentially a lonely man, who had happened never to fall very much in love—just as he happened to become an executive. He was reminded now that there was such a thing as love, and he was challenging the evanescent glow which had flashed at him from her face. Not that glow but the office mask answered him:

"Yes, I am sure we'll all miss you. Mr. Giddings and I were saying just now that there could never be such esprit de corps as———"

"Oh, hang the corps! Will you miss me?"

"Why"—as if in surprise at this breach of office etiquette—"I shall, of course. I've got so used to your dictation."

"I suppose this serves me right for making you a machine. Look! Come out to tea with me. Now!"

He felt a stirring in him, an eagerness to know what the glow meant, a discovery that he had grown very fond of her; and he was disappointed when she said unenthusiastically:

"Very well; if you wish."

They didn't talk much on the street; but he planned, once they should be snugly seated, to throw aside all the slight severity of being her boss and make her exult with him in his discovery that they were friends. But when they were in the smart hotel tea room he was unable to find anything to say to her. The best he could do in the way of affectionate intimacy was stammer: "Well—uh—well, we've had a good deal of fun working together."

"Yes," she said more prosily than ever.

There was between them, not glow and discovery but the peculiarly solid phantom of a peculiarly solid oak desk, and three years of such amorous murmurs as:

"Say, Mis' Arroford, could you get out a letter P.D.Q.?"

They talked—now when he wanted to make a touching farewell—they talked of the appearance of the brass name plate on the new carburetor! He saw her anew as a woman, an attractive woman. He tried to drop notes of tenderness into the conversation. But she went on discussing brass stamping.

She looked at her watch, which had been a timepiece to him before, but was now a slender bracelet on a sentimentally white round wrist, and exclaimed:

"Heavens! It's five o'clock. And I have two hours' more work. Must have your records ready for the new chief."

"Wouldn't you like to consider coming with me to the Pistoflash Company? I need you for my secretary there."

"No—you have been good to me, but I've identified myself with auto accessories so completely now that I can't turn to anything else. I'm—I'm married to them. . . . I must hurry now."

He had no excuse for returning to the office with her. He had done complete justice to a Washingtonian last farewell to his troops. So he put her on a bus, and felt that he had lost the chance to acquire something fine and good. He walked slowly to his club.

He called up the Magnus office and suggested to his successor, the former sales manager, that he come down to the club for a last drink and talk.

The purpose of this talk—and drink—wasn't to give his friend the benefit of his wisdom. It was to insert carefully the hint that though, of course, they both knew that women were out of place in business, yet Mrs. Arroford was the best man in the shop, and it would be for the good of the concern to advance her beyond a secretaryship.

"Let's see," Price craftily mused: "you're raising your old sales assistant to sales manager and you haven't chosen his successor. This is butting in—just a suggestion; but why don't you just try out Mrs. Arroford as assistant sales manager? Send her out on the road for a while, and then try her? I've watched her for three years, and I'll bet a hat she knows more about the stock and the quirks of a lot of the trade than either you or me, Billy. She can handle the crankiest customer———"

"By golly, that's a good idea!" said Price's successor. "I'll try her out. Though, of course, a woman———"

"Oh, of course you couldn't expect any woman ordinarily to stand the hard knocks like you and me, Billy; but still———"

V

If Price could have gone to the Pistoflash Company as a subordinate, could have worked slowly into the gun business, he might have learned something about it; but he arrived with a fanfare of trumpets as the big executive who already knew all about executing—executing almost everything.

They had provided an obliging young man to insulate him from anybody who wanted to annoy him with details. He didn't need to see a single employee except his secretary, the factory superintendent, the purchasing agent and the advertising man; and as for the powers above him, he was responsible to no one but the board of directors. Officially Vorhees, the majority stockholder, was president of the company; but he interfered as little with the actual workings as though he was only chairman of the board.

With such a royal position ready made, Price could not help sliding into a notion that he was rather above the average run of business men. He was the executive; whatever he did, that must be right. His decisions were papal bulls.

They all encouraged him in that belief. He had come to them as the expert, the man who was to make Pistoflash sell. It wasn't his fault entirely—he really was a pleasant chap and popular at the club—if he felt that it wasn't necessary for him to study things minutely. He kept himself for the big decisions.

As he didn't know much about the business, those big decisions didn't consume any too much of his time. He complacently came to conceive his job as a twiddling of the thumbs, an agreeable siesta in his enormous chair, and frequent absences from the office during work hours, while the anxious young men of the company wrote the advertisements or tried to persuade the jobbers to take large consignments of Pistoflash.

It was easy; and Voorhees said nothing—except that at the end of the first year he murmured:

"Price, after your experience with auto accessories, I thought you'd make a more direct appeal to individual motorists—good way to get the Pistoflash introduced. Seems to me you let the jobbers do too much of your pushing. Fish for the direct consumers. You ought to know them, if anybody does. The people who buy cars and speedometers and cameras and photographs, they're the ones that can afford to buy Pistoflashes. Spend whatever is necessary in national advertising."

Price was rather jarred by the criticism and tried to profit by it. He turned his publicity department upside down that second year and made a real advertising campaign—well, fairly real, but not quite alive and breathing. He did not follow it up by getting at the small local dealers and by this time the oversolicited jobbers were bored by Pistoflash.

His first year had resulted in a loss to the company; the second year increased that loss.

He began to realize that he was up against it for the first time since he had been a cub salesman; up against the reality of struggle. But he was unable to shake off the hypnotic spell of sloth into which he had drifted. There was no one to stir him. He remembered how Mrs. Arroford, as his secretary, had always roused him to activity. Even when he had not been ashamed to be indolent before himself, he had been ashamed to be so before her trusting eyes.

He wanted to see her—have her inspiration. He asked his successor at Magnus' about her and found out that she had made good as assistant sales manager; that she was in line for sales manager, and was none the less valuable because, as a woman, she was a novelty. He had asked for her home phone number; rang her up once at home and once at the Magnus office, planning to call. She was away both times.

He gave her up—gave himself up to the despair of mental beach combing.

His peril was increased by the expensiveness of his establishment and habits. He had a large apartment, a Jap, dinner parties, two cars, occasional vintage champagne. He had saved out of his considerable salary only seven thousand dollars at the end of that second year, when Voorhees and the board of directors called him in and fired him as uninterestedly as though he were an impudent office boy.

VI

He had, for the first time in twenty years, to hunt a new position like a young clerk, not like an executive for whose services firms contested; in fact, the job-hunting clerk had the better of it, for Price was a twenty-thousand-dollar man now and he couldn't take a position at less; he couldn't even visibly economize without admitting that he was a failure, on the downslope. So many eyes were watching him———

He told himself that he wouldn't take the first thing that was offered; he would wait and choose. He waited, all right! He waited four months; and he did not receive a single offer of any kind from any firm.

They were bitter months. At first, he enjoyed sitting about the club all day. Voorhees had permitted him to maintain the fiction that he had "resigned from Pistoflash to look after interests of his own." Inasmuch as twenty-thousand-dollar men are never fired, but always "resign," many fellows at the club were a little cynical; most of them, however, in view of his unreduced expenditures, and his ruddy blandness, believed the jolly tale and envied him his armchair leisure. But behind his well-trained face muscles he wasn't comfortable. He worried. He kept making estimates as to how long he could hold out at this rate of living.

He became bored by idleness. What had been a refuge from business was infernally dull as a regular abiding place. To drift all day long from library to grill to card room, and then to go out for a poky walk through undiversified streets, or even to sneak into a movie—that existence was more arduous that the stress of anxiety during the most critical days of Magnus Accessories.

Price began to meditate about himself. He remembered his business career as a series of half-done tasks, half-seized opportunities, half-understood purposes, half-lying self-satisfaction. He felt that he had been a plain shyster at the Pistoflash Company. He longed for another chance to make good; less and less he saw himself as a Napoleon in exile. But unfortunately no one else could see his real spiritual change, and a bad reputation of him had crept through the circle of automobile men who might have ben glad—once—to give him the chance.

At the end of four months, during which he had used up a good deal of his seven thousand dollars in small smart parties and a general attempt to appear more prosperous than ever, Price decided that it was time to stir things up; to give a few hints that he might be persuaded to consider a new position.

He called on an acquaintance who had formed an aeroplane company. He was received with heartiness and a cigar. The aeroplane man acted as though he considered Price a genius, but he didn't make any suggestions about acquiring the genius; and Price could not bear to get down on this cheap rug—it was so much cheaper than the Iran in his office at Pistoflash—and beg for employment. He pretended that he had merely "dropped in," and awkwardly went away.

For a month more he could not get himself to ask for work; but this month saw him becoming haggard, and he began to economize, to recall the systematic, frightened saving of the days when he had been a cub salesman, and to try to stretch his inelastic middle-aged dignity to this mean carefulness. He had only twenty-two hundred dollars left now. He had spent about five thousand dollars in a few months; had leant five hundred to the club tattler—a man he had to keep in the belief that he was still prosperous.

He gave up his apartment, sold or stored his furniture, took a two-room suite in a family hotel, and cooked his own breakfast over an electric stove. He was a rather pathetic, blundering figure—this solid official personage in tailored clothes and a silk shirt—endeavoring to fry an egg and getting the yolk all over his fingers.

He sat in the silence of his room, trying to read library books, and longing for the days at the Magnus Company when, to himself and to Mrs. Arroford and all his young men, he had been busy and secure. When he could no longer stand the seclusion he would go and sit in the lobby of a Broadway hotel, one of the line of intruders and loafers and pompous failures in the big chairs.

He had at last come to real humility; and he started a campaign to get a job—not a position, but a job. He made out a list of all the motor firms he knew and offered them his services. He even planned to see Magnus.

But he read in a trade paper that Mrs. Nancy Arroford had been made general manager of the Motor Accessories Department of the Magnus Company. The paper commented that she was the first woman to hold such a position in the accessories world, but that her record as salesman and her invention of the Magnus Bumper had "so splendidly qualified her for the position that there is no man in the business who does not heartily approve of her appointment and wish her good luck."

So Price could not go to the Magnus Company. He could not contemplate working for a man who had worked for him—especially when that man was a woman! Take orders from a person whom he had taught the very meaning of an office memo? That was asking too much, he decided; and his remembered affection for Mrs. Arroford was inescapably dulled by envy as he began to bombard the motor firms with written applications for a job. He received a number of chatty replies, but not one single offer.

Where now was the born executive? At last he was considering the details—details of cutting down the cost of breakfast by a nickel and making a collar last two days.

He was in actual want. True, he still had eighteen hundred dollars, but he who has eighteen hundred dollars and no prospect of ever getting more is as much in need as he who has nothing. So at last he turned back to the Magnus Company, to beg for any sort of chance to start over again. It was three years since he had been near the Magnus office or her.

VII

There was a new office boy in the outer office at the Magnus Company, one who knew not Joseph and didn't want to let Joseph go in and see Mister Pharaoh. He stared at Price's spats and piped: "Whacha wanna see 'im 'bout—heh?" But Price's old filing girl was passing through and cried:

"Oh, Mr. Price! It's so long since we've seen you. My, you're looking fine! Eddie, you beat it right in and tell Mr. Magnus that Mr. Price is here."

As Price passed through the inner offices to Magnus' coop, it was through a lane of smiles and handshakes. He was home, and glad to be home; and his old friends were glad to have him. But Magnus himself wasn't so flattering.

"Magnus, I'm on the rocks!" Price felt the luxury of absolute frankness and confession. "I was a damn fool ever to leave here. I want to come back."

"Well! Well——— Just a moment, Price. Forgot to tell———"

So, in the rush of his gallant self-exposure, Price had to wait while Magnus telephoned. Chilled, uneasy, he tried to start again; but he could only mumble:

"As I said, I'd be glad to make a connection with the firm again, Magnus."

"Yes, yes; 'course we'd be glad to have you back; but—uh—I don't know just how you'd fit in now, Price. You see, we've completely reorganized the department. The big business now is in direct appeal to car owners—they're getting educated now. You're trained to handle big consignments to manufacturers; but Mrs. Arroford—she's boss now—I told you she was a bright little woman. Hee! Hee! Lord, a small-car owner can't go ten miles in his bus without her coaxing him to some local garage to buy a speedometer, or maybe a whole electric starting-and-lighting system. I don't know how you'd be———"

Price wanted to say "All right, then. Go to the devil!" But he couldn't afford even this first, most valuable privilege of an executive. He said uncomfortably:

"I'd like to look over the situation."

"Then you go see Nancy Arroford. She's boss now, Price. She's boss! 'Fraid I can't do anything for you; can't go over her head, you know—hee! hee!—though, of course, personally———"

Price saw that Magnus was looking at him with a fuzzy leer of amusement; but he said nothing. He stalked out and took the elevator to the next floor—to the Motor Accessories offices.

Mrs. Arroford herself came fluttering out to greet him; but it was the flutter of a cordial woman, not of an embarrassed girl.

"So nice to see you! Won't you come right in!" she said.

Her office was solid and masculine, except for a huge bowl of roses on her flat-top desk and a Canton hourglass chair for visitors. To Price, after a certain hardness of the chair hitched up beside old Magnus' desk, the Canton chair was comforting. As they sat down, Mrs. Arroford's secretary poked her head in the doorway and remarked:

"Hubbard wants to see you, Mrs. Arroford."

Mrs. Arroford stared blankly at the secretary; looked worried, fidgety—feminine. Price watched her closely. "She can't make decisions like a man," he concluded. He had wondered whether he would be stirred by her, and found only a tired, busy everyday woman; pleasant, smartly dressed, and with more character now to her prettiness; but with none of that lingering magic that had, in his memory, seemed to melt about her. And she wasn't even a decisive boss! But Mrs. Arroford's face cleared and she spoke very concisely:

"Tell Hubbard he's to go to Buffalo. Let him fuss, and listen sympathetically, but tell him I can't see him—and sympathize with him about that, too—and get him started off. That's all."

In her voice was shown a perfect understanding with her secretary and a perfect readiness to fight with this invisible Hubbard person; but she dismissed her interest in the problem and turned on Price a smile of real welcome.

"I'm so glad you came in! I think you'll be pleased with your old pupil. We've increased receipts thirty percent this past year; and we——— But tell me about yourself, first. I heard somebody say you'd retired from Pistoflash after a mine of your own. That's awfully exciting! I knew you wouldn't always be working for somebody else."

It was hard, but into the lamp of her enthusiasm Price had to throw a brick:

"No; I'm not working for anybody else—or myself either. I'm broke! Flat! I'm a failure! I'm through pretending. I want a job—from you. Anything from twenty a week up. I haven't admitted to anybody but you and Magnus———"

"Oh, I am so sorry! But it doesn't really matter. You couldn't be a failure even if you are broke. You'll be back where you belong—soon."

Mothering pity gave color and warmth to her voice. Price hastily decided that business women excelled men in one thing, at least—they could show compassion without seeming weak. He burst out. He confessed that he had made a botch of Pistoflash, and of job-getting since.

"Probably I'm a fool to tell you all this when I ought to make an impression on you; but I've needed somebody—no; needed you!—to buck me up."

"I'm glad you told me. I———"

She walked over to the window and stared out. When she turned back to him he saw that her eyes were teary; and as she passed his chair she patted his shoulder—just once, shyly and delicately.

"Of course I'll do anything in the world to set you going again," she said quietly. "We've been reorganizing here and I'm not satisfied with my new sales manager. Sooner or later I'll have to let him out. Would you like to try that? It's only five thousand a year, because——— You won't be offended, will you? I'm really sales manager myself—and all the rest of the managers too. And, oh, you'd have to—well, I'm afraid it would almost be taking my orders."

"Dear lady, I'll take them without questioning. I mean it! I ——— "

"Don't! I know. I just wanted you to understand the situation. It's——— It will be wonderful to have you here again. We all loved you. . . . I'll let you know in just a day or two about when you can start in. Leave me your address."

Then she waited for Price to go—she who had so often awaited his permission to go! At least, she hadn't been so crude as to rise as sign that the interview was over!

He thanked her with mingled affection, gratitude, and an unavoidable resentment that he should have to come and sponge on her pity.

"I'll make good," he vowed in the elevator; "but it will be a stiff fight. To get myself to take orders from my own secretary—Lord, that's the last slam for a failure! . . . But Nancy—poor, sweet kid! It will be just as hard for her, I suppose."

VIII

There were many differences between Mrs. Arroford and the typical man chief. She was at once more impatient and more generous; more interested in the fortunes of everyone who worked for her or encountered her. She overworked too frequently; like a girl grind in college, she couldn't put away her work and go jovially off to loaf. She talked too rapidly; she was rather too insistent on the fact that she played no favorites. But for details she had real genius; and her "big decisions" didn't have to be undecided afterward, because they were not flip-a-quarter guesses, intended to bluff a waiting subordinate.

She never hesitated to reprove savagely anybody who came to her with a "Well, my little woman, I will give you my masculine advice" manner; but for the clerks she had a never-exhausted tolerance that made them adore her and give her the loyalty which enables executives to succeed.

In all this she was not so very different from the girl secretary Price had known—merely a little surer; a little more independent. Two things, however, kept warning Price that she was very different, an enormously larger person now: She had a certain luxury of living; his position of inferiority was crudely but clearly indicated by the fact that she could spend more than he could now. Like most business women, she decidedly retained a love for pretty things—flowers; frocks; charming apartments; a woman's club as elaborate and self-dependent as the most exclusive man's club; her own car; her overnight bag, with silver fittings. But more important than her luxuries, as a hint of how completely she had passed him, was the fact that he had to take her orders.

Price was sincerely trying to accustom himself to the new methods in Magnus' distribution; to organizing data about garages and hardware dealers and small jobbers; to advertising not just for technically trained minds but for amateur motorists. It was hard for him to skip quickly over a million details and be an authority on them when Mrs. Arroford called on him for information—and it was harder to realize that he mustn't give her advice all the time. When he noticed her using an old-fashioned desk calendar instead of a box tickler, when someone was impudent and she was unnecessarily aggressive in her resentment, Price would catch himself giving her suggestions as though she were his secretary.

She listened impatiently. They grew dangerously polite in their conferences. He began to doubt himself and felt useless. In this frame of mind he couldn't get up the energy necessary for that most demanding of tasks—starting over again.

Oh, he knew it; he blamed himself as savagely as any boss could have done; he sat and watched himself, unable to originate ideas, to put any fire into his salesmen—even to keep decently busy. He descended to the sordidness of pretending to be busy; of rustling papers and looking up abruptly when somebody came into his office. Before even small office girls he played out this shameful game. He could not get his mind to take hold. He glowered through the window at a chimney-pot skyline, and hated it. He did want to get to work; but there was no force in him.

In his nervous idleness he felt himself becoming irritable. He was irritated by Mrs. Arroford's tricks as manager—the tricks she had learned from himself, but which she presented as her own. Because he was ashamed of that irritation it was harder to go to her for orders; go to that small pretty woman behind a bowl of roses! And always he had the fear—which every delinquent clerk has in the presence of every chief—that some day she would "blow him up."

But she did not blow him up; and for months he wavered between that fear and slight contempt of her because she allowed him to go on merely marking time, and a bitter contempt of himself for everything.

Suddenly, one evening just before closing time, she sent him a memo:

"Please see me before you go home."

He ambled into her office rather patronizingly and sat down beside her desk. She called in her secretary,

"Please don't let anyone disturb us," she said. "You can bring in my letters to sign after Mr. Price has gone."

Her voice was very weary. Price felt as though she was turning to his masculine strength. But as she faced him she seemed not woman to be petted—neither man nor woman, indeed, but merely a brain behind cold eyes.

"Mr. Price, we must come to an understanding now; and let's get it all threshed out at this one conference. What are we going to do? I've tried my best to give you an opportunity and not be bossy, and you haven't responded. Do you realize that you are making it harder than ever for me because I've been doing most of your work? What can we do?"

"You've been doing————"

"Yes; I certainly have."

"Then, in that case, my dear Mrs. Arroford, I suppose there is nothing further desired from me, except my resignation."

"As you wish—though I really am sorry. I had hoped————"

"And I do resign. Now!"

"Oh, please don't be so stiff and dramatic. Can't you see I'm not talking in any unfriendly way? But I can't—oh, I can't, just can't go on carrying any more work. I'm overworked now. I thought you would take some of the burden off my shoulders. Please understand. I'm not talking like a boss, am I? I don't feel like one, but like an exhausted woman. And yet I am the boss and have to take responsibility. But I can't if my courage goes smash. What am I going to do?"

His stiffness was gone then.

"I know," he said. "I've been rotten! Now I resign again—but this time for your sake."

"No; I won't accept your resignation tonight—not for at least a week. See, oh, please see if you can't think of some way of getting hold of your job, so that you can help me. Good night."

He stood up. He took her hand—a small, tired, relaxed hand—and smiled down at her, not as the naughty boy who has been scolded but as a man does smile at a woman.

"I'll try—dear," he said.

He sat at dinner, alone, for two hours; and suddenly he threw overboard his whole philosophy. He saw that he had been working for himself first; for the firm second—a far-distant second; and for her, who needed him, he had not been working at all. Now he would work for her first; then for the firm; and as for himself—oh, his self had become confused, useless, and he would forget it entirely. Her presence in his plans made it not an impulsive desire for reformation but warm, thrilling, human. He went to her next morning and said:

"I want to work for you. And please give me the devil whenever I need it."

"I will!" She smiled.

What he had to do was simple enough—he had to work! . . . The same being a solution of many complex problems in life. . . . He had to attend to every detail; have information on which she could depend ready for her; not let his desk get choked with papers; not delay his assistants nor give then snap judgments. But to get himself to do this work required some change in himself. His new determination was a fine, earnest, youthful little determination; but determinations to reform are generally worth about as much as the "never again!" of next morning. He had to change.

So, at fifty and more, he began to make an art of so living that he should again have fire and joy in his work.

It is possible that he recalled the régime to which young Mrs. Arroford, of Mt. Vernon, had once subjected herself. He gave up ease and the precious routine comforts of middle age. He was up at six-thirty; took a cold bath, though every square inch of his sleek skin protested; walked before breakfast, and then cut out most of the breakfast, omitted the waffles and lamb chops—just as later in the day he shook off his lunchtime habits of a cocktail, coffee, cigars, and familiar gossip with the male old women at the club. He lunched when he could with small-garage men, with his salesmen, with men from the factory; and their close-to-the-machine energy enlivened his dull office view of business.

He was too busy now to stop to consider whether he was a born executive or not.

IX

Between failure and success there is, sometimes, only a thin partition; an inconspicuous difference in system or in not having headaches, in philosophy or in not smoking too much, in will power or in not forgetting to sign letters. Leonard Price knew a great deal about business; and, once he was willing to use that knowledge not to glorify himself but to serve the world—and a woman, it was not very hard to come back.

In a little over a year he was making so much of his position that Mrs. Arroford herself insisted that he ought not to be merely an inferior of hers. They had a two-day conference—Magnus and Mrs. Arrofrod and Price; and the department was again reorganized, with price in charge of negotiations with manufacturers and in possession of independence equal to hers.

He had come back; and now he had a far more puzzling problem to study.

X

When she had been his secretary Mrs. Arroford had turned all her femininity into discrete loyalty; when she had been his chief she had turned it into kindness, complicated by resolve that no one should walk over her. But, now that she was his equal, now that she was day by day his more quickly responsive companion, sharer in his every ambition and enthusiasm, he began to see her as a woman, with vanities and petulance, and a smile that was dearer than laughter; with ridiculous little hands, and mystery not to be deciphered. A woman—but a business woman, iron rigid in system, who laughed with him, but was swift to resent any undue familiarity in the office from him or from any other man!

He seemed never to get nearer to her. If his hand fell on hers as they said good night at the elevator she would respond with a casual grasp, but instantly withdraw her hand and speak with an impersonality that was harder to pass than scorn or hate.

He had to pass it, he told himself. She was necessary to him. When he spent an evening at the club he was equally lonely for her illuminating shop talk and for her woman's gentleness.

But if she was determined to be businesslike about everything—very well, he would be businesslike in love-making. He made a plan of which he was just a bit proud. Never, he told himself, had any staid middle-aged loved had the genius to think of being businesslike. He would discount all this romantic stuff, as Mrs. Arroford had done, and made a regular campaign of selling the attractions of Mr. Leonard Price.

On a winter afternoon, when the streets were irritating with squalls of dirty snow and the office was a warm refuge, Price sat beside her desk in conference.

"See here," he said prosily; "I know you're tired, but there's one other matter I must bring up and get all threshed out. There's one feature you've been neglecting."

"Go ahead."

"Nancy, you're always evading me when I want to talk about—well, about us————"

"Heavens! Is that your neglected feature?"

"————but I'm going to make you take it up systematically. If you're so darn businesslike, then I'll simply have to be a good salesman for the Price line."

"Very well. What goods are you showing this season?"

"A very nice line of heart and hand—heart tobacco-marred, but very warm."

"I'm afraid we're all stocked up."

"Well, madam, how about heroic male protection?"

"No; we don't deal in male protection—or any other windshields at all. We prefer open ears so that we can drive right into the rain and feel it on our cheeks. Sorry!"

"No lady's car can be sold with just a bare chassis, though—no upholstery or anything. How about something neat in an upholstery that you can simply jump on if you want to—and it won't complain?"

"No; no upholstery, Mr. Price. I've got so used to riding down next to the crank-cage of life that I like the heat and smell of it—even the spattering oil. Business has made me afraid of all the upholstery that most women start out riding on, and find themselves sunk in, lost in————"

"Will you stop evading my attempts to propose to you! I'm so terribly afraid you'll get away from me again. And I do want to give you the chance to rest, to work for you———— Oh, hang it, I say—will you marry me, Nancy?"

"Business has made me so————"

"Confound business! Nancy, you make me go back to my old belief that women don't belong in business. You business women ruin yourselves for love."

"No! That isn't true! It's you business men that ruin us for it. When we go into offices you expect us to be either flirts or nuns. If we aren't obviously nuns you keep bothering us. So we have to freeze out all the habit of love. No! I'm sorry. I am glad to have you for a friend; but—that's all! Ever! You see, we're both being practical and frank, and—decisive."

"Nancy"—he hesitated—"I wish I could kiss you—just once!"

She smiled; but:

"No," she said; and he unhappily ebbed away.

XI

Upon his birthday old Magnus gave a Company dinner at his big house on Riverside Drive. The businesslike Mrs. Arroford was radiant and soft and utterly feminine in a cloud of silver and pearl; and Price stared at her all evening.

"Walk down the Drive with me on your way home," he had the chance to whisper. "There's moonlight on the snow."

"Moonlight?" she said. "Oh, yes; I remember—that's what they used to have on spring evening when I was a girl."

They came chattering and laughing out of the orange glow of the doorway. They crossed to the river side of the Drive.

A yacht was fleeing up the Hudson, its lights red and yellow and vivid green upon the water, its searchlight shifting over the snowy heights of Weehawken. They stopped to watch it.

"It's so startlingly beautiful by night," she sighed, as they stood there.

He watched her, in her white furs, become hypnotized by the river's shining light; saw her grow tender with that faint sadness which is the heart of all solemn beauty. Without a word he put his arm about her, felt the warmth and softness of her furs. He was not shy of her now, nor did he plan to seem businesslike. To be close to this dear woman comrade was as natural as that most ancient naturalness of snow and moon and wide, listening sky.

She shivered a little and leaned against him. She said no word. Deliberately he smoothed her cold cheek and kissed her.

"Oh!" was all she said; her hand slowly slipped into his and stayed there.

He had the inspiration to keep silent for a time before he whispered:

"I shouldn't have asked you, before, if I might kiss you."

"No!"

"And I shouldn't have been so practical in making love. Always it's you who are the wise executive! I should simply have been plain human, and—and made love!"

"Oh, yes; yes! A business woman wants to be just a woman when it comes to love. Oh, we're so old-fashioned, we practical modern women! Like you men! I want moonlight and romance, and chance to cry a little because I'm happy; and, oh————"

"And lumbering old me?"

"And gentle old you, my dear!"

THE WHISPERER

I

Through the office of the Bowen Drug Manufacturing Company there was a rustling like the bird gossip and stir of trees that give the twilight its secure tranquility. It was an honest business and a happy shop.

Purdy, the vice president and general manager of the Bowen Drug Company, talked frankly with the two superintendents; the superintendents were human with their stenographers; the stenographers were not too ladylike with the office boys; and the office boys could whistle in the hall without starting an avalanche. They all did their work; pride and loyalty they had, and eagerness in team play; and through the clatter of typewriters sounded a contented whispering—whispering—whispering.

Yet the Bowen Drug Company was being hard pressed by the Vanvick Pharmaceutical Supply Company, and at the weekly conference of heads of departments there was agitated discussion. Behind the discussion was an unexpressed fear of the power greater than Purdy—of Bowen, president and chief stockholder of the Bowen Company, a figure as gloomily mysterious to them as a Hindu idol looming beyond an incense-darkened corridor. Their purpose in life, aside from such insignificant personal matters as rearing families, was to make money for Bowen. But Bowen never came near the office; usually he was off in Canada, buying lumber lands. He let them alone, and it was Purdy, that stooped rustic with the pale blue eyes and the hesitating kindliness, to whom they turned for leadership in the war on Vanvick.

The Bowen Drug Company was not large. It was not a national concern, though it was popular among the druggists of six or seven states; and almost national was the fame of its hypnotic preparation, Hippogen, founded on the tri-chlor-tertiary-butyl formula. Now that the Vanvick Company was entering the Hippogen field with a rival preparation, it was agreed at the conference of heads to take more space in the local pharamacists' journals, featuring Hippogen, together with Bodent, the Bowen dentifrice.

Purdy was comforted by the cheeriness of the heads—the superintendent of the proprietary-medicine department, the superintendent of drugs and biological products, the treasurer, the sales manager, the purchasing agent, the chief chemist and the advertising man. But he was secretly perturbed, after the conference. He believed that Hippogen would never regain its lead. He saw future profits only in the ethical drug business. They would have to retrench.

Then came to Purdy's office an optimistic man who promised much gain and glory to the Bowen Company.

R. Chester Doremus, M.D., was that optimistic lad, that bringer of good news about making more money. His card announced that he was the editor of *Therapeutic Tidings*, and instructor in therapeutics in Minturn Medical College.

Doctor Doremus was as neatly engraved as his card—neat black hair parted in the middle, neat rimless eyeglasses on a silken cord, neat gray flannel suit, neat tan oxfords, and an enunciation as neat and bright and helpful as that of a popular duchess or even a telephone girl.

"Not going to bother you about advertisements or anything to do with the magazine," he chuckled, briskly producing a plain silver cigarette case. "Just been getting a couple of ideas, and I like your firm's reputation for square dealing, so I thought I'd hand 'em over. How would it do to use a cap on your Bodent tube with a glass jewel set in it? That might make it distinctive, and maybe rather attractive. Second thing is this—just a bit of psychology—

great believer in applying scientific psychology to business: You know if a person is using a new brand of toothpaste, by the time he has finished the tube there's nothing but a roll of metal to show what kind it was. Why not print the name across the very top of the Bodent tube?"

"Well, that's worth thinking of," droned Purdy. He was always impressed by words like scientific and psychology. But he was not a rapid thinker, and, before he could digest the ideas, Doctor Doremus had popped out of his chair, grinned, and shot:

"Glad if they prove of any use, old man! Like your firm. Fine people. Be in to see you again some day." And was brightly, neatly, hand-wavingly gone.

Purdy decided to experiment with a limited number of the jeweled Bodent tubes. He sent a check for fifty dollars to Doctor Doremus, and asked him to call when he had more ideas.

Now the doctor had for a month been planning to get a job with the Bowen Company, and he had twenty high-colored suggestions already cached. He brought them in, three or four at a time, and after a few months he permitted Purdy to hire him as assistant to Jordan, the heavy-handed superintendent of the proprietary department, and as general suggester to all departments. The doctor gave up his private medical practice, his editorship of *Therapeutic Tidings* and his instructorship at the medical college. He dove into business and came up wet and smiling.

There are two blighted beings who are lavishly hated by all regular office men, whereof one is the suggester, that person who sits in a padded chair, and out of the rich fullness of his lack of experience with practical details advises comic changes which the chief expects you to carry out at once. The other pallbearer is that outsider who is suddenly elevated above men trained in the business because he has a college degree or a beautiful handshake. Both of these was Doctor Doremus.

The bosses of the proprietary-medicine department—Jordan, the superintendent; Zitterel, the chief chemist; and the advertising man, who was himself a prolific maker of typewritten schedules of suggestions calculated to upset everything in sight—received the doctor in the manner of three honest suitors being introduced by the beloved to a tango lizard. But the doctor was so sunnily deferential that they forgave him for being an outsider and began to accept his invitations to lunch.

After that it was easy for the doctor.

II

Rochester Doremus, M.D., sometime Robby Doremus, was the son of a poor clergyman. He had been ambitious, and almost honest, at the start, and had frugally worked his way through college.

As a doctor he was a good salesman. While he was a young and poor general practitioner he had an itch for money and intrigue. He advertised himself by the free treatment of such poor patients as were certain to talk, by his small editorship and by his instructorship in Minturn Medical College, which is a diploma mill with evening classes for students who aspire to be quacks or fashionable physicians in second-class cities.

He was successful. His bedside manner was inspiring, and he was brilliant in the cure of those imaginary invalids who are the most demanding and the most advertising of patients. He invested in suburban real estate, meddled in ward politics, and made trim semiscientific little speeches before conventions of undertakers, sportsmen, church societies, and earnest women.

But he wanted a larger field. He could not see a practice of more than seven or eight thousand dollars a year. He made himself honestly believe that he honestly believed that in business he would have more power for good. He tried to get the fast-growing Vanvick Pharmaceutical Supply Company interested in him, and failed, though he wrote the most intimate and informal letters on the stationery of *Therapeutic Tidings*. He planned a campaign to "impress his personality" on the competitors of Vanvick, the Bowen Drug Company, and came skipping in to see Purdy, as has truthfully been chronicled.

He was going to be an influence for pure drugs and ethical methods—and incidentally climb to a larger income, to be used for the most charitable purposes.

He glowed with loyalty to the Bowen Company, to Purdy, and to Jordan, his immediate supervisor. He told his shy, pretty, insignificant wife that Purdy and Jordan were the finest fellows he had ever met.

Doctor Doremus was not merely a suggester. Despite his medical prestige he had to become a practical part of the business. He was assigned to assist the purchasing agent in negotiations with new manufacturers of cartons and labels, and he was sent to the factory to study the processes of manufacture, packing and shipping. But he did make suggestions, and these he took to Jordan, and was not jealous when much credit shone round about Jordan by reason of them. He liked Jordan's bluff frankness; at all hours he was to be heard saying that it was an inspiration to discover an establishment where everybody thought for the good of the firm, and said honestly what he thought, and never held a grudge.

Despite a fair salary, Superintendent Jordan had no money to waste. He had a son in college, and he was paying for a farm. Doctor Doremus so frequently invited Jordan to lunch and, in his delight to be a big man, he was so like a sparrow discovering a crumb that Jordan got into the habit of letting the doctor pay for the bill—and manage the conversation. So Jordan was led to tell everything he knew. He not only hymned Purdy's glory and admitted how impressed he was by the doctor's ingenuity, but also admitted that there was one man he didn't like—Zitterel, the chief chemist, who might some day be a claimant for Jordan's job. Doctor Doremus purred, and encouraged Jordan to talk; made gibes at Zitterel's accent and pompadour hair; and finally, whispered to Jordan "Why don't you get rid of him?"

"We-ull, I don't know—I don't know. Wouldn't want to bounce a man because I don't like him personally. Besides, Zitterel is a good chemist. Doubt if we could get another one like him. Besides, Purdy likes him, and he would have to O.K. my giving Zitterel the gate. Besides——— Oh, Zitterel is all right. . . . Here, it's my turn to pay the check. Well, since you have it——— But I pay for the next lunch, remember."

The open season on Zitterel began.

Jordan was not a large man; rather he was thick and lethargic, a thorough commercialist, and always one day behind a shave. But Doctor Doremus genuinely admired Jordan's strength. He felt toward his superior that patronizing affection which a wit may feel for the famous but stupid athlete whom he is towing about. He decided that he had to save Jordan from the peril of Zitterel's rivalry, and win the lasting gratitude of his beloved chief.

Zitterel not only failed to worship good old Jordan, but also seemed to dislike good old Jordan's pal, Dr. R. Chester Doremus. The doctor had once tried to buy Zitterel a lunch, and learn his version of why Jordan and he did not get along so well as the rest of the heads, but Zitterel had snarled "We go Dutch in this shop!"

So the doctor made three hunting trips.

He informed Purdy, the general manager, that he was sorry Mr. Zitterel seemed to be unable to find time to take up the learned advice the doctor had given regarding the Bowen supply of chemical in which the doctor professed the most passionate interest. That chemical was the universal parlor favorite, hexamethylenetetramin-anhydromethylencitrate.

The doctor pronounced all of it once, and quite large portions of it another time. Purdy didn't pronounce it. He looked hot and awed. His favorite words were simple, pleasant ones like "window display." He remonstrated with the doctor for not appreciating Zitterel's virtues—but he listened.

Then the doctor went out to Minturn Medical College and persuaded the chemistry shark that academic work was ill-paid and dull, and that, by grace of Doctor Doremus' memory of his former colleagues, the chemist might some day be able to get a good job if he applied to Jordan, of the Bowen Company. The doctor had, as a result of his talks with Jordan, been able to draw up a little schedule of mistakes Zitterel had made. This schedule he confided to the Minturn College chemist.

Finally, at another lunch, Doctor Doremus wailed to his brother, Jordan, that he was worried about this man Zitterel. Zitterel was trying to block every suggestion he made; Zitterel didn't like him; Zitterel wanted to get rid of him. The big brother snorted: "Nonsense, doc! Zitterel's all right. He isn't after your scalp. You must get nervous and imagine things. You do too much confining work, and—if—I—caught him at anything like that I'd break him! You don't want to be anxious about that chump."

"All right, chief. But, say, Lord knows I'm not a school tattler; but I will admit I was pretty sore last week when Zitterel looked over that new label for the commercial art company, you remember, for Sanisav, that you and Purdy O.K.'d. Brer Zitterel said he'd always realized he knew more about chemistry than you, but he never realized he had better taste too!"

Jordan's eyes pinched together, and he grumbled:

"Oh, he did, did he? Well, then, I just want to tell you a little story about Mr. Zitterel's beautiful taste! . . ."

They had quantities of French pastry, large cakes with garlands of brown sugar and pergolas of white sugar, and together they made fun of Zitterel. At the zenith of their confidences the doctor declared:

"Look here, old man; I don't suppose there'll ever be many changes in the Bowen Company, because there's such an *esprit de corps*; but if there ever should be any I want you to know that my biggest ambition would be to have a good solid alliance with you, so we could stand together through thick and thin."

Jordan was much moved; partly by three cups of coffee, and partly by such an expression of affection as had rarely come to him in his prosaic life. He thrust out his paw, shook hands and boomed:

"You bet, doc! You're on!"

That afternoon, when Zitterel came to Jordan yammering about the quality of the new supply of coconut oil, Jordan was curt with him.

That evening Doctor Doremus telephoned to his friend, the chemist at Minturn College, that it was time to drop in and see Jordan.

A week later Jordan noisily discharged Zitterel for refusing to O.K. a run of Hippogen, and hired the Minturn chemist, who was a talkative young man and believed that Doctor Doremus was a genius and the protector of the poor.

Purdy was sorry to lose Zitterel, he said. But he made Doctor Doremus a member of the weekly conference of heads of department to replace the chemist, and when the publicity man offensively declared that they were making a mistake in letting Zitterel go, Purdy and Jordan looked angrily at him, and the conference was not as chummy as previous ones had been.

Now it has been noted that this same publicity man was a rival to Doctor Doremus in the making of assorted suggestions. Yet so generous was the doctor that it was he who most warmly agreed with the fellow.

Two months later this publicity man was discharged, for mistakes that had happened to come to the attention of Jordan. His place was filled by a newspaperman who had been of value to Doctor Doremus in the way of free publicity when the doctor had been a general practitioner.

Beecher Drew, the big surly treasurer of the Bowen Company, called the doctor into his office and privately thanked him for having helped get rid of the former publicity man. The doctor denied having had anything to do with it; but Drew, who was an abrupt, canny man, said:

"All right, doc! Just the same, guess you're the only one here who was keen enough to see what a bluffer that fellow was."

Doctor Doremus was safely settled in his department, with no obstacle to helping his friend and chief, Jordan. If Purdy ever should want to give up the general managership Jordan would take his place, and the doctor would be in line for Jordan's position.

After that it was easy for the doctor.

III

Doctor Doremus was not merely an office politician—he was a hard worker by day and an extensive student during his evening at home. Though the year following the removal of Zitterel was a bad period for the Bowen Company in general, with Vanvick competing savagely, with profits only a little exceeding expenses, and with rumor of thunderous memos, to Purdy from the absent Bowen, yet the sunny-natured doctor was philosophical about such details. He was happy in getting a grasp of the business, and in his assurance that he could trust Jordan.

Play with Jordan he could not. On the one occasion when the doctor had taken him for a Saturday afternoon drive in his little roadster he had been bored to a shivering cold sweat by the boss' elephantine comments on mileage and signboards. But he could manage Jordan, and he loved power as well as the finer arts of diplomacy.

When he had learned all of Jordan's opinions about their fellow workers, and most of his plans for the business, Doctor Doremus began to wonder if he had not made a mistake in tying himself too cleverly to this lumbering fellow, and in not sufficiently appreciating his *confrères*. . . . The doctor liked the word *"confrère"*; it had class, and was pretty easy to pronounce.

A narrow wrinkle began to reveal itself on each side of the bridge of his nose. That probably came from his increasing habit of scowling as he sat alone. They were the first wrinkles in his smooth face, except for smile furrows beside his mouth, which were less often seen now. The doctor was still a very cordial man, but his eyes became irritable immediately after a caller went away.

He was a success. But he had reached the limit of advancement in this job. He saw that a bright young man who desired to plow deep in this wider field of usefulness must learn a great deal besides correspondence and inspection of lab products. He must have an altruistic interest in all of his associates.

He began to notice McCabe, who was the superintendent of the drugs and biological products department, and, as such, of equal rank with Jordan. McCabe was a simpering, check-suited little man, with an imperial; bland and joky, but shrewd. Doctor Doremus felt that McCabe appreciated his scholarly references and sly humor better than did honest-dog Jordan.

He decided that it would be fairer to all concerned if he investigated McCabe's business methods and private morals before betraying affection. An earnest young worker could learn a good deal without exposing his yearning for knowledge to the rude public gaze. The doctor believed it was dishonorable to read the correspondence of others; but after all, wasn't it his duty to know all about the affairs of his beloved firm? He found that if he was passing a door, and there was a discussion within, it was possible for an innocent lad to stop and blow his nose, and overhear half a dozen sentences without looking like a spy.

He also found a way to check up on Jordan and make sure that his chief was worthy of trust. Their offices were side by side, and their telephones were on the same extension. If he lifted his receiver from the hook before Jordan lifted his, when the boss' ring was given, it was possible to catch a conversation without having Jordan suppose, from the betraying click, that someone was listening in—a supposition that might easily have led to a misunderstanding.

One result of the doctor's intensive study was a slight lessening in the ardor and volume of his compliments. At first he had gone bouncing about the office, chirruping his admiration for Jordan, but now he saw that he had been young and naive; and sometimes, when Jordan wore a funny old hat or made a mistake in a manufacturing order, the doctor permitted himself to whisper to McCabe—oh, not in a condemnatory way, but just to let McCabe in on the humor of the thing. For the doctor had a sense of humor, and loved to share it.

McCabe appreciated these innocent little jokes. One day a sudden warmth of friendship came over McCabe and the doctor, and they made boyish caricatures of the heads of the firm. Bowen was portrayed as a savage peering out of his cave and brandishing a club; Purdy as a chin-whiskered farmer; Beecher Drew, the treasurer the company, as a wrinkle-browed bulldog; and Jordan as a traveling salesman anxiously inquiring a druggist, "Say, do you know what this stuff is I'm trying to sell you? Darned if I do."

Doctor Doremus had a thought that he could add McCabe to the list as an old woman with a goatee, but he didn't suggest it—it might have hurt McCabe's feelings.

They giggled over their drawing, and whispered slyly.

Through corridors and offices, down factory aisles and round about the packing rooms, crept a faintly breathing ghost. Vanvick was getting their business; Bowen was not satisfied; Purdy was frightened; and somewhere in the Bowen Company they all felt, without knowing that they felt it, was a stealthy figure whispering—whispering—whispering.

IV

Despite the general bad showing of the Bowen balance sheets Jordan's department was paying expenses, thanks to the suggestions of Doctor Doremus. The doctor traced increased sales of Bodent to them—though apparently no one else did. It was Jordan who got the credit; Jordan whom Purdy thanked at conference meetings. The doctor was tired of this. It had been a pleasure to go trotting to his big brother with assistance, but after more than a year it was wearisome to have big brother think he had done it all himself. Jordan was as unprogressive as a tombstone. Not only did he fail ever to have a new idea for vitalizing his department, but also he failed ever to have a new way of remarking that the weather was too hot or too cold or too pleasant to stay in the office.

Doctor Doremus had learned his business. He was a better man than Jordan now, and he perceived that in merest justice to the firm he must not be fettered to Jordan. And it was now not just to himself to be always going out to lunch with Jordan when he could enjoy himself more with McCabe.

McCabe was a little cricket of a widower and, as he himself admitted, a favorite of all women over thirty-nine and under ten-thousand-a-year. Doctor Doremus felt that the man had many of his own social graces. He sent his wife off to her mother's and invited McCabe out for a weekend. McCabe seemed to appreciate the sound observations regarding scenery made by the doctor, who was always moved by kittens, wild roses, children and honesty. McCabe praised him, and during their duet about the beauty of a rustic glade McCabe said that it was a pity they two had not become intimate earlier. The doctor agreed; and without apparent connection the talk drifted to Jordan.

For Jordan, announced the doctor, he had a loyalty so great that he could not express it; he admired the man's integrity, he was touched by his simplicity, he appreciated his knowledge of business, but as a lunch companion he found him damnably dull!

"Yes; he sure is!" giggled McCabe; and they looked knowingly at each other and began to give the most generous encouragement and commendation to autumnal Nature.

On Sunday morning Doctor Doremus admitted that, with the best intentions in the world, dear old Jordan was making a mistake in introducing his new product, Saltylic, to a market already stocked with standard preparations of acetylsalicylic acid.

McCabe yelped: "You're dead right! Saltylic never will be a profitable item, and even if it could be made to go it ought not to be put out by Jordan for popular counter sale; it ought to belong to my department. I've told Jordan so, and Purdy; but they won't listen."

Sunday afternoon Doctor Doremus made mention of the facts that the correct designation of Phytolacca was *Phytolacca Americana* Linné, and that *Xanthoxyli Fructus* ought to be spelled with a Z instead of an X. McCabe looked impressed. He had not, he fawned, known that the doctor was a botanist as well as a chemist. And indeed he ought to have been impressed. These stirring truths were not only sound but quite fresh, having been secured by the doctor only two days previously from a magazine article on the Pharmacopœia.

Sunday evening the doctor remarked to McCabe, as they sat on the porch, friendly and poetic in the dusk:

"Jordan says you are a crack chemist and manufacturer, old man"—McCabe made a pleasing sound—"but he says you don't know anything about druggists. He claims that if you had your way you would compel them to stick strictly to filling prescriptions and give up soda counters and gifts, and incidentally about nine-tenths of their profits; and when I told him———"

"Oh, he did, did he? Well, then, I just want to tell you a little story about Mr. Jordan's idea of increasing profits."

McCabe presented himself as one who had slaved and died in his devotion to Jordan, but who was beginning to see that Jordan was unappreciative, and ignorant both of drugs and the psychology of druggists. Doctor Doremus was grievously shocked by this attack on his friend, and defended him, retreating from each new position with a brave-hearted "Well, maybe that's so, but still ———" He called attention to Jordan's fairness, which merely roused McCabe to gossip about Jordan's stubbornness in the office and his stinginess outside.

When McCabe had told all the stories about Jordan that he knew, and had turned to the subject of the misty trees in the yard, Doctor Doremus broke in with:

"Well, let's not talk of Jordan; let's talk about the trees there, or something else that's pleasanter. Can you hear that robin? Drowsy little cuss chirping there! I'm a sentimentalist, I admit; but these poor weak little creatures somehow touch a man's heart."

"Yes; don't they! Yes; let's forget Jordan. I suppose he's had something of a struggle, with family sickness and expensive fool sons and all—though I must say I wish he wouldn't always be reminding the rest of us about his bloomin' heroism! But still——— Listen to that cricket! Lively little fellow. I'm like you, doc; I'm touched by the least hint of beauty or weakness."

The two friends sat quiet in wicker chairs on the porch, rejoicing in their discovery of each other in this hard world. There was a felling of fraternity that was audible as a whisper, and before them the trees whispered, the grass whispered, and through the tremulous night stole an uneasy whispering—whispering—whispering.

The chums returned to the office on the commutation train Monday morning, talking so intently they did not notice the landscape. They hunched up with their heels on McCabe's suitcase, and smoked sulphurously, and pounded on the plush seat. The doctor seemed to be outlining a plan. McCabe listened, argued, but apparently agreed; for as they got out at the city station, still so absorbed in their talk that they were unconscious of the parade of commuters in which they trotted through the ringing train shed, McCabe consented:

"Well, all right then! If Jordan thinks he knows so much about it let him try and see where he gets off!"

V

McCabe and Doctor Doremus must have been confused as to their opinions of the merits of Saltylic as a selling proposition, for certainly they had ridiculed it during their weekend drive; yet during the next week, when Jordan came to McCabe and inquired: "Say, Mac, I'm ready to take up Saltylic now. How about it? Still feel you got to hide it away in your dark and mysterious department, old hoss?" then did McCabe reply, in the same spirit of friendly jesting:

"Well, I don't know as my department is as mysterious as some I could mention, old slacker; but seriously, I've been thinking about Saltylic, and if you want to push it go ahead!"

As for the doctor, when he was called in to talk over Saltylic he urged Jordan to make a big drive on it; to send it out liberally to the trade, on consignment.

The Bowen Company sales manager was only a record-keeping clerk. The superintendents of departments were the responsible sales heads. Purdy, who knew as much about Saltylic as he did about crocheting among the early Etruscans, O.K'd the reports of Jordan and the chemist whom Doctor Doremus had brought from Minturn College; and the Saltylic campaign was on. Thousands of bottles were on consignment, and were backed up by posters, window-display material, and by page advertisements in druggists' journals, medical magazines, and even in popular mediums. The Bowen publicity man came to his longtime patron, Doctor Doremus, with a worried query about the advisability of the extensive use of space at a time when the advertising budget was so low, but the doctor reassured him, and the publicity man said nothing to Purdy.

The first response to the campaign was a letter from a physician, in a medical magazine, complaining that Saltylic was an inferior preparation of acetylsalicylic acid, as well as an unnecessary addition to standard brands. The second response was the laconic return of five thousand bottles that a salesman had persuaded one of the jobbers to stock.

But most of the jobbers and retailers merely let their supply get dusty, and on worried inquiry from Jordan blandly reported that it was not moving yet.

About the time when Purdy began to ask where were all the nice little checks from Saltylic, Bowen returned from Canada to preside over the annual meeting of the board of directors—which meant a reunion of the Bowen family—and to look into the details of operation of the company. He did not go near any part of the establishment except Purdy's office, but everybody got strong telepathic currents from him.

Purdy postponed the weekly conference of heads. He asked for various detailed reports. Doctor Doremus made sure that, in his report of stock on hand, he gave full credit to Saltylic.

He went to see Purdy two or three days after making his reports. He got there at twelve-thirty. . . . Now, Purdy always went to lunch from twelve to one. . . . The doctor was quite willing to wait. He couldn't go back to his office, because Purdy might come back early. He dismissed Purdy's secretary.

Purdy was old-fashioned in regard to desk order. He let his paper accumulate, and when he wanted one of them he dived into the mass. . . . The doctor sat beside Purdy's desk in a gracious pose, his trim knees crossed, his toes tapping. He lighted a little cigar. He looked benevolently at the door. His right arm carelessly rested on the edge of the desk; his right hand carelessly patted the pile of papers. He heard Purdy's secretary, who sat just outside the door call "Yes, I'm coming!" and heard her hastening away. . . . Then he threw away the lady-size cigar and the benevolent look.

He snatched the papers from the desk and flipped through them, glancing at the bottoms of sheets, looking for the rough familiar signature, "Bowen." He found three such signatures. He yanked the three memos from the pile. Two sentences in them he studied:

"If the present staff can't even pay expenses you will have to make important changes; weed out the merely mechanical workers who, however faithful they may be, can't meet changing conditions."

"I like what you tell me about this new fellow, Doremus."

The doctor replaced the papers and reverently laid the pile back on the desk. His expression was more benevolent than ever. He strolled into the drugs department. McCabe had not yet gone out to lunch. They went out together. McCabe seemed frightened and obedient.

Next noon Jordan invited the doctor to lunch. Jordan did not mention business except to say:

"Well, old Bowen's here with his annual rumpus and four-flushing. I'll be glad when he goes back to Canada."

The reason for the lunch invitation seemed to lie in Jordan's desire to tell somebody about the record his son was making in college. The superintendent's dull eyes were wet as he said:

"I tell you, he's a great boy—a whole lot better than his big-footed pa ever had any reason to expect. I'm going to set him up in law if everything goes right."

"That's fine; that's fine, old man!" cried Doctor Doremus with that ready sympathy of his.

The doctor had to hurry back. He had an appointment with McCabe. For some reason he hesitated for fifteen seconds before he went into McCabe's office. He pinched his lips and shook his head. Then he threw back his head and darted into McCabe's office, and the two of them went together to see Purdy.

McCabe sighed: "Chief, you know I've always been a friend of Jordan's. But at the same time I feel that my first duty is to the firm rather than to any individual, and I want to talk to you about the way Jordan insists on wrecking everything in this attempt to cram Saltylic down our throats. I'd take this up in general conference, with Jordan right there, but you know how stubborn he is."

"I don't think we need to worry about it anymore. Even Jordan must see by now that Saltylic isn't going," Purdy said mildly.

"Doctor Doremus thinks not," insisted McCabe, and the doctor permitted himself to be pumped to the effect that:

"I'm afraid McCabe is right, chief. I tried my best to make Jordan see that we aren't getting any reorders, and that all the consignments apparently are dead, but all I could get him to see was 'I'm running this! I'll show all you fellows that the stuff will sell. What if it doesn't bring the bacon home for a year or two,' he said; 'it'll pay in the long run.'"

Purdy was pricked into wailing:

"But it's just this year or two when we can't stand any loss! To be frank, boys, with the Vanvick Company giving us such a run we can't afford to have money tied up this way. I know you love Jordan, as I do; but, just between us, I do wish he wasn't so pig-headed sometimes!"

After that it was easy for the doctor.

VI

No one has ever learned what was said between Purdy and Jordan during that interview which took all of one afternoon. But two days after Purdy had been visited by McCabe and his comrade in appreciation of arts and charities, Dr. R. Chester Doremus, it was announced at the weekly conference that Jordan had resigned to go into the retail drug business. Jordan said that he did not know just where he would locate, but he had always wanted to have a little business of his own.

The announcement grieved them all, particularly Doctor Doremus, who was so stunned by the thought of losing his first friend at the Bowen Company that he did not cheer up when Purdy added that he had taken up the question of Jordan's successor with Bowen himself, and that he had decided to appoint, as the new superintendent of the proprietary department—here Purdy's lean dry voice became full and emotional—Doctor Doremus!

The doctor had one more lunch with that first friend. Jordan's voice was bewildered, his motions clumsy. As he crossed a street he hesitated like a blind man. The doctor took his arm, in the most affectionate way, to guide him to that chophouse where they had had so many lunches.

Jordan said that he didn't care for much to eat; he wasn't hungry, and besides—he smiled stupidly—it was a good thing for everybody to economize in these wartimes. He looked grateful when the doctor, with his invariable gay graciousness, declared: "Oh, this farewell lunch is going to be on me, old boy. . . . Made your plans about your store yet?"

"No; not exactly. To be perfect frank, doc—now I wouldn't say this to anybody else at the shop, but it's different with you—I haven't got such a scad of money right in reach. But still—oh, it'll come out all right! I see here in the drug journals where there are several stores I can get for only a thousand down, and I can get that by mortgaging my farm. The one thing that worries me is how I can go on sending the boy any money. He makes a little extra by tutoring, but he's interested in legal research, and I wanted him to give all his spare time to that. He's a good boy, Carl is. I hope he won't have to leave college."

Doctor Doremus hoped so, too, and he hinted that, as the new head of the proprietary department, he would be delighted to slip Jordan upon longtime-payment consignment anything he might want for a retail business. Jordan was grateful, but he said he didn't think that would be quite honest, somehow.

At the end of the lunch he gave to the doctor a little list of memorandums and hints, which he had been drawing up for the doctor's assistance.

Beecher Drew, the treasurer of the Bowen Company, had sent the doctor a memo asking him to drop in at his office after lunch. It was Drew, that morose, bow-shouldered, stupidly dressed watchdog, who had thanked the doctor for having got rid of the former publicity man, and had, in a manner rather annoying to the doctor's limpid-eyed good-fellowship, looked at him as though he was searching for hidden schemes.

The doctor went to see Drew, who said, without preface:

"My boy, you did well! Jordan was blocking all our progress. Glad you got him out."

"Look here, Mr. Drew, I don't understand what you mean, with reference to Jordan! Surely you can't mean to imply that I had anything to do with his—why, he resigned to get into the retail game— why, he was my warmest friend in———"

"Sit down and be cool! Doc, you and I are the only wise ones in this shop, the only ones that are able to help the concern get on its feet. Of course you got Jordan canned. And quite right! I'd have done the same thing. Now don't let's say anything more about it. I just want you to know that I understand you are the livest wire on the producing end. And I want you to get a little better acquainted with me. I'm not so slow myself, even if I do sit back here among the dusty ledgers. So, shake, doc."

The two men smiled slightly at each other.

The doctor began to reorganize his department. He was head of it now, with nobody in his way except Purdy and Bowen. He had a feeling of irresistible power. And he was glad to know that back of him he had Beecher Drew. He felt the treasurer was a force yet unmeasured.

He knew just where he was: He was headed for Purdy's position, as vice president and general manager of the company! It was Fate, and who was he to oppose Fate? Hitherto he had been almost childishly merciful to his confrères; from now on he would have to be sterner. He saw his destiny—saw that he was a Napoleon!

Hadn't Napoleon also been a small, neat, educated man—for that matter, not half so neat or educated as he himself was? Like Napoleon, he would have to climb over the bodies of other men, he courageously philosophized. Hard on them? Certainly; but that was how the world was run; and there was no sense in fighting the beneficent principle of evolution. Survival of the fittest! Sure!

Well, he meditated, he would have to make outside alliances. With the possible exception of Beecher Drew, who might be worth studying, no one in the business was worthy to be trusted with the confidence of a Napoleon.

He was a member of a dozen associations or physicians, chemists, pharamacists. He looked them over and began to select his field marshals. He liked the drama of picking out a struggling young man at an alumni banquet and whispering to him "How would you like to have a five-thousand-dollar job in a year or so, m'boy?" When the youngster gasped and became deferential, Doctor Doremus felt large. The young men courted him; if he lunched at the University Club a dozen of them would stop at his table, one after another, flushing, stammering, looking humbly down at him.

As part of this war to gain the vice presidency he had to give full information about the wicked and contemptible enemy. Where once he had shyly listened in on telephone calls and craned his neck down passages, how he hired a complaisant porter to bring him private letter files, and he learned Purdy's plans day before they were announced at conference. He was amused to find that poor Purdy's letters said precisely what the man himself said publicly. He pitied the weakling for his lack of finesse.

At the conference of heads it was increasingly hard for the doctor to be excited. No longer did he bounce in his chair with desire to give them his helpful plans. He was bored by their droning hesitancy. He wouldn't have any conferences when he became vice president!

Doctor Doremus didn't merely go about being diplomatic and mysterious. He worked. He was moving the proprietary stock faster than Jordan ever had done—by granting large discounts to the cut-rate trade, and by reviving the sale of a headache nostrum that Jordan and Zitterel had discarded as injurious. The doctor's tame chemist had been so good as to report that it was merely ignorant prejudice, this objection to the nostrum.

His good work was going to count. Often he was deliciously stirred by a plan that was indeed worthy of a Napoleon. Since he had to break through the line of McCabe, Purdy and Beecher Drew—see to it that they were discharged lest they dare to rival him—then why waste time on them and their petty office politics, as a lesser man would have done? Why not go straight to Bowen? Bowen was still in the city, apparently keeping an eye on affairs. The doctor knew that Bowen must be impressed by the increased sales in his department. He would meet him, let him know what Purdy and Drew and McCabe really were, and step right into the vice presidency. Simplicity of genius!

He had never seen Bowen, but he had heard that he was a soft, white grub. Lazy profit worm! Be easy to handle! He took every excuse to hang about Purdy's office, hoping that Bowen would come in. But unexpected was his first meeting with Bowen. He was hurrying out of the building when the old elevator man muttered: "That was the boss with the brass mitt that come down in the elevator with you, doctor."

"What do you mean—Bowen?"

"That's him, doctor; that was Mysterious Mike himself. Gee, I'm afraid for me job every time he gives me the double O with that snaky eye of his."

The doctor gamboled down the street after the round figure that was paddling toward a trolley line. He would capture Bowen, be lively and learned with him, go some place with him and buy him a drink, and make a quick contest of his heart. He caroled: "Oh, Mr. Bowen!"

Bowen turned slowly, stopped, stared. The doctor was uncomfortable. Bowen's face was puffy, an ordinary, unimportant face; but his eyes were inhuman with contempt for strangers who hailed him on the street. Doctor Doremus was dismayed. In this commoner he felt the power of big affairs.

"Well?" Bowen was stuffily saying.

"I am Doctor Doremus, head of your proprietary department ———"

"Well?"

"Always thought—like to meet you—admired you so much from afar." The doctor coughed, tittered, and waited for the great man to give him his hand to kiss.

"Well?"

"Well, I was going your way—walk tr-trolley—thought maybe some day—get chance to meet you—talk over many problems in my department—uh, my department—new problems preparing—I mean appearing—since Jordan left———"

"Well, well, well! What can I do for you?"

"Oh, I don't want to bother you, don't want to——— Though maybe sometime, when you had leisure, you might honor me with your company at dinner at the University Club, and we could talk over—problems—great ambition see firm advance———"

"Well, Mr.—Doremus, wasn't it?—if you have any ideas I'd be glad to have you make memos of them and forward them to me—through Mr. Purdy. Now if you will pardon me——— I'm in something of a hurry."

Without a bow, with his malevolent eyes steady to the last, Bowen left him. The doctor stood like a boy sent home by his elder brother. A flush crawled up his face, while he hopelessly cursed. "The dirty, ungrateful swine!"

He almost decided to keep Purdy in his position as vice president, and to get hold of Bowen's interests. It was outrageous to think of himself and fine gentle old Purdy working for this egomaniac!

He began to tiptoe about Purdy. He got himself invited out for a weekend. Purdy insisted on inviting Mrs. Doremus, too, though doctor delicately tried to hint that his wife, while she was a very worthy woman, was not brilliant. It was an exasperating visit. The Purdys lived in a shambling house, and were irritatingly enthusiastic about chickens and gardening.

When the doctor got Purdy away from the gabbling women and tried to talk business sensibly, Purdy showed his weakness in the way he sighed: "I hope things will go better in the business." He alarmed the doctor by his frequent expressions of admiration for McCabe, and made it worse by taking it for granted that McCabe was the doctor's dearest friend, so that the doctor had to smile and bob and echo the praise.

He had been lunching with McCabe often, and in the chattiest way, but he was shockingly weary of the man's twittering. He saw that he would have to get rid of this sneaking rival at once; and he saw that his Napoleonic vision had, as usual, been inspired when he had guessed that he could never depend upon Purdy as an ally.

The first thing Monday morning he flew in to see Beecher Drew, and bluntly said:

"Come on out to lunch with me this noon. Things going to the devil round this shop! You and I have got to take hold."

The treasurer slowly nodded, and agreed.

"Yes! Sure I'll come! At your service!"

It took them less than a month to get rid of that jocose Jackass, McCabe.

Napoleon Doremus didn't waste time on him, as he did on Jordan and Zitterel. He discovered that he didn't have to explain all his reasons to Drew. The treasurer seemed tacitly to understand that they two were to run everything to suit themselves. Indeed, it was Drew who suggested that he might go to Purdy and complain about the amount of money McCabe was spending. At the same time, by agreement with Drew, Doctor Doremus had a very clever chemist, with drug-manufacturing experience and a large, open, florid manner, call on Purdy and hint that he would like to go to work for the Bowen Company, as he did not "see a sufficient future in his present connection."

Purdy whined and regretted. Drew bulkily insisted and McCabe went. The doctor did not have a farewell lunch with him. He had passed his youthful desire for such wasting of energy upon the soft organisms that were being disposed by evolution, assisted by evolution's closest friend, R. Chester Doremus, M.D.

Drew was daily in franker and more admiring communication with him. McCabe was gone, and McCabe's successor never got an order from Purdy without coming to ask the doctor about carrying it out.

After that it was easy for the doctor.

VII

Doctor Doremus and Beecher Drew had for six months been in complete control of Purdy, who leaned upon their strength and took the clever advice of the doctor, which Drew usually seconded. They were a triumvirate; they all went to lunch together, and talked without restraint about every detail of office work and personnel— that is, Purdy talked without restraint. He admitted to them that Bowen had brusquely told him he could have another year of control of the company, inasmuch as Bowen was occupied with the more important affairs of lumber-land deals. If he didn't pull the business out of the hole in that time Bowen would discharge him and everybody else in sight, and take hold himself.

Purdy wasn't pulling it out of the hole. He was exhausted. He desperately tried every suggestion that the doctor made—and the doctor was still a good suggester in regard to everything, from the quality of their gum guaiacum to the best make of clock to prod the office force into punctuality. The doctor was surprised to find out how much harder it was for him to produce really original suggestions, but he could always think of some change to make— and he did.

Somehow, probably because Purdy was unable to carry out even the best ideas, the business kept seeping away to the Vanvick Company, despite the doctor's inspirations. Purdy looked very shabby these days, in a suit of blue serge so worn that in a cross light it glittered like metal. The doctor, however, was anticipating the day that was bound to arrive when the boorish Bowen should come to his senses and put the business into his hands. He looked tailor-made and new. He was spending every cent he made, and he borrowed money to buy a larger car. A man of affairs like himself needed the relaxation of luxury.

He spent more time at the club, and he actually gave some of the promised jobs to his young followers. Indeed, one of his chief functions to Purdy was getting rid of subordinates; and whenever the triumvirate went out to lunch together, when they stood waiting for an elevator, intimate and low-voiced and exclusive, lords of destiny to the office peasantry, they were secretly observed by a hundred anxious glances followed by a hundred unspoken queries as to who would next be abruptly—though almost always cordially—fired by Doctor Doremus.

For there were subordinates in the office and factory—oh, yes, beneath the rarefied plane upon which our Napoleon moved in cosmic meditations there were some hundreds of inconspicuous privates who dared to have families and ambitions and hungers of their own! When Doctor Doremus had succeeded Jordan as superintendent of the proprietary department he had "made important changes" in the lives of thirty employees within one month.

Once, the comradeship of the conference had extended down the line; no one had been uncomfortable in jesting with his assistant. Now round the office there was an incessant, shaky murmur. Clerks started when the doctor or even Purdy passed their desks, and began to shuffle madly through work. Clerks were always peering over the tops of their desks, watching, speculating, studying the chiefs.

Whether he spoke to underlings so justly that they went away gouging their palms and chewing their lips, or whether he encouraged them and promised them that if they would keep on working a little harder every day he would speak to Purdy about a raise for them just as soon as business picked up, Doctor Doremus was careful never to let them know what he really thought of them. He saw that the first high duty of a silken diplomat was to keep everybody guessing.

He had become a genius at indirectness. He couldn't even walk straight to a water cooler to take a drink. He would stalk out of his den, stop before the office clock, compare it with his watch, frown at it, discover with surprise the existence of the cooler, sneak up on it and taste the water suspiciously, glancing about as though to say that the fact that he drank water like any simple-hearted plebeian did not indicate that he was going to allow anybody to be impudent to him.

It has all happened before; this story of Doctor Doremus might be told of thousands of offices of hundreds of kinds; and always it would have to register the intangible electric shocks that flash through the office, making big upstanding men as jumpy as schoolgirls, and making women weep for hours.

Epidemics of hysteria swept into the Bowen Company; swept from the crisp stenographers in the office to the gray-haired pensioner women and the grubby little girls down in the bottling and packing rooms of the factory. A typist would sob with sudden unhappiness, and lay her head on her desk, her thin, shabby shoulders hunching and shaking; then down the line would run the liquid fire of madness, and half a dozen women would be disheveled and crying. . . .

Usually someone was neatly discharged by Doctor Doremus after such a ridiculous attack. He had become an expert at hiring and firing. Once he had hated to see tears, but that had been in his salad days; now he was quietly efficient at getting rid of these obstructions to the blessed powers of evolution. . . . It was not true, however, he hotly told Purdy, that he had discharged that girl who had killed herself and her little sister by asphyxiation after failing to find another job; the girl was highly emotional and he had spoken gently to her.

Among the men of the office there was a different form of hysteria. They took to logrolling and scandal fetching. A factory hand tattled to a foreman, who tattled to a clerk in the proprietary department, who tattled to Doctor Doremus' immediate assistant, who came faithfully bringing the information to the doctor, all in the jolly manner of the House that Jack Built.

There were distinct alignments in three cliques. The dull-witted older employees thought that Purdy was still in charge. But the wise men saw that the doctor and Drew controlled everything, and they wore out their soles running to them, and their tongues saying

"Oh, yes, Doctor Doremus! Oh, yes, indeed, Doctor Doremus!" A third faction was composed of would-be deserters. More than once, on his rubber-heeled rounds of inspection, the doctor overheard subordinates telephoning to people at other firms. They spoke softly, and never used names—only initials and code words:

"You know what I told you about Pussy-fingers? Well, B. D. is standing right behind him. Say, see if you can't slip a hint to J. that I'd like to go to work at your place. Oh! Here's Pussy coming. Call y' up again. No; say, listen, meet me tonight—same place!"

It was very silly of them, smiled the doctor. He was paying the telephone girl five dollars a week to bring him all interesting information. She was an agreeable girl.

The employees often gathered in tiny groups that dissolved as soon as a chief appeared. They were always looking up when a friend came out of a chief's office, and muttering "What'd he say to you, Bill? Was D. D. in there?" All through the office everybody was strictly attending to everybody else's business; peeping at letters, listening to conversations. The soft confidences of Doctor Doremus and Beecher Drew were caught and repeated by hundreds of human microphones in a quaver of whispering—whispering—whispering.

Doctor Doremus was determined to get new business. He didn't care whether that hog of a Bowen received any income from the firm, but he did want to exhibit his own rare qualities. The thing to do was to put out a number of new brands, and let the Vanvick people keep the business they had stolen in competition with old brands. Drew agreed with him. But Purdy wanted to retrench, and also asserted that they hadn't enough cash on hand to experiment with new lines.

"Then we'll borrow it. You have the authorization from Bowen to do whatever you want to," boomed Beecher Drew.

It was an evening conference of the triumvirate. The main office outside of Purdy's room was dark and ghastly still.

Purdy shook his head feebly. Drew and the doctor, one on each side of him, pulled their chairs closer and glowered at him, under the unshaded electric globe, which betrayed Purdy's face as bristly, deep-creased, twitching. Impassive was Drew's face, and the doctor's was small and passionate.

Drew spoke slowly, tapping on the arm of Purdy's chair, at every word a tap that beat on the silence outside:

"See here, Purdy; come down to cases! You're an older man than the doc here. But so am I, by a good many years. I've got the sense to see that he has more brains than you or I. I stand ready to follow his lead. New brands, that's the stuff! The doc is the man to find the chemists to find the novelties. Are you going to wreck this firm by your stubbornness? I can borrow the money that will save us, man, save us!"

At midnight they were still arguing, as they came out into the dead factory street, and wavered across into a carmen's lunch room for ham and eggs.

But ten days later Beecher Drew borrowed the money—on a call loan.

Doctor Doremus had a lot of excellent ideas for using up that money.

After that it was easy for the doctor.

VIII

Somebody was to blame—probably the obstinate retail druggists who declined to take the Bowen novelties urged upon them, even with the containers, labels and advertising inspired by the doctor himself.

The doctor sat alone in his office after hours. So scrupulously fair was he that he wondered if he could have been to blame. Had he not been a little hard on men like Zitterel, Jordan, McCabe? But he saw that his disposition of them had been necessary; he saw that he was not bothered by any injustice, but merely by loneliness. Yes, he was lonely. He had grown apart from his wife. It bored him to go home in the evening. Beecher Drew was a heroic ally but not an amusing companion. His new associates were too obsequious to be interesting. He wanted Jordan and McCabe. Perhaps when he became vice president he could do something for them—give them minor jobs.

He did not trot about his office while he was meditating, as once he had been wont to do. He sat dumpily, smoking a very strong cigar. He was getting fat about the neck and shoulders. He took a mirror from a drawer in his desk and studied himself. Yes, and he was becoming gray.

He tossed the mirror on the desk, and in imitation of Drew he slapped the arm of his chair. Rats! All this was merely nerves. Trouble was, he decided, that his assistants were so stupid and treacherous that they made him fretful, instead of suave and merry, as he wished to be.

He walked to the University Club and dined alone, wishing that he knew just one decent chap with whom he could go to the theater. He walked two miles on his way home.

The exercise made him feel younger, and when he arrived at the office the next morning he was more calm, less impatient of that old idiot, Purdy.

But he landed in revolution let loose.

It was a little after ten. Drew pounded into his office, groaning "Just got phone—bank's going to call our loan!"

"Saints' sake! Don't tell Purdy! Wait! Let me think! We'll have to raise————"

"Had to tell Purdy. He's phoned to Bowen. Bowen is on his way here now!"

The doctor slumped down in his chair and simply breathed, long and noisily.

That afternoon Bowen called all heads into Purdy's office and in about seventy-five words informed them that he was going to accept a long-standing offer of the Vanvick Company for the plant, patents and good will of the Bowen Drug Company; that he himself would take care of all debts and contracts; and that he would now wish them all a good day. If they would call tomorrow they would find salary checks for a month ahead at the cashier's office.

In a curiously shrunken voice Doctor Doremus piped: "You mean I'm fired—me?"

"Hell, sir!" said Bowen dispassionately. "Do you think you are the only one?"

The doctor looked for comfort to Beecher Drew, who threw out his hands in token of astonishment at this ingratitude on the part of Bowen.

IX

The piled-up anxiety of two weeks spent in looking vainly for a new connection tumbled down when Doctor Doremus heard that

Beecher Drew had been made first vice president of the newly organized Vanvick-Bowen Drug Company.

For a week more he expected word from Drew. He had been foolish to worry about debts and lack of employment!

As he received no summons he went splendidly in his new motor car to call on his playmate. Drew came out immediately in response to the doctor's card. He stood at the inner door of the reception room, holding the card and beaming. He crooned:

"Well, doc, I been waiting to hear from you."

"Ye-es," fawned the doctor.

"Yes! Wanted to thank you for wrecking the Bowen Company! Ed Vanvick had sent me to the Bowen Company for that purpose. But I didn't need to do much except let you have your way. Quite a feat on your part. I might not have been able to put the Bowen Company on the rocks for a year more, except for your genius as a hypocrite and meddler. Oh, I know; I've watched you every second—and every time you dug a trench under somebody, I've underlaid it with a real trench of my own, and I was ready with the dynamite. But you always helped me, and I especially appreciate your volunteering to do it. I don't mind confessing all this to you, because nobody will ever believe a word you say now—with all the stories about you that are going round in the drug world."

While Doctor Doremus was gulping like a hungry pup Purdy passed through the reception room, amiably waving his hand. He looked prosperous. He had a new suit.

Beecher Drew commented: "Yes. Sure! I got Purdy here. We're glad to have him. He's an honest man. Not so inefficient, either, when he has subordinates he can trust. And I'll see to it that he does have! Fact, I'm thinking of hunting up Jordan and Zitterel. But not McCabe!"

"Then I guess you'll need me," the doctor whispered archly.

"You? I wouldn't have you round the place! But I do want to show my gratitude by giving you this."

Drew held out a five-cent cigar. He turned in the reception-room doorway. Doctor Doremus had never realized that Drew's back was so broad.

After that it wasn't easy for the doctor.

SNAPPY DISPLAY

INTRODUCING MR. LANCELOT TODD

Mr. Ad Man, YOU are the priest and poet of the commercial age. It's YOU that finds wares insensate as ditch-water, and etherealize them into a success that shines like the cumulus clouds of sunset. It's you that transmute Pittsburgh steel into African bridges and teach the pinch-minded provincial to read and travel. BUT—say, wait, brother! There's one gosh-awful great big BUT, get me, a B-U-T, broad as a barn door. BUT your ads must be founded on the excellence of the goods. You can flash up a rust-eaten stove on a full page set in seventy-two point Gothic BUT never make Doc Ultimate P. Consumer believe that the stove is honest-sure heating his little old shack. Top of the column, next to reading matter, with peppy copy done by Henry James of John J. Shakespeare or Billy Sunday, never yet turned a punkin into gold nugget. Brer Ad Man, get hooked up with a by-jiminy firm that produces the honest goods, the good goods, before you attempt the Snappy Display.

From "Yes, YOU, Mr. Ad Man," by Lancelot Todd.

Lancelot Todd isn't a whited sepulcher. His taste is too playful for whitewash. He prefers crimson, with polished brass trimmings. But he is one of our best sepulchers, and the inscription on him reads, "Lancelot lies."

Lancelot is an artist of advertising; a compound of punch, power, pep, and purest rot serene. You have doubtless heard his addresses, "Upward and Pupward," and "The Smash and Lash that put the Zing! in Advertising," which are so inspiringly delivered before Chautauquas, Y.M.C.A. business classes, and commercial clubs. In dozens of magazines you read his page poems regarding time-clocks and God and patriotism and daisies and What Gladstone Said to the Idle Young Man. You have noticed his editorials in syndicated house-organs, and his signed advertisements of everything from cocaine to arts-and-grafts coffins. You may even own one of his books; perhaps "Fishin' for Effishincy," or "Are You Toting Old Man Sloth on Your Shoulders?" or "It's the Bald-headed Boss that Keeps the Tops of His Desk Bald, Harry."

The pictures of Lancelot Todd. which are used as frontis-pieces to his books, present him as a refined person with a high-church top hat, white cord on the decolletage of his waistcoat, and a ribbon on his eyeglasses. In real life Lancelot is a youngish man of thirty-seven, who never looks natural without a striped waistcoat and a large highball. He usually looks quite natural.

He will sit and hypnotize you with an eye like a trusting aunt, while he tells you that he knows more about motor cars than a corner bootblack, more about politics than a Cape Cod barber, and more than enough about poetry, traffic routing, fallen arches, and cocktail-mixing. He lets you in on the dramatic inside facts about how often J. Pierpont Morgan, General Goethals, and David Belasco have to come and get his advice about their business. His manner is so quiet that it doesn't seem possible that he may be almost exaggerating.

He is framed for success. He has a smile, and an excellent memory for everything except debts, and his epidermis is so thick that it must have been the original model for concrete trenches.

Lancelot came from a little town. He was a grocery clerk, an excellent salesman, who could get rid of the mildewed prunes and the broken crackers. He was a good-looking youngster, with a straight nose, and a smile which he could switch on like an electric light. The girls looked into his eyes when he did the weighing. But his methodicalness was his ruin. He was too methodical about tapping the till.

He drifted as a boy tramp for a year. He got religion at a different mission every night; and by strict attention to business he became one of the most stirring converts and backsliders in the trade. He encountered the drunken editor of a small-town weekly, and was employed as his devil, reporter, valet, collector, and private bartender. The editor had once been a real newspaperman, trained in the use of ideals and Caslon Old Style. He taught Lancelot to look up every new word in the dictionary, and never to write "dainty refreshments were served" or "Peter Smith is on the sick list." Lancelot really mastered his craft as printer and item-chaser, and he had the native genius to apply to advertising the editor's principles of originality and directness. The town stores were glad to have him write their notices. By copying a list of sharp-sounding new words out of metropolitan dailies, walking out to Big Lake, and there standing thoughtfully kicking his left calf with his right foot in a transport of creation, Lancelot was able to think of new ways of saying that good shoes are good shoes, and he could get a half-page advertisement out of the Jewel Shoe Store.

Lancelot ventured to Boston, and became solicitor for an advertising agency. He was one of the first to think of taking a completed advertisement to a "prospect" and getting his order on it. He dressed like an actor, he talked like a medicine-show spieler, he always laughed at all jokes of all prospects, and he told the truth whenever he suspected that he was being tested. He joined every possible organization, from the Jolly Bowlers to The Young Men's Wesleyan Circle, and made a business of being familiar and agreeable with every member who had an income of more than four thousand dollars a year. He was so successful that he was no longer dishonest in money matters. . . . Scarcely at all.

With the pleasure of a movie actress in her first orange and lavender car, Lancelot acquired a secretary of his own—a man stenographer for the advertising agency, one Benny Simpson, who drew more salary for keeping his lips in a position of cloture than did most of the solicitors for opening them wide and often. Benny was about Lancelot's own age, twenty-nine. When Lancelot was, with pomp and salary, summoned to San Francisco to manage the advertising department of a newspaper, he took Benny Simpson along as private secretary.

With Benny to attend to details, Lancelot could give all his time to thinking of ways of making his assistants brisk and uncomfortable. He made good. He married the daughter of a real estate business, a girl little and pretty and believing. She died within the year. It is said that she was not sorry to die. . . . He made ten thousand by that deal.

In San Francisco Lancelot began to make speeches at public dinners; dynamic speeches, like the sort of dressing you put on oysters if you are not in a hurry to get off to the theater—tabasco and horseradish and lemon and pepper and salt; lively speeches, all about Initiative and Snap, and From the Siskiyous to the Golden Shores of the Southland, and It's the Worm that's Quick on the Trigger that Gets the Early Bird; plenty of humor and good rough humanness; not afraid to refer to pants and hell and sweat, where the stately college-bred speakers bored the guests by referring to Culture and Sound Conservatism. Lancelot heard that his newspaper had a bad reputation for being too humble to advertisers, and whenever he made a speech, whether it was about water power or his own specialty, gas power, he would state in a sacred ecstacy that he never asked the editorial staff whenever anything they wrote would affect the advertisers. "Gentlemen, I never ask them but one thing: 'Boys,' I say—and they are indeed The Boys to me; my own pals in the crusade to let the sun shine into every crevice of the affairs of mankind—'Boys,' I tell them, 'my department asks of yours but one thing; that every lad of you tell the grim-jawed, iron-fisted, by-thunder TRUTH!'" It is recorded that no one applauded this sentiment more than the large advertisers. But the reporters doing the story of the dinner rarely applauded.

Lancelot always went into the editorial department of his paper on one and the same errand. He advanced into the managing editor's corner, protectively holding a twenty-five cent cigar in front of him, and smiled rapturously.

The editor got ready to dodge, and examined the cigar to see if it was loaded, while Lancelot tilted his chair, rocked a little, and sang, "Great sheet you're getting out, old man."

The editor still looked suspicious, though he took the band off the cigar and put it into his pocket, to show it to his wife later.

"Yes, sir," said Lancelot, "it's a great comfort to work on a paper with a real live managing editor, old man."

"Ug?" grunted the editor.

"There's just one thing: I was kind of sorry to see you run that story about the elevator that fell in the San Dinero Building."

"Why, that was a good story."

"Yes, but, my dear man, I was just about to close a contract with the owner for ten thousand lines. Now you know, old man, I'm the last to ever think of soft-soaping advertisers, but at the same time, I would like to know how you expect me to get advertising when your bright young reporters can destroy a month's campaign by writing any irresponsible thing they please about big interests. Bad for business, yes, sir; destroys confidence. What the readers like is bright, boosting, constructive news—not all this darn destructive stuff about divorce scandals and murders and accidents. Trouble with you fellows"—Lancelot beamed softly, to show how friendly he was—"is that you don't know Common Folks the way we business men do! You literary fellows get off by yourselves too much. Now take this San Dinero accident. Who wants to read about an elevator dropping a little, and some boob Dago getting shaken up? If you'd run a story about the new real estate developments at Alameda, that would interest the whole section. And don't forget that really you hurt a business man's feelings when you insinuate that just because of some one slip, he isn't O.K. You know we're all fallible. I'm back of you boys, first, last, and all the time, but I don't see how you can expect us to finance you, if you alienate the influential guys that are our meal tickets."

The editor got his head above the cataract, swam desperately, reached shore, and sputtered, "All right! All right!"

"You see, old man? Uh, say, by the way; I don't see any use of our running a follow-up on that San Dinero elevator accident, do you?"

"No, no!"

On his next visit, Lancelot would be just as comradely and hurt and surprised and explanatory as on the visit before, and by this means he got the editorial staff into a mood of dull apathy in which it seemed easier to keep out news offensive to Business Interests than to endure another call from Lancelot.

There was but one markedly disagreeable incident in his San Francisco period. He had found Benny Simpson, the secretary whom he had brought from Boston, incapable of understanding his finer aspirations. Also, after the death of his bright little bride, Lancelot was lonely. He had discovered a pretty stenographer with large eyes and a hundred words a minute and great sympathy for his secret soul. He wanted to help her make a career. He explained that to Benny, and told Benny that he would be glad to find him another job.

Benny looked at him stolidly, and said, "Nope, boss, nothing doing. I like my salary, and you amuse me. I decline to be fired."

Lancelot was as red as his noble mahogany desk, then as green as the carpet that gave an unjournalistic splendor to his office. "Well, say, Benny, I knew you were a willing little worker, but I didn't know you'd reached the position were you could tell me————"

"Can the persiflage, boss. I'll do you work, but I don't have to stand for the high-minded stuff that you write to advertisers. Nothing doing on your carrying this girl away on your next trek. I don't trust you. I stay right on the job. By the way, boss, I still got a carbon of your agreement with the Jannsen Ink people to use your influence to land them in solid here. Get me? Now I like you, boss; you do amuse me. But if I were canned, I might almost get so I disliked you, see?"

Lancelot called Benny different kinds of a modified fool, and dropped the subject. When he was called to New York, as advertising manager for the new Taconite Lode Mining and Smelting Company, he took Benny with him.

His lovely little books with embossed covers and four-color cuts are still classics of encouragement to the unthinking mass to make twenty-five percent, and clear off the mortgage, lift the burden from Father's shoulders, and give little ones an education. . . . Before the Federal investigation of Taconite, Lancelot had severed connection, and become advertising manager for a motor company. He was one of the creators of the Out to the Broad Smiling Land school of motor advertising. And his job was but a quarter of his activity. On the side, he carried a full line of prophecy and wisdom.

Even as the poet's poet is Shelley, and the prizefighter's prizefighter is the press-agent, so was Lancelot Todd becoming the advertising man whose moral injunctions every would-be advertising man had to read. He began that series of Tip Talks—about being honest, writing business letters with Punch, Developing Personality, and keeping your fingernails clean—which were to develop into his famous books.

He was frequently asked to give addresses, and he spent his weekends in going from town to town, spilling wisdom, and receiving dinners, silver-headed canes, praise, and other junk to which public characters must submit. He started a house organ which he syndicated among forty establishments of forty different sorts. Employers purchased them and distributed them free. He kept Benny Simpson busy an hour a day finding anecdotes about the frugal boyhoods of great men, for use in the house organ; and he got an artist in reduced circumstances to do, for two dollars apiece, wash-drawing of James J. Hill working in a general store, John D. Rockefeller discovering golf, and Benjamin Franklin eating Philadelphia rolls. The house organ brought Lancelot seven thousand dollars a year, and it was worth it. It has been estimated that in one year, it kept sixteen employees from bothering their good, kind bosses by asking for raises.

In a few months he saw that his work for the motor company was merely a waste of time, and he became a freelance.

Power, sheer power, that's what makes a man kind to the kiddies in his shop, Mr. Boss. It's only the big, honest-to-God he-car that can do a pussy-foot pace of two miles an hour on high in the peerade. If you have the power, you'll be big enough to sympathize—understand, and you'll be able to so understandingly and sympathetically handle every man jack and lassie jill of your staff that there won't be a sub-microscopic one of 'em that will knock you. Don't ask for Loyalty—give 'em JUSTICE, and you couldn't duck their loyalty, not if you tried! I've never had a human working for me yet that didn't regard the Old Man as his best friend, on stage and off!

From "Loyalty, Lies, and D——— Lies," by Lancelot Todd.

Low persons have asserted that the one way not to succeed as a lady-killer is to be too respectful. One chuck deftly placed beneath the chin is worth seven decorous kissings of the hand, they declare, and they uphold the Code Napoleon, which is: Treat 'em rough. The same treatment is at times efficacious in wooing words. Mr.

Lancelot Todd treated words rough. He slapped them and tickled them and made them bounce and giggle; and the advertisers who were accustomed to pay thirty-five dollars a week to a well-bred college man who treated words respectfully and made them grammatical and neat, were anxious to pay Lancelot thousands for his special advertisements.

In his own private plant, he manufactured moral articles and books and addresses and house organs. But his best line was signed advertisements. The great common people were beginning to recognize him as the bard of bacon, the sweet singer of shotguns, and they seemed to like it when he yawped, "No, siree, Ned, this ain't an ad for you, if you believe that Progress stopped with our grouchy granddads."

His staff consisted of Benny Simpson, as general manager, with two copywriters, a combination solicitor and publicity agent, six stenographers, and a scared office boy. Lancelot trained his copywriters to go out and get facts about goods, and to prepare copy in imitation of his own saffron style. Then he split up their infinitives, and introduced a few errors and a couple of handshakes into their efforts, thus giving them the genuine Todd flavor.

For the first time Lancelot had a number of people responsible to him alone, and as he became more busy, more nervous, he had the advantage of being able to take it out on his staff. No one could snap at an office girl, for powdering her nose or being late, more efficiently than he. . . . Benny Simpson says that Lancelot had to have a glass top to his desk, to keep it from being warped by the tears shed over it by the stenographers. Lancelot used to sit and watch them interestedly, and hasten to dictate rhapsodies on the pathetic romances of a poor office girl.

In fact, he was enjoying himself thoroughly.

He was cashing in on success. His earnings had risen from fifteen thousand a year to forty thousand. He was hysterical with it. He had all the stammering excitement of a small boy who has found a dollar. When he wasn't working he was letting the world know how rich he was. He bought a striped roadster with an enormous gas tank behind the seats. He sometimes kept a taxi waiting for him all day long, with the meter running. He hired a restaurant for an evening, and invited all the showgirls of the *Kiss Me, Kismet*

Kid company to be his guests, on champagne and otherwise intimate terms. He was particularly small-boyish in his delight in telegrams, wireless, long distance telephone calls, and private cars.

These diversions kept his forty thousand in mobile circulation, and to keep up, he had to drive his staff even harder. Whenever he came into the office they bent to work like willows crouching before a tornado. Lancelot would have been almost sorry for them, at times, if he had not realized that soppy sentimentality would be a bad influence upon the youngsters he was training. So he put aside his own impulsive desires, and saw to it that they worked ten hours a day. He was everywhere praised as a friend to the laboring classes, and by no one was Lancelot more eagerly cheered than by Mr. Todd.

The cheers were echoed by all the other members of the Big Boosters' Club, which is an informal organization of optimists. The Reverend J. Murray Sitz, the much interviewed pastor of the Church of Modernity, which meets in the Frou-frou Theater, declared in an address before the Real Estate and Religion Club of Brooklyn that "Lancelot Todd is a better preacher than I ever expect to be. He has the pen of an angel. It lets sunshine and pep into gloomy minds. He has the voice of an angel. It carries to the farthest nations the good tidings about American enterprise. I am a firm believer that the heathen Chinee gets as much good out of Lancelot Todd's publicity for Dimpletoe Stockings as out of theology and psalm-singing."

By the most amazing coincidence, in the very next number of his house-organ Lancelot chronicled a Little Talk with the Big Man, the big man being the Reverend J. Murray Sitz of the Church of Modernity. Said Lancelot, "There's one preacher who gives a snap to psalm-singing, and keeps theology from being logy. He is an upstanding, handmade, he-man, and he preaches a gospel that a business man can practice. Murray Sitz is a booster, not a knocker; an up-building and regular guy; and he don't have to wear a nightie in the pulpit to make you feel the reality of his religion."

In the stress of all this brotherly love, and commercial missionary work, Lancelot was getting slightly brown under the eyes. He found it necessary to be tolerant toward a good many cocktails every evening, and a good many headache powders every morning. His celebrated exhortation to young men to "rise at five A.M.—not as a duty and a goldarnbore, but as a priceless privilege, since thus you have two hours the jump on the stuffy-heads and drunks who lie abed" was not dictated at five A.M. It was given forth at one P.M., Lancelot being at the time recumbent in a walnut-and-cane-treatment bed, with his voice still dusky from an all-night spree. . . . Nevertheless, the oracle certainly did increase the sales of Cheery Chime Alarm Clocks.

Peace, and stars, and the light of a robin's laugh—these are the luxuries of the poor. Did you never hear the fable of old man Ulysses who, with argosies swelling to the pompous might of the booming billows, went down the long sea-road questing—no, little one, NOT the purple question mark of new empery, but the quiet period of his own small home? Gets me how any man can be so much in love with biting off his own foolish red nose as to desire the insincerities and queasy plotting of SOCI-ETY! Breaking into the Smart Set! Right, Gustavus, that's the worst BREAK there is! All I want is an old friend, and a quiet fireplace, and let the fools scatter their hard-earned corn for the chic chickens. I'll never catch 'em at their foolishness! They can be in society like a mice and I'll never know! I'm too busy reading the Bible, and a fragrant bouquet of poetry, and a few books about engineering, and a hey-bo! letter from an old pal, to have any time to read the Sassiety Colyum and learn about their triumphs!

From "The Little Gray Home in the —Everywhere," by Lancelot Todd.

Mr. Todd was now ready to take up the solid duties of a leading citizen and ally himself with all that was most comely in the body politic. He saw that he belonged in society, delicately dallying with the fine old families who know about polo, Tagore and custom-made towncars. He looked back with pity on a certain young Lancelot who had wasted his time on mere business men.

Mr. Todd put himself into the hands of a conservative tailor, a dancing master, and a teacher of auction bridge. He got himself proposed at the Avenue Club. He got acquainted with the smart young men who were solicitors for *Piquant Pickings*.

Good old *Pickings*, as its regular readers call it, is the most consistently moral publication in America. It never contaminates its columns by the mention of anyone with less than twenty thousand a year, and that income must not be made by pork packing, authorship, or any of the other less aristocratic trades. It gives the most stimulating details of the loves of really nice people. Many a humble clerk has been roused to ambition by reading in *Pickings* about what Whimpy Vanscutte said to his mother's maid when he was humorously drunk.

To be an advertising solicitor for *Pickings* is one of the few gentlemanly jobs which a young man about town can hold. It is almost as gentlemanly as having no visible means of support except a wife. The *Pickings* solicitors are a body of young Samurai. They are level-eyed and courteously insolent; they are scholarly in regard to trouserings, and they all have mustaches like camel's-hair brushes— small camel's-hair brushes for use by quite little children. They go about to the offices of vulgar manufacturers and coldly permit these common fellows to force space contracts into their hands. Mr. Todd had met the young Samurai, and remarked that they were "sap-headed snobs." But as he made a business of reading *Pickings* and *Boudoir* and the society columns of the High Class Circulation newspapers, and discovered that they were related to some of the most prominent residents of Newport and the Atlanta Penitentiary, he began to appreciate the manner in which the young Samurai cut their business acquaintances on the street.

He saw that their cars were not striped, but solid black, with slippery black upholstery, so he bought a black expensive car that was so much the real thing that it looked like a hearse. He spoke admiringly to the Samurai at the Avenue Club, and whenever they condescended to listen, he offered to introduce them to valuable clients. Sometimes they permitted him to buy them champagne. But if he went so far as to say, "I see your sister is back from Coronado," they would say "Oh?" exactly in the manner of a sparrow with sciatica.

He made a practice of telephoning business tips to them, on Saturday, and saying wistfully, "You live at Tuxedo, don't you? I'm going to be motoring out near there tomorrow." Never did the Samurai invite him to drop in and take jackpot luck. They piped, "Oh? I fancy yuh find very decent roads. G'bye."

He knew that if he could get past their guard to their women-folks, he would have a chance to bore into society. He did have a way with women; he grinned at them as though he knew what they were thinking, whereupon they were wildly curious to find out whether he really knew.

His good little heart was now in a most trustful state; it was ready to be very tender toward any of the oppressed race of women, providing only that they were smart, beautiful, rich, and not too exacting about drinking, gambling, and slang. When he was in this democratic mood, Miss Cordelia Evans came out for suffrage.

Miss Evans was the only daughter of Mrs. Blenkheim Evans, who invented society. Miss Evans was tall and white and stately. Dukes made love to her, when she went abroad. She was gay of manner, and had read all about economics, and played a game of tennis which Molla Bjurstedt had praised. She announced to the reporters that she was going to campaign for suffrage in New York. She was appointed assistant in the publicity bureau.

Mr. Todd had his clipping bureau send him every item about Miss Evans. He had a strange feeling that here at last was his lady of dreams, for whom he had kept himself so pure and unspotted all these years.

He called upon Miss Evans to offer his services to the cause of suffrage as an expert publicity man, free. He spoke to her reverently, and made two quite good repartees, and in five minutes showed her how to reconstruct a pamphlet about Suffrage and the Home. His manner was brotherly, modest, friendly, with just a touch of delighted awe, and Miss Evans and he smiled at each other a good deal.

She sent him copy to revise. She telephoned him for advice. She went out to tea with him, and became tearful over his splendid tirade against office managers whom he had heard nagging their women assistants. She invited him to address a Newark meeting at which she was chairman, and at the end of the ringing eulogy on the business women he knew, she ran forward and shook his hand— a boyish, comforting handshake which pledged comradeship.

He scientifically charted the progress of their acquaintanceship, and in less than a month he felt it time to release the following advertisement:

Dear lady, I must be very stern with you about one thing! You are mistaken in supposing that I can really add anything to your splendid campaign. Service, yes, I give that gladly. But I am merely a man-at-arms, following the banner of you, who are our dear Joan of Arc.

She answered that she wasn't really very good at Joanning; that it was she who must serve and he who must lead; that they needed Mr. Todd not so much because of his eloquence and skill in publicity as because of his "great-hearted passion for justice to women, all women."

Then he was invited to an Evans reception.

Society, like business, was capitulating before the sterling worth of our handmade man.

He had never been able to tell whether Miss Cordelia Evans really was fond of him. But at the reception, which was an ant-heap of males with distinguishing eyeglasses and females with well-bred dowdiness, he found Miss Evans coming back to him as often as she could get away. She laughed low with him, and at his deft praise she bridled like a girl.

As he rode home he chuckled to himself, "My Lord, she falls for me like a thousand of brick. She isn't as good-looking as I thought she was. I never did care much for these horses of women. But still, she has got some brains, and an awful drag with the inside bunch in society. And if she bores me, after I marry her, there's plenty of cute kids in this old burg to play with on the side."

Just when Mr. Todd was most burdened with business and with falling thus passionately in love, his ungrateful general manager, Benny Simpson, took occasion to become obnoxious by introducing a low "lady-friend" into the office.

I knew a man who knocked advertising—He's out of business.
I knew a man who knocked every boss he had—He's out of a job.
I knew a man who knocked his home city—He's down and out.
I knew a man who knocked the fair name of a woman—He's out of
    jail BUT HE WON'T BE LONG.
            From "Boosters and Boobs," by Lancelot Todd.

In his capacity as Doctor of Human Chemistry, as the Reverend J. Murray Sitz had so justly called him, Mr. Todd was able to observe with amusement the clumsy attempt of Benny Simpson to spy on him in his social triumphs. Benny was not only ill-bred, but he was also a failure. Mr. Todd and he had started even; Benny was still at the movie and subway level, while Mr. Todd felt perfectly at home in a box at the French theater, and even understood several words of the French.

Benny jeered at him, "Must be swell to go to all these receptions, boss. What do all you aristocrats talk about? Do you ask old Mis' Vanastor how Pa's rheumatism is, and Reggie Widenfish how he's getting along carrying his paper rowt?"

Mr. Todd ignored him, and secretly wrote a seven-line masterpiece about The I-Knew-Him-When Guy which is today carried in the pocketbooks of more than one hundred self-made capitalists.

The most amusing thing to watch was Benny's reverence for Miss Cordelia Evans. Miss Evans called at the office, tall and brisk in her blue serge suit and smart boots and broad black hat. From his private office Mr. Todd could see how Benny ran to receive her. Mr. Todd realized that Miss Evans was a good-looking wench, but it did tickle his renowned sense of humor to see how Benny acted as though Miss Evans were the amateur champion lightweight Joan of Arc of America.

When Mr. Todd was compelled to discharge his girl secretary for supposing that he meant to be insulting when he playfully stroked her wrist, he ordered Benny to get a new secretary, and Benny brought in one Miss Bangs, a prissy woman of thirty, with tight brown hair and dark blue glasses which Mr. Todd's aesthetic soul could not endure. She was as inspiring as a pair of rubbers.

Mr. Todd tried her on dictation. She was quick and accurate, and he had to find some other reason for getting rid of her. Benny seemed to be a friend of hers. Mr. Todd saw them talking in corners. Just for the fun of it, to see what their reactions would be, the Doctor of Human Chemistry said to Benny, in Miss Bangs' presence, "Say, Simpson, this young lady is good enough to hack, but I can't stand those blue glasses. You'll have to get me something a little livelier to look at."

Benny resented this clever thrust at his lady-friend with all the swift wrath of a mud turtle. His chest bulged, his eyes opened, he curved his tongue out round his lips. But Miss Bangs was violently shaking her head at him. Mr. Todd was diverted to see how much these females will stand in order to hold down their picayune jobs.

It took him a whole week to find a good reason for firing Miss Bangs, and not till the day of his greatest social triumph was he able to get rid of her, though he went through his regular scientific system of blaming her for losing every paper that he himself had mislaid. But on a Saturday he told her to stay till eight o'clock, to get out some rush work. With the usual clock-watching laziness of women employees, she whined that she had promised her brother to go out to his house in the country. So Mr. Todd was at last able to discharge her with propriety. He saw Benny Simpson glaring at him. He felt that he would have to have a fatherly talk with Benny. Then, whistling cheerfully, swinging his stick and looking down on the poor home-going mob who were not invited to a Great Social Event, Mr. Todd walked to his hotel.

He had at last been welcomed to the real inner circle of the Evans set. He had been bidden to one of their intimate dinner parties. He planned to get a chance to whisper to Cordelia, during the evening. He had, he chuckled, yet to see the female he couldn't "make fall for the whispering stuff."

Just once, let me toot my own bugle. Step by step, making sure the old feet—big, but solid, by heck!—are firmly planted on one rung before I take the next, everlastingly checking up on how I stand with my fellow men and women and the spirit of the cosmos, thus do I go ahead. When I'm THERE, I'm THERE, and I don't hit the greased slide for the Down and Out Bin.

From "Then Go Ahead—or Afoot!" by Lancelot Todd.

Mr. Todd shaved twice and tied his dress tie three times. He must have been a valet! He thought more about the valet than about Cordelia Evans. Cordelia was a cinch; these big bossy women were twice as easy to handle as the wiry little devils. He gloated, "*Quelque* evening, kid; think of Old Man Todd's little boy Lance knocking out Sassiety with a cake of soap in a sock, and dragging it off!" He did a small dance, and went imperially down to his waiting car.

It was pleasant to have his own chauffeur waiting; to give the Evans' Park Avenue address; to be received by an English butler.

Mrs. Evans greeted him with blinking dignity. Miss Cordelia held out her warm hand to him. "I want to talk to you, when I get the chance," he whispered. She hesitated, flushed, then confessed her admiration with, "Yes, I—I want to learn about the real you!"

Miss Evans turned him over to a bouncing squab, and till dinner was announced, Mr. Todd enjoyed himself enormously. He took the squab in to dinner, and found that she didn't mind his squeezing her arm.

He was too much interested in her to notice the other guests till they reached the table. Then he found that the girl on the other side of him was somehow familiar. She was small and trim, with wonderfully waved brown hair, and a delicate throat rising from a frock all silver tissue and straight lines. But she was at least thirty, and her eyes were too serious. Mr. Todd had no time to waste on these serious hens. He did not look at the stranger again till they were seated. Then he realized, with a feeling as though the butler had dropped a bucket of ice down his back, that beyond the serious woman sat Benjamin Simpson.

An hour before he had left Benny Simpson at the office, snuffy in spectacles and an alpaca coat. Here he was in eyeglasses and reasonable evening clothes.

Mr. Todd felt that there was something fatally wrong with a social success which let Benny Simpson in. He began nervously to study the serious woman beside him. If she were tabbily dressed, and masked with blue spectacles, she would resemble Benny's lady-friend, the clumsy stenographer whom he had discharged that afternoon.

Mr. Todd's glance sneaked about the table. Miss Cordelia Evans was oblivious to him. He had a sense of spies and danger.

"Listen, my children," announced Miss Evans' clear voice. "I want you to hear an amusing story. You know what an earnest soul Rose Bangs is—she drove frivolous me into suffrage. Well, there is a big manufacturer of, oh, it doesn't matter what, who wanted to get a contract out of a charity I am interested in. We almost gave it to him, but his general manager, who is a splendid, rigidly honest man, awfully quiet but beautifully on, hated to see us taken in, and he came to me and made me promise to investigate the manufacturer first. So Rose Bangs went to work for him, ostensibly as a humble stenographer, and I want her to tell about her adventures.

The serious woman beside Mr. Todd spoke. Her voice was that of the stenographer whom he had just discharged.

"It wasn't really such an amusing experience. It was tragic. This man told our charity society that he spent all his days and nights trying to free women. I found him about the most pretentiously ignorant and conceited and casually cruel puppy I ever encountered. He kept everyone till six-thirty or seven, when they were breaking with weariness. One man in the office had a chance to get another job, and this boss lied to him about intending to raise his salary, till it was too late for him to get the other job. Once the manufacturer gave my friend, the general manager, the man who got me in there, the most frightful scolding for advancing a girl ten dollars, when her mother was sick—and he had the cheek to put it entirely on moral grounds; said it would get the girl into bad habits! He lied to everybody in the office—in a way it was funny, the naive manner in which the poor silly supposed the staff was taken in by his bluffing. One time———"

When Miss Bangs had finished her tale, the whole table broke out in a babble of discussion.

The squab thrilled to Mr. Todd. "Don't you think a man like that ought to be lynched. I'm going to get Rose Bangs to tell me his name, and I'll let people know about him."

Across the table a man was asserting, "Don't suppose there are many rotten cads like that in business, though. I always cut connections with any man in my line who lies to his own people. Who is this fellow, Miss Bangs?"

"Oh, he doesn't really matter. He will die of heart disease from loving himself so much," said Miss Bangs languidly.

Mr. Todd could not look at her. He gawped toward the squab, who was urging him, "What do you think ought to be done to a man like that?"

"Well, you must remember he may have some excuse," said Todd feebly.

"Yes, that's so. Perhaps he's just a poor common fellow who's been raised above his station," agreed the squab. She had charming manners; she had been trained by a careful mamma to assent to all the statements of marriageable men.

Mr. Todd did not enjoy his dinner much. He had, he explained to the squab, a sudden affliction of the throat which made it hard for him to talk.

The affliction grew worse so rapidly that he had to go home directly after dinner. When he said good night to Miss Evans, she was bright but not loquacious.

Benny Simpson was standing beside Miss Rose Bangs in the drawing-room. As he came near them, Mr. Todd saw that they were, in the most simple-hearted fashion, holding hands. With an excellent assumption of carelessness, Mr. Todd observed, "Good night, Simpson. By the way, you needn't report at the office Monday, dear chap. I'll send your personal belongings to your home."

"Thanks, I've already taken them home—*and* my salary! By the way, Miss Bangs and I are starting an advertising agency of our own; the kind where we get the good goods before we do the snappy display, dear old chap."

SLIP IT TO 'EM

BEING A STORY OF LANCELOT TODD, THE PROPHET OF PROFITS

It is perfectly easy to choose a motor car. Most makes are reliable, today. You won't waste money even if you excavate a secondhand Twin-Asthmatic, and have to add wire wheels, slip covers, a hand-warmer, a cigar-lighter, a tire pump, an ammeter, a dammeter, a private massage parlor, a new top, a new body, and a new chassis. You are safe if you heed just one caution: Don't Buy a Vettura Six.

Yet even a Vettura isn't so bad if you care more for impressing the family across the street than for getting the milk cans to the station in time for the early train. While the Vettura isn't much good for running in traffic or on boulevards or on country roads, it looks robust, and the axles almost never break when it is in storage. The thing to do with a Vettura is to walk home, and have dinner quite early, and run the car carefully out of the garage and round in front of the house. Then the family can sit there all evening, while the neighbors admire the splendid line and big hood. When everybody in the vicinity has gone off to bed, you can push it back to the garage by hand—under its own power it probably would not stand up under a trip to and from the garage, not both in the same evening.

Another way to get the best results with a Vettura is to remove the engine entirely. Of course it won't run very fast that way, but it will give much less trouble. You see, the Vettura engine is a sensitive, shrinking blossom. You can't expect it to stand rough pounding, as though it were a truck, for it is the creation of the poet of pep, the superman of snappy displays, the father of the slap-'em-on-the-back style of advertising—Mr. Lancelot Todd.

Mr. Todd is a freelance publicity expert and business consultant. He is so broad-minded that he can write notices for the prohibitionists and the distillers simultaneously, and so loyal to the Better Classes that he devotes as much attention to choosing light, tasty spats as he does to the lectures he delivers before audiences of nice, clean, ambitious young men, inspiring them to save money, so that he can come and take it away from them on his next trip.

He is as talented in giving first aid to wounded corporations as he is in writing optimistic prose poems for the magazines. Butler Ballard was indeed wise when he came to Lancelot for advice about creating a higher standard of mechanics for the public—and a higher standard of living for himself.

It is true that Lancelot is not noted for his practical mechanical knowledge. He couldn't adjust the carburetor on a dollar watch. But he does pre-eminently understand what the People need. They need to have their money kept in circulation, and Lancelot is the human circulation pump.

Ballard had just inherited the control of the Ballard Coach Works, which had been making carriages for a hundred years, and automobile custom-bodies for ten. He was a gentleman debutant, with a nine-dollar silk shirt, squirrel teeth, and invisible eyebrows.

He asserted, "Say, uh, Mr., uh, Todd, I have been thinking— I've been thinking———"

Lancelot tried not to look incredulous at this improbable statement. He brought out the cigarette cabinet, and the smile with which he encourages the widows and orphans. It is a kindling smile; it spreads from rounding mouth to steely eyes, and beams love for everything from the human race to the lesser fur-bearing animals. Young Ballard toasted his chilly soul in the smile, and hitched onward:

"I been thinking, the Ballard-made body for motors has such a thunderin' big reputation, we ought to put out a car of our own. And we have the capital to back it. Fellow, club, advised me to see you, said you were a wiz at advertisin', maybe get you to give me some suggestions, or even take charge of advertisin'————"

"Have you engaged your engineer?"

"No."

"Then I'll consider it, if you will agree to give me complete charge of organizing the business—manufacture, distributing, service, publicity, and everything else."

Ballard looked as though he wanted to escape, and be allowed to play with his own company. Lancelot suddenly became energized. He leaned forward, shaking a surgeon's forefinger and glaring. If he had bellowed also, Ballard would probably have been frightened into a peep of defiance. But Lancelot's voice was quiet, as though he was accustomed to being obeyed.

"My friend, I hope you will not think I am a crank about psychic investigations if I tell you that I can read your thoughts. You are wondering how I, an advertising man, can control a motor business; and you are trying to think of a polite way of questioning my knowledge of motors. You are quite right. I may not know all about motor manufacture but"—for an instant he rattled his teeth and looked savage—"I do know men! Some critics of my inspirational books have been kind enough to say that I am a Doctor of Human Chemistry. Very well! Do you think you could tell how truthful, how dependable, how ingenious an automobile engineer is, after five minutes' talk with him about the weather? No? Well, I can! Look here!"

He whirled in his desk chair and yanked from the top drawer a set of scrapbooks bound in crushed levant, hand-tooled and stamped with titles in gold. As indifferently as though they were paperbound catalogues he tossed them into Ballard's lap, and sniffed, "There! You can see what I did with the Merry-oh Corn and Bunion Salve campaign. And there's the Raw Gold Perfume smash. Was I an expert on perfume? I was not! But I invented the name Raw Gold. Get its fine barbaric splendor? Well, I took it up to the perfumers, and they stuck a fool perfume onto the name, and we got out a slick line of pictures showing Byzantine courts and elephants and kinks and dancing girls. And go? Man, it's been estimated that every woman in the country has bought one and seven-tenths bottles of Raw Gold in the last thirteen months."

Ballard gave up the problem of how a woman buys seven-tenths of a bottle of perfume, and uneasily glanced over the advertisements in the scrapbooks, and the laudatory letters from managers of concerns. Lancelot turned his back on him, and over his shoulder said pityingly:

"And now you are thinking that you wish you could go away and examine those at your leisure, and get the chance to ask more about me. Go to it! Get hold of the president of the Rock of Ages Letter File Company, and ask him what I did for their output. No!" as Ballard was about to speak, "let's not talk about even a tentative arrangement today. Go think it over first."

"Jove, you do read a fella's thoughts!" whimpered Ballard.

Lancelot nodded to him curtly. "Come lunch with me at the Avenue Club tomorrow—no, hang it, I'm lunching with a railroad president. Well, let's see. I can put him off. So drop in here at one. G-bye."

He became extremely busy making annotations on a mysterious document, scowling at it as though he were a federal investigator, and Ballard tottered away. When the door had closed, Lancelot dropped the weighty communication, which was a begging form letter from a charity, into a waste basket. His captain-of-industry expression changed into a cynical smile, and he murmured, "Poor ham! He's falling for it. Some car you'll build, Lancey! Give 'em a fine big steering wheel and a running board, and that's all."

Next day at lunch he was begged to take charge. He would not consent. Ballard wept into his demitasse till the philanthropist agreed to help him out for two years, for a retainer of ten thousand dollars, and twenty percent of profits.

"First thing is to find a good name for the car; something nice and foreign, and yet easy to pronounce. I got it!" said Lancelot.

He sent a club servant to the library for a dictionary. Leaning back, lanky and immaculate, cigar-chewing and excited, he flipped through the back of the dictionary to the section "Foreign Words and Phrases."

"Course you understand," he condescended, "that my knowledge of foreign tongues is rather unusually large. In fact, the last time I was in France—uh, do you speak French? No? Well, M. Ribot remarked to me, when I met him at a diplomatic dinner,

'*Musheer, vous parlez Français comme un Français homee.*' But I do find that this list refreshes the memory." Down the page he ran a forefinger almost as slender and hard as a top section in a bamboo pole. "Let's see. Hm. '*Gitano*. Spanish. Meaning gypsy.' Not a bad name for a car. Ah, here's a nice juicy word: '*Tripotage.*' Er no. It means 'a mess, a jumble.' That wouldn't hardly do for *our* make of car! Oh, here we are! '*Vettura*. Italian. A four-wheeled carriage.' That's the stunt, Vettura! Foreign, classy, deluxe sound, eh? Boy! A pint of Château O'Riley, '96! Ballard, old man, we'll drink to the success of the Vettura!"

"But say, we got to have a car to go with the name!" wailed Ballard.

"Nonsense, m' boy. We got to have an advertising phrase to go with the name! Then we'll see about adding a car!"

Lancelot had a list of acquaintances who could be depended upon to assist him in promotions, and who would not annoy him by being so humorless as to mix up morality with business. Upon the list was Randall Thayer, a mechanical engineer who had been discharged from the chief engineership of a motor concern upon a charge of selling the company's plans to a rival. Lancelot knew, however, that Thayer would never sell him out. They were kindred souls. Curious thing; they both liked Scotch better than rye, gray gloves better than tan, "When the earth's last picture is painted," better than "The Psalm of Life," and plump brunettes better than tall blondes. No, Lancelot knew that Thayer was his true pal, and would never betray him. . . . Also he had the goods on Thayer in regard to the sale of ten thousand floatless carburetors to the Allies.

Thayer was tired of drifting from scheme to scheme, and he was boyishly excited when Lancelot engaged him to organize the manufacturing and selling end of the Vettura concern; to build assembling plant, enameling ovens, sidings, on the tract adjoining the old Ballard factory, on Long Island. The Vettura was to be an assembled car, the company manufacturing only the body. Lancelot and Randall Thayer, with Ballard wistfully listening in the background, held conferences with makers of units—power plant, axles, bearings, magneto. The untrained grafter, however gifted naturally, might have supposed that Lancelot would double-cross the firm, take rake-offs, contract for inferior parts. He did not. When salesmen suggested it, he was pained to hear that such things could be. He held up his pure white hand in reproach. The Vettura was to start off as a thoroughly good car, with fair commissions and profit, would be worth fifteen hundred dollars and, by a startling coincidence, also sell at fifteen hundred.

To constructing the factory, Lancelot devoted only a few hours a day. He was able to continue the supervision of his own bureau for special advertisements and syndicated house-organs. But once he had left Thayer in charge of finishing the plant, he took a week's leave and went up to the Berkshires, to concentrate on the really important task of outlining the publicity.

He took the bridal suite at the Blossom Wold Inn. He had the curtains changed from rose to a delicate green. He ordered that a pint of champagne, a pot of coffee, a game patty, and an orchid be sent in to him four times a day. He arranged a big chair in front of a window, and on a marquetry table beside it he set out a box of a thousand cigarettes, a quire of rich orange paper, a quill pen, a bottle of dead blank ink, a picture of the new cabaret hostess of the Tapestry Tavern, and his favorite three books: *The Sermons of the Rev. William Sunday*, *Poems of Passion*, and Dr. M. J. Fitzhouse's fundamental Nietzschean energizing philosophical pronunciamento, '*Ataboy*.

Of Lancelot in his artistic transports, of how he leaped from his chair to chew the stem of an orchid, to gulp down a coffee-cupful of champagne, or of how he gnawed his knuckles and played the xylophone arrangement of the *Peer Gynt Suite* upon his skull, no one save a fellow poet could tell. From this unveiling of our laureate of commerce in the very exaltation of art we turn in awe. Masterpieces worthy of a quarter page in any magazine he dashed and heedlessly cast upon the floor.

Then in one lightning flash of inspiration he struck out the first complete lyric:

Silk and steel, couleur de rose and crashing power, luxurious as a powder puff and mighty as a locomotive, foreign grace and hand-made American honesty.

So much for poetry. Lancelot now turned to the production of a life philosophy. He decided that the average family, hesitating among different makes of cars, can never remember which car costs fourteen-forty and which fourteen-seventy. Again he flung out a classic:

You can remember the price: Fifteen hundred dollars flat.

Finally, for a touch of romantic fiction, Lancelot brought right out of his magic brain cells a picturesque but most unpleasant person, the Old Garage Man.

There was one dear thing about the Old Garage Man. He did have an imagination. Though not one single Vettura had yet been assembled, this seer, using Mr. Lancelot Todd as Ouija Board, described in detail that slim rakish body—which was still being drafted by the coach-designers of the Ballard Company—those seats "like a chair in a rich folks' club," those headlights "that bring every pebble of the road crashing into view," and the almost brutally sincere construction of frame and engine. Lancelot wanted to go right out and ride in a Vettura, when he had read over his psychic report, and was restrained only by the remembrance that there weren't any Vetturas to go riding in.

A sarcastic, disagreeable carl was the dear Old Garage Man, but he had a tender heart beneath his gruff exterior, for he admitted:

"Old friend o' mine, 'tain't no fun t' hump Bennie Back under the cars that most of these here Sunday automobilly-goats brings in, with the bearin's all loose and like, and the bolts a-droppin' off. But when I crawls under a Vettura, I know I'm gonna find the Works in O.K. shape, allee samee like when it left the shop. That's my luxury and reward, old hoss! I know that the wust wheel-yanker can't put a Vettura on the fritz. And then the ladies—God bless 'em—they all sez to me, 'Dad,' they sez, 'we ain't uncomfortabilious when we drives a Vettura. The engine sings like the laughin' larks o' dawn, and the clutch is soft as a chiffon veil beneath the dainty tootsie-toe,' they sez. I'm mighty much 'bleeged to Boss Ballard because the firm that's been his'n and his foredaddies for a hundred honorable years have took a whole century makin' plans and ripenin' 'em 'fore turnin' out their brand of buzz-buggy, 'stead of goin' off half-cocked. Well, old friend o' mine, must get to work again. Where's my rim-stretcher? Good day to ye. Wait! O boy! Have a look! See that shiny miracle sky-boomin' down the road, steady as a clock and swift as an aeroplane? It's a Vettura!"

When he had exhausted the higher flights of ecstasy, Lancelot chastened his style to the solid simplicity of Tolstoi or the butter-and-egg quotations, and prepared a series of notices for the motor-trade journals. He did say a good word for Initiative, Enterprise, Driving Home the Idea, Thomas Edison, the Firing Line, General Joffre, and other virtues, but mostly he confined himself to warning dealers that very little territory was still open to agents—the only territory now remaining consisting of the United States, Canada, Europe, and a few continents—to admitting what excellent discounts and delivery the company could offer, which was the more remarkable as the company hadn't delivered anything yet except orations, and to pointing out what a strong "talking point" was the slogan "You can remember the price: fifteen hundred flat."

Then Lancelot sighed and came out of his trance, a little wan about the cheeks and red about the eyes. He packed his bag with everything in sight, including the hotel soap and the Gideon Society bedside Bible, put on his wealthy Panama, and went out to while away the hour till train-time by being bucolic, and trying to get acquainted with a red-haired beauty whom he had noticed passing the window.

Randall Thayer really was a clever engineer, and now it looked as though he had not been comfortable as a jolly privateer of commerce. He admitted—while Lancelot grinned internally at the naïveté of the poor ex-crook—that he had enjoyed being straight for a change, and creating a reliable car. The Vettura Six, first series, was composed of excellent units; it was assembled by thorough workmen; it was road-tested on hill, sand, mud, and track. The dealers liked it, and began to ask for territory. They were backed by Lancelot's full-page advertisements, which shed a glory of steel sparks, glistening leather, and twenty-four coat paint o'er all the land. The public read his cunning references to boudoirs, clubs, polo fields, and English manor houses, and wanted to ally themselves with all this aristocracy as well as with the red-blooded virility of the Old Garage Man. The Vettura sold. It was a success.

Randall Thayer was thrilled over being again a somebody. He

tested, experimented, inspected; spent his days with workmen in the shops and his nights in the office; hunted for experts and kicked out lying salesmen and hands; systematized the distribution; polished the whole organization—and then was amiably fired by Mr. Lancelot Todd.

He gasped and whined; he babbled that he was going to go to Ballard and complain; but Lancelot showed him photographs of the letters in the fraudulent carburetor case, and Thayer drifted on, discouraged. It was later rumored that he had been arrested in the West, for selling worthless tractor stock. That shows how little the scoundrel had appreciated an intimate association with Lancelot Todd, the lay preacher whose lecture "The Nest Egg for the Kiddies and the Honest Egg for the Boss" was a favorite on the Lyceum Circuit.

The defection of Thayer left Lancelot frightfully busy. He had to keep his own publicity bureau going, yet rush to the Vettura office or factory every day. He had to discharge almost all of Thayer's favorites, and get a really practical set of men, now that business was solidly founded and ready for expansion. Despite a slight whimper from Ballard, Lancelot engaged a successor to Thayer at thirty thousand a year. . . . Every month, just to show his gratitude, this successor sent Lancelot a check for five hundred dollars.

The second series of Vetturas was almost as good as the first, and by this time the recommendations of friend to friend had started a steady sale. They were always behind on deliveries, which is the S.R.O. of industry. Ballard loved his benefactor Lancelot, and began to invite him out to his country place, an old Long Island mansion which was open the year round.

Lancelot had a weakness for country places. He liked breakfast in bed, and white pants, and the chance that low persons passing the estate might mistake him for a gentleman. It is true that it was slightly dull at Ballard's. There were but few squabs for the weekends, and you got only one cocktail before dinner. But he came often, and hoped to get in touch with the livelier Long Island set.

On an April day he met that old friend of Ballard's mother, Mrs. Gansevoort Cole, dowager widow.

Mrs. Cole was twenty-five years older than Lancelot. She was vain and varnished; she sat pompously, and hated to be contradicted. But Lancelot took one look at her, then sneaked off to the village drug store and telephoned to his business agent in town to find out how much she was worth. The agent said she had a million and a half, and Lancelot went into another trance, not of poetic creation, but of admiration for the lovely Mrs. Gansevoort Cole.

Lancelot was a willing widower, and a quick worker. When he set his mind to it, he could do almost anything. Now he set his mind to liking Mrs. Cole, and discovered that she wasn't a bad sort, in her tart independence. Her heart became God's little garden, and a peony of love began to flower there.

There were three men in the party who tagged at Mrs. Cole's heels, and obsequiously accepted her preposterous statements about architecture, earache, and catching trout. But Lancelot raided through them, and growled at her in his best Intellectual Caveman pose, "Come for a walk. These gigglers make me tired, as they do you."

He didn't offend her by contradicting anything she said, as they strolled along the oak avenue and across the meadows. That was because he didn't give her a chance to say anything that he might contradict. He overwhelmed her with a lamentation about the foolish virgins of today. They didn't understand the labors and artistic ideals of a big business man like himself. Only an older woman could do that. Having thus established himself as an interesting man of affairs, powerful and tired and a little unhappy, he showed her that he could also be young and jocund as the frisking lamb. He sang a loud, cheerful-sounding ballad, and swung himself up into a tree. Also, he was a knight upon whose might a woman could lean, for he defied that peril of the pastures, Elizabeth, the Ballards' oldest cow, the brazen-horned monster. Having thus ingenuously disclosed the frank, rustic side of his many-colored nature, he became a cynical man of society, and said a couple of clever things—that is, a couple of bitter things about people whom Mrs. Cole disliked.

He had a tenor voice, and he had been playing siren songs upon it to entice Mrs. Cole's million and a half. But he had a masculine wile that was still better—his knowing smile. When they stopped on a cliff overlooking Long Island Sound, he glanced at her as though he knew everything she was thinking.

"Why do you turn that growing expression on me, young man?" Mrs. Cole demanded.

He merely continued it, patted her hand, and whispered, "You are a nice person—oh, I wonder if many people know how terribly nice?"

She bridled, whereupon Lancelot winked at a squirrel and informed himself, "By golly, I could turn the trick. I believe I could marry the old girl. O you winsome little wad! You rollicking roll! Come to Lancelot's bosom! When I can't stand her, I can have a trip out of town. I'll open a branch office in Chi, and have to duck out there———"

He looked at her with enlargement of the heart. He teased her and mocked her and listened with rapture to her opinions of Zuloaga and rare roast beef. He picked arbutuses for her, and lured her into telling how lonely she was.

By Monday morning Lancelot seemed to the yearning Mrs. Cole a combination chow dog, financial adviser, prattling playmate, and grim man of granite. She couldn't take her bicarbonate of soda after each meal without his assistance and counsel.

Lancelot bought a new morning coat when he got back to town, and skimmed through manuals on Mrs. Cole's hobbies—architecture and sauces. To his half dozen business absorptions he added chivalric devotion. He gave every afternoon from four to six to Mrs. Cole, as he gave his mornings to the Vettura Company, his early afternoons and early evenings to his own publicity office, and his late evenings to studying food and liquor control with a commission composed of members of the Honolulu Highlife Burlesque Company.

It occasionally made him ill to realize how aging was Mrs. Cole, when he held her parched hand or peeped at her streaked hair. But he did find in her a hovering sympathy that was lacking in younger women. When they were alone at the gray and quiet of tea hour, she threw off the covering of loquacious touchiness with which she protected herself, and let him be silent, and with understanding eyes pitied his fagged nervousness. In return he was always at her service, and he was a valuable young man, who could dance, play cards, pass tea cups, wag his head in tune at the opera, tend bar, and talk respectably to New England relatives. He kept his top hat in the bottom drawer of his desk, his evening clothes in a wardrobe, and six new dress shirts in an envelope under "T" in his letter file. He could work at his office till nine, yet be in her box at the theater at nine-seventeen.

When she went up to Connecticut to open her country place for the summer, Lancelot wrote to her every day. He was ready to marry her now, and to drop Ballard. While he might be able to bully Ballard into signing another contract, it was better to make a quick haul and go into another "proposition" than to plod on in a stupid steady business. He had to get the Cole option first, because she was crabbedly fond of young Ballard. It is true that she did not show her affection by using the Ballard make of car, but stuck to her French-made Moriceau-Stanislas, which had cost twelve thousand for the chassis, 1909 model. But in Ballard she saw his dead mother, and Lancelot was not sure that she would side with him against Ballard unless she was attached to the Todd staff of useful persons.

While he prepared to bring her into camp, and to get out a third series of the Vettura, Lancelot looked into a couple of ripe fields in which he had not reaped. The grain was gold for the garnering, the clear sky was alive with his little brother the cowbird, and our young husbandman rolled up his sleeves, took his sickle, and went singing to the harvest.

Dr. Professor Gustavus Sibelius Harrarskjold Von Ingennojd of the University of Uppsala in his celebrated "Neutral Study of the Teuton" made the cyclonic discovery regarding the German common people that "Some of 'em are good and some of 'em are bad." The professor might have made the same report regarding automobile service stations.

The Vettura service stations had been properly started by Randall Thayer, during his attack of virtue, and as Lancelot had, till this private harvest festival of his, been too busy to touch them, they were still being conducted with decency. You could take a Vettura in to have the battery charged, and not have them bill you for tightening the spring shackles, repairing the radiator, putting in an anti-rattler, and dropping a loose bolt into the magneto, while incidentally forgetting to do any of these things except dropping the bolt.

Lancelot spent only two weeks of his valuable time in increasing the efficiency of the service stations, but in that time he reduced their running expenses thirty percent. He made them abolish the custom of giving in advance a flat price for repairs and sticking to it. He discharged the expensive and fussy testers who actually ran a car so slowly that they could hear a low noise, say that of a broken ball-race, and instead he hired agreeable vocalists who would take customers out at forty miles an hour, at which speed there are no disturbing noises to indicate minor faults.

He got rid of the mechanics who used up too many repair materials, and for an average of ten dollars less a week, he engaged pleasant youths who could dance and tell conundrums, and not get a car done too quickly. When he walked through a service station and saw one of his new repairmen lying under a car half-asleep and occasionally tapping the muffler with a heavy wrench, to make the foreman think he was busy, Lancelot smiled out of fellow feeling for the rogue, and didn't discharge him. It was unfortunate that the customer should pay a dollar an hour for the man's time, to the end of having the muffler broken by the tapping, but Lancelot liked originality, and he made a note of the man's name for possible future use.

With equal success Lancelot turned to reaping in the salesrooms. The salesmen had been accustomed to give as much as an hour to a customer, in return for their hundred dollar commission, but Lancelot taught them not to waste time on a fool who thought that an expenditure of fifteen hundred demanded thought and investigation. He laid down the great moral business principle: "Slip it to 'em."

He himself took command of the salesroom for one day in each city, and taught them efficiency.

When a salesman promised an old lady to have the upholstery changed so that she might ride more softly, Lancelot suggested, "That's a cinch. Keep the car for three days, and slip it to her the way it is. She won't know the difference. Rats! Our upholstery is deep enough for anybody." When a man wanted to buy a car right off the floor, but hesitated because there was a scratch on one door, the salesman came tiptoeing to Lancelot, who inspired, "Slip the same one to him! Take it upstairs and turn it around so the scratch is to the wall. Tell the boob you got another car for him, and take him up and show him the same one. Have one of the other boys kid him along while you're getting the car upstairs. You got to learn not to let these hogs run over you with their idiotic demands."

Because of the freight car shortage, there was difficulty in obtaining Vetturas at the agencies, and they were run in by road, under their own power. A driver punctured an inner tube three times on such a trip. When the purchaser had a puncture in this tube, and it was taken out at a repair garage, the old patches were discovered. The purchaser came with much unseemly lamentation and demanded a new tube. Then, while the salesmen stood in a ring and admired, Lancelot gave them a lesson. He convinced the man that his garage had substituted an old tube in place of the magnificent new one he had unquestionably had from the agency, and sent the fellow off roaring for the blood of his garage man.

Thus did Lancelot, from his comprehension of human nature, which was so much more important than any mere technical knowledge of motors, so much more manly than giving way to this weak craving for honesty, cut down the expenses of distribution and service. Having finally counteracted the influence of Randall Thayer for slow and unlucrative methods of business, he went into council with Thayer's successor, and got out the third series of Vetturas.

He didn't take Ballard into that council.

He had whispered to certain manufacturers that they might be able to cure him of his mania for perfection in materials, and make him listen to reason. He replaced the Vettura's carburetor by a valuable new sort which saved gas by never letting much of it get past into the cylinders. He installed a generator which didn't keep pestering the batteries by charging them. He saw that he had been Quixotic in lavishing such expensive curtains and top on the ungrateful public, and corrected that ungentlemanly error. He made thoughtful changes in spark plugs, tires, axles.

Each of the salesmen for the new set of unit-manufacturers recognized Lancelot's kingly favor by sending him a little check. On the single detail of the clutch spring, Lancelot made four thousand dollars. . . . He completely forgot to tell Ballard about these checks.

Lancelot also instructed Thayer's successor to make improvements in the methods of assembling. The units were now tied together with not too expensive string, and they were not tested.

Despite these economies, the third series must have been an improvement, for the Old Garage Man, whose name was a synonym for integrity of the old oaken bucket brand, confided to the public, in double-page spreads adorned with a faithful limning of him standing bespelled before an automobile of the size and general appointments of a Pullman chair-car:

"Dogonum, them Vettura folks have put one over on me! I reckoned to guess 'twan't possible for them to turn out a better car than they had done at first—but they have! Every one of the male men-folkses that drives a new-series Vettura, when he stops t' my place for a little gas or some free advice, tells me he likes the new carburetor—the boat now accelerates faster, and starts better when the frost is on the punkin and the radiator. The women-folks seems real took with the nifty new side-curtains—and don't forget it's Maw as has to slap up the rain-kickers, while Paw just glares ahead and drives and c-u-s-s-e-s! But I'm horngeswoggled if, while all these other benzine-boys are histin' the price of their mills a notch, the Vettura bosses, in their light and palatial New York factory, ain't kept it the same—YOU CAN REMEMBER THE PRICE: FIFTEEN HUNDRED FLAT—by hecklelum! Full specifications follow."

The third series sold fast upon the reputation of the first two series. Before the purchasers came complaining to the salesmen more than ten or maybe twelve times, Lancelot would make his quick turnover, his contract would run out, and he would be wed to one million, five hundred dollars, accompanied by a Mrs. Cole who would be useful for quieting any doubts Ballard might acquire regarding Lancelot's value.

He ran up to Mrs. Cole's place in Connecticut to close the marital deal. She had invited him for a weekend in October, before she shut up her house for the season. He was to be the sole guest. He could hold her hand uninterrupted, and confess his boyish affection for her.

Only once had he been a guest at her house, which was a Tudor castle, with a deer park and lawns, but situated among abandoned farms in the rough hills near West Eastford. On that visit he had been met by her chauffeur in the huge old Moriceau-Stanislas car. But on this critical second coming, Mrs. Cole herself was waiting for him at the station in a shabby dogcart. She was wearing a faded khaki suit, and gardening gloves.

He groaned, "She looks like a cranky farmwife. Gee, I hope she hasn't got sore at me, or lost all her money, or anything." But when he had fitted on his most innocently childish smile, and trotted across the station platform to her, he saw that her eyes were hungrily kind.

"Why the jolly old chariot?" he said gaily.

"This is the result of my belief in you and Bertie Ballard."

"Eh?"

"I've discharged my chauffeur."

"Eh?"

"Don't 'eh' at me . . . But here's what happened. I've had rather a guilty feeling for a long time that it wasn't very nice of me to stick to my old Stanislas, as though I don't believe in your splendid Vettura, so I talked it over with my chauffeur, and he said he liked the looks of the Vettura on the road, and just a few days ago I turned in the Stanislas and bought a Vettura. I thought I'd have it down here as a pleasant surprise to you." She sighed. "But when I got it, the chauffeur—you know what temperamental virtuosos these Swiss chauffeurs are—he looked it over and said, think of it; said to me that he wouldn't be found dead driving it; and, of course, I let him go. I haven't been able to get a new man yet, so here I am in this frightful old shay. But you can drive me about in the Vettura while you are here."

"Yes," said Lancelot feelingly.

If her Vettura was second series, his life was safe even on these rocky, abandoned roads; but if it was a third series, he hated to think in what peril the pontiff of publicity, as well as a million and a half of marriageable dollars, would be. When he had the chance, he sneaked out to the garage and examined the car. It was third series.

He started the engine—it really did start, but it sounded even looser than he had thought. To make up for that, the windshield was a good deal tighter. He was unhappy. The million and a half seemed larger than ever, and more lovely and pastoral, and a lot farther away.

He expressed a desire to sit still and rest, but Mrs. Cole assured him that driving the car would rest him far more than lolling about, and he had to take her out that afternoon. His attitude toward this monster which he had created was half fear, half hatred, but he drove slowly, and nothing happened, except that the motor knocked so much on grades of more than one-seventh of one percent that he didn't care to tell Mrs. Cole how madly he loved her.

All evening, while they played bezique, he was haunted by the horrible forms of third series.

But in the morning it was raining—a thick, bleak, unimaginative October rain. He chuckled over his breakfast in bed, and made up his mind to take the car away, under the pretense of having it tuned up, and replacing it with a repainted Vettura of the first series, if he could find one in perfect shape. This inspiration convinced him that the Providence which looks after the enterprising benefactors of mankind had not deserted him.

All day long he was the little dancing sunbeam in the house. His lean, long face, above a beautiful wing collar, was effective against firelight. He played fourteen games of bezique without looking bored. At least once an hour he elaborated his regret that the weather prevented his driving her all over Connecticut, Massachusetts, Vermont, and adjacent portions of Canada. He listened to her recollections of parlor maids, and praised her forbearance with these persons in such a tenderly insinuating manner that she hung her head and blushed.

Lancelot was, even while thus swayed by youth's wild romance, systematic in all things. He decided to propose to her at eight-thirty that evening. They would have a large dinner, and Mrs. Cole was always most mellow after dinner.

But at six-thirty, just after he had dressed for dinner, there was a telephone call for her, and she came back to the fireside wailing, "Lancelot, dear, oh, it's a telegram from my nephew. His regiment is sailing for France tomorrow from Boston, possibly before daybreak. I must see him. I'll have to catch a train tonight. You'll have to drive me. I can't get the Boston train this side of Hartford, and it's forty miles. We must start right away. And we were going to have mushrooms *sous cloche* for dinner!"

"Why, that's easy, dear. Slip it—I mean, just get him on the long-distance telephone, and say good-bye that way. I, uh, I wouldn't want you to risk catching cold————"

"I'd catch anything to see him once before he sails. My affection for that boy is the one fine thing in my coddled life. I brought him up————"

"Yes, I know, dear, and I, uh, I don't want to be conceited, but can't I make it up to you for, uh, him? Do you realize how, uh, fond I am————"

"You? Ye-ou? Oh, I suppose you like me; possibly, for once, you do care for me instead of for my money. But let me tell you here and now that I would sacrifice you body and soul to save him one heartache! You make up for him? You couldn't make up for one letter from him! Now do you want to drive me, or shall I telephone to the village for one of their wretched jitneys? There is hardly time————"

"Of course I'll drive you, and gladly!"

He tried to make it cordial, but she went off muttering, "He or any other man make up for Billy! Cheek!"

Lancelot put on his unsuitable top-coat over his dinner clothes and edged out of the warm house. Not only was he going to give the Vettura a test which made him shiver, but also he wasn't going to have any dinner. But he would propose to her, just the same. "When I get the old hen back into good humor—gosh, that was a break about her nevvy—I'll propose steady from here to Hartford. Every time we hit a thank-you-ma'am, I'll kiss her. But wait—wait till we're hitched! Ugh! I'll show her!"

He tried to get the gardener's son, a milky-eyed youth of no great intellectual powers, to help him put on the chains and the side-curtains, but the boy merely stood and yawped and got in the way and lost things till Lancelot yelped, "Oh, getell out of here." He stripped off his coat and perspiringly tried to fit the curtains. They were curtains of the new series, and, aside from the fact that they wouldn't button and wouldn't fit, they looked almost all right.

He was in a state of mind when he drove the car around to the carriage entrance. Lancelot Todd was careless about money and women, but he did have physical courage. He was not afraid of grilling driving. He demanded savagely of Mrs. Cole:

"Are you ready for a bumpy ride?"

"Anything—so long as you make that train."

Between them was still a strain from his having presumed to

play favorite nephew, but in a fury of driving he paid no attention to her. There was exhilaration in racing from the smooth drive out on the rutted roads, in thrusting up the upper half of the windshield when it became streaky, and peering out along the path of light, which made every puddle glower like a deep black hole, and warned of skidding with every shining stretch of clay.

Mrs. Cole was silent, though the shoddy curtains were letting in blasts of rain, and drops were beginning to ooze through the porous top. The inside of the car became chilly and wet and wretched. As soon as they were accustomed to this discomfort, a state convention of canary birds assembled; a chorus of squeaks arose from every possible part of the car. The springs whimpered, the wheelrims creaked, the doors rattled, the mudguards clanked, the rear seat slapped, and no sound was in tune with any other. Mr. Roget, the author of that book of whimsical ballads, the *Thesaurus*, must have been thinking of a damp Vettura when he rapturously trilled:

"*Sudden and violent sounds:* V. rap, snap, tap, knock, click, clash, crack, crackle, crash, pop, slam, bang, clap, brustle, burst on the ear, crepitate, flump."

Especially flump. Flump exactly indicates the noise of the axle as it came down hard in mud holes. Mrs. Cole also flumped, in her one observation during a quarter of an hour: "It sounds as though this dratted car was going to fly to pieces. I wish I had the Stanislas."

Lancelot could not think of any affectionate or advisory remark to offer upon the occasion.

It wasn't really a very good road, not for a Vettura, series three. There was a long stretch which the selectmen had been going to repair, but which they had forgotten after having it plowed up. All the way it was tediously up hill and down. The grades were so riveted that he used the foot brake constantly to keep from turning over. . . . Perhaps he used the brake too much.

His collar and the bosom of his dress shirt were soaked to flabbiness by the gusts that kept darting between windshield and curtain. His wet cheeks felt frozen. But he was too miserable to care. At least he was keeping going, and he would make the train.

Then a cylinder began to misfire.

The car bucked at every misfire; staggered and plunged; boiled and steamed as she took the hills. But Lancelot did not stop. He had often admitted to Mrs. Cole that he knew more about motors than Mr. Flivver or Mr. Jitney, and now he did not care to own that he hadn't the slightest idea of what was the matter. . . . Perhaps the spark-plug salesman with whom he had been in such loving conference a short time before could have enlightened him.

But our handmade man was able to get much credit for heroism out of the misfortune. He unbuttoned the curtain beside him, thrust his head out like an engineer peering from the cab of a locomotive, and stared sadly at the hood. His stare didn't have much effect upon the missing cylinder, but the slap of rain on his exposed head made him feel daring, and impressed Mrs. Cole. When he came back into the car to thaw out his cheeks, she patted his shoulder and cried, "It's wonderful—it's darling of you to take these risks for me."

"I could stop and fix this funny bucking of the engine, and that would make it easier to drive, but it would take so much time that we would miss the train—and I won't miss it!" he declaimed in the assured tones of the Old Guard at Waterloo, or at a national convention; and her gurgling sigh of admiration restored his confidence.

He determined to propose to her right now before she became irritable again. As they started down a long descent he began:

"Evelyn—hang that rock—Evelyn, dear, I have long wanted _____"

Yes! He had used the foot brake too much. The brakes of the third series were lined with tissue paper and great expectations. A single, hard word would burn them out. Just as he reached "wanted," and automatically put on the brakes to ease a sharp drop, he had the unhappy sensation of the machine shooting ahead, accelerating frightfully on that gravelly grade, which shot down into nothing but darkness. He jabbed down the pedal more sharply. It went clear to the floor, and still the machine coasted, faster and faster. He jerked the emergency brake toward him. The machine jarred, then rolled forward again. The emergency wasn't holding. It had not been adjusted.

He slammed into first speed with a shriek of gears. They went slowly down to safety, while he hung feebly over the steering wheel. He was sick with shock, as though he were merely an ordinary, contemptible purchaser of a Vettura, third series, and not the master of motors.

He hoped that Mrs. Cole did not know what had happened, but she was piping, "Both brakes gone?"

"Uh-huh."

"This is certainly a well-inspected car! I begin to sympathize with my chauffeur."

That was all she said for a while.

With only the gears for brake, he could not make time on down grades, and all of that journey that wasn't up hill was down. Mrs. Cole looked at her watch by the dash-lamp, several times, then fidgeted:

"Can't we go any faster?"

"Not downhill we can't, not without any brakes!"

"Huh! It was insane of me to buy this car on faith!"

They passed the village of Heatherhampton. After two more miles they would be out on the state road, with a smooth surface all the way to Hartford, she said.

The headlights showed the beginning of an upgrade, long and rough and narrow, but not steep. He put the car at the slope on high, hurled it around a bend—then hastily started to change to second speed, to slow down for a deep hole that sprang into existence in front of them. He rammed down the clutch. It stayed down. . . . That change in the clutch spring on which he had thriftily saved four thousand dollars might be costly. The clutch spring was broken. The engine ran merrily for an engine with a misfire, but it was no more attached to the drive than to the pyramids of Cheops.

The machine halted, then irresolutely began to run back downhill. Mrs. Cole wailed in fear. "Jump—we must jump!" she groaned.

Lancelot was too angry to be afraid. "Sit still, will you!" he shouted. Making out as much as the road as he could in the glow from the tail light, steering steadily, he let the machine shoot down the hill, reeling and threatening to run off the road.

On a tiny level space between hills it came to a halt. The gears would not enmesh; he could hear them rolling mockingly. He shut off the motor. They would not make Hartford. But he was glad to have got out alive. And he was reformed, oh, tremendously. He resolved to have the Vettura engineer get out a better fourth series—after his own contract was up. He would be glad to throw all of the third series on the junk heap; but, of course, they could not afford that.

Through his moral meditations ripped her sharp voice:

"Well, well, well! What are we going to do? Can't you go on?"

"Nope."

"Then go someplace and telephone for help! Am I to sit here all night?"

He wormed his way out, dropped off into a pool, felt the cold, dirty water above his pumps, shook the mud off, lost a pump, found it, gave up trying to keep dry, and through water that splashed up to his legs he clumped toward the light of a farmhouse on the hill.

He telephoned to the garage at Heatherhampton to send out a wrecker-car. The garage man's wife said that he was off on a trip, but said that she would send him to the rescue as soon as he returned.

Lancelot hated the outrage of having to go back and waste his time on the unpleasant Cole person who had so unjustifiably made him her chauffeur, but he dared not stay away. When he crawled into the car again he tried to be cheery of voice. "Man's away, but they'll send———"

"Huh!" Mrs. Cole's voice was the only dry thing about the car. "I've had a chance to think. Now you'll begin to explain away the faults of this abominable vehicle. Well, I'm going to have a talk with Bert Ballard. Not all of these things could happen to a decently made car. I'm sure I'm properly grateful to you for trying to get me to Hartford, but I want you to understand that hereafter I shan't ever care to have the man who is responsible for this contrivance, as you have often boasted that you are, as my guest. O dear! To think I almost———"

There was nothing to say. Far off there was a rumble. Lancelot realized that a railroad embankment ran above them. It was probably the main line into Hartford. A train was coming, a long train with Pullmans—her train! The fireman opened the firebox in the cab. Lancelot could see the rosy glow transfiguring the underside of the whirling trail of smoke. He glanced at Mrs. Cole. There was just enough light to make out her eyes steadily fixed upon him.

The train left them alone. Time crawled past him, imprisoned with her and the detestable car in this pit of silence. He was taut. He wanted to scream. There was no sound of a wrecking car; nothing but the raindrip.

GETTING HIS BIT

LANCELOT TODD AND PRUDENT PATRIOTISM

Mr. Lancelot Todd, that playful pussywillow of publicity by the brook of commerce, hasn't taken part in the Great War officially, but he has taken part officiously. The only thing that has kept him from rushing out and doing his bit has been a preoccupation with getting his bit.

Lancelot loathes sauerkraut, the Kaiser, the Leipzig theory of paleogenesis, and all those Teutonic verbs that button up the back. He has, when merry, been known to stop singing, "It's always good weather when press agents get together," and chase a terrified dachshund three and a half blocks. But he is as practical about belligerency as about follow-up systems. He is a Prudent Patriot.

He stops short of getting into khaki—or of losing money. You see, Lancelot has so many dependents that he belongs to Class 13Z. Nineteen bartenders, a maker of monogrammed cigarettes, two haberdashers, five showgirls, and the red-haired manicure girl at the Hotel San Dinero all look to his brotherly generosity for their support.

Lancelot is a large embodied sunbeam in spats. He is a Professional Optimist, which means that he sees everything as all-for-the-best. He most decidedly sees the War as all-for-the-best—for Lancelot. While others have been doing such conventional things as enlisting or buying Liberty Bonds, Lancelot has given a lot of

Spiritual Value to the conflict. By January, 1915, he had already contributed nineteen pages of magazine poetry to war literature, and contributed an extra nineteen hundred dollars to his bank account.

When the United States went in, Lancelot had to chain himself to his desk to keep from entering the army. That was very, very fortunate, because within a month he had an idea which must have added immensely to the cheer of our soldiers. He was the real creator of the Khaki Khomfort Trench Bench. He had been hurt by the thought of other men getting all the contracts for munitions and chocolate. You might, on a day in May, 1917, have beheld him working fiercely at his desk. A cigar in an elongated black-and-white holder was savagely rolling in a corner of his mouth; his face was wrinkled with imperial cares; the air rustled to his low cursing; in fact, he was giving an imitation of an oversize Napoleon hunting through the royal card-index for a new nation to conquer. Spread out before Lancelot were the cards listing his former advertising clients. He was looking for a chance to do what, in speeches at banquets, he called "constructive and imaginative merchandising."

He banged the desk-tablet till it clattered. He bawled, "That's the lead! Here's where we show our patriotism by increasing our income tax!"

He was holding the card of the Hinterland Furniture Company, makers of canvas fittings for camps and porches. Within twenty minutes he was sitting by the desk of the president of the Hinterland Furniture Company, talking like an aeroplane engine. Within an hour the Khaki Khomfort Trench Bench had been born and christened.

The Hinterland Company had for years manufactured a folding canvas stool—the familiar kind used for funerals, fishing, and to provide an extra seat for Uncle Amos in the back of the flivver—the kind that simultaneously bites you on the underside of the knee and threatens to give way beneath you. It was covered with brown canvas, and to change a seventy-five-cent, brown-canvas stool for Uncle Amos into a special, warlike, khaki stool for Uncle Sam, all they had to do was to give it a name and add two dollars to the price.

Lancelot himself chose the mediums and wrote the advertising.

A classic of prudent patriotism is that half-page notice which queries:

The solicitude of the Hinterland Company for the laddies was proclaimed in all the public prints and emotionally announced by traveling salesmen to the jobbers, and the Trench Bench blossomed as the sunflower. It is true that no Trench Bench ever got nearer to Europe than the Hudson River. It is true that, though the fishes in that lordly and dirty stream may have enjoyed reclining on the Benches, no soldier ever took one to the shell-craters. It is true that hordes of infuriated soldiers were nightly seen in all cantonments making bonfires of brown-canvas stools sent to them by aunts, office-mates, pastors, and enemies. But cheerfulness and music pervaded the Hinterland offices, and Lancelot weekly received a check for two hundred dollars.

Then something happened—Lancelot never learned exactly what. Apparently some government official whispered to the Hinterland president that the officers of the Q.M.D. were aweary of throwing away Trench Benches. The manufacture of the Benches stopped abruptly, and Lancelot was informed that he would not receive any more checks.

He was furious at this gross inappreciation of his imaginative merchandising and his Prudent Patriotism. He was so disgusted that for weeks he simply refused to give any more assistance to the country. He let it go to ruin in its own willful way. Besides, he was busy with matters which, as he laughingly told Mr. Cyrus T.

Jasbrook, "might not be so pretty and sentimental as all this Red Cross stuff, but sure did show a quick turnover."

Mr. Jasbrook was himself a gentleman who combined an enthusiasm for prettiness with an appreciation of turnovers. He was the most influential layman in the national council of his church. He was famous for his donations to denominational colleges, for his sanctimonious whiskers, for his rose garden, and for his manufacture of Tonah, the Sensible Tonic. Tonah is not one of these panaceas which are presented by unscrupulous persons as a cure for everything from sabotage to ink stains. Not at all. Tonah is a Specialized Remedy, and intended only for coughs, colds, lassitude, biliousness, and all diseases of the liver, kidneys, lungs, throat, and stomach.

The Digest of the Northern Medical Assembly has been so thoughtless as to suggest that Tonah was also a specialized remedy for that Saturday evening thirst in dry counties. Mr. Jasbrook indignantly sued the *Digest* for libel. He engaged Lancelot as the most important member of his legal counsel—in charge of the publicity. The courtly old gentleman, stroking the silken skein of his whiskers, and from a thirty-cent cigar blowing out an aroma like strictly evangelical incense, informed Lancelot, "I don't care a tinker's fiddle"—Mr. Jasbrook was rigidly against the degenerate practice of profanity—"whether we win the case or not, as long as reporters write lots of pieces about Tonah."

Lancelot assembled a convention of witnesses who looked like the judges of the cake, pie, and doughnut section of the county fair. They all swore that they found so much innocent benefit in Tonah that they used it in place of syrup on their flapjacks. Lancelot was busy. He gave his witnesses a fish-chowder dinner to which he invited the reporters. But he didn't let them have Tonah. He wanted to keep their heads clear.

Unfortunately there was a low humorist on the legal staff of the defense. The *Digest* lawyers produced a solemn mariner who swore that the skipper of the *Pride of Manitoba*, after drinking one bottle of Tonah, had insisted that the steward was a U-boat, had chased that unhappy man down a hatch, then sat on the hatch-cover and sang:

They buried my Evangeline

Beside the old mill-pond,
And here I sit and mo-o-ourn,
Because she's went beyond.

The jury indicated that they wanted to hear more about the skipper. So did the reporters. But Mr. Cyrus T. Jasbrook didn't. He demanded that Lancelot call off the newspapers. Lancelot urged that this was all good publicity, and that he would have to shoot the city editors to get them to kill the story, anyway. But Mr. Jasbrook insisted, and a perspiratory wreck that had recently been the leery Lancelot rode soggily about in cabs, begging the editors not to run the fictions which their bright young men were joyously writing about Eskimos getting through the Polar nights by throwing Tonah parties.

At the end of the suit, when Mr. Jasbrook received damages of one cent, Lancelot had to see a nerve specialist. "I've been working frightfully, doctor. I can't sleep. I can't eat," he wailed.

The doctor was a large, calm, horn-spectacled person. He snorted, "Probably. But that wouldn't hurt you if you didn't want everybody to give you credit for overworking. My experience with men like you is that if you have to go out and see a man, you first telephone a few times, send a couple of wirelesses, light a cigarette, discharge an office boy, set the wastebasket on fire, yell for a taxicab, stop to wing a cocktail, and get there five minutes late, with everybody impressed by your importance." Lancelot tried to look haughty, but the doctor stared back, moon-faced, tapping his teeth with his thumbnail, and droned on: "I want you to put on a flannel shirt and disappear for a month. Backwoods—small town—seashore—anywhere. Don't even leave your address at the office. No telephones. No little second pot of coffee at lunch. No trying to make headwaiters think you are Charlie Schwab. Above all, no cocktails—" The doctor smiled as roundly and blandly as a 37 x 5 1/2 smooth-tread tire, and snorted, "and no Tonah."

That was the origin of the astounding spectacle of Mr. Lancelot Todd languishing in the village of Ramsaye, Canada. Ramsaye had meadows, meditative cows, and cottages among large oaks. During his first half hour the poetic soul of Lancelot was sure that it would enjoy this pastoral vacation. He rapidly outlined ten or fifteen poems on cows, cottages, and oaks, to be assembled immediately, with standardized parts and sped-up production, and stored for delivery to editors whenever they had an unfilled two inches in make-up. But after a whole hour of strolling and being gentle and looking as much like a meditative cow as was compatible with his new belted coat, Lancelot discovered that Ramsaye seemed to lack plumbing, hors d'oeuvres, and Al Jolson.

He walked out to a dairy farm and drank a glass of milk. He liked milk—in milk punch—but he believed in being temperate about it. The walk got him through from 1:27 P.M. to 2:19. He sat on the porch of his boarding house and for nine minutes counting the number of times Aristide Botteau's roan mare flicked her tail. He tried to go to sleep. His mind went round and round like an electric fan. He considered, "Let's see. If I needed to get back to New York I could catch the 11:42 and be there next day, and I ought to telephone to Jenkins from Hartford—and oh Lord! I've got to find out how the steel-cable house organ is pulling with positive appeal, and I'd step in at Dubb's and get a couple of new ties and—*oh damn that horse's tail!*"

The buzzing of a fly, the jar of a closing window, the flapping tail, were the only sounds in the world. Seven times in succession ———— You know how you reach for your watch, when you have pawned it, and each time discover blankly that it isn't there? Thus for seven times Lancelot had the inspiration to jump up and get a drink, and seven times did he remember that Ramsaye was dry.

"And they say it takes nerve to dodge bombs in a nice exciting trench!" he lamented.

He sprang up, he raced down the street, he stopped at the first place that showed signs of life—the shop of the cobbler. Like a yellow pup on a Sunday afternoon, when all the folks have gone to the picnic, he longed for someone to talk to. And in the shop the cobbler was chatting with a tall pale man in the uniform of a Canadian captain.

Lancelot entered the shop with a smile like lollipops soaked in crème de cocoa. "Good awfternoon!" he said with all the cordiality and English accent he could get into his voice. He wanted to meet the Canadian officer. Association with officers always gave him a feeling of caste and courage, without entailing any risk of getting shot. They had to be in uniform, though. What was the use of his being a hero if passersby didn't know it? The Canadian captain looked well in his uniform. And probably played a sympathetic game of poker. As he glanced at him, Lancelot came out for hands across the sea, across the border, across the kitty.

"Well, sir, what can I do for you?" inquired the cobbler.

Lancelot saw that the captain—delicately trying to hide a stockinged food behind his chair—was having rubber heels put on, and he affably suggested to the cobbler, "Pair of rubber heels, governor, when you get around to it. No hurry." He wasn't really sacrificing himself to international amity. He approved of rubber heels—not because they made walking easier, but because they were handy for sneaking up on stenographers.

He turned a Cooper-Hewitt smile on the captain and lisped, "Some coincidence! Big rush on rubber heels today!"

"Quite so," observed the captain. He made it a cross between a question and an insult.

"Just came from the States. Almost a furlough, as it were. I'm a newspaperman—journalist?—pressman, you Britishers call it? Been doing so much war work that my nerves went to pot. Begged to be allowed to stay on the job strafing the Hun propaganda, but the doctor simply said 'No!' Ordered me off for a complete rest."

"Ah?" The captain was almost interested. "You are a war correspondent? You have been at the Front?"

"No—tried my best—went down on my knees to get them to let me go, but Washington said I would be more useful on this side. You know: Confidential work. Spies. But how I have longed to get into action! The trenches. You know. Red-blooded."

"But they aren't. They're muddy."

"Of course. In fact I, uh——— Did you ever read these advertisements for Khaki Khomfort Trench Benches?"

"I have! If I could get my hands on the blackguard who was responsible for the profiteering swindle———!"

The red-blooded Mr. Todd anxiously moved back and cooed, "You have been at the front, though?"

"Two years. Invalided home. Going back."

"My dear chap! How terrifically fine! How I envy you! If I could only manage to go along! Let me shake your hand!"

This time it was the captain who moved back in alarm, but Lancelot captured his hand, and shook it with the fervor of an insurance agent who has been mistaken for a real acquaintance. He won. Twenty minutes later the captain admitted that he found Ramsaye dull, now that he was almost fully recovered. Two hours later, over tea, the captain admired Lancelot's tale about the daring of a reporter at a big fire. Lancelot didn't exactly *say* that he was that reporter. . . . And he wasn't.

That evening they played poker, and Lancelot was content to let the captain break even.

For three weeks he spent most of his time with the captain. He chastened his normal seventy-two point boldface manner to the neat seriousness of the *Boston Transcript*. Secretly he believed that the captain ought to be examined for insanity for wanting to go back, but expressed a dry admiration, while he skillfully fished out of the captain his stories of the fighting.

The captain's name was Edward Edgerling, and he was an infantry officer. There were few kinds of daring and sudden death that were not commonplace to him now. He didn't want to talk about them. But Lancelot, who was trained to question reticent business men, knew just when to nod and be silent, just when to demand, "What do you mean by a salient? And how did you happen to see these Germans?" Even he could not get the captain to talk of his own exploits, however.

Lancelot had often said that he never read anything or listened to anything that he couldn't check against. He did not gather Captain Edgerling's stories merely for the pleasures of being thrilled. He knew that he would be able to use them. But for three weeks he didn't know how. The solution came to him when he read in a Toronto paper of the success of a lecture by Fistlethwaite Barnes, the war correspondent. Lancelot reflected that since he was so much more eloquent than Barnes, it was a national disgrace that a little detail like his not having been in France should keep him from lecturing about having been in France. Then, with the sound of distant applause and dollars, it came to him that practically he *was* in France. No one save his general manager knew where he was.

And what correspondent had better material than the information he had gained from Captain Edgerling?

He sent to his general manager a coded telegram signifying:

"Feeling fine. Back in week. Let it ooze out that have been on mysterious secret mission to Western Front, seen unusual phases, unusual opportunities through personal friendship with Foch, Haig, returning with most quickfire description actual fighting yet brought America. Will land Atlantic port next week, be indefinite. Send out press notes, get after lecture bureau, book dates. Subject: An American Business Man in the Hunnish Hell, the First Real Story of No Man's Land."

He pounced on Captain Edgerling. "I've got to wake America up. You give me the dope, and I'll do it. Here's a way for you to do your bit though you're on leave. Come across!"

And the captain came across. He told of the night when he had been afraid and had sneaked out of danger; of the silent, lonely struggle with himself; of his mastery of fear; his raid into the German trenches next day; his tears and stolid fury when a cousin was killed beside him—all the bitter treasures of his soul he gave to his friend, the Prudent Patriot.

Lancelot felt exalted; for a time he believed that he believed in loyalty and courage. When they were not walking and talking he studied maps of the War in the tiny public library. He redrew them till they were clear in his brain.

By this time he was convinced that he really had been at the Front. He remembered his own coolness. But he was modest about it. It was natural for him to be calm in danger. The only thing that kept him from being so calm as to get the D.S.O. and the Croix de Guerre during his last week on the Ontario and Western Front, was the arrival of the captain's younger brother, Lieutenant Tom Edgerling, once a lawyer in New York, now a lieutenant in the American army. Tom Edgerling was a lean, tanned, golfing young man, with a club haircut, a love for his brother, and instant dislike for Lancelot. When the captain introduced them, Lancelot made the mistake of hailing him, "So here's our kid brother! Glad to see the youngster in uniform." Tom Edgerling looked at, over, and through Lancelot and said, "Hmgh." Which was practically all he did say to Lancelot during his two-days' leave.

Lancelot's working time was worth sixteen dollars an hour, and during these two days he was perfectly willing to give three hundred and twenty dollars' worth of it to promoting fraternal confidences. But Tom Edgerling was so pointedly silent whenever Lancelot skipped into view that Lancelot's feelings were hurt, and he refused to have anything more to do with the fellow. He returned to his boarding house and to the notes of his coming lecture he added the outline of a terribly clever burlesque on a young Plattsburgher being superior to a fire-tempered, hard-tack-hardened old war correspondent.

Lancelot's vacation was over. He returned to New York from his perilous station on the battleline. He let himself be interviewed—he saw to it that he was compelled to let himself be interviewed. He rushed to the costumer's and the photographer's, and was portrayed in a war correspondent's uniform, which included a sun helmet, a puggree, binoculars, a camera, an automatic, a typewriter, a cartridge belt, a money belt, a Sam Browne belt, a year's supply of food pellets, a Khaki Khomfort Trench Bench, an expression of three A.M. courage, a cricket jacket, golf trousers, and puttees presumably intended to protect the limbs during the fierce rallies of croquet. Scenery by Rothstein and Keppell. Expression by Lancelot himself. Walk, not run, to the nearest exit.

Within a week this portrait was decorating the walks of Penn Yan. The press carried brief but hysterical accounts of Mr. Lancelot Todd. By an amazing coincidence these accounts had been written by a man named L. Todd. On the day before his first lecture there were quarter page advertisements in the papers. No ordinary cheeping announcements that Lancelot was a worthy journalist were these. The master of coloratura publicity had himself written them, and they softly bellowed:

> Spite of this-here bellicose get-up———
> He isn't a real war correspondent———
> He is a tall excitable guy who ordinarily sits in his office with stenogs
> and phones cluttering up the landscape, and slings out big business
> campaigns———
> He went to Europe to see for Plain Folks in vests what the War is

really like, and he tells about it with the forthright, punchsome, acidly honest clearness of a reg'lar fellow.

Two thousand plan business men with their somewhat less plain wives came to hear that first lecture, and they glowed and applauded. For it was a good talk. That must be understood as the chief explanation of Lancelot's success. He was an efficient salesman. In the language of a sales manager, he "sold the idea of war." He told the little things that people wanted to know. He didn't lead a small pointer up to a large map and mumble, "With your permission we will now review the strategy of the first three phases of the second development of the first campaign. Doubtless you all know that Jonghoer is the focal point of the Flanders railway system————" Being a T.B.M. himself, Lancelot guessed that doubtless they didn't know anything of the kind, and didn't want to. He explained exactly what the soldiers ate and wore and swore, and he was coy about rats and mud and other minor but interesting acquaintances of the trenches.

Then, with deepening voice, he told of the night when he himself had been afraid and had sneaked out of danger; of the silent lonely struggle with himself; of his mastery of fear; of accompanying a squad in a raid on the German trenches, next day; of his tears and stolid fury when the officer detailed to guard him was killed beside him. The audience rose, shouting, and the reporters went to their offices to write appreciations of the lionhearted plain business man.

For two months Lancelot had to conduct the affairs of his office by telegraph. He didn't mind that. It amused him to step up among the traveling salesmen who had nothing more important to wire than "Reserve a sample room," and to hand the admiring operator a two-hundred-word message filled with lightning and dollar signs. For two months he lived in hotels, parlor cars, and applauding lecture halls. Reporters interviewed him on an average of once an hour, and in measured kindly tones Lancelot settled for them the questions of barrage, camouflage, and sausage; of the just terms of peace, the state of public opinion in Silesia, the amount of barley on hand in Germany, and how long the war would last if it ended before 1920.

To no one did it occur to wonder whether he had actually been in Europe. The public was so accustomed to reading of secret arrivals, of dignitaries who had slipped across the ocean, that they saw no reason why Lancelot should not have slipped also. That is——— Well of course a commercial statesman like Lancelot cannot go on forever without being annoyed by some low muckraker who doesn't look at things in a practical manner.

When Lancelot had finally brought his lecture to New York, and was giving an afternoon address at the Lapidary Theater, he noted that several real soldiers were present and appeared to be taking him seriously. While his epiglottis mechanically continued to produce the most pinkly pleasing medley of sounds, his eyes glanced from one to another of the soldiers, and his heart was filled with kindness for his fellow warriors. One of them, an officer, seemed especially intent. But as Lancelot studied him the officer scowled. His face was familiar. Lancelot was so accustomed to regard himself as one who had really been in France that he wondered if he had met the officer there. As he started to tell about the night when he had been afraid and had sneaked out of danger, he realized that the officer was Lieutenant Tom Edgerling, brother of a certain Canadian captain.

It was fortunate that this blow fell near the end of the lecture. Lancelot had difficulty in being anything like as quietly heroic as usual. He watched Tom Edgerling's unkind sneer, and wondered if the captain had told Tom certain stories. He planned to be called away as soon as he had finished. But he was trapped by a crowd of people who wanted to shake his hand and ask whether he had happened to meet Cousin John over there. In the rear rank of the seekers Tom Edgerling was waiting.

Never had Lancelot shown such delicate modesty as he did that afternoon. He admitted that there were some things about the War that he scarcely knew at all. While he was establishing this spiritual alibi he was praying for an earthquake.

His face as blank as that of an old, bored fish, Tom Edgerling waited till the others had gone. He shook Lancelot's hand, then shook it again. At last, with his upper lip curled up, making wrinkles from his nose to the corners of his mouth, Edgerling growled, "I was very much interested in your personal recollections—strangely interested."

"Ver' pleased," said Lancelot, clearing his throat.

"I wonder if I haven't met you before—possibly in France—seem to remember your face," pondered Edgerling.

Lancelot had an excited hope that he was safe. He caroled, "Yes, I'm sure I've seen you somewhere. It must have been in France."

"Undoubtedly. Though the fact is, I haven't been in France yet!"

"I don't—uh—why————"

"But what's a little thing like that between friends? Oh! Now I know! Aren't you the man who was so kind to my brother when he was recuperating? Just willing to let Edward drool on by the hour?"

Lancelot grabbed at Edgerling's hand, and though he didn't exactly catch it, owing to the fact that Edgerling folded his arms behind his back in the rudest manner, he gurgled, "Why of course! Now I know you! You're Tom. And what do you hear from old Ed?"

"No. I am not Tom. I am Mr. Edgerling. But I am dear old Ed's brother. Dear old Ed is back in France. Isn't it a pity that dear old Ed couldn't give his lectures personally! But, then, dear old Ed isn't much on lecturing. His style is cramped by having actually been on the other side."

"See here, are you insinuating————"

"I am! Lord, I'm insinuating! I say. I didn't care much for you in Canada. When I got back here I got hold of a friend who's in the advertising game. He says you're the kind that makes honest advertising men want to commit homicide. He says you're the man responsible for the Khaki Khomfort Trench Bench frightfulness. You see, dear chap, I was detailed as quartermaster for a while, and I spent most of my time trying to find shipments of cabbages among the carloads of Trench Benches. Get me?" The theater was deserted now, save for the two men standing in front of the stage, and a janitor, who was gathering the rubbers, candy boxes and war books left under seats. Lancelot looked patiently over the sleek brown top of Edgerling's head, and, like a martyr, waited for the torture to be over. Edgerling was going on: "I'm sure you get the idea. You're great at grabbing other people's ideas! No more modest ferocity, Todd! No more lectures, at least within traveling distance of Yaphank, where I'm stationed. No more lectures, Todd, no more!"

Edgerling marched away. Lancelot stood alone. He put on his chamois gloves, and pulled them off, and tucked them into his pocket, and took them out, and dropped one of them, and stopped, and lost his fountain pen, and said, "Damn!" He started slowly up the center aisle of the darkened theater. He met the puttering janitor at the baize door. It was an old, feeble, trusting janitor. Lancelot fixed him with a savage look, and snapped, "The ventilation was rotten today! I'm going to complain about it!"

Lancelot was eager to cooperate with the army as represented by Lieutenant Tom Edgerling. He didn't want to give any more lectures within two days' travel of Yaphank. But he was under contract for several in Manhattan and East Orange. He engaged a large detective, and instructed him to watch for Edgerling. He was to sit near Edgerling if he appeared, and if he made a disturbance to drown it out by starting a fight with any small, meek family man who happened to be handy.

Though Edgerling twice appeared at lectures, he did not make a disturbance but merely annoyed Lancelot by sitting down front with fellow officers, and cynically whispering to them. Like all poets, Lancelot needed sympathy, and this nastiness so affected him that he began to refuse all engagements.

He was offered a contract for an extensive western Chautauqua tour with his war lecture in the summer of 1918. But he hesitated about accepting it. He told himself that the office needed him. That highly lucrative magazine, *Naughty! Naughty!* had asked him to conduct laboratory experiments to find out whether it was possible to have a summer magazine cover which did not picture silk stockings, parasols, canoes, or young females in bathing suits. Like all the art editors, Lancelot doubted it, but he was glad to assist science by inquiring.

Late on a spring evening Lancelot was working alone in his office. The only light was the bulb over the desk in his private room. In the dimness, hidden, were all those extension-bracket telephones and dictation phonographs and charts showing what Mr. Lancelot Todd had done for selling campaigns; all those Doric files and the Ionic ticker and the Corinthian stenographers that by day decorated the outer office. A lean, strong, intent, light-centered figure in shirtsleeves, Lancelot was wearily sketching layouts for covers. Before him was his letter to the Grubb-Wiffenbury Chautauqua Bureau, accepting their offer for a war lecture tour. The letter was not yet signed. He wasn't yet sure he wanted to sign it.

One by one he got ideas for vital, red-blooded, rompsome, gripping, dramatic, powerful covers—bathing girls and silk stockings and canoes—and one by one he destroyed them, cursing in a methodical, unconvincing manner. He looked up, thoughtfully scratching his chin. Standing by his desk, only half real in the duskiness, were three men in uniform.

His heart gave one terrible sick throb that left him dizzy, With a scared dullness he saw that one of the three men was Tom Edgerling.

"Good evening, Mr. Todd," said Edgerling. "May my friends have the honor of meeting you? This is Captain Hanbridge, and this is Lieutenant Meyrick. Mr. Meyrick has been especially keen to know you. He has heard your lecture, and he once met my brother—-*you* remember, dear old Ed!"

Lieutenant Meyrick was an enormous young man with a smooth, annoying smile. He swooped on Lancelot, gave Lancelot's shrinking shoulder such a frightful whang, and bellowed, "Such a pleasure. You and I must see a lot of each other, Brer Todd."

Edgerling added, "We've decided that I was wrong in knocking your lecture. I'm glad you kept it up after I told you to stop. In fact, we're so impressed by your valor that we want you right with us in the regiment."

"You think you can kid me," Lancelot mumbled feebly. "As a matter of fact, I could have had a commission any———"

Edgerling broke in, "Toddy, Toddy, your manners pain me! To let your superior officers remain standing like this!" Meyrick had roamed over to the wall switch, felt along the wall like a young elephant in the dark, and snapped on all the lights. The three intruders drew chairs up to Lancelot's desk and faced him in a grinning semicircle. Edgerling was continuing: "So you could have had a commission? But, you see, we have lots and lots of officers in our regiment, and yet we must have you along. Oh, yes. Positively. Oh, yes, indeed. But as a private, Todd. Unless you get to be a corporal. And personally, I don't think you'll live long enough to be a corporal. Terrible hard to arrange your enlistment with us, but we'll cut the red tape and slip you in. Rotten shame, man of your nerve—remember the time you accompanied that squad on the raid?—shame you haven't a chance to get into action. We'll attend to that. See your right into the first-line trenches."

Lancelot felt a solid earnestness behind the taunting. He crunched down in his chair and pulled at his lip, looking from one to another. He was aware that they were rising, rolling toward him, over him; that while he shrieked they had seized him, switching off the lights, and started him running through the outer office, down flight after flight of clattering marble stairs, out to the deserted business street, into a taxicab.

Ruffled, bruised, desperate, wedged in between Edgerling and the large Mr. Meyrick, he could only moan as the car started:

"What does this mean?"

Edgerling inquired, "You've got a lot of courage, Todd?"

"Why, uh, why I suppose————"

"Of course you have. You told us so in your lecture. . . . And you'd like to serve your country?"

"I am serving it."

"You sure are! You're enlisting in the Xth Infantry!"

"I am what? Huh? Whadyumean?"

With his thighs turning cold and his hands trembling, Lancelot decided that they actually meant this horrible thing. The trenches—fighting—danger—coming inescapably!

"I won't do it!" he shrieked.

They did not answer. They sat rigid. He stupidly noted that the car was passing the Café du Pom-Pom, where he often went for the peculiarly excellent golden fizzes. In the swaying taxicab he tried to struggle to his feet, snarling, "You can't get away with this fool joke stuff with me!"

They did not answer. Lieutenant Meyrick thrust out that bear-paw of his, and plumped Lancelot back into his seat.

The drew up at a building on Sixth Avenue. There was a restaurant on the ground floor, but they did not go into it. Lancelot looked for a policeman vainly. The three men edged him up a flight of stairs, through an evil hall, to a door on the outside of which was hung a pasteboard sign with the legend "U.S. Recruiting Office."

His knees had almost given way. The three men had to support him into the office. It was a bare room, with two windows in front, a desk between these windows, and at the desk a sergeant, filling out a blank. As the sergeant rose Captain Hanbridge said to him, "This is the man who is so anxious to enlist, sergeant. He has had his physical examination, you know. See that he is accepted."

The three officers hastened out of the room. Lancelot heard the key in the lock. He glanced about. At the back were old-fashioned folding doors. They were solid, and probably were locked. The two windows in the front were closed. And the sergeant was a man on the lines of a motor truck. It was not going to be easy to escape, unless——— Lancelot felt the roll of bills in his pocket.

The sergeant, seated, as sharply inquiring, "Name?"

"See here, sergeant. Those officers are friends of mine, and just playing a little joke———"

"Name, Jake Brown," said the sergeant, writing it down. "All right, Jake, how old are you?"

"Look here! I'm sick of this farce!"

"Age thirty-four. And a very nice age for enlisting, too." The sergeant was putting it down.

"I'm not! I'm forty-two! In fact, forty-four! Much too old ———!"

"That's what I said—thirty-four. Occupation?"

"I'm a newspaperman and advertising man of con-si-der-able importance, and I'm going to raise the most particular hades about ———"

"Occupation: Raising most particular hades. I'll put that down as Agriculture."

"I'll get a writ of habeas corpus! I'll have you arrested, court-martialed!" Lancelot shrieked, hanging on by the desk, bending a palsied head toward the sergeant.

The sergeant finished the entry "Agriculture," and purred:

"Don't worry about having your corpus habeased, Jake. You're to be assigned, by special favor, to the Xth Regiment, company of Captain Hanbridge—and of Lieutenant Edgerling—and you sail for France *tonight*. The transport leaves in the morning. The enlisted men are already aboard. Presume Captain Hanbridge and the other gentlemen are on their way there now. You'll be out of sight of land by morning, Jake. In about three weeks you may be in action. And if there's any trouble about you on the other side, Jake, all we know is that you came in here drunk, gave your name as Jake Brown, and begged to be enlisted. Not sure but they can get you for perjury and————"

Sobbing, pounding on the desk, Lancelot shouted—while the sergeant remained as red and hard and unimpressed as a sandstone sphinx:

"This is murder! It's murder! You're all in a plot to get me! I'll do———— Look here, sergeant, I'll make it worth your while." He pulled out a roll of bills, began to snatch twenties from it.

"I don't want your money! I know how you got it! But I would like to hear you do a little confessing, just for the good of your soul!" growled the sergeant, seeming to Lancelot's blurred vision to grow bulkier and more terrible, while he wagged a heavy forefinger and demanded:

"You admit you've been lying in your lectures, Todd?"

"Yes!"

"You admit you're a slacker, a profiteer, a coward?"

"Yes!"

"Well then————"

"Then you'll let me go? I guess I'm not fit to serve————"

"Oh no! Then I guess we'd better send you to the Front and not let you come back!"

While Lancelot tried to think of something annihilating to say, he became aware of a titter behind him. He looked back. The folding doors behind him had been slid open—how long they had been open, he did not know. Beyond them was darkness, but out of that darkness came a rising chuckle, then a voice sighing, "Let the poor devil go. I'm ashamed to listen," and another voice, "Not at all. He laughs at the public, and all we can do is to get the chance to laugh at him."

As Lancelot gaped, the room beyond the folding doors flashed into light, and he saw the officers of the Xth Regiment, saw Edgerling and Hanbridge and Meyrick and the rest, all at a horseshoe table, facing him, watching him perform.

The colonel of the regiment rose and addressed him across the two rooms: "Thank you, Mr. Todd. You have made our last night in the States very interesting. In the hall you will find a Trench Bench to rest on—a Khaki Khomfort Trench Bench. It will doubtless restore your death-be-damned, lilting, laughing nerve."

One block from the restaurant, walking toward his office, feeble in his shame, Lancelot decided to win the right to face the colonel by really enlisting. Never again would he touch a drink or a lie, never eat an expensive dinner or tack about in taxicabs. He would walk, exercise, get into shape, and quietly enlist.

Three blocks and two drinks farther on, he decided that enlisting would be rather hasty, but he certainly would give a thousand dollars to the Red Cross.

Four drinks beyond that, as he got into a taxicab, he decided that he needed the thousand dollars, just now, but he would buy a fifty-dollar Liberty Bond.

He reached the office. With disgust he picked up that still unsigned letter, which would have bound him to giving his war lectures in the West. He pulled the wastebasket toward him, and held the letter in his two hands, to tear it. Then he remembered that Lieutenant Tom Edgerling was sailing for France that night. He smiled benignly, neatly replaced the wastebasket, signed the letter, and strolled out to mail it.

JAZZ

LANCELOT TODD VIGORIZES THE HOUSE ORGAN

There are three kinds of house organs. The first is that musical neuralgia that stands between the patent rocker and the pink-soap statuette, and is adorned with diamond-shaped mirrors, with battlements and a donjon-keep in mahogany-finish pine, with the *College and Heartthrob Songster*, with pedals (clutch, reverse, and brake), and brackets for lamps or harmonicas. The other two kinds of house organs are different in appearance, though not dissimilar in sound.

Both of them are pamphlets, with coy titles and articles reluctantly suggesting that Orinoco Tires or Fairy Tale Leather Belting are so much the best that it's a shame not to stock them and pick up the easy money. Of these, one is intended for the employees of the company; the other for jobbers, retail dealers, and such final consumers as can be hypnotized into taking it out of the severe, classical envelope.

The house organ intended for dealers should never be so lacking in taste as to suggest that the proprietors of the tires or the leather belting would like to make a little ready cash out of them. They should start out with essays on the power of the will, on the value of courtesy in selling, and the duty of never letting a customer who has come in to buy a box of matches leave the store before he has also bought an eggbeater, a pair of shock absorbers, a box of Gloucester codfish, and a three-volume life of McKinley.

At the bottom of the each page the editor should run a few epigrams about the great art of gladvertising, such as "It's the early worm that gets the bird," or something in a Vermont-Hoosier dialect reputed to have been uttered by one Si Perkins. When the mind of the dealer has been thus coaxed into a condition of wisdom and merriment, the editor may justifiably slip in, not praise of the belting or the tires, but a heart-to-heart confession about the efforts of the chief chemist of the company to find the best raw materials.

Now it must be added that most house organs are worthwhile. They do sell the goods, and they do unite the trade. They give that human interest which distinguishes college spirit. But some of them have all the value of nine pounds of sea wind, and the sincerity of a German peace offer. Of these imitations, the most interesting are the house organs for which Mr. Lancelot Todd, the freelance advertising man, is responsible.

In his early days Lancelot had edited one of the first house organs in the country. For a wide circle of oil-lamp readers he had described the ease with which gold could be taken out of Chair Y Mine—if the operator ever happened to find any gold there to take out. Since Lancelot had reformed and become a poet and philosopher of business, he has frequently planned the policy and layout for house organs. One of them he continues to manage, though not to write. He permits an assistant to do the actual work. Lancelot always is willing to give the bright young men and women a chance, provided he gets ten times as much for the product of their labors as he has to pay them for laboring.

This house organ is that smart, chic, *katische*, clever, *décolleté* publication *Aux Dames*—dames, not damns—which is devoted to creating an interest in Dimpletoe Stockings. It has regular departments: "Madame Shops on the Avenue," signed by Elizabeth Van Goock; "Madame Honors the Play," by Contessa Olivia; and "Madame Finds *le Secret de la Toilette*," by Sandra Sanbœuf. These departments are vignetted with photographs of their editors—sturdy Elizabeth in a suit, the Contessa in evening wear, and Sandra in negligee. But it is a fact that all three of these perfect gentlewomen are jointly included in the person of Mr. Eugene Hicks; and that Mr. Hicks is a large, slow-spoken, solemn male, with a face of the general dimensions, shape, and texture of a manhole cover, and a personality like underdone cornmeal mush.

Mr. Eugene Hicks sits all day long at a desk in Lancelot Todd's office, and obediently writes whatever he is told to. Some days he is domestically gladsome about Mother Nature Catsup; some days he states in a dignified manner that all scientists admit that Hydine is the best tonic for the rundown business man; and four days a month he devotes to writing *Aux Dames* and being clever about Dimpletoe Stockings.

Miss Melody, the redheaded stenographer in Lancelot's outer office, says that Eugene probably wears Dimpletoe Stockings himself. She swears that if it weren't for Lancelot's hard-hearted supervision, Eugene would come down to the office in a boudoir cap.

Lancelot usually takes the credit for *Aux Dames*. He certainly did so when the president of the Universal Grocery Company surged into the office and asked Lancelot to turn out a house organ for the employees in the Universal Company's chain of stores. The president screamed:

"Want something with punch in it. A lot of these clerks keep thinking about raises instead of tending to business. I have the district superintendent of the chain tell them that if they would think first of my pocket, then I would think of theirs—you know—the good old paternal employer stuff—used to go down easy, ten years ago. But now, somehow———" The Universal Grocer sighed a disillusioned sigh—"what with these blame Socialists and agitators and fool magazines, the clerks don't seem to believe me. So I want a nice little monthly house organ—not too expensive, y' understand—but friendly and lots of dynamic thought, that will wake up these fellows and give them espreedy core."

"I get you," quoth Lancelot.

To create a mere magazine was to Lancelot but a waving of the hand. He could always go out on the labor market and hire one or two educated, college-bred, horn-spectacled, sensitive, literary young men, promise them an Opportunity for Advancement, and put them to work—a little harder work than the elevator-starter downstairs, and a little less pay, but oh, so much more experience! This time he didn't even trouble to do that. He called in the large, gentle, milk-fed Eugene Hicks, told him that the name of the Universal house organ would be *What's Up, Boys?* and instructed him:

"You can steal the contents of the first issue out of almost any of these magazines that the railroads get out for their employees. Practically all of them do pepowerpunch and the 'Young man, we are your best friend' stunt. Meanwhile you can gather in some news items for the next issue. Get hold of some easy mark in each district to send in the news, and hash it up with red pepper and couple cheap line drawings. Oh say, and first I want you to do some good, sound, deep, philosophical junk for introduction."

"Uh-huh," said Eugene throatily.

Eugene went solemnly out and produced the introductory article. He wrote it on one of these spidery typewriters that have the bottom left off, and he used the type-spool that contained the lady-like script. He brought the essay in and laid it before Lancelot in the manner of a wet Newfoundland depositing a ruined frog before his mistress at party tea. Lancelot read:

"When Madame daintily trips into the *bazar des comestibles* and from the gaily colored congeries of smart edibles chooses—but what *shall* it be today? Is it *le pois*, greenly shimmering in their silken pods? Or perchance the artichoke, like a cameoed palm from the Southern resorts of *le beau monde*? Or the artful truffle that to scrambled eggs *à la Turque* gives that last flip of sheer deliciousness————"

Lancelot carefully laid down the sheets of copy paper, dusted them with his handkerchief, and faintly implored, "Say, did you ever eat a truffle?"

"Who? Me? On my salary?"

"Well this sounds as if you were stuffed full of them! Right into the garbage can for this. For heaven's sake, don't let the janitor find it in one of our wastebaskets! Say, don't you get my idea at all? We don't want to remind these grocery clerks that they have to wait on dames that trip daintily. We want to make 'em *forget* their misery. And we want to fill 'em so full of ambition that they'll sell the counter and the breakfast-food posters. Red-bloodedness! Efficiency and the Superman! Will Power! The Soul Victorious! The Success Attitude! Push, Pluck, Persistency, Prosperity, and Progress! Con and Concentration! Blazing New Trails! Violent, Vigorous, Vicious Vitality! All that kind of dope! See? Apparently you haven't gotten onto the fact that the modern live-wire guy has a new vocabulary with zippo to it. Go back and pound out some real copy. What I want you to give 'em is triple-spaced hell!"

Next day Eugene presented to Lancelot a prose poem which began:

"Are you one of the kings of men? Do you find your Psychological Empire widening? Does your mind echo the masters of vigor and vitality?"

There were two more pages of impertinent questions for indignant grocery clerks, but Lancelot tore them up with a quick yank, and blared, "Say, what is this? A valedictory? Where do the class motto and the thanks to our dear old teachers come in? I'll have to take you off this job, Hicks. Back to the dignified ads for yours. Beat it."

Lancelot called up his acquaintances at the agencies and trade papers, and made it known that he had an opening for a literary person who, if he proved to combine the gorgeousness Milton with the salesmanship of Billy Sunday and the amiability of George M. Cohan, would be permitted to try to qualify for a position with remarkable opportunity—though, of course, with only a moderate salary to *start*. Three days later there was brought to him the card of:

> WILLIAM JOHN BUCKINGHAM
> *Editor and Manager*
> Thought Power Magazine

"It listens good. Let it in," said Lancelot to his secretary.

From the card he had an impression of a man nine feet tall and four feet broad, with a Henry the Eighth beard. Yet William John was but a small little man, with a thin neck, thin arms, no legs worth mentioning, and a vast bald head, on which the fuzziest, shabbiest, tiniest round cloth hat in the world was perched, like a wren trying to hatch an ostrich egg. The edges of his sleeves were rubbed through to the interlining, and his shoes were patched. But his manner was not diffident. He was apparently too bored to take the trouble of having any manner whatever. He strayed in, followed by a giggle from Miss Melody in the outer office. He flumped on a chair, and piped in the voice of an unoiled sewing machine:

"Heard you had a job. House organ. I would like to try it."

"You are Mr. Buckingham?"

"Yes, sir."

"Why do you want to leave *Thought Power Magazine*?"

"I'm not exactly on it, just now. I still write some for it, but ——— Well, in fact, I've taken up a new aviation journal since I left it. Do you realize that the interest in aviation———"

"Well, then, why do you wish to leave the aviation sheet?"

"Oh, I'm not with it anymore. Since then, I've taken the managing editorship of a society monthly for divorcees. Fine idea. Do you know that there are sixty-two thousand wealthy alimoniacs in———"

"Um. A great light begins to dawn. Why were you fired from this—or from the *Plumbers' Gazette*, or the *Family Knitting Magazine*, or whatever you've been on last of all?"

"Booze."

"Well, I'm afraid———"

"Aw, thunder, boss, listen. I can make any kind of house organ. I may seem light-waisted, but I'm dandy at slinging copy. *Honest* I am! And I don't get drunk till after the paper has gone to press. Hardly ever. What's this new house organ to cover?"

"Jolly-'em-up rag for the employees of a chain of grocery stores—the Universal stores. It's called *What's Up, Boys?*"

"If you'll excuse me for saying so, I don't care an awful lot for the name. I'd call it after this new kind of motorboat-exhaust music—call it *Jazz*."

"Not a bad idea."

"Now I'll show you what I can do, if I may."

Without an invitation, William John rambled to Lancelot's private typewriter, and suddenly it turned into a machine-gun battery at close quarters. In twelve minutes William John had snatched out of the typewriter a screed that yawped:

"Hey, you Universal fellas—here's your magazine—*Jazz!* Full of jazzazza, but nix on the psychological guff and the optimism omelets! The editor is old Jerry Ginger, which he is a regular guy that used to be a grocer hisself—used to drive the chicory acrost the counter, and explanation the old dame that she didn't ought to expect us to deliver one sad-iron holder when the hoss was lame. His mission is to let the blobs of darn-good-fellowship flow from the dandy bunch of scouts in the main office out to every clerk in the chain.

"Ye editor will pass on practical hints from the president. The Big Boss could sell rings around Jawn D. Rockymorgan, but he can't spiel his ideas in swell-elegant magnolious langwitch like you and I can. (Gosh! Hope he don't read this! Maybe he can't read!) Frinst. This coming moon we're gonna stock heavy on Falluzo's Olive Oil. Tween you and I and the lamppost, the stuff is all O.K., but with a splendorious margin of profit. To the first five stores that clear it out we're gonna give credit marks————

"Heh? Whazzat? Betchanek! Thassakid! Some good news is done came from the grocery trenches. Firm's instituted a system of credit marks for individool stores, and when your shugar-shop gets enuff of 'em, every man John can glom his eye onto a BIG RAISE! (Yezzur, Brer Local Manager gets in on the joy-jump, too!) The Big Boss has shure got his Easter perspicacity on straight. He'd enthuse a morgue. If you fellas could meet him mitt to mitt like I do—well, you'd go over the top!

"Roll up yer shirtsleeves and spit on the cat and get the brass kenuckles ready and listen to the next spasm. We also want you to put a mighty shove behind McGigelum's Oat Flakes and Joleo, and get some system into your vegetable trade—use a little mental cup grease in your differential. Huh? Oh, we caught you, cutie! We know it should be transmission oil. Ne' mind! You Omaha-ha, give a cheer! You K.C. and Peoria! All together! Shove!

"Last year we increased the biz from 6 turnovers to 6 1/4. Thatsnuff, you say? Ye deities and lil red sardines! Sherlocko, tote in the jazz needle! Last year's ooptarara was a mere practice sprint. This year we're gonna whup-tee-by-doodle GO! We're on your toes, limber-jointed, hope-souled, hearts bumpity-bump-ti-bump, then the signal, and it's OFF, down the stretch, dust in your noses, crickety-crunch, feeling like we could just everlastingly run circles round an aeroplane, bound to increase the rapidity of turnover to a grand sweet 6 1/2, and all come in on the better biz. Yes, Aloysius, wife can order them summer furs!

"It's scintillating, sizzling, startling, stellar, staminatty, stalwart, stentorian Success for all the Universal stores this year, brother boosters, and here's a hand on 't for auld sake's sake, my lads!"

"Say!" said Lancelot Todd, "you're hired! But on one condition. You get drunk only three days a month. Is it a go?"

The creator of sizzling success wailed, "Gee, have I found a decent boss at last?" The tears oozed from his weak red eyes, and he moaned, "Honest, I'll do it. Say, could you————"

"Yes. Here's a five. Now be here on the job Monday morning."

The first number of *Jazz* was actually prefaced by the quoted lyric, with no change except the insertion of actual wares in place of the imaginary ones. To get the president of the Universal chain to consent to the suggested system of credit marks for stores, Lancelot had to prove to him that the marks did not bind the firm to the expenditure of real money. Nowhere was it stated just how many marks entitled the staff of a store to raises. If, Lancelot suggested, the *Jazz* fever did so increase the income of the company that the directors didn't know what to do with the money, it wouldn't hurt to give a few bonuses.

The president did not meet William John Buckingham. It was Lancelot who took the dummy of *Jazz* to the Universal office—and took the credit away.

There was only one obstacle. The advertising manager of the Universal Company did not like Lancelot, nor Lancelot's rock-of-ages handshake, and as for Lancelot's books on gladvertising he viewed them as mental German measles. His name was Anderson, and he rather looked like Lancelot—the same taut energy, the same suave smoothness, the same imagination. Only Anderson happened to have honesty, a pride in advertising, and the ability to read and write. He hinted that Lancelot was lowbrow, crooked, and noisy. Lancelot considered him highbrow, impractical, and snobbish.

Anderson quietly objected to the outlined style and policy of *Jazz*. He stated that the contests were unfair, and that the style was the best example of the ideal of smart-aleckism in literature that had been inflicted on an ailing world. But the president sided with Lancelot, and informed Anderson that he had taken the house organ out of his department.

So with line cuts portraying a highly idealized Big Boss handing out bags of money, and of customers mobbing a Universal store, the first number of *Jazz* was issued. In the Olympian grove where thoughts float on the cool sweet morning air, the golden scroll of *Jazz* sprang from the Jovian head of William John Buckingham.

Miss Mary Theresa Melody was a stenographer with red hair, one hundred and twenty words of shorthand a minute, and a snicker, which last she devoted almost entirely to the male of the species. The anti-suffrage gentlemen are absolutely right; if women are to be impressed by the lords of creation, they should be kept out of offices. After Miss Melody had seen Eugene Hicks sucking his fingers and craning his neck outside Lancelot's door, in the hope of a word with the chief, she could not take him very seriously.

Never had she seen so perfect a proof of the theory of evolution as William John. To him was given a small brown desk in the dark corner behind the water cooler, where he turned out *Jazz* copy, and dictated letters to Universal clerks, asking for news notes. He had no talent for discipline. Whenever he asked Miss Melody to take dictation, he pattered to her desk, waited till she had finished her conversation with Miss Rosie Hiltz, and implored, "Could you take a few letters?" He put himself into Miss Melody's power when he disclosed the fact that he was not receiving enough salary to live on.

He had forgotten in the first interview to ask Lancelot how much he was to be paid. He found himself put down at twenty-five dollars a week, and likely to remain that, till the inevitable time when he should be discharged. Now William John had a wife, two children, and a bungalow, concealed in Weehawken. He needed thirty-five a week. He had to make the extra ten by outside writing. Two weeks after he had gone to work for Lancelot, he remained in during lunch hour and for *Thought Power Magazine* composed an essay on "Getting a Raise." He boldly stated:

"Don't ask the boss for a raise—hit him! And hit him hard! First put so much originality in your work that you stand out among the other fellows in the shop, then walk in and tell the boss what he's GOT TO give you! Look him square in the eye and say, 'Here's a schedule of what I've done. I'm WORTH this raise, Brother Boss.' He'll listen—he'll treat you square—he'll remember the time when he used to want raises himself! If he wasn't square he wouldn't be boss!"

Miss Melody, returning from lunch with the battered remains of a dill pickle still in her hand, caught him chuckling over his writing, and queried, "What's all the humor, Mr. Buckingham?"

"Kind of like something I've been grinding out. Want to hear it?" asked the little man wistfully.

Miss Melody perched on a desk and condescended, "Shoot!"

When William John had recited his bold words, she gurgled, "Say, that's swell! Why, don't you tackle Mr. Todd that way?"

"Ddddddddo you ttttttthink I dare?" quavered William John.

"Sure. Look him square in the eye."

It was noticeable that for an hour afterward William John was too upset to work. He begged pardon of the office boy who walked on his feet. He glanced bashfully away when Eugene Hicks cast a roving, bored look his way. When Lancelot returned from lunch, William John fumbled across the office, knocked at Lancelot's door. At the blare of "Well?" he ducked. He crept inside. He tried to look Lancelot square in the eye.

Ordinarily, when he had matters of *Jazz* policy to discuss, this was easy. He was not in awe of Lancelot as penman. But as keeper of the purse, Lancelot seemed to have turned into a brazen monster with eyes of fire. William John despairingly picked up a ruler, tapped it on the back of his hand, and muttered, "Say, Mr. Todd, with the rent and grocery bills going up this way————"

"Nothing doing till we see how *Jazz* goes!" rumbled Lancelot, so that his voice could be heard all through the outer office.

As William John trailed back, Miss Melody looked sympathetic. But Eugene Hicks was laughing, in his widest, pastiest manner.

Eugene Hicks, editor of *Aux Dames*, and failure as editor of *Jazz*, had been the lowliest creature in the office, till the coming of William John. Anyone could tease Eugene. Through his layers of fat he would dimly perceive that something was wrong, but he never knew what it was all about. The office boy gave a good deal of honest labor to catching flies and drowning them in Eugene's inkwell. Eugene realized that here was somebody he could make miserable in turn.

Miss Melody had praised William John's essay on boldness. Eugene went to William John's desk ostensibly to borrow the Thesaurus, and fished about till he got hold of the essay. At five, when

Lancelot had gone out to tea, Eugene took the middle of the floor and made oration:

"Gemmuns and ladies. You may not know it, but we have among us Kid Waldo Emerson, the featherweight philosopher. Let me read you his ringing words, which will, I am sure, encourage you all to imitate his manner of addressing tyrant Todd." With his big soft flabby voice mimicking a schoolboy, Eugene read the essay. William John looked as though he were going to weep, then became tinily belligerent, finally locked his face in an expression of patient amusement.

Eugene began daily to find new jests to practice, and William John did not turn in wrath. He bent lower at his desk each day, spoke more diffidently to Eugene and Miss Melody and Mr. Todd, slunk in among the gossiping crowd in the elevator at night. He did not go to war even when Eugene smashed the international office code by borrowing his new fountain pen, pawning it, and wittily buying a box of candy for the office out of the proceeds.

But the more humble he became as a private person, the mightier was William John as editor and chief contributor of *Jazz*.

By the middle of the second month he had obtained a staff of volunteer correspondents from among the Universal clerks and managers who liked to see their names in print. He was receiving a dozen letters a day, choosing the best news items, and revising these in the puristic manner of *Jazz*. His columns of gossip were as buoyant as William John himself was depressed.

Under the heading "An' Everything," the delighted clerks of the chain stores were enabled to read:

"'Lo, folks! Are you creeping up on the increase of turnovers and gonna soak it with brick in a sock? But don't expect to find it napping. These turnovers are spry birds to ketch, Claude.

"Shy old Chi store No. 16 may be put out in the smello packing house district, but it sure is prodding 'em prizely. Get into the procesh, youse other Chicago stores!

"Our good friend Miss Mamie Fallups, the capable cashier of Birmingham store No. 3, writes us there's a new clerk down thataway as oughta chase the rest of the bhoys offn the map. He's a wonder at handling milk, and has some idees about a lil side line of safety pin. Notherwords, Local Manager Martin is grinding and passing the seegars. Bring him up to the Universal ideals of Service, Hustle, and Increased Sales, Brer Martin.

"Special Representative Carl Skovgaard sends us the following interesting facts about the six Minneapolis stores: Among the twenty-seven clerks are nine Norwegians (Ay tank so!), six Irish (arrah, yez spalpeens, the top o' the mornin' begorra!), five (we dassn't say it, these wartimes, but these five WERE G-rmans!), three Yanks (nix on the wooden nutmegs, boys!), and one Icelander (brrr! that makes us cold!)."

William John encouraged communications from clerks, but the most popular department of *Jazz*—as was indicated by scores of letters—was that in which William John spoke from the pulpit, under the name of "Uncle Jerry Ginger." He made of Uncle Jerry a real person; chattered about his rheumatism and the shortage of heat in his flat; recalled the most convincing—and mythical—experiences as a grocery clerk. It was Uncle Jerry who uttered that distinguished philosophical dictum which was copied by eleven other house organs:

"We aren't satisfied with clerks that spend only eighteen hours a day in working or thinking about work. What are you doing with the other six hours? Huh? What's that? Sleeping? You remember what happened to Rip Van Winkle. He slept forty years and all he had to show for it was a load of chin-alfalfa!"

It was Jerry Ginger who composed that delicate lyric which a printing house begged permission to quote on a card to be sent to all its customers; that inspired yet playful call to a nobler conduct of business affairs:

> O r U gonna B a busy b, b, b?
> O r U gonna * or merely c, c, c?
> O g! the lazy js will cuss a big d-d!
> Kum kan the t-talk, boys, and in ur B-V-D,
> Y, work like l, and get the $$ same as me!

It was Jerry Ginger who originated and judged the contests. Each month he picked the three individual clerks with the largest salesbooks, and the town with the largest percentage of increase over the previous month's sales. He was elaborate in his remarks about the contests. He described them as aeroplane races, or base-ball games, or donation parties to Old Pastor Universal. Perhaps the most esteemed of these comments was his description of the success of Lima in winning the city contest:

"My Land o' Goshen, ef Pop ain't gonna take us all out Sunday P.M. ridin' in the flivver. And who's that in the front seat beside him? Why, it's Lima, Ohio! But come on all you other near-wases! Where's Gramma Hartford's bonnet? Jax, have you got the cold tea—no, not feet, *tea* I said! Tell lil Eau Claire to crank the bus—he's one bright enfant, and oughta climb into the top-prize-winning class P. awful D.Q. All you birds, pin the hustle-buttons on your chist, shake up, wake up, and come on. With the Big Boss driving, we're all riding to the town that's built of dollars!"

The only persons whose salaries were increased as a result of all this clamor were the three prize-winning clerks each month. But so many paeans were sung over these increases that almost every clerk in the chain was stirred to frantic energy. Lancelot estimated that the Universal company, in three months, received an additional three thousand a month in net income, at a cost of not over a thousand a month for the expense of issuing *Jazz* and for all the raised salaries. The president of the company was so cheered that Lancelot felt safe in demanding a jump from two hundred to four hundred a month as his salary for supervising the publication of *Jazz*, a task which took at least one afternoon a month. The president assented. Lancelot was moved to generosity, and added eight dollars a week to William John's wages.

The only visible effects of this wealth on William John were his purchase of a new suit, price eighteen dollars in a "climb one flight to save ten dollars" shop, and his increased attention to *Jazz*. He was able, now, to drop almost all of his outside writing, and to devote all his days and evenings to searching for new and more splendidly nauseating ways of saying. "Work hard, you clerks, hear me?"

His real reward was in the letters from clerks to Uncle Jerry Ginger. They wrote to thank him personally for all the raises in salary, for his prose poems which encouraged them when they began to wonder if every clerk in the chain would indeed become president of the company. He had become to them a more real and incomparably more respected person than any officer of the Universal. They urged him to make the round of the stores and get acquainted. William John smiled as he thought of what they would say if he did come cheeping in, and he answered with good sound lies. Once, after reading a round robin from the enthusiastic San Diego clerks, who agreed that Uncle Jerry in real life must be "a big tall fellow, probably about fifty-five, with gray beard and jolly voice and a big laugh," William John bowed his head on his arms.

Even Anderson, the nonconforming advertising manager of the Universal Company, said that Jerry Ginger made him less ill than some other features of *Jazz*. Jerry's remarks had, said Anderson, the same chewing-gum manner as the rest of the house organ, but at times seemed almost literate.

As for the president of the company, he developed real affection for the unknown Uncle Jerry. Once, in Lancelot's private office, he asked, "Who is Jerry Ginger, anyway? You told me you didn't write this stuff personally, but who does? Some well-known author or somebody?"

"You bet! And that's why I can't tell you his name. You'd know it, all right—magazine headliner. And say, that fellow is a wonder at looking out for Number One, too. That's why I had to ask you to come through with a bigger budget for *Jazz*. I don't really make hardly anything out of it personally, because Uncle Jerry demands so blame much that I have to shell out practically all I get!" confessed poor Lancelot whimsically.

"What kind of fellow is he personally?"

"Oh, a prince! Big, fine-looking chap, dresses well, and repartee—say, *man!*"

"Yes, I figured out by myself that he must be quite somebody. I don't care much for this literature and guff, but I do know a sound, sensible, progressive, successful man when I read his stuff," said the president proudly. "Well, I wish I could meet him."

As he spoke, a small man with a bald head and weak red eyes peeped through the door. The president did not notice him, while Lancelot merely snapped, "Busy, Buck. Come in later."

William John did not take advantage of his legal period of three days for a spree, the first month. The four months following he merely disappeared for a day each month. During the sixth, he was trembly; his hands shook; his voice broke unexpectedly. Though he turned out copy as steadily and spicily as ever, his typing was slow, and his neck sunk vulture-like between thin shoulders, as he stooped over his rickety desk.

The office discussed his nervousness with pleasant dread. Miss Melody protected him; helped him pick up the pages when he jumpily dropped a manuscript. The thing which stirred her hussar soul gave joy to Mr. Eugene Hicks.

As a large boy of twelve, Eugene had been whipped by every ten-year-old in the neighborhood. Back in the shoe store, he had been ridiculed even by the scrubwoman. This was the first time that he had found a butt. He felt virile, red-blooded, pushing, plucky, persistent, and progressive, as he regarded William John. Miss Melody protested, "You think you're a Charlie Chaplin, Mr. Hicks, don't you? No office but a bum one like Todd's would stand for you. Why, a real copywriter in a real agency—like the one I used to work in before I got jinxed and came here—would whale the daylights out of you. Funny: whenever you find a tyrant like Mr. Todd, there's always a bunch of leeches like you hanging around him."

In the joy of having a victim, Eugene ignored her. He became a patient and methodical office pest. He used William John's pencil—with the good eraser. He hid William John's hat, when the butt had worked past his lunch hour and was in a hurry to get out.

One Wednesday morning Eugene surpassed himself. William John was gasping in a queer, puppy-like way. Eugene got a house-connection with William John's telephone, pretended to be a neighbor, and till Miss Melody interrupted and spoiled the game, he had the nicest time telling William John that his daughter had been taken ill. Also he hung on William John's desk a wonderful new sign: "Yesterday was my busy day—today I'm drunk." The smaller stenographers giggled. William John tried to smile, and went out to lunch extra-early.

Not till four-thirty did he return. At that time, just after Lancelot had gone on the rampage because the stenographers could not find the carbon of the Aurora Borealis Gunnysack Company proposition, there was a sound of smashing glass, and Mr. William John Buckingham entered.

He had on a new crimson tie, and from his breast pocket trailed a saffron silk handkerchief. His chin was up, and he was stepping wide and high. He was singing a recitative:

> I lost a valoolable pipe,
> A v'loolable pipe,
> A v'loolable pipe,
> I lost a valoolable pipe,
> V'loolable pipe.

At the racket, Lancelot bounced to the door of his private room. Now Lancelot was in many ways a wise man. When he beheld the state of William John, he nimbly shut the door, and was as the deaf.

William John sat on the edge of Eugene's desk, and remarked. "The hiding of hats is a merry game." With that he threw Eugene's derby through the window, which was twelve stories up. "Hanging signs upon desks? A zephyr of wit!" He yanked open the waistcoat of the trembling Eugene, who tried to pull away. With one hand William John seized his throat, and while Eugene's face turned to a fairy lavender, William John lettered his shirt-front in ink, "Hicksie, the human two-em dash."

"Now, Eugene, my desk likes me not. 'Twere befitting that you should hide in yon sequestered nook, while I be here enthroned. Take your violet stationery and powder puff over there, while I go in and tell Todd the gladsome tidings that he has forced a raise on me." He leaned down and looked into Eugene's eyes. Eugene shuddered, and tried to duck behind his upraised elbow.

William John climbed into Lancelot's office, without knocking.

Lancelot was not angry. He was grinning. "Say, Buckingham, you think you're the drunkest bird this old town has ever seen. Well, I was about four times as drunk last Saturday, and I bet it took more than four times as much liquor to do it. And you think you're going to bully me into raising you? Well, I'm bullied. I raise you—ten bones a week. Here's the first ten in advance. Now run along and play till next Monday, and don't try to compete with a *real* booze-hoister."

William John opened and shut his mouth silently. Abruptly he sat on the floor and raised his voice in protestation: "Then I can't quit! And I was going to wreck your office, and go back to the bread line! When I get over this jag, I'll find I'm still on the same rotten job I had when I started in. That's never happened to me before in twenty-seven years of gin and journalism. Damn you, you're an intellectual forger, gimme fifteen."

On Monday the office was creamy with peace. Eugene was respectful at a small brown desk behind the water cooler. At Eugene's former desk, by the window, was William John, very hoarse and suddenly grown fond of water as a beverage. In the private room Lancelot was making plans for the publicity features of the coming national convention of the Universal Grocery Store's employees.

The convention had hitherto been merely a gathering of managers and district superintendents. William John had suggested that it be made a real social event, and that the company pay half the expenses of all the ordinary clerks who wished to attend. He had planned rides to Coney Island, visits to food factories, and that religious rite which the New York *Sun* says must not be called a "banquet."

He had invited hints from all readers of *Jazz*. Glancing over the letters sent in response, Lancelot was disturbed to learn that one thing the clerks most wanted was a chance to meet "Uncle Jerry Ginger." They assumed that at last they were to find out who he was. Lancelot wasted no time in considering the fact that William John might also wish to meet them. His only feeling was that at all costs the readers of *Jazz* must be prevented from learning that Uncle Jerry was an unsteady, red-eyed little hack. Someone large and imposing————? "Yeah, cinch!" Lancelot caroled.

He rang for William John and informed him, "You can announce in the preconvention number of *Jazz* that Uncle Jerry will be at the banquet, and after it be glad to meet every delegate personally."

"That's awfully good of you, sir. I'll get a new suit and—I'd really enjoy it. Kind of got interested in these Universal fellows————"

"You? Now, Buckingham be reasonable. Do you really suppose *you* could throw enough side to impress these guys? I'm sure you'll understand. No, we'll train Eugene Hicks. Of course, we know he's a boob, but he can look like a hundred thousand dollars, and if we tell him what to say————"

"But don't I even go to the banquet? Gee—and—there—will—be—champagne!"

That was William John's only complaint. He was sulkily obedient. He composed a banquet speech and some impromptu epigrams for Eugene to utter, as Uncle Jerry, and coached him in casually tossing them off.

When Miss Mary Theresa Melody heard that William John was to be robbed of his glory—and his champagne—she delivered soapbox speeches in the office. "We've got to do something about this. Let me think," she said maternally to William John. A week before the convention assembled, William John was trying to dictate to her an answer to a letter from Anderson, advertising manager of the Universal Company, in which Anderson had courteously hinted that the enthusiasm roused by *Jazz* was about as real and enduring as the Belgian Hare craze. As she slashed out the sign for "Very sincerely yours," Miss Melody whispered, "Got it! Quick! Come out in the hall!"

When they returned William John was smiling so pacifically that Eugene reached for a lead paperweight and prepared to sell his life dearly. But William John did nothing more violent than croon: "I lost a valollable pipe."

The Universal convention was attended by hundreds of clerks, who were roused to a suitable hysteria by the speeches of the president, the sales manager, Anderson, and Lancelot. It wound up in the banquet in the Gold Room of the Hotel Riviera.

Lancelot was there. During convention week he had rented himself to the Universal Company—for a large rental. But the feature of the banquet to which the clerks had look forward was the appearance of Uncle Jerry Ginger, and at last they were able to hear and see him—words and music by William John, face and clothes by Eugene. Front, center, at the speaker's table, was Eugene, a beauteous thing in evening clothes, with a rococo facade of shirt-bosom, and a gardenia which Lancelot had anchored to his lapel and warned him not to touch.

Now and then Eugene drank inspiration from a typed list of Uncle Jerryisms which William John had prepared for him. When he found nothing good to say, he obeyed instructions and smiled knowingly. More reputations for greatness have been acquired by the use of a knowing smile, dignified whiskers, or a deep voice, than by the use of brains.

Beside Eugene was the toastmaster, Anderson. He was curious about Uncle Jerry. He detested Jerry's coy misspellings, but did expect to find in him a cynical humor. In Eugene he discovered nothing but dust and odor of jimson weeds. He tried to get Eugene's theory of advertising. Eugene's theory was, it proved, "Well, aw, well, I think advertising is a very valuable means of, uh, in modern selling."

"You really think so?" marveled Anderson.

Lancelot, sitting just beyond Eugene, tried to protect his strawberry lamb by interrupting, "Brer Anderson, d' I ever tell you the good one about the traveling man in the Pullman?" Anderson listened gravely, and wondered whether he would kill Lancelot with a carafe or a hotel roll.

Eugene realized that he had failed to make an impression of Knowledge Abundant and the Soul Victorious. He didn't know exactly what a Soul Victorious was, but from the career of Lancelot he judged that it must be closely allied to noise. He burrowed in the dark recesses of his lack of intelligence, and brayed in what he conceived to be the best manner of Uncle Jerry. "Well, Anderson, ole socks, we've sure got the boys together and handed them the glad hand, uh, handed 'em, uh—certainly jazzed 'em up! Ha! Ha! Ha!"

"Yes, aren't these roses charming," replied Anderson.

The banquet struggled through the remarks of the president and the sales manager. The clerks had been willing to throb over efficiency speeches at the business meetings, but now they wanted a good time, a table-pounding time, with an uproarious address by Uncle Jerry. Shouts of "Uncle Jerry! Jerry Ginger!" were beginning to crackle. Anderson nodded to Eugene, and suggested, "Go to it."

Eugene loomed up, vast, shiny, and, thanks to Lancelot, entirely sober. He smiled like a maple-nut sundae, and opened his mouth, all of it. Then he closed it again. Anderson's quizzical look had made him forget the talk which William John had written for him. He fought for time while rumbling on in his own pretty, native way:

"Well, fellows, old Uncle Jerry Ginger has come to meet you at last, uh, meet you; and, uh, I guess he doesn't seem so awful old at that. Ha! Ha! I am reminded of the story, uh, the story about two Jews; no, it was too Irishmen; their names were Mike and Pat, and one of 'em says to the other————"

It took Eugene two minutes of stalling to remember just what was the very humorous thing which Mike had said to Pat. The guests looked at one another in surprise. This didn't touch the insurance man's annual speech at the I.O.O.F. banquet back home. Anderson was frowning—wondering.

Eugene struggled on, decks awash and boats carried away. "Now, fellows, you know we all just work together—work together—wish I could make you see how we all work together—I at my desk and————"

"You at my desk, you mean!" shrieked a voice from the back of the room.

Everybody turned. All they could see was a crack between the entrance doors. But Eugene appeared to recognize the voice. He became distinctly shorter as his knees sagged. He tried to go on: "————you at yours, each of us doing—doing duty, full of energy and————"

"————and prunes!" added that diabolical voice.

Eugene came to a full stop and looked imploringly at Lancelot. As the guests glanced back again the doors swung open, and between them stood William John Buckingham, Esq., beatifically waving his oldest, smallest, fuzziest round cloth hat. He advanced into the room intoning, "Somebody has been feeding meat to that sheep again. That ruddy ram isn't Unk' Jerry Ginger. I am! And if toas'masser will lemme, I'll prove it! How 'bout it, Misser Toas'masser?"

"This is an outrage! Call the hotel detective!" the president was observing, while Lancelot growled, "Anderson, I know that fellow. He's a drunken panhandler."

"Throw him out!" demanded the dignitaries at the speakers' table. "Give him a chance!" yelled back the enlisted guests. The captain of waiters was swooping on William John, apparently intending to bury him under a silver platter-cover.

Quick, keen, knife-like, Anderson darted to the edge of the dais and commanded, "We will give him a chance. What's the idea, old man?"

"Conjure process—shesh—sesh'n—caravan from Damas'us comes—spishes of Eash—camels and bellboys—whoosh!" explained William John. He waved his magic hat, and through the doors he evoked a procession of four Hotel Riviera footmen in buckled shoes, knee breeches, and blue and silver coats, carrying two light typewriting tables with fixed typewriters. The rearguard was a bellboy bearing typing paper and wearing a cocked hat made of newspaper, which was presumably not part of his regulation uniform.

"Put 'em down here in front!" commanded William John.

The president was protesting, "By the great Jehosophat———"

Anderson turned on him earnestly. "Wait, chief. I've got a hunch there's something to the little man."

While the banquet hall snapped with curiosity, the typewriting tables were set up in front of the dais. William John addressed the toastmaster—whom he seemed to be trying to locate on the ceiling.

"Zhis fellow they rung in on you as Unk' Jerry is mere error in syntax. Prove it. Let him and me sit down here and write spiel on any subjeck Misser Toas'masser chooses. Shee which of us soun's like Unk' Jerry."

"Fair enough!" bellowed the enchanted guests.

Eugene looked piteously at his commander, Lancelot Todd, and besought, "What can I do?"

"Aah!" snarled Lancelot, turning his back.

"Whash subjeck?" demanded William John.

Anderson announced, "I should think an appropriate topic would be 'The Beauties of Prohibition.'"

"Sosh—soc'logical interest," acclaimed William John. "Shay, Misser Toas'masser, forgot consideration high impor'—import. If I win, do I get some champagne?"

"You sure do!" confirmed Anderson.

"Whoosh! Come on, Eugene, you pair of brackets, you parasitical parenth'sis marks!" William John rejoiced.

Eugene mournfully descended from the speakers' table and forced his fat legs beneath one of the typewriter-stands. William John attacked a chair, vanquished it, yanked it to his stand, held up his hands like Paderewski about to play a scherzo, and hit the keys one terrific swat. He sprawled all over the machine. He used only his two forefingers in typing, but he seemed to write a whole sentence at once. He jerked back the roller with a bang. He kneaded the keys and slapped them; he punched them so that they stuck together and had to be pulled apart with a lightning swoop of his tiny little finger. And while his forefingers flashed like knitting needles, he hummed, "Lost v'loolable pipe."

Eugene seemed shy of his machine. He poked at it and dodged back each time.

Two on each side of the contestants were ranged the footmen, their four majestic chins and eight haughty eyes aimed toward the ceiling, and their forty pure white fingers glued to their sides.

For five minutes the hall was filled with the crash of William John's machine, the slow ticking of Eugene's, the muttering of the president of the company, the giggles of the clerks, and the opening of champagne bottles. Then William John tore out his second sheet of paper and rose.

"Time's up!" declared Anderson.

With a sulky rattle of ratchets, Eugene pulled out his single sheet.

"You big fellow, you read first," directed Anderson, and Mr. Eugene Hicks offered:

"Hello, you chaps. I want you all to know that I think Prohibition is certainly one of the big questions of the day. We all admit that in running Big Biz, the boozer isn't as dependable as the steady and sober————"

"That's enough. Now you!" said Anderson, and William John, standing bandy-legged and wavering, but lifting his voice to the glad eventide, recited:

"Prohibition? Rats! Dunno the word! If I had to be all bound round with a woolen string 'fore I could cut out some swell little habit like eating ground glass, or cutting Gramma's throat, or wearing earmuffs in August, I'd apply for Class 1 in the bobby-hatch draft. Nozzaree! I canned the blind-stagger stuff all by myself! Me and the Missus got our own private Anti-saloon League on the front pazzazza, and *our* kids never have to yip, 'Gee, I wisht they would pass the Prohibition Law, 'cause there's dear Pop weaving home again, with a cop's ear in his side pocket, and a summons in his hatband, and in his wobbly fist a lil letter saying, "Dear employee, the razoo for yours!" ' "

Anderson interrupted to state, "Gentlemen, I swear to you that I don't know what the trick has been, but"—pointing to William John—"I do beg to introduce to you the only genuine Uncle Jerry Ginger!"

Among the guests who rose, cheering, were not only all the clerks, but most of the local managers and district superintendents, and it was the sales managers who shouted to the captain of waters, "Bring Uncle Jerry a full quart of champagne."

In the lee of the retiring footmen Eugene had disappeared. William John, very shabby and calm, took Eugene's place at the speakers' table, refused all such annoyances as food and salad, and applied himself to the champagne. Lancelot Todd looked like the prisoner during the summing-up by the district attorney—impersonal and uneasily easy, recrossing his legs a different way every time somebody glanced at him. The president of the company was red and sunken in his chair, and beyond his mental depths.

The crowd began to yell, "Speech, Uncle Jerry! Speech!" William John ignored them till he had finished his quart. Then he rose and pronounced, "Boys, no need for a speech. Got it all written out for you." He raised his voice: "Minions! The court circulars!"

The silver-laced footmen again entered, with piles of pamphlets, and distributed them to the guests, while William John explained: "Gotten out special convention number *Jazz*."

He sat down, and the others glanced through the magazine—the clerks with frowning thoughtfulness, the managers with uneasiness, the president with fury, and Lancelot with complete nausea.

The special edition contained only four pages, printed in large, boldfaced type, beginning:

"I've been lying to you Universal clerks, but I've come to like you. Here's some truth. Have you noticed how few actual raises follow these desperate contests we've been running? The bosses want you to get so excited over the contests that you won't think about how much you're paid.

"And let's analyze this glorious philosophy of hustle-jazz-pep. It sounds like heroic progress, this working twenty-four hours a day; but what it means is never taking time for friendship, courtship, reading, music, the fineness of leisure. The firm wants you to become machines, and for what? If you increase their income a thousand percent they may give you back, as charity, a ten percent increase————"

When the president had read thus far he bellowed, "I want all of you men to bring your copies of this filthy, lying rag up here and leave them————"

Turning a friendly eye on his disciples, William John piped, " 'S all right. I've mailed two copies to each clerk at his home."

Then did the patience of the combination Job, Jeremiah and Joshua of press agents, Mr. Lancelot Todd, go beyond the boiling point, and, poking a ramrod forefinger at William John, he thundered, "You're fired, right now!"

William John rose. "Boysh, before you bring copies up, glansh at last page. I go sadly hence, but Uncle Jerry will hold reception at bar, downstairs, for now till one—merry but strictly Dutch."

On the last page of *Jazz* they found printed in Gothic caps:

"Uncle Jerry to *his* boss: No, Todd, I'm not fired. I've quit. I've saved up twenty-five dollars. Do you think that anyone with twenty-five dollars would work for you?"

BRONZE BARS

Valory sits in a cage and looks through bronze bars, and from nine to three he never sees anybody's feet. But he is general advisor to English actors, Greek bootblacks, policemen, and the widows of colonels.

He is senior paying and receiving teller of the Palladium Savings Bank, a small stuffy institution not far from Broadway. He is thirty-three years old. His dark, thin, sulky face is considered romantic by his landlady and sardonic by depositors who watch him scowl over their vanishing accounts. But he is neither romantic nor sardonic. He is as sentimental as a maiden aunt. He sympathizes with the little people among his customers. He sees so many tragic comedies that after banking hours his soul is drained, and whenever he tries to make gallant plans for his own advancement he ends by wilting into a seat at the movies.

Valory is, at our first view of him, as chillingly regular as a clearing-house certificate. From his furnished room, with its matting and its photographs of an undesirable child posed as Cupid, he regularly comes by way of breakfast at the Eats Garden to his cage. He has never experienced wheat fields glaring in the sun, nor a steamer's bridge slanting in a gale. His world is a space six feet by twelve. He knows every inch of it as an ant knows every grain of sand on its hill. For almost ten years he has been profoundly familiar with the watery blue label of this paste pot, with this small brown spot on the side of the coin till. Thirty times a day for three thousand crawling days he has caught this sharp nick on the edge of the elbow desk with the heel of his palm, and uttered an abstracted "Ouch!" All his perilous mountains and climbing seas are in this nick in a slab of oak.

Yet he remains alive. He has never yet carried out his ancient fond desire to assassinate the president of the bank, kick the porter, choke the cat and become a hobo. For he lives in and through the line of people who all day long come past his grille and peer in at him, asking for the means to purchase bread and sorrow and satin slippers.

He lives in them, yet at times he seems to detest them. For his job is not merely to hand out money, but to keep people from wanting it. There are the drunkards who—ever since the most important July 1st in history—come unsteadily to the bars, breathe in on him and demand a ten with which to continue their vacation from human cares. If Valory can coax them to go away, they are likely to come in grateful next week and deposit an extra ten.

There are messenger boys who have heard that if you put a dollar in the bank it almost immediately turns into a thousand, and after you get the first thousand you are practically over the difficulties in becoming a Rockefeller. The boys put in a dollar a week for five weeks, and after this large proportion of eternity discover with pain and disillusion that they have only five dollars. What's the use? They come cynically to Valory and try to withdraw it.

Valory viciously dislikes the bland, soft gentlemen with hardboiled foreheads who do nothing but go about lecturing to young men on optimism and early rising, but when the young depositors need coaching he gives an imitation of the inspiration jobbers. He smiles down on the boys and commends their thrift. He snaps at them that they are nuisances to expect the bank to do all this extra bookkeeping. He tells them not very historical anecdotes about Napoleon and Earl Kitchener. Somehow or other he usually keeps the money in the bank, and once in a dozen times the five dollars grows to a hundred—and once in a dozen, dozen, dozen times the boy is grateful to Valory.

When the scrubwomen come shuffling in on flapping shoes, when they mumble of sickness and the rent, and want to draw out all they have, Valory begs them to leave in just one dollar. If they leave a dollar they will try again.

Watching them, protecting them against themselves, Valory has almost as much interest in expanding accounts as have the depositors. He knows his people better than their ministers do. They ask him questions about the correct time, hiring cooks, the name of the man who played the crocodile in *Peter Pan*, and the shortest way of getting to Williamsburg.

Actors send him money from Terre Haute and Spokane, till the summer day when they appear in new, green, high-waisted coats, and begin their tedious season of drawing it out, fifteen dollars a week. Young scared girls starting out as public stenographers talk with him about their balances till the day when they excitedly confide that they're going over to the national bank to open a real drawing account.

He sees a noisy young man, who has been depositing three dollars every month, suddenly begin to save ten a week. And sometimes there is a girl waiting at the bank door. On the day when the waiting girl's cheeks are pinkest and her fingers most fluttering the depositor draws out most of the account. Then Valory knows that the time for furnishing the new home has come and he shyly cries: "Good luck!"

It must not be supposed that Valory is as constantly in a glow of benevolence as a Dickens Christmas story. There are many days when customers are as stupid to a teller as they are a to bootblack. To the bootblack people are merely tan boots or black oxfords or slimy mud on thick soles. They are equally irritating to Valory on days when his brain is dry and rusty—only he sees them at the other end from the bootblack. According to his experience people not only lack shoes but, to a surprising degree, they lack legs. They are objects with heads, shoulders, and hands designed to stick bankbooks at him.

On such days he peevishly divides all human beings into three classes: Those who paw at money in a blasé way, those who clutch it betrayingly, and Account 112,761.

Account 112,761 had long been the one person who took the trouble to be frivolous and inspiring and gay and shocking to his professional conservatism. Account 112,761 was the one person who invariably stood out of the drab, preoccupied line creeping past him. Account 112,761 was the one flower on his dust heap; the one person who understood that he wasn't a mechanical device, an accessory to the adding machine and the charge counter. When the others said, "Good morning," they didn't really care a hang whether he was having a good morning or not. But account 112,761 looked at him quizzically, and made impertinent comments in a voice that suggested drawing rooms.

Account 112,761 had come in a year before—a girl of perhaps twenty-six; a plain beaver hat, all lines and no trimming, one side rolled up like an Australian's campaign hat; a high collar; a small black bow clasped with a diamond bar; white chamois gloves. He never was able to describe her face; there were no irregularities to get over, but he was conscious of the fineness of her nose and brows.

It was the sweet sure lines of her wrist, where a ring of delicate flesh peeped out above her turned-down glove, that he best knew and remembered. And everything, eyes and nose, glove and flippant hat, was accented by her nervous way of throwing herself at the teller's window. She was a human exclamation point.

She dashed at the grille, the first time, poked a badly rolled wad of bills beneath it, smiled at him, and suggested: "Will you take care of all my nice money for me?"

He was thinking how pearl-textured were her ears, almost concealed beneath her chestnut hair, while he droned: "You wish to open a new account?"

"No, of course not. I do not wish to leave the money. I wish to take it all out and spend it. But as man to man, do you think I shall save anything of if I put my patrimony here?"

He tried to look serious and financial, but her lips were lifting, and he admitted: "I doubt it. We might try."

"Will you be frightfully disagreeable when I come and try to coax some of this away from you?"

"I will!"

"Will you be good for my soul?"

"Certainly. We are a very moral institution."

"Oh, I'm sure of it. The dear old gentleman spending his dotage at the desk beyond the railing looks like a bishop."

The dear old gentleman, who was the president, was approximately a hundred and ninety-seven years old. He had been cursing frightfully for a hundred and ninety-four. He was a pirate and a crank, and one of the most dependable bankers in New York. He considered Valory a maudlin young fool, and Valory considered him

———

Well, Valory leaned his brow against the cold bronze of the bars and begged: "Won't you go tell him so?"

The girls eyelids did not move, but she gave the impression of winking at Valory.

While she was filling out her signature card he counted her first deposit. It was four hundred and seventy-six dollars. He made the entry in her virgin bankbook in his shockingly refined thin script. She took the book, tapped it with restless fingers, airily inquired: "What do I do with this literature?"

"Bring it in with you when you want to draw or deposit."

She peered into it, her eyes as curious as those of a mouse. She murmured: "Confidentially, has anybody ever read all these funny rules in the front of the book?"

"Why, you're supposed———"

"Have you ever?"

"I think——— Why certainly. I must have."

He tried to sound responsible and official. She merely grinned at him. She carelessly dropped the bankbook into a handbag and soared out, while he worried about her.

"She'll lose that bank book in seven minutes by the clock," he said, cynically, solemnly, disapprovingly.

He examined her identification card:

> NAME: *(Miss) Marcella Page*
> OCCUPATION: *None*
> RESIDENCE: *99,999 West End Avenue*

"Who the deuce is she?" he wondered. "Don't get many accounts from up there. Society, I guess. Father given her an allowance. She doesn't know what money is. Confounded idler. Ought to detest her. Yet—she's so much friendlier than some of the haughty waitresses and high-minded elevator girls. She——— Yes, ma'am—

deposit five—that's fine!" His awakening eagerness was lost in a line of hurried little people as twelve o'clock came and the lunch-time depositors began to gallop in.

Not till three o'clock did he return to the thought of Miss Page; then merely to sigh: "Wonder if I'll ever see her again? Probably not. Oh, well, thunder————"

He did see her again—at nine-thirty the following morning. She drew out ten dollars; and complained: "I thought you were going to keep my money away from my fevered clutch. The idea of spending all this on a lace dickey!"

"Why do you do it then?" he said gruffly.

For a second he was scared, not frightened, but plain, vulgarly scared. Her thin eyebrows went up in peaks, her eyes became impersonal, her hands twitched. She snubbed him with intensity and dispatch. But she relaxed and sighed: "You're quite right. Do keep after me. But—if I need the dickey. Man, would you have me walking the streets unclothed and shameless?"

She was gone and he was troubled. The girls he knew, the jolly girls back home, the wife of his friend the insurance man in town, did not talk that way. Yet he seemed to feel in Miss Page a fine, sure, penetrating honesty, a fundamental goodness, which he never caught sight of in their indignant respectability. She was————

"Idiot!" he snarled. "You'd think this was my first day in the cage. Me, that have banked for the star of the Follies and the secretary of the mayor, mooning over a pretty girl depositor!"

That, he felt, settled it. But in the evening, when he took Miss Clara Schweitz, buyer for the glove department at Golthrop's, to the theater, he found it so hard to talk to her that he merely listened to the play. Miss Schweitz had been so interested in his plans for a country bank that she had made him eloquent. Now something was between them, something tenuous, choking, thick, phantasmal as mist and more impassable than bars of bronze.

Account 112,761 did not come in for a week. Then at lunch-time she was suddenly visible in the line, a scarlet butterfly among gray moths, an exclamation point among commas and battered periods. A man made way for her; a frayed old woman looked back at her uncomfortably.

When she had edged up to the window she volleyed at him:

"Heavens, so many people going out of here with money, what a good profession picking pockets must be. I like your bank, the marble columns are so sweet and dumpy, like cream cheeses. Please let me have ten of my beautiful dollars."

Now she had not made out a withdrawal receipt, and for Valory to fill one out would hold up the line behind her. He was particular about customers writing their own. He worried that he ought to send her back to the wall desk—and he also managed to get in a good second of worried wonder as to whether he hadn't become as fussily red-taped as the old treasurer. He felt guilty that he should be stern with newsboys and lenient with her. "It's snobbish—unfair—rotten of me," he assured himself—and reaching for a slip made it out and beamingly slid it to her for signature.

"What's this ten for?" he said fatuously.

"Hat!"

He stared at her hat of that date—a martial affair, turned up in the front with a flourish of blue plumes.

"But you have a new one on."

"Yes. Isn't it nice?" She snapped up the bill he had handed her, tucked it into her pocket. "Is there any way of making me keep this in?"

"I'm trying to make you."

Her lips were impudent, her eyes rollicking. "My dear man, you must bully me.

"You must say a lot of overwhelming things about how Lord Rothschild saves threepence a week by never throwing away an inch of string."

He looked helpless, while she nodded and dashed away.

It was a glittering, intoxicating October day when she next appeared, just after the bank opened. No one was in line, and he cunningly held her there to chatter. This time, it seemed, she wanted fifteen dollars for a dozen bars of soap. This soap was worth all of five dollars, too, she insisted.

"How can I bully you into keeping up your account? You've drawn thirty-five dollars now, and you haven't deposited a cent. Don't you see that your entire account will soon be gone, at this rate?"

"Oh, no! Not all those beautiful four hundred dollars! The interest ought to cover my tiny drafts. By the way, I do get some interest, don't I? I forgot to ask," she said engagingly.

"Oh, Lord yes, but———"

"Don't sound so abysmal. The voice from the tombs went out when females stopped swooning. It must be dreadful to stay in a bank and have so much integrity and responsibility and everything. I'm glad I'm a butterfly. If I were a cashier—or whatever dreadfully imposing object it is that you are—I'd steal every lovely adorable dollar in sight, and go out on a day like this and blow in the whole thing. Pouf! Like that! Every cent!"

"And then go to jail."

"Oh, of course. Entrancing! Delightful porch climbers and safe blowers for company. They must have such a sense of humor."

"There is nothing humorous about crime."

"There is nothing criminal about humor."

"Then you haven't been to a vaudeville show lately."

"Bless me, the man turns on one! But—don't be discouraged. Keep after me. Poor Marcella, she wants so dreadfully to save money, but the fates are against her. This divine day—the sky over the white stone of the Pennsylvania Station is like tight-drawn blue silk. The sunshine is in all the shop windows—on velvets and polished satinwood and sapphires and sleek black furs. I'm drunk with it. I've simply got to spend money. And—*voilà!*"

As she raced away the cage was tight about him, like a choking collar.

Her voice remained with him, a lyric voice, not mumbling or rasping like most voices, but softly ringing. His cautious diligence seemed folly to him in the memory of her polite impertinence, her cheerful unwisdom. He knew that he was right, and he was not in the least comforted by the knowledge. He want about for hours spiritually washing his hands of her—and not getting her off.

But the Monday after she came in proudly, laid down ten dollars, and boasted: "I did save some! I'm going to make a deposit!"

"That's great!" he shouted.

He was aware that his normally thin voice has risen in such a clamor that the bookkeeper was staring at him, alarmed.

"You are nice," she meditated. "I hoped you would be. You make saving a pleasure. If you hadn't given me lots and lots of praise I should never have tried it again. And yet I suppose people keep bringing you hundreds and hundreds. I suppose you're about as much excited by the sight of ten dollars as a major general is by the sight of a second lieutenant. You have an amiable mind."

She shot out; as always, she left the conversation unfinished, palpitating, flying on by itself.

It occurred to Valory that this was the first time that a depositor had realized that he had any mind whatever. Even when they asked him financial advice—which in sumptuous, wholesale amounts they did ask, regarding stock investing, lease breaking, mortgage buying and the price of theater tickets—they poked queries at him as though they were jabbing nickels into a slot.

She thought he had an amiable mind.

It was lucky he wasn't shopping with her. He would uxoriously follow her into every shop and buy everything she liked. But not for long, he wouldn't. He had, these years, saved four thousand, two hundred dollars. Account 112,761 would make that last about one week.

Then he was stern with himself. How unjust he was to this lovely, gentle woman. Here she was saving money, already learning habits of thrift. And he had done it. He, who had never touched her hand, had influenced her.

From Monday morning till two-seven Wednesday afternoon he went about so like a stick of radium that the irritated bookkeeper inquired: "What the devil are you looking so virtuous about?"

At two-seven P.M., Wednesday the eighth, Miss Page trotted in, smiled upon him, and caroled: "I think I'll take out that ten dollars I put in, with two more dollars feebly clinging to it."

And this time the money was for tea to three girls at the St. Candido. She volunteered the inspiring tidings. She added: "I'm dreadfully trying. I have no idea of the value of money. I'm a parasite woman, aren't I?"

"You are," he growled.

He deliberately went to the telephone to order the florist to send some tea roses to Miss Clara Schweitz.

But after hours he stopped in the midst of running up items paid out, stalked to the president's desk, borrowed the Social Register, and looked up Page—Marcella. He found her.

Now Valory was not afraid of the Social Register. He had a perfectly good Rhode Island family. He knew a few people in the

New York register, and his cousins, the Gingery girls—the wife of the major and the one who married the judge—were very much in the St. Paul register. But he had given some study to his own limitations. He knew that he was not likely ever to be anything more conspicuous than the cashier of the Palladium, or assistant cashier in some big bank downtown. Whereas Miss Page's father——— He looked again. Her father must be dead. But anyway——— Probably a big gun—surgeon, corporation counsel, that sort of thing.

He sighed and went back to his adding machine. He yanked the receipts furiously from the spindle. He glanced over at the dignified ledger and told it bluntly that it looked like a butter tub. When the junior teller came festively up and inquired, "What's eating you? Great short arm jab you've got on the machine," Valory said, "Don't be vulgar," which was an entirely new form of repartee in the Palladium cage.

Through the winter Miss Page burst into view at least once a week and conversationally abstracted money from her account. She observed that she had heard George M. Cohan was going to stage the "Ride of the Valkyries" in a blimp. She confided that the real news of the day wasn't the peace conference, but the fact that since she had grown a bang she could wear a hair net without chopping her forehead in two. She asked his advice about selling a couple of shares of an industrial which she owned. She confessed her limited Manhattan life by snorting about a departing depositor: "What a terrible walking stick that poor dear man is carrying! He must come from out West—Buffalo or someplace."

But he realized—he who had listened to confidential people, to boasters and drunkards and the women who weep always—that she talked a great deal about herself without telling anything; that she was more reticent than the merchants who growled "G'mornen'." He never dared, for all his desire to coax her into thrift, to bully her. It was only with whimsical despair that he wailed, "What's this for this time?" when she came in and flippantly drew ten or fifteen or twenty-five.

Twice she said that it was for shoes. Once for an evening petticoat. Once imitation pearls. Once for another hat. And that time he noticed that she already had a new hat—a baskety kind of thing with a white satin facing. He begged her not to waste her money.

What on earth did she need a new hat for when she had this triumph?

She remarked: "Do you like it? So glad." She took her money, grinned and departed—flippant, alert, clean, provoking and distracting and gaily aloof.

In July her account was down to seventeen dollars.

And she was not aloof or flippant on the July noon when she entered the bank and, instead of rushing into line, stood back till his window was clear. Her lips were white and tight across her teeth; between her eyes a wrinkle came and went, came and went, while her brows twitched. She rushed to him when he was free, laid her bank book down carefully, begged: "Will you please let me know whether I have any interest coming?"

Normally, interest would have been computed for her at the bookkeeper's window, but Valory himself took the book back, hustled the process through. She had never had the interest entered. While he waited Valory looked down the length of the cage and saw her standing rigid, tapping the counter.

"There is five dollars and eighteen cents," he told her hopefully.

"Oh!" she wailed.

A bulbous, short, pushing man, a prosperous and unlovely person from the garment trades, had fallen in behind Miss Page and was making sounds of haste.

"Is there some place—may I speak to you a moment?" Miss Page begged.

"Certainly. Come down to the Liberty Loan window." To the impatient one Valory suggested: "Would you mind going to the other teller?"

From the Liberty Loan window he looked owlishly, while he ached at hearing her sure quick voice break under doubt, at seeing the stain of sorrow on anything so bright and unscarred. She clutched the edge of the counter with both hands, her thumbs beneath. Valory noticed that her gloves were not as sleek as formerly. There was a distinct darn in one chamois finger.

She was hesitating. "I've heard—I'm a ghastly dub about money matters, and I don't own any real estate or anything, but I've heard something about the possibility of borrowing money from banks.

Especially if you're a regular customer. And I've been frightfully regular, haven't I? You don't know how hard I've tried to heed your suggestions about saving. But———— I must take out the twenty-two that is coming to me and I should like to borrow fifty more."

"Why—why————" He could not tell her that her perfect lack of security would not greatly appeal to a conscientious bank examiner. He fenced. "Of course it would be a pleasure, but———— Please let me be frank with you. It's on your behalf. I've ventured to take a good deal of interest in your account. Frankly, why don't you try to get along without this? I know that a—a—well, a pretty girl of your type loves clothes, but honestly—and you are a very honest person—won't you admit that if you go and spend this loan for clothes and hats and stuff, the way you have————"

"I need this money to send my mother to the hospital. I'll need some more later for the nurse."

"Oh, I'm—I'm—I'm dreadfully sorry. B-but surely you have other funds? It's just that I don't like to see you in debt."

"What makes you think I have other funds?"

"Why, a person who gets all these expensive hats and————"

She laughed. She said rapidly, looking straight at him: "My dear man, I haven't had a new hat since last October. I haven't had one on my head except this one I'm wearing." She touched it with a tapping finger—and it was another new one, a close-fitting toque blurred with dark blue tulle.

"B-but————"

"This is the same black beaver I had last fall. Seven times now I've retrimmed it or faced it, and this last time I had to cut the brim off, it was getting so wobbly. Heavens, if I had actually bought a new hat—well, my kind costs shamefully more than the benign ten dollars that I've been optimistically giving you as the price. And I haven't had a pair of shoes since—no matter. My father died and— well, mother and I moved into two rooms, and I deposited the four hundred dollars of family wealth, and got a job in a real-estate office at nine dollars a week. All these frivolous teas at the Ritz I've been drawing money for have been rent and porridge at home. I don't like to whine, but—may I have the fifty now? I—I rather need it."

She drooped suddenly, as though she had been on the witness stand under desperate strain. Her hands feebly flopped down out of sight beneath the counter. She went on with difficulty: "Must I tell all this to the president of the bank or someone, too?"

"No, oh no, I'll take care of it," he assured her. "Please wait here." He turned his back, rushed to a ledger, pretended to examine it while he thought.

The Palladium Savings Bank had a considerably smaller fund for unsecured personal loans to Account 112,761 than it had for the purchase of mouse traps. But Valory wanted her to have the loan more than he had wanted anything in his life. She was his life. In lending to her he was lending to himself, to a larger self than he had ever known. She was the one thing above and beyond making marks in books. And he believed her story.

He'd lend it himself. He had over four thousand dollars saved, and he could think of no use for it so deeply pleasurable as lending it to her.

He made up fifty from his own pocket and funds hastily and severely solicited from the assistant bookkeeper and the junior teller. He brought it back and casually shoved it under the grating, droning: "Do you wish the balance of your account, too, Miss Page?"

"Yes, please. But don't I have to sign something? A note or whatever they call it?"

"Oh, of course, of course. But—uh—the personal-loan blanks happen to be out of print. Just write me a personal I.O.U. on the back of a deposit slip—that will be perfectly legal."

As she gave him the I.O.U. made out in her trim, smart, nervous script, she murmured: "You have been very kind. I was so afraid I'd have to be catechized about my religion, politics, and favorite filling for éclairs."

Now in his good works and assistance to the poor Valory had been a perfectly pure and noble young man. He hadn't performed them for praise. But when he received the praise it made him hungry. His fingers tightened, his biceps crept across the bone with his shrugging desire to yank the bars apart, come out into the open, seize the hand of this girl whom he had never met without the bronze grille between them. He tried to say something arresting, and wanly stammered: "It's—glad to be able to do anything."

"Damn it, I sound like a scared bus boy," he reflected.

"You have taken care of me. I'm not sure, but I think you're the one person who has kept me going in this world of business. It hasn't been so awfully easy. I was pretty soft. And the absurd pride that made me fib to you—oh, it doesn't matter. Thank you. Good-bye."

Two weeks later she returned for another loan—of a hundred—and got it. Valory was not such a hero that he didn't secretly hope she would not keep this up, but his only protest was a suave: "I hope you can soon start saving again."

"Yes, I think I can. I'm not going to borrow to pay the surgeon. I'll pay him two dollars a week. I'm to be raised to eighteen before long. I'm learning real estate."

"How did your mother's operation come out? Is she well?"

"I hope so. She was very sweet. I hope she can get the happiness she earned. She died on the operating table."

Miss Page had said it quietly, without tremor, but she turned quickly, was gone.

He was conscious that the bookkeeper and the junior teller were staring at him while he stood at the empty Liberty Loan window. He was conscious that he was shocking them by violating the etiquette of the bank—dreaming while the irritated junior teller had to take care of all the customers. But he did not care that he had become queer to them.

He was stormed and betrayed by an immensity of thoughts. His mind was like scarlet and golden scrolls on a fabric of black velvet. It was like fireworks, red streaks and saffron zigzags and a pattering of colored sparks against a sky of starless jet. And the sable background of his mind was the thought of death. It gave dignity and vastness to what had been a kindly romance. Suddenly he was not a capable young man whose day's grind had been diverted by courtesy to a pretty girl. He perceived thoughts and emotions so large that he could not encompass them. He had in the raw tragedy of Miss Page touched all the terror and glory of life. He had in his sorrow for her lost for a moment his neat propriety and tasted the strong salt savor of danger. He could fight for her now.

While he returned to his window, while he smoothly took in money and glanced at bank books, he was devastated by a thousand thoughts of her. Could he send her flowers? Would they be banal? Weren't there books to give people in grief? Could he write to her? Only, what could he say? And—where did she live? Cynically, even in the tumult of his adoration, he jibed at himself that he could be certain of one thing—if she moved she'd never remember to change her address at the bank.

After hours he took the subway and, telling himself he wasn't going to do anything of the sort, he went up to West End Avenue. Halfway down the block from Broadway he stopped, stood with his watch in his right hand, his left tapping his chin. This was entirely for the benefit of a group of small boys with two balls and a hoop stick and a dog, assembled on a high stoop. Having tacitly established in the eyes of all whom it might concern the theory that he wasn't really insane, but had recalled an engagement, he turned round, and stalked toward Broadway somewhat more rapidly than he had just come from Broadway.

But he hadn't recalled an engagement. He had asked himself what he would do if he did find that her address was unchanged. What would he say to the maid or to the elevator attendant? That it was a fine day, and he was just asking for exercise? And then turn round and go away? Certainly he could not go up and call on her. Suppose Miss Page was in. Suppose she stared at him and demanded: "Yes, what is it?"

What was it, anyway? What could he say?

Wherefore, keeping clear of West End Avenue, he walked for a hundred blocks, and contented himself with a conversation with Miss Page. She stood before his window at the bank and admitted that he had helped her to bear the heavy hours. He thanked her modestly and explained how near to him were her financial interests———

"Oh, the devil! That's probably just about the sort of thing I would say," Valory snarled aloud, standing by the rail of the Riverside Drive bridge, glaring at the Fort Lee ferryhouse below, the trucks like beetles, the river and the glowing brown cliffs across. "Why, it's perfectly simple. All I have to do is come right out and ask her if I may call. I'll do it! Gee—I—hope—I—will! It won't take any more nerve than facing a machine gun or asking the Old Man for a raise!"

She did not appear at the bank for two weeks. Then she stood in line, smiling at him between the shoulders of two men ahead of her, so that Valory gave one customer fifty cents too much and the next three dollars too little, and heard a great deal about it—from the latter customer.

She thrust ten dollars at him. "There's the first payment on the loans."

A slaty lean man with a slaty lean umbrella was behind her, but Valory kept her while he put his lips close to the bars and murmured: "Look here. Aren't you saving too much? With paying the surgeon in installments and all————"

"No, really. I'm enjoying it. A sort of spiritual adventure, a new power, finding how many things I can do without."

She was slipping away. He snapped at her: "Here now! Wait! There's no need of paying us till you get the surgeon paid. I won't have you. M-miss Page, what did you have for breakfast this morning?"

Her lips widened in two distinct motions of growing friendly amusement till their sharp clean points were overshadowed by rounded wrinkles. "You're worse than a lawyer or a father confessor."

"I want to be. I'm worried about you," he grumbled.

"It's nice of you. But I must do my job." This last she said over her shoulder. Instantly she was hidden by the impatient form of the man with the umbrella, who was piping, in the voice which his umbrella would have had if it had spoken: "Hustle this through, will you?"

Valory thought how pleasant it would be to pop his fingers through the bar and pull the man's nose. He thought it so intently that it was three minutes before he realized that he had not asked Miss Page if he might call. Then it occurred to him that she might have answered: "But why should you?"

What was the answer to that?

He was smothered in the cage. He was at once drowsy and angry. He had to get out of this, to fight somebody. Years might go by while he tried, in moments which he merely caught by the skirts from behind the grille, to impress her as a human being. She probably thought of him as she did the ticket chopper whom she saw at the subway station every morning, or as she thought of her nail scissors! He pulled at his collar, he clenched his fist, even while he was saying colorlessly to a woman who was looking at him with bored, ignoring impersonality: "Yes, ma'am, seven tens and a five."

After dinner, when he was passing a Forty-second Street theater, he had the most curious psychic experience of his life. He was suddenly sure that Miss Page was in there in the audience. Her presence came out to him, penetrating curtains and walls as a fire shines though a dark and plaited hedge. He quietly asked the box office for a seat in the front row of the balcony—and did not get it. He stalked a speculator to the corner of Seventh Avenue, was shown into the back room of a shoe-shining hall of mirrors, and got a ticket for two dollars more than the marked price. He paid it stoically. But when he flopped into his seat, the pit dim beneath him, he was trembling. He heard nothing of the first act. The instant the lights went up he was bending over the rail, hastily glancing along row on row. Then he examined all of the balcony; made himself a little conspicuous—he who hated conspicuousness—by leaning out to look up at the first row of the gallery.

Gradually, incredulously, he owned that he could not see her. His remarkable psychic revelation had been plain and simple madness.

He grouchily turned his attention to the play. Fortunately it was an easy piece to follow. It belonged to the great New York school of drama. No remarkable intelligence was required to watch the pleasant round gentleman with the bald head pop under beds and into box couches. Valory betrayed the fact that for all his admirable appearance of maturity and trustworthiness in the bank, he was still young. When he caught himself laughing he stopped he stopped, and with all the beautiful plaintiveness of a Freshman he reproached: "You're a fine lover, you are! Laughing at a cheap farce like this!"

Walking to his room near Gramercy Park, Valory longed for the noisy absurdity of the farce. The city, his city, which he had found a diverting background, was lean, grim, gray. The street was an echoing emptiness, a trap lined with ambushes.

He sullenly got ready for bed in his still room. He poked contemptuously at the special editions on his center table—the big book on decorative textiles, with colored plates; the handsome souvenir of the hundredth anniversary of the Fort Vincent National Bank. Till tonight he had admired the air they gave his room. They had lifted the curse of the landlady's blotchy lithographs. Sleepily he wondered why they now seemed so depressing.

The instant he had turned out the light and somersaulted into bed he was flamingly awake.

"Now I know," he worried. "Those books aren't human. There's nothing human about me. The bookkeeper, with his family and his flivver in Yonkers, he's not much of an accountant, but oh, he's living! And I! The years sneak in on me. I'll be bald before I know it. Death will come—before I ever live."

Frightened, he watched the darkness kindle and glow and revolve in dizzy whorls. He folded his pillow four different ways. He tucked it over his head. He furiously slapped the flap of it out of his eyes, slammed it on the floor. He turned over and over, and tried to lie quiet, and gave it up.

He sought to defend himself: "I'm a good banker. And I've helped a lot of people to build up accounts. I've been honest with them. But—no, it isn't enough. I haven't gambled with life. I've never gone to any man or woman and said: 'Here's my heart and soul and honor. Take them and kick them—or make me happy.'"

Then: "Hang it, lying here worrying like a schoolboy!"

He burst from bed, swiftly dressed himself, let himself out of the lower hall, strode to an all-night lunch room on Fourth Avenue. He ate two bowls of crackers and milk, and ardently discussed prize fighting with two men in overalls. He knew nothing whatever about prize fighting, and the men in overalls were not particularly interesting persons, but Valory coaxed them, flattered them, listened to them, tried to keep them, tried to postpone the hour when he should again be dismayingly alone. But they deserted him. He sought to continue the conversation with the cook, but the lord of the night lunch was contemptuous of late conversationalists. So Valory sat silent in a light yellow oak chair, with a broad arm used as a table, while he smoked and stared at the electric fan, a collection of miniature boxes of breakfast food on a marble shelf, a huge bowl of crumbly loaves of sugar, and a sign insinuating: "Try our special Denver sandwich on toast, 20¢."

When the cook began to look belligerent behind a pile of sand-wiches in oiled paper, Valory rose in a genteel and disarming man-ner, said that it was a damp night, and went away. But as he came out on the street he found himself happy. Without having known that he was thinking about it he had thought out his problem. He submitted that he was frankly in love with Marcella Page. He had decided that he was not going to stay back of the bars and let her slip away. He knew now, with a certainty quite different from his previous bravado in imaginary addresses, that he was going to ask her to let him call.

He felt extremely heroic and competent.

The next morning he said to the junior teller, "Son, aren't you ever going to get a new zero key to your adding machine?" and he said it so masterfully that the other teller was impressed, and sighed: "You're right. I've got to 'tend to that."

Only—Miss Page did not come that day. Nor did he see her for two and half weeks. And after the two and a half weeks, his vaca-tion time arrived, and he reluctantly left for New Hampshire. He thought about her through a fortnight of fishing and apple sauce. He came to know her and to know himself.

On the Monday of his return he entered the bank briskly. The junior teller gaped at him, and the bookkeeper rushed over to grunt: "Say, the president wants to see you. Bad! What the deuce you been doing?"

"Doing?"

"Them was the word I denunciated."

"Don't know what you mean."

"Well, I don't know what's up, but the Old Man comes in here roaring like a World Series after a three-bagger and wants to know your vacation address, and then he says: 'No, I'll wait till he comes back, but by the gods———' Oh, he was sore as a crab!"

Ten minutes later the junior teller informed him: "Say, the presi-dent wants to see you about something."

Ten minutes after that the porter-guard whispered through the bars: "Say, Mr. Valory, the Old Man was peeved at you for some-thing while you was away. Don't know what it was."

The president came in at half past ten. As he passed Valory's window he glared. But not for half an hour did he summon Valory to his desk, behind the railing at the back of the bank. Then, with a booming mock courtesy, he begged: "Do have a chair. I want to have a conference with you. It's a pleasure to know that we have a financial genius and an intellectual giant in this humble institution."

"I don't quite get you, sir."

"Ye don't, heh? You will! But first perhaps you'd like to give me a little advice about some investment that I might make a million out of. I have no doubt you're an expert on Pretty Polly Oil Stock and that class of sound ventures. Or do you confine your genius as an innovator to banking methods?"

"I'm sorry, chief, but I don't understand."

"Ye don't, heh? Then will you kindly tell me since when savings banks in the sovereign commonwealth of New York have been permitted to invest in the unsecured personal notes of pretty girls?"

"Oh! Oh, that. Well, of course that wasn't———"

"Don't tell me what it wa'n't. I know what it wa'n't. In all my years of banking, since I started in sweeping floors in a bank upstate, I've never had such a scene. Here comes her Royal Highness, and she wants to see the Honorable Mr. Valory and oh, no, the other boys wouldn't do at all, she must see me if the great Mr. Valory wa'n't home. And she looks me over——— Well now, without prejudice, I must admit that I haven't felt comfortable in these congress shoes since the day she looked them over. Well, she allows she'll take out another loan for fifty, and this would be the last. I didn't seem to catch the idee, and she condescended to explain that the bank, through our Mr. Valory, had loaned her a hundred and fifty dollars. Oh, no, certainly not: 'twa'n't a personal loan by Mr. Valory. The idee! I tried to explain the law of savings-bank investments, but she wouldn't listen. Now was she crazy, or was I, or are you?"

Valory explained.

"Well," the president puffed, "it's beyond me. Of course, it's a case for a commission in lunacy, and we certainly will have it understood that it's never to happen again. Cat's sake, think of what would happen if every loafer in town learned we were making personal loans to everybody that cared to come in and apply! But still, I don't suppose it was criminal. Hm. Curious. Sort of the opposite of embezzlement—giving funds to the bank. You don't care to buy a new tile floor too, do you? Well, one good thing—I'm glad to know you're making so much money you can throw it away. That means you won't ever need another raise."

Valory looked coldly upon his chief. For once, with Miss Page behind him, he was not embarrassed by the ancient roarer.

"On the contrary, it means that I'll need one right now to keep up the good work. I want to stay here, but I found a wonderful location for a country bank in New Hampshire————"

"Then ye better take it, I guess!"

"No, sir, it isn't that, but—I may get married."

"Oh, well, I'll talk to the director. Mind you, though, don't go getting false notions. I'm not saying but that I may advise them against it. New bank! Huh! Absurd. Leaving a sound, conservative institution like———— If you must get ideas and notions, why don't you try to work out some schemes to get a little new business for us?"

"Have."

"Oh, ye have, heh? Since when?"

Valory's new scheme had been conceived and developed during the time the president had been sneering "Since when?" and patting his whiskers as though he were congratulating them for having said it. But it was in the authoritative manner of one who had revolved his problem for years that Valory whipped out: "How about sending a man round to the biggest offices near here on pay day? And maybe some East River factories? To accept deposits on the spot? Lots of clerks would put in something every week if they didn't have to take the trouble of going to the bank."

"Huh. Well, it might be worth thinking about. We'll talk about it."

Valory paraded back to the cage. Twice during the day the junior teller was distinctly polite to him, and once the assistant bookkeeper asked his advice about writing movie scenarios. He became agreeably superior, and he thought up sixteen distinct ways of promoting the Palladium Bank. But at two-thirty-three his new dignity collapsed into gasping apologies. For at that time he looked up from counting bills to discover Miss Page standing at his window, glowering.

"I want to see you alone," she said impolitely.

"What was it?" he begged.

"Alone and at once, if I may, please."

"Y-yes. Please come this way."

While the junior teller, the accounting department, the president, the treasurer, the porter and two depositors watched his feeble progress, he got through the cage—his knees perfectly worthless for walking—and led her back to the directors' room. In his nervous progress he wanted to turn back to look at her, but he kept on.

The directors' room was dim—and he wanted to see! He yanked up a shade and light so thick with dust that it glistened like honey crept over the long rosewood table, the cobalt blue of the carpet, the deep crimson and black and rusty brown in the portraits of the ex-presidents of the bank. He turned toward her and for the first time he saw her without the bronze bars between them. She was more slight and tired than, in the spell of her frivolity, he had ever realized.

She was staring at him in turn. For a second a smile rose to the surface of her anger. But it sank, and she flung at him:

"I couldn't make much of the explanations of your fussy old president, but I've finally thought it out. The loans you made were personal loans advanced by yourself."

"Yes."

"Why did you do it? I'm not a charity patient."

"Why shouldn't I? I'd have charged you the same percentage as the bank would."

"But it makes me furious to have been treated like a child, fooled, teased———"

He sat on the edge of the directors' table, looking at her in the ooze of thick sunshine, amid the richness of tapestries and dark wood. He said casually: "I never realized you wore pumps. When you turned away I could only see your heels."

"For that matter, my dear man, I never realized you wore shoes at all. I'm relieved to find that you have legs too. I thought you were a statue bust."

"I'm not. I'm practically human. But I will admit that taking care of you is the first amusing thing I've done in years. I don't apologize for having fooled you. In fact, I'm going to continue it. You will be sick of this city struggle in less than a year. You're not trained for it. You need care."

"But"—angrily—"does it occur to you that I may already have a number of charming young males desirous of caring for me?"

"No, I shan't let it occur to me. Did it ever occur to you that I was a human being? The only trouble with a young woman of your kind—I suppose you're what's called 'a well-bred girl'—your chief fault is that you can't conceive that people you meet in business may function almost like the people whose families you know."

"No, that isn't true. I've wondered about you—as a person—with your funny, dark, sophisticated face, there in the cage, like a poet behind bars."

"Honestly?"

"Yes, but———"

"Miss Page! Are you engaged to be married? I mean, very fatally and unavoidably engaged?"

"I'm—I really don't see why I should tell you. Please let's return to the business———"

"Are you? Oh, I know how unimportant I have been to you ———"

"Oh, please, please, please don't bully me! Can't you see I'm trying to be sane? You—you've been only too ridiculously important to me!"

She walked swiftly to him, held out her hand as she went on: "I think you're trying to tell me you like me, and I think I'm glad. You see, the day you gave me the second loan, for a hundred—well, I hadn't eaten but one meal in forty-eight hours, and I was going quietly back home to kill myself if I didn't get the money. You reached out from the bars and gave me back my life."

Then she was in the seat vacuously occupied at directors' meetings by J. Swann Ebenflicker; her face was on her arms, and she was crying, while he shyly stroked her hair.

She raised her head to say furiously: "I never thought I'd fall so low in egotism that I'd be grateful. Thank heaven I'll get over it. In fact, right now let me say that I never have liked your collars."

"Please come out and help me buy some you do like," he said meekly.

WAY I SEE IT

I

A tale of unparalleled woe, as related by young Mr. Ray Moller, former salesman for Tribby, Burkett & Day, real estate, to his friend, Mr. McNew, of the Crescent Sign and Poster Company. Diligent research has determined that these confidences were revealed at the Good Red Beef Chop House in the city of Vernon; and it is believed that at the time Mr. Moller was lunching upon hash creole.

Let me tell you right now, Mac, I'm not going to boast or anything, but believe me, there's nobody that can give me the razz and get away with it; and that's why I threw up my job and simply refused to work for Tribby, Burkett & Day one second longer. Bum firm anyway, to tell the truth.

You know how I am; you've seen me there in the office. I'm awfully easy to get along with if anybody hands me a square deal, but nobody can put anything over on me. I stand up for my rights. I guess Homer Huff felt foolish when I up and quit him. But he got just what was coming to him. Course it's a good firm, but I wouldn't stand Huff. See how I mean?

There's one funny thing about me; I can tell just what a man's like the first time I lay an eye on him. But I did get fooled for once in sizing up Huff. That's why I wanted to tell you what happened.

You don't want to get the idea for one second that I cared for my rotten old job. I just want to illustrate to you how hard it is to tell about a crank like Homer Huff. It's like I said to Sim Jenson.

"You can't most always sometimes tell," I said, and Sim said to me: "Ray, that's exactly the idea."

See how it is?

Way I see it, Huff's character is just naturally soured. He doesn't got any ideals or sense of humor. Man like that, you can't do anything with him; mistake to go on tolerating him; only thing to do is to tell him he can throw his old job in the lake, way I did.

You know we salesman used to call Huff by the nickname of Old Huffy. Pretty good takeoff, don't you think that is? Well, I guess I was the first fellow to give him that name. Get it? Huff—Huffy. Way I look at it—and I don't want to hand myself anything, but I just see a thing once I guess I can come pretty doggone near getting onto the philosophy of it, all rightee—that's how he is. Kick him in the face—that's all he can understand, see?

Well, here's how it all happened—huh? No thanks; no coffee for me; I find it hurts my digestion; never touch it at lunch, hardly ever—hey, wait, don't know but I will, too, just this noon. Large cup with cream—or say, waiter, might's well make mine a pot.

First time I met Huff I got to admit I did like him. I was selling lots out at Arbutus Villa—you remember that bum development behind the tanneries that Harry Jason flivvered on? Good sales proposition, though—swell commission—and I was ace high with Harry Jason—fact, I named all the streets—swell names. You know I always did kind of have a fancy for poetry and that stuff—Magnolia Lane and Beauchamps Terrace, and so on. High-class stuff.

I ran into Huff at the Commercial Club banquet; sat next to him and told him what I was doing with Arbutus. Well, make a long story short, Huff offered me thirty cold bucks a week to go to work for him in the rental department at Tribby, Burkett & Day's. He'd just recently been made manager of the department. And say, you'd of thought that night that nothing was too good for me. Huff gave me a cigar and slapped me on the back and called me "my boy" and said: "You're too bright a fellow to be hitched up with a fly-by-night tinhorn like Harry Jason. You want to come to a real firm where you can grow up with the business."

And I fell for it—me, that there aren't so very many ever put it over on me, if I do say so. I walked with Huff over to the Randall Avenue car line and told him about my ideas for triple-deckers, and you'd have thought we were a couple of old college chumps, you might say.

But the first morning I showed up to work for him—the very first morning—once I'd quit Harry Jason and was at Huff's mercy—was old Huffy chummy? In a pig's eye he was! I blew in about ten o'clock—course no boss that was a human being had ought to expect a fellow to be a stickler about office hours on the first day when he was just learning the ropes—kind of on a vacation, you might say. I breezed up to Huff's desk and looked at him in a way that'd show any decent fellow that I wanted to be friendly and work together with him, and I told him: "Well, boss, here's little Ray all ready to save the country."

You'd of thought he'd of laughed, wouldn't you? 'Stead of that he looked me over like I was a book agent, and he snarled—oh, he's got the meanest, nastiest, doggondest unpleasantest way—he yelped at me: "In this office the saving of the country begins at eight-thirty A.M. daily."

Well, d'you know, I had a good darn notion to quit right there. Bawling me out because I showed my good will! First crack out of the box! Can you beat it? But thinks I, "Oh, he's just fooling," so I kind of looked dignified to show him he'd better not presume on his position, and I says perfectly cool and businesslike: "All right, jus' you say. Which is my desk?"

At that, he's so *dumm* I bet he never got the fact that I was practically snubbing him.

I didn't like the desk he assigned me. I've got some idea about office lighting; fact, I suppose I'm the only fellow in the realty game in the entire city of Vernon that's got what you might call anything like a scientific knowledge of lighting problems. I'd made a study of it, see? So I kicked about the way the desk faced the window, and old friend Huff, he looked sore as a crab.

If truth were known, guess he felt kind of cheap that I'd showed him up about this lighting proposition, and to cover up he shot his face off about what a swell desk it was and all. Well, I let it go. I never start anything; I'll stand a lot; anything for peace, long as nobody's trying to put anything over on me, you understand. And I got busy, and darned if I didn't rent two houses to a couple of tough old prospects the very first day, and say, maybe the other fellows weren't jealous of me! But Huff didn't say anything; just grunted—him that had been so mouthy at the banquet when we met. Yes, sir, it was the big boss, old Burkett himself, that congratulated me and told me they were tickled to death to have me with 'em!

Guess maybe that didn't grind Huffy, to hear his own subordinate getting a swell line of appreciation from his own superior—from the president of the firm! He looked mad as a wet hen. You bet! But I didn't rub it in. I just grinned and told Burkett I'd do all I could to put some pep in the firm, and got busy digging into the prospect file.

What you might call the first real fracas between Huffy and I was over my car. Huffy wanted to get me a bum old secondhand flivver to take prospects out to see houses in, though both the salesmen of the Guarantee Realtors, that handled about the same line of business and customers that I did, had swell Disselbourgs. I put it right up to Huffy! And do you know—not that I believe in brass or anything like that; I think a fellow should be modest and hep to all his faults and study to improve 'em way I always do. But still I always have prided myself on having enough nerve to tackle most any kind of proposition. But do you know—and I hadn't been with the firm but four days—Huff had almost got my goat? And darned if I didn't find it hard to brace him for a decent car.

And he turned me down like a mice. Turning down is the easiest thing that old grouch does. And whadyuh think finally sold the idea for me? Why, the big boss himself, old Burkett, happened to waft in, and he asked what the big stew was about, and I told him. Burkett suggested I might use the nifty little Schnitzel sedan that was assigned to Huff himself whenever Huff wasn't using it—and that was most of the time.

Well, Huffy blew up like a molasses factory. Said he wouldn't trust me with his boat. You know how I am, Mac. I'll stand any amount of joshing, long's a guy is a gentleman, but when they step beyond the bonds—and it don't make no never-minds if it's my boss or anybody else—yes, by golly, even if my girl, Sue, got too fresh with me—why, then I just get as cold and dignified as a United

States senator. That's how it was this time. I just shipped old Huffy one frozen visage, charge collect, and I says: "Mister Huff"—just like that; chilly as a lemon ice-cream soda—"Mister Huff," I said, "I've taken the full course in motor repairing at the Y.M.C.A.," I said, "and I guess I'm not going to have the ears scared off me by chuffing a car round on city boulevards."

Burkett got it. Tickled him stiff to see me call Huffy. He said: "Let him have it, Huff," and walked off.

And do you know, Huff never even looked at me! Too everlastingly crushed to let a single yip out of him. Just said, "I keep the key in this box with the rubber bands," and turned his back on me.

Honest, I was sorry for the poor *zob*, having put it all over him. And that was one sweet little darling of a car—that sedan. And say, Mac—now for Pete's sake, don't go telling this; Huffy never got onto it, and of course I was always careful of the machine—but say, maybe I didn't have one-two nice little joy rides in that sedan with Sue and Sim Jenson and Sim's girl!

But's I was saying. I saw there were bad times coming. It made me sore. I really wanted to glom onto that job for keeps.

There's some knockers in this burg—course I never pay any attention to 'em; there's some folks that it don't seem as if they could be happy without they're shooting off their faces and trying to get somebody in Dutch; and way I figure it, it's beneath a fellow's dignity to notice 'em; but there's some hammer throwers in this little ole hamlet that say I ain't steady and that I don't hold onto jobs. And I wanted to show 'em I could keep this one, and I liked Burkett. Not wishing Huff no harm, still I figured out that in the course of time I could just neatly lift the old crab's job off him, and with me as manager the rental department would show a little speed, and Burkett and me would get along like a coupla sunbeams in the merry springtide, ho!

And I had a swell five-dollar room at Ma Stirner's, right next to the bathroom practically, and there was a dandy joint where I could get breakfast right round the corner, and me and Sue were thick as thieves—engaged, you might say; and believe me, if there's any prettier telephone girl in town than Sue just lead me to her, that's what I say! So, you see, I was settled down like an old ladies' home, and I wanted to coax the job along.

But I saw there was going to have to be an understanding between Huffy and I, and one of two things—either I'd up and quit, or sometimes when he got just a little too flip I'd make him eat his words.

And now I'm out of a job and Sue don't hardly seem to know whether we're sure-enough engaged or not—but, Mac, I'm going to stick to her through everything. There's no other girl I'll ever look at besides her. When I go to New York—I figure that there, where they'll appreciate a fellow, I ought to be making five thousand bucks a year inside eight-nine years, and then I'll send for her, and oh, you joyous weddink bells! That's the kind of fellow I am—count on me to stick. And she's too swell a skirt for this bum city. New York, that's her class.

But—well, 's I was saying. I guess about the second real scrap I had with Huff, not counting lots of time he was sarcastic and I let him have it right back, you bet—second row was over that punk stenographer, that Tillie Groat; stuck-up little nit; can't write "cat" without getting too many Z's in it, and the way she wears her hair, prissy stuff, parted in the middle like she was a saint—some saint, all right! Worse temper than old Huffy himself, and ignorant as a Finn lumberjack.

Trouble started: I was nice to Tillie same's I am to everybody— you know how I am, Mac. I guess maybe I jollied her a little, but nothing but a little fun, you understand, like calling her Millie the Monk and Willie the Catawampus, and things like that—you know how I can make up funny names for people—I don't claim any special credit for it, just comes natural. Did you know I was the first one to call Huff old Huffy?

Well, it used to get Tillie sore. She thought I was trying to be flip, and she insisted I had to call her Miss Groat.

"Sure," I said; "you got the right idea, sister. Us highbrows is long on the formal stuff. All right, kiddo; I'll call you by your full name *mit* the handle on it."

And then whadyuh think I called her? Miss Goat! Sa-a-y, maybe I didn't have her wild.

Then bimeby I kind of got to liking her. Me and Sue had been having a little spat, and I will admit Tillie looked good to me, though I can't say I care much for those skinny, serious dames with no pep and fun to 'em. Neither Tillie nor Huff got a sense of humor, and whatever ails me, I do have one elegant sense of humor; it's just natural with me. Don't you think a sense of humor and the ability to see your own faults are the most necessary things a fellow could have, Mac?

Well, 's I was saying. I didn't care much for Tillie. But I could see she was getting moony about me, and one time I sort of patted her on the head—made out like there was something the matter with the way her hair was fixed. But, my heavens, just kidding her—same's I would the Queen of Patagonia if she walked into my office!

But Tillie—it does beat all Hades how seriously these dames can take themselves and any little thing a fellow says to 'em—she goes and gets an idea I'm making love to her, and she gives me to understand she's all plenty engaged up *mit* a young dentist out in Rosebank, and will little Ray can the flirtatious chatter? And she didn't think I was such a much-a-much anyway, even if I was her superior, and she'll take my dictation, but she wouldn't take my lip and—man, you never heard anything like the way she threw it into me! I mean, she thought she was handing it to me. But Lord, I never paid the slightest attention to her squawking, no more'n a rabbit!

Well, that got me kind of irate—her having the fall to think Ray Moller would think of falling for her. Why, say, when I marry it's going to be somebody with class, like Sue, that can put up a front anywhere! And I'll back Sue to kid any of these sassiety wrens up on the Boulevard and get away with it to a fare you well—yes, and in New York too, and just between you and I, Sue thinks I'm the candy kid myself!

So I says: "All right, Miss Goat; we'll strictly observe office eti"—what was it I said now? Oh, yes! Sure; that was it! "We'll just observe business etiquette," I says.

And I did. When she made a bull in my letters maybe I didn't bawl her out for fair! She'd gone and asked for it, hadn't she?

And then—you remember how it was? I had to share her time with Huffy and two other salesmen. Believe me, that was some punk arrangement. It cer'nly did use to give me a pain to have to sit round waving my feet in the air waiting for Tillie to get through with Huff's long-winded dictating. Why, say, that fellow Huff may know a little something about real estate, but he's so plumb illiterate that when he tries to compose a letter he Fletcherizes his words—like this:

"Dear—uh—dear—uh—dear sir—In reply to your—in reply to your favor would you say that—uh—that—uh—would say that—uh—the house regarding which you asked about is still unrented—no, cross that out, Miss Groat. Make it, is still available. No, no! Leave it the way it was."

Oh, it used to get me simply wild to have to listen to him, and me all ready to sling out a nifty little epistle if I could just get hold of that scrub stenog. Well, after our talkee-talkee, blamed if Tillie didn't try to take it out on me by deliberately putting the other fellows' letters ahead of mine, and if I spoke to her about it she'd do the injured innocent and pipe up: "I'm very sorry, but I have to finish Mr. Huff's mail first." Oh, gee, girls, aren't we the snippy little schoolma'ams! I could have slapped her!

But I got even. She wasn't very long on vocabulary—I don't want to toot my own horn or anything, but I will say that all through my two years—almost practically two years—in high school I put it all over the class in English, and I used to read *The Merchant of Venice* aloud. The English teacher said I could spout it like a regular actor, and if I haven't got anything else I certainly have got a three-ring vocabulary. So 'stead of giving her a lot of lowbrow junk like she was accustomed to from Huff and the other roughnecks I'd gabble off something like this:

"Dear Sir: As to further details regarding the many elegancies and refinements of apartments mentioned, would say that situation is salubrious, and architecture strictly A Number One and up-to-date." You know—regular college-professor stuff.

Well say, she muffed about one word out of four. And then, oh, Clarence! Say, can you blame me? I cern'ly did soak it to her. Asked her why she didn't read the dictionary. Asked if she was going to make me go clear up to Burkett and squeal on her. Asked if she expected a high-class thirty-a-week man to waste his time spelling s-a-l-u-b-r-e-u-s—salubrious for a twelve-a-week machine pounder.

Well, I was having a good time stringing her along—and mind you, I'd of told her afterward it was all a josh and made friends—

I was having so much fun I never noticed that Huffy, the darned old sneak, was pussyfooting right up behind me till I let 'er rip.

"Mr. Moller," he says—and oh, maybe he wasn't trying to be nasty, though—"I wonder if you expect an intelligent stenographer to waste her time listening to your misspellings of inappropriate words."

Oh, zowie, just as raw as he could make it! Or anyway, I mean, he tried to be, though course I never noticed it. I'm not thick-skinned, but when the human wasp, like Huffy, tries to sting me I feel it's simply beneath a fellow's dignity to pay the slight-est attention to him.

And then he went on and called me down some more—right in the presence of my own stenographer. Fine for discipline! Oh, fine! Just lovely! Sure! And expect me to be able to get away with giving her orders afterward!

And that wasn't the worst of it. As I said, I'd just been kidding her. But honestly—I want you to believe this now—I meant it for her own good. Make her a whole lot better if she studied words, like I do. I didn't care a whole lot about her personally, but I do like to see anybody improving his mind, and that's why I zinged into her. And then him skinning me alive for it! Can you beat it?

And was I up on my ear about it? Oh, boy, I were them! Say, Mac, I could of beat his block off. But I just gave him the double O, and never took my eyes off him. I guess that embarrassed him all right. He cut out the royal razz and poked back into his den. Say, for two cents I'd have handed him one.

Well, then the paperweight championship was on. Ding! Ding! Huff and me loved each other like a coupla Wops up on the Iron Range after they been hitting the hard stuff. I'd tried to excuse him, but I could see there was no use. And I began to realize how he was treating his wife.

Mrs. Huff was as nice a woman as I ever laid eyes on—treated us fellows in the office swell whenever she came in three-four times a week.

"Good morning, Mr. Moller. How is everything?" she'd say, nice and bright and jolly. And then she'd go in to see Huffy, and you could hear—you couldn't make out what they'd say, but you could hear her voice, awful pleasant, or kind of tired, maybe. Do you wonder her being tired out, married to a brute like that? And then you'd hear him growling. You could make out he didn't want she should do this and she mustn't do that, and—oh, he was the household pest for fair!

And then—say, Mac, that fellow Huff pulled something just a little bit worse than anything I've ever run across, and I've seen some pretty gosh-awful hemale grouches, being in the rent line and getting on the inside of some of this domestic-bliss stuff, as you might say. You know what these deah chappies in England call a cad? Well, that's Huff—Homer Cadwallader Cad Huff. That's his moniker, you take it from me!

Come about this way: 'Nother salesman and I were staying a little late, and Huff was there four-flushing about working or something, and we all went out at the same time; and for once Huff acted like he was trying to be almost human.

"Tired, boys?" says he, and we answered friendly. Then he stopped on the steps and pulled a sigh to impress this large and intelligent audience, and then he yaps: "Look here, boys! Sometimes I may seem a little gruff————"

Get that? Gruff! Oh, gruff is good! Tumble up, gents! See the humanitarantella from Mexico! Only one in captivity! Stings the bars of his cage till they turn green! Gruff! Whee!

"You may think I'm gruff at times," he says, "but I hope you boys won't take it too seriously. Fact is," he says, "since you've probably guessed it—well, there's a little trouble at home now and then, and it gets on my nerves, and I suppose I probably saw it off on you fellows. Just don't take it personally. Good night," he says, just like he thought he'd been awful pleasant.

Can you beat that? Him with that nice sweet wife, and hinting that she was a nagger and a crank and made him rare up.

Oh, maybe I didn't burn him up afterward when I discussed him with the other fellow! Say, I just despised him! I may have a lot of faults. I'll own up to anything that anybody can pin on me. But I can't imagine myself talking mean about a fellow's own wife. Can you, Mac? I should sa-ay not!

And then, little while after this, Huffy starts putting up a holler about my chumming round with Sim Jenson. You know Sim—advertising solicitor for the *Courier*. Comes into the office once in a while looking for ads, just the same as you come in to drum up a little signboard trade; perfectly right and proper. And Sim's like you. He sits round and chins a coupla minutes before he beats it. Well, somehow Huff got it into his noodle that Sim was stringing me—trying to get me to boost his paper and see if I couldn't persuade Burkett to shoot him in some more ads. Well, that was a darn lie.

Huff as much asked me if Sim and I didn't talk about ways of ribbing up more advertising, and if we didn't, he says, what the deuce did we gas about then? Well, I don't tell all I know. I know how to keep my trap shut. Matter of fact, Sim and I pulled off some pretty good parties, and that was what we were discussing usually. But that wasn't any of Huff's business, and so I led him to go on thinking Sim and I talked ads every time he came in.

You see I figured out Huff was pretty much of a straight-laced old codger, for all his grouchiness, and he'd of had a fit if he knew how Sim and I got away with a little hike over to St. Clair and maybe lapped up coupla drinks every time I held out the sedan on him overnight. Huffy's just the kind of crank that claims a fellow can't drive if he has a drink under his belt, but you know me, Mac —why say, I can drive anything, plastered or sober! I just got kind of a natural taste for mechanics, you might say, and—oh, not that I really drink anything to speak of, you understand. Course I don't believe a fellow had ought to drink if he's driving—not regular—see how I mean—I mean—you see how I mean? Nor gamble or nothing when—but say, Mac, wisha had time to tell you about one big poker game I got into. Say, I won sixteen dollars—and right off a bunch of hard-shelled old sports, too—though of course a fellow hadn't ought to really what you might call gamble—see how I mean?

Well, 's I was saying, finally Huff up and snorts: "Mr. Moller, I wish you'd be so good and tell your dear friend Mr. Jenson to stay t'hell out of here. When we got any advertising I guess the boy can find the way to the *Courier* office."

Oh, man, maybe I wasn't het up! You know how I am, Mac; I don't hardly ever get irritated even. But say, I cern'ly was good and plenty hostyle that time! But I never said a word—not one word. I just gave him a good straight look right square in the ocular orbit.

I kind of think I threw a little scare into him. I guess he took a tumble to himself and realized that here was one guy he couldn't bulldoze the way he did the others. I was all ready to get through right then, and I got my idea all right. Anyway, he never spoke to me about Sim again, and when I got darn good and ready I hinted to Sim that maybe he better not show up in the office so often—we could meet at lunch. So that blew over too.

But that's about how things went for a whole year, Sue and me falling out now and then and making up; and me letting Huffy go just so far and then pulling him up sharp; and him getting meaner and meaner to his wife. Used to hear him phoning to her. "No, I can't!" he'd snap at her. And he was the limit with us fellows in the office. He was just simply one chronic morning-after. He never appreciated a thing we did, and he was suspicious about our expense accounts and our time out of the office. Say, he made me so mad by suspicioning all the time and I used to get away with a few games of poker in the afternoon once in a while just to get even with him, and never got on—naw! The poor boob thought he was keen, but he was just mean. Say, gee, that's a regular poem, eh? "He wasn't keen, he was mean!" Say, I ought to send that to the newspapers. But———

And Huffy was always so sarcastic. That was the worst of it. He'd say: "Just what was your authority for telling this party that the owner would repaper the drawing room for him? Did you dream it, or did Mr. Simple Jenson suggest it?" Or maybe I'd be a little sleepy after lunch—you know how you get; just want to pound your ear for maybe two-three minutes, with your feet up on the desk and a house plan in your mitt like you was looking it over; and if you can get away with it, why, you feel all O.K. again, and hoopla, all ready to play, girls! But Huff—say, that guy just nachly hates being human. He'd dot over to me just when I was going bye-bye, and he'd yell: "If I may intrude into your slumbers, Mr. Moller, would it be too much to ask you to try occasionally to quote rentals right?" Like that—sarcastic.

I couldn't imagine myself ever getting sarcastic to anybody, Mac—honest I couldn't. I may have my faults. I can get peevish, and if anybody tries to ride me I'll cuss him out—yes, and I don't care how husky he is, the big stiff! I don't pretend I'm perfect. In fact I do a whole lot of frank analysis of myself, and I'm pretty fair to middlin' good at it. I guess I'm kind of a natural psychologist, you might say.

And I know myself.

You see, I'm telling you just how things are. I want to illustrate how it is with a fellow like Huff, and believe me, I'm sorry for you, Mac, having to get him to have signs painted. You're like me; you'd rather lose a good sale than get sarcastic—ain't that the way it is?

Well, I guess about steen million times that year I felt like going right up to Burkett himself and telling him what Huff was getting away with in his department. But pshaw, Burkett'd of have him up on the carpet and given him the gate so p.d.q. that Huffy'd of wondered when the cyclone hit town. I didn't want to do that—him with a nice wife—and besides, thinks I, it wouldn't hardly be what you'd call loyal. But believe me, I was tempted, all rightee, seeing Burkett so polite and nice—so different from Huff.

Well, then I had the big grind with Huff late September. We were busy as a cat—big demand for houses to rent—and I was showing twenty people round every day, I guess, besides all the phones and all. There was a Mr. and Mrs. Sanbœuf—funny name, Wop I guess, but they certainly were high class, smart people, though, and don't you forget it—came from New York, and Mr. Sanbœuf was going to open some kind of picture store.

Say, them people knew more about house furnishing than I did! Yes, sir, I cern'ly hand it to them! And they were awful pleasant, and I had a lot of fun with them. I suppose I'm a roughneck some ways, but I swear I do like people with elegant manners. I had such a picnic with them that I guess maybe I did give 'em a little more time than was coming to them, looking at it one way. But I wanted them to be suited, and that's my business, ain't it? And they told me all about New York and how much money I could make there. I slipped them into the Vandevelt house on Chestnut, and that's the best buy in town.

Maybe Huff had intended the Vandevelt house for one of his own pet clients, but anyway, he didn't like the Sanbœufs a-tall. Said they were four-flushing tinhorns and cranky about the plumbing and wanted four-hundred value at one and a quarter, and a lot of lies, and said if the Sanbœufs felt so superior to Vernon they better go back to New York. Outrageous the way he talked.

Well, I'd stood a lot, but I wasn't going to stand his jumping on my friends.

"Vernon may be all right for you," I says to him, "but maybe there's some people that think it's a bum town. I suppose they're nuts of course. Oughtn't to be allowed to have artistic tastes, maybe. Better have a law passed against it," I said.

Oh, I soaked it to him—showed him he wasn't the only *wütt* that could be sarcastic.

He comes back at me with: "Well, when you get too much artistic taste or too many millions for Vernon you better take 'em on to Wall Street and tell J. P. Morgan what's what," he says.

See how I mean? Sarcastic, all the time!

Then we had quite a set-to about Vernon. I said it was crude; no stimulating influence, like the Sanbœufs said: bunch of commercial kale grabbers. He said it was the livest burg in the Middle West, and believe me, he came pretty near hinting that if I ever got so I was fit to associate with some of the big bugs here I'd be hitting up a whole lot hotter pace than I had been.

I let him have it back right hot off the bat. I don't remember just what I said, but—oh, I stood right up to him. You know this motto about so living that you'll be able to take any big slob that tries to climb your neck and give him the hard-boiled eye and can tell him just where he heads in at. I don't remember just the wording, but it's something like that—and say, that's pretty good philosophy, eh? And that's me.

But the whole scrap left me feeling kind of mean, allee samee, I got to thinking about quitting—in fact, I made one or two passes at going to Harry Jason's, where—say, let me tell you Harry was crazy to get me back. Yes, sir! Now, say, there's a guy that can appreciate a good salesman. And Harry'd of paid me more money, too, if business hadn't been kind of slack with him. Told me so himself.

So things got to going from fierce to rotten. Tillie Groat was tattling about everything I did—oh, I got this straight. Maybe there's some people think they can pull the wool over my eyes, but believe me, I keep 'em peeled! Whadyuh think she had the nerve to blab to old Huffy? Said I told Sim Jenson I could get the sedan for a party any time I wanted it! And what I really told him was—well, I didn't say anything like that—practically. Besides, it's none of her business to go horning in, listening to phone conversations. And, of course, Huffy got sarcastic about that, too, and—oh, things simply got intolerable!

Then something happened that made me forget my grouch against Huff. I was really sorry for him—honest I was. It was pretty serious business—knocked out all the fun. His wife got pneumonia sudden—you may remember if you were in the office along about that time. And I must say it made a big change in Huff. I guess he realized and was sorry he'd been so cranky to her. Poor devil, he was calling up his house ten times a day, and ordering flowers to send up to her; and once his door was open and he was all broke up. I must say he isn't a man to give his feelings away, but he wound up his phone conversation by blurting out, "I don't know that they will do any good or that she'll ever see them, but—send up, two dozen tea roses—and hurry, oh, hurry 'em!"

Honest, it got me hard. I darn near sniveled standing there in the door. And afterward I tried to say good night to him nice, and I wasn't a bit huffy when he hustled out by me. I guess he never saw me at all, he was so worried. And the next day he wasn't there, and I suppose she must have died the day after that. But he came back to the office for a few hours before the funeral.

Now you know how I am, Mac—rough-housing and joshing. But gee, when I own up to it, I guess I'm pretty sentimental. And Lord, I did want to do something nice for old Huffy! So I took up a collection—put in five simoleons myself, too, if I do say it—and we thought we'd send up a special wreath from us boys in the department, besides the regular office funeral piece. But I thought maybe Huff would like something special. Then I got one large big idea that afternoon while he was in the office.

Why not give him our check and let him do what he wanted with it? thinks I. Well, you know how I am—impulsive. Minute I got the idea I was so full of it that I jumped up and busted right into his office and I started, "Oh, Mr. Huff!"

He was sitting there staring at some papers. He jumped about a mile, and he turned on me and hollered: "Good heavens, have you always got to be dragging me into your rows? Get out of here!"

I kept my temper, and I just said, "Why, I came in to ask————"

"Ask hell!" he says. "Go do your whining to the janitor. You know your work. If you can't do it by yourself for a few days, then you better jump the job. And I don't care to hear any of your office quarrels either. Get out of here! Git!"

I got all right.

I honestly meant to quit that afternoon. But I kept telling myself to keep my shirt on; no use taking a man seriously when he's crazy with grief, though I bet a lot of his grief was thinking and realizing how mean he'd always been to his wife, and now it was too late. Poor old duffer, he was sitting there trying to collect his thoughts, and he supposed I was butting in to start something, I told myself. Oh, sure! I argued it all out. But I was up on my ear just the same. Lord, Mac, I'd meant it so nice, and wanted to comfort him! Well never mind. But honest it did hurt. And I gave the money I'd collected for flowers back to the fellows, and I darned near blubbered.

Why say, I was so down in the mouth that evening that Sue called me for being the human gloom, and we had some set-to, believe me—haven't hardly got over it yet. But I don't care. Nothing can shake my love for Sue. Though she'd better understand which of us is the big noise, and she ain't going to be the only trolley in our car. I guess I got just as good a right to be temperamental—that's what she calls it—as she has.

When Huff came back he had enough savvy to know he'd been pretty raw, the way he ordered me out of his coop. But he wasn't man enough to own up; and believe me, I wasn't going to go in and yelp, "Dear boss, I want to apologize for your kicking me in the face." So we just kind of kept circling round and watching each other, ready to bore in, and then—yippo! The old k.o. right on the point of the chin, and don't wake me, nursie dear, I'm in Paree.

It wasn't much in itself.

Huff couldn't find a letter he wanted. Swore he'd given it to me to have it filed. Of course I'd be the goat! I suppose I probably ate it on him to save lunch money. Or maybe I made an auto tire out of it. Anyway, he bawled everybody out for our carelessness about mail, and when he went out to feed his face he poked round on his desk, and darned if it wasn't right there under a bunch of junk under his elbow.

Well, I held it out on him, and 'bout midafternoon I sailed in and said—oh, I was the meek thing! You see I was kidding him. I kind of snickered like I was naughty Willie, and I said, "I found that missing letter, Mr. Huff."

Well old Nero the lion licks his whiskers and figures out here's where he'll heap ketchum plenty big meal, and he howls, "I told you you'd lost it!"

Then I let him have it—zingo!

"But I didn't. It was right on your desk all the time. I found it this noon."

Say, maybe he didn't look cheap. He knew I had him, but he tried to bluff out of it. Whadyuh think he has the gall to say?

"Then why did you put it there?" he says. "I certainly never did," he says. "I want you to be more careful. You're the most careless man I know," he says.

I looked him right square in the eye. I kind of got up my dignity, and I was quiet, and you know how it is, Mac. A guy that'd studied human nature and frank self-analysis would of known enough to look out then and not get flip—you know how it was in the West in the old days. Gee, maybe I wouldn't of liked to have been a cow-puncher. Some life, riding round on the buttes and shooting up Indians! You remember in those days if there was a big husk shooting off his mouth he was nothing but a false alarm, but a little runt with cold gray eyes and polite—say, watch out, he was dangerous. I guess I'm the same way. So I says, "Mr. Huff," I says, "I like my work, but I don't like to be persecuted. I ain't careless—not more than what there's an excuse for in rush times—and I don't think it's fair to roast me."

See, like that. Quiet. But make an impression on him? Say, does a sparrow make an impression when he lights on a tin roof?

He never got it at all. He just snorted, "So you don't think you're careless, eh?"

"No, I don't," I says, still polite, just like a holdup man in the movies, where you find out afterwards he's a secret service man.

But my line was too smooth for him. The rough stuff, that was all he could savvy. He came back: "Then you might explain how you happened to fail to keep your engagement with this R. T. Bradley and show him an apartment."

Say, by golly, he had me there, but I wasn't going to let him get me going! And I'm never afraid to own up to my faults. So I come right back: "Yes, that was careless. Go on. Any other times you can think of?"

That stumped him, and he wanted to crawl out of it. Why, to save his life he couldn't of thought of four times when I'd been careless! So he was plumb buffaloed, and he just grunted, "Well, you don't want to be so careless," and turned his back on me.

That got me peeved. So I said, "Mr. Huff, I guess you and I have ended our usefulness to one another. I quit! I'm through!" And I walked out on him. Never looked back once.

Well, maybe he wasn't floored! I stayed on till Saturday, and I bet there was more than fifty times when he tried to get a chance to jolly me up and persuade me to hang on. But I never paid any attention to him; never passed any remarks with him; and Saturday, I walked out and I wouldn't go back, not if he offered me fifty bucks per each week every week! No, sir!

So I'm thinking of going to New York and getting next to a real job. I can't do much for this burg. Too blame slow.

"Ray Moller, Realty, Forty-second Street, New York." How does that sound, eh? I bet some day I'll be making five thousand good iron men a year.

But old Huffy——— I haven't seen him since I got out of the office. But I'm hoping I'll meet him. And believe me, if I do, no matter when it is or where it is, I'm going to light into him and tell him just exactly what I think of him, and if he gets funny I'll just nachly up and pound the daylight out of him. Lord help him when I meet him again!

So that's how it is, see? I just wanted to illustrate how you have to handle a man like Homer Huff.

II

The confidences of Mr. Homer Huff, manager of the rental department of Tribby, Burkett & Day, as given to his friend, Mr. McNew, of the Crescent Sign and Poster Company, at lunch at the Good Red Beef Chop House.

Well, Mac, how are you today? Oh, pretty fair. Well, I've let this Ray Moller go. Remember him—salesman? Huh? Quit? Moller? Why, no; I fired him. Don't like to fire any of the boys, but it was as much for his sake as for ours. He's a little too self-confident.

You know how I am, Mac; you've seen me in the office. I'm always easy to get along with, and friendly. Way I see it, I always take a chance on being easy on the boys, even at the risk of injuring discipline. But this Moller is a fellow that will take advantage of you. Too brash. I tried to get him over it, but I saw I was wasting my time, so I fired him.

I liked the boy when I met him, too. Seems to me I first ran up against him at Harry Jason's office. I saw he was green and pretty mouthy, but he had a good deal of energy, and I thought he might have the makings of a salesman in him, so I took him on. Way I see it, the boy isn't bad, but just bumptious; always looking for trouble, and I guess there's plenty of trouble in the world without having to look very hard, Mac. I've certainly found my share without much prospecting.

Why, the lad hadn't been in the office—I don't suppose it was over two hours—before he became lippy about—what was it now? I can't remember. Oh yes; we had a set-to about the way the office ought to be lighted, and—well, I hate to have to show up a young fellow and dampen his enthusiasm, but I had to explain some of the fundamental principles of lighting to him, and I guess he was a little chagrined when he found out he'd been going off halfcocked.

Then there was a little discussion about the car he was to have. I forgot now, but I think he wanted a flivver of his own. Anyway, the big boss, Burkett, butted in. He told me privately that he didn't care to spend any good money for a car for this youngster, flivver or anything else, and I was to let him take my sedan that the firm had bought me, when I wasn't using it.

Now I resented that. You know how Burkett is, Mac. I like to be loyal to my boss, but old Pussyfoot Burkett sticks in my craw. You know his game; always smiling and loving out in the front

office; treats every stenographer like a daughter and every salesman as if he were the Prince of Wales; and then calls us department
heads into conference and tells us we have to call down our subordinates.

Minute he laid eyes on this Moller boy Burkett disliked him,
and he told me: "Homer, you've made a bad break hiring this boy.
Better let him out."

"What's the trouble with him?" I says. "Give him a chance,
boss."

"He's altogether too fresh," says Burkett. "Acts as if I were his
roommate. I don't want to butt into your department————"

Oh, no; not at all; he didn't want to butt in a bit more than a
dog wants a beef bone!

"I don't want to interfere," he said, "but if you keep this boy
on he's your responsibility, and you'll have to try to lam the big
head out of him."

And just to put one over on me Burkett let the boy use my sedan and kept hammering at me to scold him. He'd meet young
Moller on the street and pass the time of day with him, and then
come to me and grumble, "Boys of this generation—too fresh—
too fresh."

Nice position a department head has, Mac. Buffer between the
big boss and the staff—kicked by both sides. Young Moller thought
I was a crank if I begged him to interrupt his afternoon naps and
answer a phone call, and old Burkett thought I was a shyster if I
didn't haul the lad up on the carpet and just naturally skin him
alive every time he stole a postage stamp—which was frequent,
Mac, frequent.

Most of the real trouble started over our department stenographer, Tillie Groat. You know what a cute, nice, bright little girl she
is; and got the best sense of humor of any girl I ever saw. Looks so
demure and quiet, but never misses a trick. She almost died laughing over the way this Moller boy swelled round talking about what
a sport he was and how he and his lady friend always dined at the
Royal. Tillie used to imitate him when he was out of the office—
say, she took him off to the queen's taste.

Well, after about two months, I guess it was, of trying to make
a killing with Tillie this Moller seemed to tumble to the fact that

she wasn't lying awake nights thinking about him, and that hurt his vanity and he turned mean. Tillie asked me what she ought to do about it, and I advised her to overlook a lot, same as I always do—the rock you don't kick doesn't hurt your foot any. So she stood for his bragging about how well educated he was till I happened in one time and just gently made fun of him a little and shamed him out of it.

Not a bad boy, you see; just weak, unstable—awfully young and callow—no power of analyzing people or situations. You could see that in his relations with a fellow named Sim Jenson. You've met him? Well, you and I know what Jenson is. But he certainly is a glib mouth artist, and he fooled poor Moller. Simply used him. I never said anything, but I know they took the office sedan out for trips constantly.

Perfectly innocent trips; though say, it's funny to listen to Moller trying to make believe he's a wild joy-riding devil.

And Moller always paid for the gas. How do I know all this? Why, I used to keep an eye on the speedometer, to see how much the car had been used after office hours. And the gas station I patronized is the same place where Moller used to get his fuel. Say, the fellow working there almost passed out laughing at the way Moller would swell up in the sedan, with Jenson and a couple of girls, and try to show off, pretending he owned the car and insisting on paying for the gas, while Jenson would make a bluff at wanting to pay himself, but always making Moller shell out. Oh, it was rich! But I never let Moller know I was on. Poor kid, I was sorry for him.

But by and by things did get a little raw. It was when I was going through my trouble. You know what my wife was, Mac; we've talked of her enough times; don't need to go into that again. You know how the poor girl nagged me after her nervous collapse, and how extravagant she became. I can forget all that now. But there was a time she had me on the edge; I couldn't be patient with her or anybody else. I never knew where I was at. One minute I'd hear her in the outside office joking with Tillie or some of the boys; then she'd sail in and cuss me out because I didn't make more money.

Poor old Mac, you've had to hear my troubles a lot of times. Well, all this time I tried to be considerate to the men under me, and I must say I got away with it mostly. Just to show you how considerate I was: One time I caught myself getting grouchy I hinted to some of the boys one night when we were working late just what the basis of my trouble was. I made it as delicate as I could, but I wanted them to know they could discount about seventy percent of any bad temper I might be betrayed into showing. Course that wasn't hardly necessary, but I always believe in giving the boys the squarest deal I can, and they appreciated it. When I hinted about my wife I could see in this Moller kid's face that he understood me a little better now.

You see, I don't believe in blowing up my men way a lot of these fellows do. Instead of scrapping with them I just jolly 'em—some joke that clarifies the situation—sense of humor so much better than being gruff.

Take for instance: There was this couple from New York name of Sanbœuf—why, you must know the fellow—this grafter that calls himself an interior decorator and sells a lot of junk to fool women at about triple prices? That's the fellow. Well, he and his wife were looking for a house, and they kidded Moller into wasting a lot of time on them, so I called him in and I said, "My boy, these Sansbœufs are first class tinhorns," I said.

"I don't know—maybe they're fakers, but they've got artistic taste," he says. "They're awfully important in New York," he says.

"Yes," I says, "and you and I are important New York millionaires, and we better try and buck Wall Street," I says.

Moller laughed and said, "Well, maybe that's the way it is."

"Sure!" I said. "Don't ever take any man's estimation of himself."

See how I mean? I always had a little joke, and the boys appreciated it. So we got along fine, even if Burkett did keep after me, telling me Moller was no good. But then came the bad time when —— You remember how quick my wife took sick? I was simply dazed, and I forgot how nervous she'd been. I just thought of her as the jolly girl she used to be. And then she died, and I was about all in. And oh, Mac, I felt so darn lonely for her!

Say, I oughtn't to be talking this way, whining like a schoolboy, but you and I've been sort of chummy so long. Mac, offices are hard places sometimes. Here I'd done everything for these boys, but there wasn't one of 'em cared, now I was up against it. Way I see it, they simply didn't have enough imagination to understand. Just because I didn't wear my heart on my sleeve I suppose they thought I didn't suffer. But Mac, not one of 'em came up and patted my shoulder and said, "Sorry, old man. Anything I can do?" And at the funeral——— Burkett sent some flowers for the office as a whole, but the boys in my department never peeped, never showed any recognition of the funeral. And there was one thing

———

This was what really started me being sore at young Moller. I came down to the office for one afternoon between her death and the funeral. I was sitting there at my desk thinking about her. I suppose I was terribly wrought up. I'm especially sentimental most times, but that afternoon———

I don't know anything definite about the future life, but that afternoon I felt perfectly sure that was someplace where she could start life all over again, with her nerves all right. Poor kid, she'd been so lively before her prostration. As I sat there in my office I was thinking how maybe she was someplace now where she'd got back her feeling of fun in little simple things, and—it was strange, Mac; it was like a vivid dream. I felt as though she was talking to me from beyond the veil, and I was saying to her: "Never mind, lass, we'll try it again over there and make a better go of it." And I could see her smiling the way she used to, and———

Then, crack! Smash! This gawk of a Moller had come slam-banging into my office without so much as knocking, and he'd started shouting about some trouble he was having with somebody or something.

I interrupted him, and I said nice as I could: "Old man, I'm sorry, but I'm afraid I can't listen to any business this afternoon. You'll have to run your own work entirely for a few days. Use your own judgment."

And instead of getting it he looked angry because for a moment I dared to be human. I didn't say anything, but as a matter of fact I was furious—no, not so much furious as awfully hurt, that he'd come in on me at a time like that. And I tried not to be censorious, but his butting in that way and his constant impertinence had got on my nerves, and after that I couldn't help noticing how careless he was.

I'd wasted a lot of time on him, trying to teach him business technique and give him a chance to go ahead. But rats, he couldn't appreciate it! He'd forget to turn in his reports, and if he took down the particulars about a flat over the phone he'd forget to put it on the list; or if he did enter it, he'd leave out the rent or the term of the lease, or whether it was a.m.i. or something.

I got more and more impatient, and finally there came a time when I was looking for a letter that he'd misplaced, and he had the nerve to insist that he'd finally located it on my own desk!

"Well," I said to him, "probably I lost it. Probably I make a regular rule of asking you for letters that I already have. But that isn't the point. The point is that you're too careless."

"Am I?" he says, impudent.

"You are," I says. "You're careless, and we're not going to argue about it in any way, shape, manner or form. Enough's enough, and I want you to quit being so careless," I said. I let him have it straight for once.

"I'm not any more careless than the rest of the fellows, except maybe in rush time," he says.

Then I lay for him. I looked innocent. I don't know how come, but suddenly I could see that for his own sake he was due for an awful jolt.

"So you don't really feel you're careless?" I said.

"No, I don't," he says.

"Then you might tell me how you happened to fail to keep the appointment that you yourself made to show Rob Bradley an apartment," I said.

He flushed up and admitted it. I was tired of coddling him. No use.

"I think you'll have to learn your lesson, my boy," I said. I was as nice as could be, but I was pretty final. "I think maybe you'd better get through next Saturday," I said.

He blurted out: "You're not firing me, are you?" The poor kid, he almost bawled.

"Yes, I am," I said. But I saw he was so broke up that——— I always was a fool. I never could stand hurting other people's feelings. I took pity on him, and I said: "We'll put it this way: You're laid off for three months. If at the end of that time you think you can be a little more careful come back and we'll see if there's a vacancy. Meantime maybe Harry Jason will give you a temporary job."

"Honest," he said, "I can't stand working for that piker. Let me try it again," he said.

"Nope, I'm sorry," I said. I was firm.

Well, here I'd gone and tried to help him by just making it a layoff, even though I knew Burkett would give me fits for being such a softy. But think that Moller boy appreciated it? He did not! He got impudent right away.

"I'm going up to kick to Burkett," he says.

Can you beat it? Then I was mad for fair.

"You come right in and do it right now!" I hollered. I grabbed his arm and yanked him to the big boss' den.

"Mr. Burkett," I says, "I've fired this yahoo. But I guess he wants to fire me instead and take my job. How about it?"

Tickled Burkett to see me so worked up.

"Why, why! How we let the angry passions rise!" he says just to get my goat. You know how he is—sarcastic. All the time. No excuse for it. But same time, course he didn't like Moller, and you've got to admit that Burkett is a master of nice polite nastiness. He turned on Moller and said: "I'm afraid we'll need your desk Saturday. We're thinking of hiring a real rental salesman, and he'll want it."

Poor Moller slunk out completely flabbergasted. I was sorry for him. But same time it's pretty hard to forgive him for trying to go over my head to Burkett. I haven't seen Moller since he left the office. But some day I'll run into him, and then I think I'll just cut loose and tell him what I really think of him. His swelled head is going to be a whole lot reduced in size when I get through with him.

Say, somebody was telling me that Moller thinks he's going to New York to tackle the realty game there. He'll last quick! Poor kid, he'll have an awful failure. Why, he'll do well if he ever makes two thousand a year there.

So that's how it is, Mac, from the inside of the inside.

III

Stray remarks of Miss Tillie Groat, stenographer in the rental department of Tribby, Burkett & Day, to her friend, Mr. McNew.

Say, honest, Mr. McNew, aren't men the simps? Did you know Mr. Huff has fired Ray Moller? They both of 'em make me tired. Always looking for a chance to row. You talk about women fretting and worrying! Say, Mr. McNew, if there was as many as two men out of every hundred that wasn't looking for trouble all the time, life would be about eleventy thousand percent easier for everybody. Ain't it the truth?

Huh? Sure, Ray's a good salesman! Did you know I could of married him if I wanted to?

Huh? Sure! Huffy is a good boss—if you know how to handle him. Laugh at his jokes, that's the way.

Huh? They sure are! They're as mad at each other as can be; just working up a fine temper. Way I see it, Huff and Ray'll never be satisfied till they have a regular fight and get it out of their systems. My, I wonder what will happen when they meet up? I hope I won't be there. It'll be fierce.

Ain't men the simps!

And me, do I ever get any credit? I do not! I take the bum English both of 'em dictate to me, and turn it into swell language and slip it back to them, but they never know the diff. Way I see it, if it wasn't for Tillie this department wouldn't be one-two-three. See how it is?

IV

Statement by Mr. Burkett, president of Tribby, Burkett & Day, to his friend, Mr. McNew.

I'll never accept another loan from the Drovers' National, McNew, and I advise you people to do the same thing. The president of the bank is too sarcastic—all the time. No excuse. Now you know how I am, McNew. I'm easy to get along with———

V

Certain events which occurred in the city of New York at a time approximately ten years after the preceding testimonies and depositions.

Mr. Ray Moller, the junior partner in the small but active real-estate firm of Dysell & Moller, on Thirty-fourth Street, New York City, is a business success. A fellow realtor has insisted to me that Mr. Moller is an accident; that Moller happened to be on hand at a time when the chief and other salesmen were sick, and thus had responsibility forced upon him. But it is certain that the responsibility taught Moller the necessity of accuracy, formed in him the habits of diligence and punctuality, and developed in him a self-confidence the lack of which his former brazen boasting had concealed. An inherent cheerfulness assisted him. He became Dysell's partner, and was the larger factor in developing Dysler Park on Long Island. But he paid for his success by becoming so habituated to routine work day and night that he had no intimates.

On a certain evening as he walked away from the office, solitariness divided him from the crowds. He turned dully into the Firenze Restaurant—one of those anomalous places which are not quite cheap enough to be popular or quite good enough to be distinguished. Thoroughly bored, he ordered an entrée, coffee, pie; then drugged himself with an evening paper in order to escape from reality—from the problem of what to do with his evening. He knew enough people; enough admirable young women upon whom he could call. But he reflected: "Oh, I don't know—don't feel like taking the trouble of ringing anybody up."

He would, he supposed, drift on to his expensive and plushily bleak furnished room, brood over a sales campaign, go to bed. He sighed and began eating his entrée, not seeing it, scarce tasting it, looking across his lifted fork at headlines in the paper.

Someone was standing at his table; a familiar voice greeting him: "Well, for the love of Mike! Ray Moller!"

He was startled. Through his blood went the pleasure of seeing a face which he had known long ago. It was a Mr. Homer Huff, once his senior in a real-estate firm in the Middle Western city of Vernon. He had not seen the man since the day on which he had left that firm.

"Well, well, well, well! What the dickens you doing in New York?" Moller chuckled, springing up, eagerly shaking hands.

"I'm living here now, Ray. Been here for six months—Tomlinson-Burke Realty Company, on Madison. Say, but it's good to see you! I've heard you've done fine. Putting it all over old Huff, I guess!"

"Oh, rats, old man, just crawling along! I'll never be a real natural executive the way you are, Huff. Dining with anybody? Can't you sit down?"

Huff sat opposite, pleasure apparent in his broad face.

"It's mighty good—mighty good to see you, Ray. This is a pretty lonely town."

"I'll say it is! And I've been here almost ten years. Well, well, old Homer! I can't believe my eyes. Tell me all the news from home. Say, whatever became of that girl—what was her name? Tillie something, wasn't it?—that used to work for us. She was a bright, nice little girl, wasn't she!"

"She sure was! Why, she married Tom McNew, of the McNew Sign Posting Company."

"Well, well, well, is that a fact? I'm glad to see hear it. Mac is a prince."

"He sure is! Do you ever hear from that girl you used to play around with, Ray?"

"Which one? Bessie?"

"No, wasn't there a—oh, that was it! Sue, that was her name."

"Say, by golly, Homer, that reminds me—plumb forgot it—been putting it off and putting it off—ought to write her. She wrote me six months ago that she'd had a fourth baby born. You know she married Sim Jenson. Remember him?"

"Can't say I do."

"Why, he worked on the *Courier*—believe he's circulation manager now."

"Oh, that's right! So he is. Sure, I remember him now! Good steady worker. Nice fellow. Well, say, Ray, I went to hear about your success. I tell you I'm mighty proud of the way most of my boys have turned out. I always believed in you, and I tried to give you the best advice I could. Probably I got cranky sometimes, but I meant it for you good."

"You bet it was! Sure, you were cranky now and then. But heavens, I had it coming to me. I must have been a brassy youngster. And tell the truth, I guess I roast my salesman worse'n you ever did me, though I wouldn't admit it to them. I've got a youngster working for me now—not bad, but unstable, weak. Doesn't analyze himself and his problems. Means well, but too fresh, and I light into him for his own good. See how it is? Say, Homer, here's a funny thing: All these years I've been thinking of you as so much older than I am, and now I feel as though you and I were about the same age. How old are you, Homer?"

"I'm forty-eight now, Ray."

"Well, I'm thirty-six, and I don't feel as though there was any difference at all. Tell me how Tomlinson has fixed you up, Homer."

"Pretty well—oh, nothing extra, but good comfortable job. How much you making now, Ray? You must be crowding ten thousand a year."

"Yes, I am. Say, isn't it funny? One time I thought if I ever made five thousand I'd be the emperor of Wall Street!"

"Yes, that's how it goes. But I always knew you'd make big money here. Say, Ray, what're you going tonight? What d'you say we take in a show!"

"That sounds good to me, Homer. Or say, I know a couple of nice girls, business women, that have a dandy little flat uptown. What d'you say we give 'em a ring and ask 'em if they're going to be home, and we'll go call? Like to have 'em meet you, Homer."

"Fine! Suits me, boss."

The girls and their mother were home. They sat on the pillowiferous divan, while Ray Moller in the wicker chair and Homer Huff on the piano stool talked about each other.

"Homer used to be my boss, and he was the greatest sales general I ever met," boasted Ray.

"I'm proud to say that Ray worked under me. He's gone ahead of the old man, but he and I worked out a lot of things together—like the principles of office lighting, for instance," boasted Homer.

At eleven, as they descended from the stairs from the apartment, Homer crowed: "Fine girls, Ray! Say, this is the best evening I've had since I hit town. Real home folks."

"Same here, Homer. I tell you it's good to see you. I haven't had any fellow to trail round with here really. Got into a bad habit of just meeting people in a business way. Then, of course, these New Yorkers aren't like us Vernon boys. Say, where you living, Homer?"

"I have a room in a small hotel. Regular old bach. Don't like it much."

"Well, look here, Homer: if you haven't any other plans, why wouldn't it be a good stunt for me and you to take a flat and furnish it together?"

"That's a great idea, Ray. You bet! Let's do it. Come have lunch with me tomorrow and we'll talk it over."

"I'll be there with bells on. I'm strong for the flat idea. We'd get along fine. We're alike in a lot of things, Homer—both of us easy to get along with, and we'd hit it off great. Always liked you from the first time we met. Funny thing about me—I can just about tell what a man us like first time I lay eyes on him."

"Same here. And I'm strong for your idea. I'd always hoped we'd meet up some day. I remember telling Tom McNew, about the time you quit Burkett: 'That boy'll make a big success,' I said."

"Quit? Why, rats, Burkett practically fired me, you might say."

"Golly, that's right! So he did, come to think of it. Isn't that just like him? Fire the best salesman in the shop! Way I see it, fundamental trouble with a man like Burkett is that he makes snapshot judgments and doesn't hold off and mull things over the way you and I always do. Well, good night, old Ray. Good luck. See you tomorrow."

THE GOOD SPORT

I

The wha-n-n-n of the foghorn, gray, crinkled water sliding past, the boats of oyster tongers springing up from nowhere and disappearing, the strangeness of a world destroyed. It oppressed her agreeable little inland soul. This was the fourth day of Emily Banning's honeymoon. They had motored for two days; they had stayed at a gold-and-onyx hotel in Philadelphia; and now they were on the *Opodnock,* a steamer like an elongated tug, trudging down the Chesapeake. She had known her husband for less than six months. Paul Banning had come to her Maryland hill town to sell Meeper trucks. Besides the changeless and heavy-footed village lads he seemed miraculous. He sparkled. He said curious things.

"That puts me all to Croatia!" he cried when he lost at five hundred.

He had wonderful accessories—a gold cigarette case, a gold cigar cutter, a silver matchbox, a thin watch chain strung diagonally across his vest with its exquisite fit and long points. He was nervous, and his wrists were thin, but he was young and swift of laughter.

Paul had first come to the house to sell her father a truck for the grocery. He took her to the Knights of Pythias dance, where with his elegant whirling step he stood out like an oriole among cowbirds. And he praised her. He said she was a little Madonna, and adorable, and steady as a church. He murmured to her on an evening walk: "I've got the business pep all right, but I'm too easygoing. If I had a wise side partner like you I'd show up every motor salesman from Broadway to Hick Center—and by golly, the prettiest girl in this ole state!"

His eyesight had shut him out of from the draft in the Great War, now expiring.

They were married.

In marriage Paul was daily more endearing. He was eager to make her happy. He invented surprises—flowers on the dinner table, candy hidden in her suitcase. To him the honeymoon was a succession of games. He played lap dog, stalking across the floor on hands and knees to bring her mules in the morning. He was a make-believe aviator when they drove—in a car whose ownership she never quite understood, so vague was Paul about it. He convulsed her by his solemn way of standing beside the wheel and crying, while they crawled along a level road: "Ah, my lallapalluza, 'tis it not thrilling to be flying above the Aleps this way! Look down hitherward ten thousand feet to the snowish top of Mong Blang! Now we will do a tailspin." And he steered the car into a ditch five inches deep.

He put the car in first, ran it at two or three miles an hour on the hand throttle and leaped out. He could keep it in the road at that speed by occasionally reaching in to touch the wheel. He raced round and round it; he stood in front and tried to push it back; he rode on the hood; and when a passing farmer saw this madman on a driverless car he gaped and lashed his horses, while Paul gurgled.

Emily hadn't known that she could play so wildly. She had been given to walking by herself, to thinking things out, though there was never anything definite to think out. But roused by Paul, she giggled, she chased him about rooms, she bounced when they stopped at an amusement park and rose the chutes, the carousel, the captive aeroplanes. She looked forward to a life adventurous and many-colored.

If she could only get used to the surprises Paul was always flinging at her! Back home people didn't do things unexpectedly. If they were going to take Number Seven on Sunday with Cousin Engelberta, fourteen miles up the line, they started planning it on Tuesday, and got a timetable on Wednesday. Number Seven hadn't changed time in ten years; still, you never could be too careful.

But Paul—it wasn't till the second day of the honeymoon, when they were driving toward Atlantic City, that he remarked, "By golly, forgot to tell you! I've thrown up my job with the Meeper truck people." That was all, and he went on as though it were much more important, "Wait'll you see the ocean! I'll show you some diving!"

"But, Paul, I thought you liked the Meeper Company. You said they appreciated you so much and made such a nice truck."

"Sure! Nice bunch of junk! I mean, they used to get out a good boat, but this year's model——— Besides, I don't want to go floating round when I've got a little wife like you. I want to get in some big city agency, and stay put. Think I'm gonna leave you for all the naughty mans to steal away!"

He abandoned the wheel and embraced her, but as they were going thirty-seven miles an hour she was not altogether gratified.

"What are you going to do? Oh, please be careful! I thought you had it all settled to take the house in Frederick and get back there every———"

"Say, gee, glad you reminded me! Must drop that fellow a line and tell him I don't want his bum house, or he might try to collect rent."

"But—but—what are we going to do?"

"Now you quit worrying! For heaven's sake be a sport—on our honeymoon, anyhow! I've got a little wad put aside. We'll float round awhile, and then I'll dot into some big agency and let 'em annex me priceless services. Don't know but what we might try Baltimore. They tell me that's a good live town. And I'm through selling trucks and cheap cars. I want to sell high-class stuff to a high-class trade. There's where I shine. I know how to jolly the boys with the money. I can travel right into their gang. Most of these pikers don't know how to handle swell customers. Let's see! We'll get a nifty flat, and meet a nice bunch, and maybe join a golf club."

"Oh, Paul, Paul! You can't do all those lovely things till you have a job. I thought you had your business all arranged. We mustn't—we can't go on spending money like this if we haven't anything———"

He ran the car to the side of the road and stopped.

"See here, don't you trust me?"

"Of course I do!" But while she swore it she reflected how little she knew him.

"Don't you think I can get an opening in Baltimore? Or do you think I'm a four-flusher?"

"Oh, no, no, no! It's just—perhaps I'm silly, but I've always lived in such a settled way that it scares me to think of everything going out and nothing coming in. Oh, I do love you and trust you—yes, I do—but———"

"I'm going to teach you a lesson. I'm going to turn round and start for Baltimore, right now, this minute! Before tomorrow noon I'll have a job in an A-1 agency there. Then maybe next time you'll trust me!"

"But you wanted to go to Atlantic City so much; you'd planned ———"

"Yep, I did. Planned it for you. Did the best I could. But if you don't appreciate it—well, I'm sorry, that's all. We won't talk about it anymore."

He swung the car about, sullenly drove south, not looking at her. She begged forgiveness. He muttered: "I don't care a hang about losing the Atlantic City trip. It's your not trusting me that hurts; your not being a good sport, with enough red blood to duck the cautious and steady for a few days. Gosh, if we can't be reckless even on a honeymoon we'd better be dead!"

He drove furiously, taking chances on curves, and she agonized that it was her fault; that with her petty complaining she had wounded him. He slackened the speed in a few miles, hastily kissed her, and cried: "It's all right now! Didn't mean to get sore. But we'll go on to Baltimore. I just want to show you what Uncle Pauly can do."

She was grateful, and assured herself that he would find the new job as quickly as he said—only she had to go on assuring herself. They arrived in Baltimore late that evening, and he drove to an enormous hotel. She began to protest, "Don't you think we better go to a cheaper place?" but checked herself. She mustn't be a kill-joy again.

From breakfast time till lunch next day she waited in their room.

He was to have had the new job before noon, and it was now one. At a quarter after one Paul quietly opened the door—he who usually came through doors as though he were making a high dive. He looked depressed.

"Is it all right?" she begged.

He sat limply in the pretentious plush chair.

"Em dear, would you be awful worried if I hadn't made my connection—if I'd slipped up for once?"

She cried stoutly, as though she were defending him against the world: "I don't care! You'll find something! Perhaps tomorrow!"

"Whee! Stung again!" He sprang up, posed like the Statue of Liberty, hurled a pillow at her and stood on his head on the floor, airily waving one foot. He rose—rather red-faced and choking and muttered: "Gosh, guess I been smoking too many cigarettes! Kind of gets your wind." But he immediately recovered his triumph and crowed: "Dear madam, you may be interested to learn, in reply to your huffy query of seventh instant, that your husband is now a salesman for the Torquay-Belfast Motor Company in Baltimore, Maryland!"

"Honestly!"

"No, dishonestly! I didn't get the job. I just stole it. I walks in—well, I did go to a couple of other places first, but the managers there were grouches, so I told 'em to go to. But I drifts into the Torquay agency and tells the high guy what a swell little mixer I am, and how much I know about ignition and upholstery, and takes me on at thirty-five per, with a bird of a commission, and I go to work there a week from Monday, when we wind up the grand honeymoon. Now do you trust the poor nut? Now do you see how much more fun it is to take a chance once in a while."

She was hiding a shamed cheek against his coat, and he was forgiving her with lordly blandness. Also he was announcing that in twenty-seven minutes they would be starting, not for Atlantic City but for a voyage among unfrequented plantations on the steamer *Opodnock*.

Someone or other at the Torquay agency had recommended the trip—he didn't exactly remember who.

She was dazed, but she began to pack, murmuring, "I must learn to like taking chances," and trying to make it sound natural.

Paul finally agreed with her that perhaps it would be just as easy for her to do the packing alone. He sat in the plush chair boasting.

"We're off to beat all records! I don't care if I spend the rest of my natural life with the Torquay-Belfast. Now there's a car! Sells at five thousand two hundred—yes, and the limousine runs up to eight and nine. Grand colors and upholstery and motor—say, that engine's built like a watch, and all the power in the world. Do you know I drove a Torquay at eighty miles an hour once? Well, I wasn't exactly driving, but I was along with a fellow that did. And there's a corking bunch at the agency here—manager is a prince—wait'll you meet 'em! Oh, you're going to have one great time here, Mrs. Paulibus Banningski! Feel a little better now?"

"Oh, I'm terribly ashamed!"

II

She had enjoyed the comfort of his car; she had, for all her worries about expenses, enjoyed the lavish hotels. But she did not enjoy the chunky steamer and their stateroom with shelves for beds. She was the inlander, the hillbilly, used to dry air and solid surroundings, and as they slipped from the security of the dock into a blind world of fog, as she caught the slippery smell of mist, salt water, rusty iron and dead fish, she was faintly alarmed. It was, she fretted, a wretched little boat, and the puffy captain didn't seem competent to get them through this wall of nothingness, past those other boats which she could hear—but menacingly not see—with their angry "Zh-h-h-h!" their wailing "Wha-n-n-n!"

She hid it; she crawled along the slippery deck, arm about Paul's waist, and tried to join in the boisterous singing of "Smile, Smile, Smile." Supper was a trial. The *Opodnock* served a district between the James River and the Potomac which was untouched by railroads. Small traveling salesmen, fishermen, and storekeepers who had gone to Baltimore on business lined the table and gobbled in silence. They ignored her, and in her brisk friendly little life she had never been ignored. Not till they had finished, grunted, pushed away their plates and produced toothpicks did they began to talk, and then only of Virginia politics.

Paul joined their talk, and in a metropolitan manner endeavored to guide it to national affairs—and the Torquay-Belfast motor. He waved his fork and chanted:

"You take it from me, and I can talk by the book, because I sold a car to a fellow whose brother is one of the biggest newspaper men in Washington and closer to Tumulty than a brother, and this fellow let me in on the inside stuff, and that's how I happen to know that in the 1920 campaign the Republican candidate will be Pershing."

She felt—and tried not to feel—that he was showing off. She was embarrassed by the way in which the old passengers cocked their morose eyebrows at him. She whispered, "Let's go out on deck, Paul, and get some fresh air."

She found nothing to say as they walked round and round the box-heaped deck in the drenched darkness. She was startled at each blasphemous yawp of the foghorn.

"What's the matter? Why the grouch?" he asked.

"Nothing—really! I—Paul, don't we stop in some town about midnight?"

"Yuh, I think so."

"Wouldn't it be fun—oh, Paul, wouldn't it be fun if we sat up till then, and went ashore, and went to a hotel, and tomorrow—oh, we could walk round and explore."

"What's the matter? Scared of the fog?"

"No, not—not exactly."

He held her two arms, spoke sternly, while she writhed with a feeling of inferiority.

"Now look here, old Em. Let's have this out. What's the rub?"

"I don't like this boat! Those men at supper, and our stateroom—those horrid pencil boxes of berths!"

"What of it?"

She was homesick for her pink-and-blue room at home, for its daintiness and its security.

"I'm used to a decent clean place, and I simply don't care for a filthy hole, that's all!"

"No, all you want is a suite with a bathroom, like a liner, on a boat making a backcountry run! This is a good outfit, with a crackerjack skipper and tol'able food, and the stateroom is all you can expect. But suppose it were the limit? What of it? You got to choose between two kinds of life: the dead-or-alive kind, where you never have any fun, and the adventurous kind, where you see the world. That's me! Maybe tonight isn't as nice as you're accustomed to, but wasn't the hotel last night a little nicer than anything you ever hit? That's the way I do things. And if you can't stand my speed—why, you got to leave me!"

He halted. They were in darkness, on a gently rolling deck, the wet planks glaring amidships from the light of the small engine room. Beyond there was nothing save an appalling emptiness and the wailing of a gull. She felt abandoned to that emptiness. She wanted to cling to Paul's protection and dared not. The flippancy was gone from his voice; he was resolute.

"I'm crazy about you, Em, but for that reason I ain't going to let myself make you miserable. Do you like me? Want to stay with me?"

A long kiss, which argued many things.

"Then you've got to be a sport. You've been brought up soft. Always had mother to skip to, and sure of your three squares. Well, sometimes I can beat that; sometimes I can afford the mushrooms and champagny water. Ain't it fair then that some of the time you should only have spuds?"

"Yes, yes! Of course!"

She determined to be very fond of spuds, though what spuds were she did not know.

"Are you going to be a complainer, a nagger? Some sense to kicking when you can get something by it, but when a thing's done, when you can't change it, will you kindly tell me what use it is to nag your spouse into the grave? F'r instance, we're late for a show. Going to make it any earlier by yelping that I started too late? And maybe sometimes I might start late. I ain't perfect. A fellow like me that enjoys life, prob'ly he won't always be as powerful on the dish-wiping as one of these fish that want to sit home and snore all evening. But can't you trust me? Can't you understand I love you? When things go wrong, won't you be a sport and say 'Better luck tomorrow'? Won't you be a good sport?"

"Oh, yes, yes, yes!"

Thus it happened that Be a Good Sport, the slogan of joy-riders and race tracks, became the sacred device of Emily Banning. The sun was brilliant on the water next day, and in a week they came back to Baltimore, to a whole floor of a jolly little house off Charles Street, and during his first two days at the new work Paul sold two cars.

III

She made of their apartment a village home, with white curtains, boxes of narcissus, a jug of cider. She went trotting about the markets, a demure figure. Paul laughed at her economies.

"You're one of these Busy Berthas that spend five dollars' worth of gas to save three cents on a bunch of carrots!" he gibed.

But he adored her, planned parties for her. To her, their happiest evenings were when they played alone. She did not like his new friends.

"Folks with some zip to 'em, real Bohemians," Paul called them, but to her they were merely noisy. They were men with small salaries and large cars—not quite paid for; with shoes having pearly buttons—and heels ground down to muddy wafers.

They scattered cigar ashes on the floor she had scrubbed and polished. They left rings from wet bottles on the book of engravings which Aunt Tommy had given her for a wedding present. They filled the quiet and fragrance of her beloved rooms with the stink of cheap beer and the rattle of coon songs. But she smiled as she saw how people and gaiety—any people and any gaiety—exhilarated Paul, and she felt guilty because she was a poor sport.

When his Bohemians were gone, Paul philosophized: "They're only a starter. We'll duck them when we sneak in on a real society bunch. I'm beginning to get good and chummy with my customers, and you can bet that any guy that can shell out five thousand clinkers for a car is in right with the giddy whirl!"

Then, suddenly, the morning of worry. A Sunday morning; Paul abed at eleven, handsome in the corded silk pajamas which were economical because, as he explained, "they're so classy that they make you feel like a gentleman, and you know all this new stuff about psychology and mental power—a guy is like what he feels like." Emily herself, in an apron, was probably unclassy. She brought breakfast on a tray, and begged: "Oh, come on now, Paul. It's a peach of a day. Get up and we'll drive to Annapolis. I want to see the middies."

"Oh, what's the use of ever getting up? I been thinking—I'm sick of the hole where I work."

"I thought you liked it."

"Well, the place is all right, and some of the salesmen. Max Kelley, he's a prince—and say, maybe he can't play bridge! But the boss is a darned old grouch."

"Why, just two days ago you were saying————"

"Well, I had a kind of a run-in with him yesterday. Didn't want to bother you about it; but I goes out to lunch with a fellow, not exactly a customer, but might's well be. Darn nice fellow—and rich? Wow! They say his dad left him one hundred thousand cold bucks! Of course I don't want to hurry a fellow like that, and I was out maybe two hours, and when I gets back the manager bawls me out. Seems there hadn't been a salesman on the floor, and maybe we missed a sale—sure, maybe we had, maybe we hadn't! Anyway, if we did, don't I lose my commission? I guess if I'm sport enough to not put up any holler about that the firm ought to take its medicine too!"

"But, dear, you must remember that selling a fine car like the Torquay probably demands so much attention and————"

"Where do you get that fine-car stuff? Know what the Torquay is? Bunch of junk! And the service station? Oh, zowie, if I told you what I know about that bunch of pirates!"

"But—but————"

She was confused, so shaken out of her feeling of security, that "But—but————" was all she found to say.

Paul rose, shaved, came out cheerful and rosy, in his new hat which "did cost a little more'n I expected to pay, but it'll last twice as long—that is, 'less it goes out of style."

He had forgotten his woes. He chucked her under the chin, he sang "My Jazzland Cutie," he took her for a drive among hills serene with autumn, and he admitted: "Guess I was cranky before I got up. The boss ain't such a bad pill if you know how to kid him along."

But the next evening he came home raving.

"I won't stand any more of the boss' lip! He had the nerve to spring the new-brooms-sweep-clean line on me today. I as good as told him he could have my job, any time he wanted it."

"What would we do? We haven't saved but seventy dollars since we've been here!"

"Don't you worry! Trust Pauly!"

A week later he was again in glow; he was master of the world. But it wasn't over the Torquay-Belfast and the manager that he glowed. With those illusions, he announced, he was good and plenty through. What delighted him was the knowledge, derived from a friend of an acquaintance of a congressman, that if he could open an agency for the new Helmet car in Washington he could make a million dollars!

He pounded the table with the bone of his lamb chop. He sprang up to put on a one-step record. It was an hour before he came down to details and, incidentally, to helping her with the dishes.

"Here's the idea: The Helmet's only been on the market about a year, and there's no agency for it in Washington yet. You know what a doggy place Washington is—senators and all that plug-hat gang, and a lot of social climbers that go there to spend the winter and get the girls married off to colonels. Class trade, and the Helmet's got class. Grand body and motor—say, built like a watch, and oodles of power. And I've learned this expensive-car selling game from A to mince pie."

"But dear, my dear! Just yesterday you were saying that these rich people are so unfriendly."

"We-ull, I'll admit they aren't as chummy as I'd thought they'd be. Snobs, looking down on a fellow just because they've got money! But I'll tell you I've learned how to handle the plutes now. The quiet and dignified and the codfish eye, that's the stuff to slip 'em. Like this."

Though his demonstration of the quiet, the dignified and the codfish eye was slightly marred by his costume of ragged apron and dish towel hung over his shoulder, he was lofty as he stalked across the kitchen, shook hands with the folding clothes rack and addressed it compellingly: "'Ah, yes, Mr. Skitamarigg. You wish to see a sedan? Very well, I shall be with you in a moment. Pray be seated.' See, like that, Em. Reserved. Then skin off for a couple o' minutes. Let 'em wait. Make 'em think you're ringing up the Queen of Poland for a date to play stud poker. Make 'em think you're important. Or suppose some high muck-a-muck comes in. Let him know you're hep to him. 'Ah, Senator Snickaree! I trust the President is well.' See? Calm and nasty."

The old "But—but———" rumbled in Emily's brain.

"If I had just a measly little sum I could put it across. You have to put up ten thousand dollars to get the agency; but Lord for a Torquay agency you'd have to show resources of ten times that amount. I know a fellow that would chip in with five thou—one of my customers. He thinks I'm the liveliest salesman in the row. If I could only get my mitts on five thousand dollars more I could make a million. No, I don't want to exaggerate. But I could make a hundred thousand. Straight! Just waiting to be picked. Oh, it's murder to see those nice juicy dollars going to waste! Don't happen to have five thousand up your sleeve, do you?"

He laughed artificially and wandered off to the living room. She stood fixed, a hand suspended in the air, because she did happen to have five thousand!

When she was ten her grandmother had left her a bequest, in bonds, which was now grown to more than five thousand. Years before she had met Paul Banning she had determined that this money should be kept for the education of her future children. It wasn't hers—it was theirs. This had become so much a habit of thought that she had really forgotten the money. It came to her with a wrench.

"Nonsense, it ain't mine!" she said—and wasn't convinced. She felt guilty at withholding it from Paul, deliberately preventing her boy from making his hundred thousand. "He's right. I don't really trust him. I'm not a good sport, and I thought I would be—oh, the next time I was sure I would be!"

Each evening now he improvised about Washington and grumbled about the Torquay-Belfast and Baltimore. When she called for him at the Torquay she hoped to find it the shoddy establishment he painted it; she wanted to be made to believe that he was right. But it looked emphatic, with its vast floor, its gilded plaster columns, its array of glass-topped desks. The enormous limousine in the center of the floor was as solemn and reputable as a trust company, and the manager, in his morning coat, was pontifical. Paul was wrong. She couldn't trust his opinion. Well, then, since everything was against giving him the money—she was going to give it to him! Now was the time to be a good sport!

On an amiable winter evening Paul came home to find candles and roses on the dinner table.

"What's the idea, Em? Somebody coming? Then what's the use of showing off?"

"Aren't you and I enough?"

"But what's the hunch? Anybody got a birthday?"

"No one that I know of."

"Well, you're beyond me. First you kick every time I want to make a hit with the bunch by blowing 'em to a feed, and then you drag out everything but the kitchen stove when it's just a family meal. And"—as he sat down—"why the plates turned over? That's hick-town stuff."

She was silent, pale, taut, as he lifted the plate and disclosed a bank draft for five thousand three hundred nineteen dollars.

He gulped. They wept together. In their vows and kisses they rediscovered the honeymoon. He soared quickly from his abject repentance. He crowed, he danced, he rushed out to buy a pint of claret from a bootlegger, he waved his glass and shouted:

"We're rich! That's what we are! We'll grab everything in Washington that ain't tied down! Lord, I wonder if you realize how down in the mouth I've been getting, having to work for that frosty face? Everything's all to the hunky-dory now! Whee! As us professors always say, *Terra firma, status quo ante, e pluribus unus, Gallis ist omna, Emibus corkeritis ist!* Whee! I will now came, saw, and conquer! You're the best sport I ever met! And we can't lose! Not a chance!"

IV

They wanted for the Helmet agency a space in the smart shopping district of Washington, but they couldn't afford the rent. They had to descend to a block filled with delicatessens, lunch rooms, laundries, vulcanizers, offices of doubtful agencies and the promotion office of a gas-saver company which wasn't in the least doubtful but plain crooked.

They had room for only one car, a pair of desks and a pile of colored circulars. But they had a tile floor and glazed-brick walls topped by a frieze of crimson and dull green. Paul's partner remained in Baltimore, and the only employee was a Negro porter who came in for two hours a day. It was Emily who shared Paul's preparations; and since she shared them, she was enthusiastic. Her love of home-making went all to the agency. They had a cheap hotel room, and almost lived at the agency. Emily admired the glossy walls, the gaudy frieze, the beautiful shiny copper drip pan; and when the first Helmet arrived she went over it after the porter, rubbed the brass hubcap and cleaned the casings with alcohol.

She became office typist. On the glittering new typewriter she learned, by the popular two-finger corn-pecking method, to write quite fast enough for all the correspondence they had. It was she who insisted on circularizing well-to-do Washington with individual letters. Her first creation, composed by Mr. Paul Banning and typed by Mrs. Banning, was:

```
Dear $ir: Do you knowthat wr have opend in Wasging-
ton an agenvy for the best car 9on the market) DO
you know that the HELMEt is un/ surpossed for
beauty, eenrgyy, power and classs Do you know that
it one all the e-vents at ghe Fort Smith Endyrance
Rest?
    We dont want to borre you though. This is just
to let you knoe we are her!
```

In a month her letters looked professional. Between times she was also the bookkeeper, only there wasn't anything to put into the books.

Paul had missed one detail in investigating his market. A good share of the possible purchasers of expensive cars came from outside, and brought their cars with them. The rest of them were sufficiently served by the existent agencies. Everybody spoke well of the Helmet; everybody looked in at the window and remarked that it was an elegant boat, but everybody did not come in and buy it. In six months Paul sold two cars. After that business wasn't so good. He had an equity in the ownership of the Helmet agency. This he mortgaged. He discharged the porter. Now, in the evening, with the shades pulled down, Emily scrubbed the floor and polished the sample car. But she did not resent it, for Paul helped her—rather helplessly. He rolled up his beautiful, his altogether exquisite trousers and dabbled at the scrubbing water, and when he splashed it on his knees and cuffs he looked at her mournfully. This year of responsibility had tamed him. He tried to be agreeable to everyone who came in to look at the Helmet. He tried to endure the impertinences of airy debutantes. He tried to persuade Emily that her five thousand was still safe.

Then in the middle of an ordinary-looking afternoon the new general sales manager of the Helmet company strolled in, took one look, growled: "You can't sell Helmets in a hole like this. Got to have a decent-looking office with some space. Can you do it, or do you want to give up this agency? Huh?"

That evening the holder of the mortgage on Paul's agency was the agent for the Helmet car in Washington D.C., and Paul sat in his hotel room with nothing in the world to do but look pitifully at his wife, who had never loved him quite so surely as then.

At eight the agent for the Denver Six telephoned: "Mrs. Banning? Hear your husband is out of the Helmet. Well, say, we need a salesman. Would he be interested?

"I'll have him call you," she said.

She hesitantly planned a campaign—reluctance, final yielding at an interesting salary. As she burbled she raced up and down the narrow room, along the mean, faded strip of carpet, while Paul reclined elegantly on the bed, his head against the wadded-up pillow, his legs crossed and one foot wagging.

"Well, I don't know," he objected. "Give me time to think it over. Say, I'm almost glad the Helmet game is up, and this being on our own. I'll lay alongside of anybody I know at selling, but I don't think much of this responsibility—waste time on too many fool details. That's all right for some piker of an office man, but not for a fellow with adventure and red blood in his system. Gee, I begin to feel human again, and I never did think much of the Helmet. Strictly between ourselves, it's a bunch of junk. Next time—we'll hook up with something with some zip to it. Zowie! No more worries! No more scrubbing floors! Let's go to the movies!"

At ten as they came out of the movies he danced upon the sidewalk, and he cried: "Oh, to thunder with this town! Too conservative! Don't appreciate a live salesman. I begin to fell like a move would be good for us. Go farther west, where there's some real hustle. Let's tell the Denver Six people to go to thunder. Just yesterday I heard there's some magnolious chances out in Cincinnati. Let's take a shot at it! Whee! And let's go have a chafing dish of good chow someplace, and start off with the right feel of success."

"Paul! Paul! You're mad!"

He glared at her.

"How many times have we got to go over and over and over the same row? How many times have I got to say the same thing? You've got to trust me! You've got to take things as they come, the lean *mit* the fat! Did I ever let you down? Have you ever starved yet? I tell you we'll make good in Cincinnati. We'll stick there and be reg'lar citizens, with a house and garden and this fambly you're always wanting. See?"

"Have you any definite prospects?"

"Well, practically, you might say. The fellow that put me wise to the big chances there, he says he'll give me a letter to his brother, who's in the Doublegood Tire place in Cincy and knows everybody in town.

Four days afterward they started for Cincinnati, and because they had less than a hundred dollars in the world they went on the day coach; they slept at night and curled on the red plush seats.

V

Dim lights along the aisle. The sharp scent of oranges cutting the soggy smell of unbathed people. Rope-tied suitcases, pasteboard boxes, derelict shoes and coats and bottles and crusts of bread littering the car. Weary people in a weary imitation of sleep, their heads on the seat arms or propped against the window panes, their legs grotesquely balanced on valises. The day coach at night.

Paul enjoyed the adventure of it. Within an hour he knew the name of every trainman; he had played a game of seven-up in the smoker and joyously assisted in the removal of a drunk. He returned to pat Emily as she lay back against her old coat—she hadn't had a new coat since she had been married. She couldn't sleep. She choked in the tight-packed air. Paul seemed to be waiting for something. She guessed that he was waiting for her to complain—waiting for the chance to say "You're not a good sport." If she heard that word once more she would go mad and leap from the train.

"Oh, don't be a fool!" she interrupted herself, and achingly shifted into a new position.

They came to Cincinnati. Her eyes were burned out. She wanted to take refuge in a hotel—alone.

"Are you going right out and capture that job?" she hinted gaily.

"What's the big rush? Let's give the burg the once-over first. Maybe we might cross the river and grab a look at Ole Kaintuck. I want to see a blue grass."

"And I want to see a bed!" She was grim. "And I want to see a paycheck. Do you know that we have just ninety-four dollars?"

"Stung again!"—cockily. "We have ninety-four dollars and eight cents and a Washington trolley ticket."

"Paul, please don't make me bad-tempered! I'm trying to be good. I'm trying to be a sp——— be cheerful. But really, dear, can't you see it's silly to take so many risks?"

Then he was off. She was, it seemed, to trust him. She was to be a sport. Indeed, she was to be a good sport. He had never let her down yet. Hadn't he always landed a job?

She was unmoved. She retorted: "You know these aviators who do stunts that no aeroplanes will stand. Nothing ever happens to them—till something happens."

But if she was more stubborn, so was Paul. He made no promise. He left her at the hotel. She went to bed, too sleepy to think and too bitterly thoughtful to sleep. Would he get the job this time? Ninety-four dollars—well, hang it, whatever the exact idiot sum was—it wouldn't last very long. They knew no one in town. They might actually go hungry. Oughtn't she to telegraph her father? But he hadn't much. No. It was a devouring day of waiting. She flew at Paul when he came in.

"Did you get the job?"

"I did not, my angel. Because why? Because I haven't asked for one! But I've given the town a good north and south. Say, there's a lulu of a bungalow on the heights that I'd like to own." He looked at her. Then he was on his knees by her. "Gosh, I didn't realize! You're all in! Did I scare you? Oh, honey, I've been a hog! I just meant to kind of teach you a lesson. I didn't realize you were so worried. Poor kid, you're just about ready to bust out crying! I'll start right out and shoot me a big fat job first thing after breakfast tomorrow, honest I will!"

After such repentance, what could she do but consent when he insisted on buying a dinner which cost thirty cents more than a sleeper from Washington to Cincinnati? But he had the job the next day. He crowed: "See? Or was I right or not? And you didn't trust your Paulibus, did you? You didn't think he'd deliver the goods this time. 'Fess up now! You weren't a sport, were you?"

She couldn't make herself say anything affectionate and apologetic. She said, "Good! Well, let's go right out and look for a boarding house."

"You wait! Someday I'll be the owner of the Javelin agency in this town, and we'll live in a marble pal-lal-lace, pal-lal-lace, pal-lee!"

He was steady and successful—for two weeks. Then he remembered to tell her that his job was only temporary. He was filling the place of a salesman who was ill. Three months later the salesman had the unkindness to be well, and with more than a hundred saved this time—a very little more than a hundred—Paul was out of a job. But that didn't matter, he explained, because he had heard from a man who knew a man that in the city of Vernon, another thousand miles to the west, there were marvelous openings for a live wire. They'd take a chance. In fact, they'd be sports! They'd hop a train and go out and give Vernon the once across and the high sign and the glad hand.

Emily said things, hateful scarring things, of which she was ashamed. If he couldn't support them, she would. She'd go to work in a store. He was fish-mouthed. He admitted there was a chance for him in a Cincinnati tire agency. He'd take it, but—his voice grew more stubborn—by golly, he was going to write out to Vernon and find out how's tricks. She was touched by his renunciation of *wanderlust*, and they wept together.

A few months afterward they were in Vernon, Paul a salesman for the Apthorpe car; and here for a time they stayed, forgot the desire of wandering, had a bright furnished flat and were happy.

VI

The Apthorpe, with its graceful streamline and its distinctive colors, sold readily in Vernon. Paul saved money, while doing his share in the way of entertaining the people they met. There was a gay group centering about the Black Bass Club—Sim Jenson, circulating manager of the Vernon *Courier*, and his wife, the flirtatious Sue; Harry Jason, the real-estate speculator; Tom McNew, who controlled miles of billboards. They played bridge, they went together to the feature movies, they drove out to the lakes for evening picnics. Emily became plumper and more placid. She did examine their bankbook a good many times every month, but she did enjoy the sight of these lively people about her flat, with its red cushions. glassed-in porch and smoker's set on a taboret.

Paul exulted: "Not a bad layout, what? I tell you it pays to take a chance. Suppose I'd stayed with that stick-in-the-mud Torquay gang in Baltimore! Think we'd ever have a swell shebang like this? Think we'd have the circulation manager of the biggest newspaper in town dropping in, thick as thieves? Class, that's me! The best is good enough for me, providing the service is good!"

But this desirable class cost more and more. Paul stopped saving. Emily tried not to wail. She was tired of having to be disagreeable, and when she cautiously suggested to Paul that it wasn't wise to spend so much on display he stumped her. For he agreed with her!

"Sure! That's right. Fool thing to do. Now me, I never spend a cent just to show off. But same time, I feel a fellow who isn't a mucker owes something to himself. If he's going to be a gentleman and keep his self-respect and his business pep he has to dress and eat and live like a gentleman."

That twist puzzled and held her for a time. Not till the night of the polysyndetonic taxicabs did she complain. The occasion was the minstrel show and grand ball of the Black Bass Club. The Bannings were to pick up the Tom McNews in the secondhand Vogue touring car which Paul had bought as an investment. But the evening was boiling with rain.

"The side curtains on my machine don't fit extra O.K. I think we better take a taxi," Paul grumbled at dinner.

"Oh, we can wrap up in coats and things."

"Yes, but we can't ask the McNews to swim there after we've invited them."

"Yes—well———"

It sounded like her old, weary "But—but———"

She reflected as they drove to the McNews', "No, I won't get a new evening frock, no matter what he says. This old thing does perfectly well."

Tom McNew wanted to pay his share of the taxi fare, but Paul refused in a high and princely way, and at one-thirty insisted on calling another taxi for the return home.

The rain had ceased.

"Why couldn't we just as well walk? I want you folks to drop into my place and have a bite to eat before you go home, and it's only just a few blocks there," objected McNew.

"What? Make the ladies hoof it, with their el-lel-egant garmentses?" chanted Paul. "Mac, there's only one more queenly dame than your beauteous frau, and that's the star of my harem, Mrs. Paulena Banana!" He waved his hat, he bowed, with one hand on his stomach. The McNews laughed, and said Paul was a sketch—a perfect scream.

High esteem and good fellowship reigned, until, as Paul was running in to telephone for a cab, Emily whispered: "Really, Paul, we could just as well walk. Be good for us. Lovely air. Taxi so unnecessary. Let's save———"

"Of course you'd spring something like that just when we've having a good time! Can't you ever——— And t' hear you tell it, you'd think a taxi cost a hundred bucks a minute. Why, 'twon't cost us more than a dollar and a half clear home."

"I know—but perhaps it's a symbol."

"It's a what? What new highbrow idea you got now? Oh, Lord, I should fret! Anyway, I can't keep the McNews waiting on the sidewalk all night."

At his apartment house McNew insisted: "Now I want you folks to come in and I'll open up something. Still got some of the stock. How about it, Mrs. Paul?"

"Thank you, but I'm a little tired."

Paul shouted: "Rats! Tomorrow's Sunday. Sleep all day. Sure we'll go in. Couldn't lose us! That open up something sounds like a letter from home to me!" He gallantly helped the ladies out of the cab, and as Emily straggled into the hall she hated herself for continually spoiling his pleasures.

It was after something had been opened up several times that Emily looked out the front window of the McNew flat. The night was fresh, grateful. Then instantly it was ungrateful and close. In the street stood a taxicab. She had been trained by Paul to notice cars, their makes, models, licenses, special marks. She knew by a twisted fender that this was the taxi in which they had come; that Paul had kept it waiting. In the early morning deadness of the small city she could hear it ticking—ticking—ticking: "Money, money, money, money, money!"

She was rather abrupt about insisting that it was time to go. She knew that Paul was watching her all the way home, and all the way his lips were pouting with the word "sport." She vigorously said nothing at all.

The charge for the taxi was five dollars and forty cents, and the generous Paul, the friend of waiters and hatcheck girls, gave the chauffeur a fifty-cent tip. This made five dollars and ninety cents, and it was a coincidence that the amount of money they had saved in two months also was five dollars and ninety cents.

VII

The Apthorpe factory was listed to port. An admirable designer it did have, and the best of salesmen, but it was scant on purchasing agents and foremen. The factory could not get steel. As soon as it got the men they obligingly and unanimously struck. For three months there were practically no deliveries of cars in Vernon. So that Paul, hustling all the time, really working, trying to be cheerful, his book filled with orders, every customer agreeing with him about the merits of the Apthorpe, was nevertheless poverty-stricken. He would have no commissions till deliveries. Emily and he had to live on a small guaranty—and on their much smaller savings.

But, he pointed out to Emily, he had to keep up his expenses, lest his friends and customers think he was a failure. She was too wretched at this sudden breaking down of their apparent security to have much of a say. She tried only once. Why couldn't he go to another Vernon agency?

"I've thought of that, but most of 'em haven't got the class. I'm a big-car man. I'm not going to waste myself on any of these small-time concerns. No, no, I guess we'll pull out somehow. If I did make a change—say, how'd you like to see a little of Canada? They tell me Winnipeg and Victoria and Vancouver are great towns, and Calgary and Moose Jaw, and do a whale of a motor business. Kind of fun to hike a little, eh?"

Anything to keep him from the subject of wandering! She accompanied him as cheerfully as she could to the parties in which he forgot his troubles. He took to poker. Poker also took to him. Poker adored him—because he so richly supported it. He played brilliantly and wittily; he bluffed carefully; he was a master of raising before the draw; he lost like a good sport—and he always lost! At least once a week he played, at the house of Harry Jason, the shifty wizard of real estate; and Emily sat back, her senses dead, her very power to suffer dying, as she watched her husband lose, as she watched him caper and boast—the village clown.

Then the Apthorpe sales manager had an idea. He reduced his sales force, and since Paul Banning was the latest addition the reduction was Paul. He came home to inform Emily that he had no job, and he added the news that he was darn glad to be divorced from that gang of pikers; and as for the Apthorpe car, well, aptly considered, it was a bunch of junk. She inquired what he planned to do; she waited for a proposal that they go to Vancouver—or Los Angeles or Honolulu or Shanghai. He looked old about the eyes.

"Oh, I'll land some other job here in town. I'd like—I'd like to chase on to some new place, but I don't seem to have the pep anymore. But—you trust Pauly! I'll be selling Darlingford trucks inside of a week. That's what I'll do! Know the Darlingford truck? Say, there's a lulu; there's a beauty! Throw a ton and a half on a Darlingford, and you don't even know you've got a load, and she'll pull up on a fifteen-percent grade on high with it, too, or something like that. And the manager and me are just like two fingers on one hand."

He returned at dinnertime to denounce the Darlingford manager, who not only did not appreciate a willing and steady salesman but was also forcing on the public a vehicle that was a bunch of junk.

"I should worry about him, though. I'll have a job inside two days. Say, there's a show in town with the original New York cast.

Lez go, old thing—lez throw on the bonny chapeaux and skate down."

"Paul dear, don't you think it would be just as well to economize, now we're so nearly broke."

"Now there you go! God Lord, I might have known you'd say something to take the heart out of a fellow just when he needs his nerve to make a hit with the high guys! Trouble with you is you don't know"—he thought it over and produced his analysis triumphantly—"you don't know what it means to be a sport!"

For two weeks he came home more quietly each evening; he was each evening more pitifully anxious to help her. He set the table, he scrubbed the sink. He admitted that there was no sign of a job. He even admitted that he'd do well not to play poker—he more than admitted it; he discovered and explained it.

"Strikes me we might economize just now for a while, Em. Not that I'm scared, you understand. Don't never think the old dogs are as frigid as that! But with these profiteers and all, if they get funny and raise prices on me too much I just quit blowing the mazuma till they get wise—see how I mean?"

There was, however, very little mazuma either to save or blow; and there were no resources. Emily's father had died during the past year. She began to slide, clawing, but sinking ever farther into the slimy chasm of debt. It had been her pride that, no matter how reckless Paul was, they owed no one. She tried to keep it up. She walked ten blocks to save a cent a pound on cabbage. But everything came at once, as though the derisive gods had been waiting. Paul had to have his teeth filled; he had to have a bridge. Then he owed the dentist a hundred dollars, and Emily felt like a sneak and hurried past the dentist's office. He had to have a new suit; he couldn't solicit work in these streaky, shapeless clothes. That same day Emily broke the handle of her only hairbrush. She wept wearily, and spent half an hour in trying to think of ways to avoid the purchase of a new one. But it can't be done; a woman's hair can't be managed with a handleless brush. She went to the largest department store, opened a charge account, bought a brush, and, while she was about it, twenty dollars' worth of groceries—charged.

The next week she was threatened with tonsillitis. There was a doctor, and a bill—unpaid.

But however much credit they might obtain, however much Emily might spend her self-respect to make up for money, they wouldn't be able to get through another month. She flung it at Paul.

"What are we going to do? We're all in. Let's stop lying."

He bent over his chair, his head in his hand.

"I don't see where I've been to blame. I've had hard luck. It makes me sore, your roasting me. Think I left the Apthorpe because I wanted to? I was canned. But sure, go on, rub it in, tell me it was my fault!"

"We might—oh, heavens, what's the use! I'm afraid we can't even afford the luxury of fighting. Well?"

"We'll borrow. I think I can raise a couple of hundred."

"Oh, I hate it! It makes me feel inferior. Besides, it's bad business, as you call it. Borrowing from a man gives him a hold on you. No, not yet, anyway. Why must you have a salesman's job? Why not try something else, just till we get on our feet?"

"Haven't I tried everything? I don't insist on selling cars. I wanted to go out on the road for a hardware house, and I tried to edge in on the insurance game, and milling, but I haven't got the experience."

"No, but I mean—you do know motors. You're awfully clever with tools. Why couldn't you work as an auto mechanic—I mean— I mean just for a while, till————"

"What? Me changing tires and getting grease all over and sitting with the lunch-pail squad, after being in the front office and bawling out the foreman? Not on your life! I'm not going to have the bunch I used to train with say, 'Banning has gone to pot. Heard what he's doing?' I'll stand a lot, but there's a limit. No, sir! I'll buzz round and see what I can borrow. That's fine!"

He bounced out of the flat. Presently she followed, walking slowly. She bought a newspaper. She looked at the want advertisements. She timidly entered an office. That evening she had engaged herself as assistant to a dentist, a young and anxious dentist who couldn't afford a trained woman, and, as an afterthought, as clerk from eight till midnight in a candy and soda shop which had a large after-movie trade.

Her first day's work was blistering torture. She had been busy enough about the house, but she had been her own manager. She was confused now by commands, by being unable to sit down or trot out for fresh air. But a change was on her. Her desires didn't matter. She wasn't Emily Banning; she was a pauper, expecting nothing but work, hoping only to get through the day. She was as divorced from her normal self as the lawyer turned soldier. Indeed, she was so outside of herself that it came to her that there wasn't any reason why she shouldn't work and help Paul! She wasn't a martyr. If Paul had been weak, perhaps she herself hadn't been as perfect as she had thought. Thus she meditated, slowly, uncertainly, while her body learned to be obedient and interested in dentists' burrs and pralines.

She had not told Paul of her work till after the first day in the dentist's office. He had raved and pounded various pieces of furniture, while she ignored him and prepared dinner. She left him in full tide, to hasten to the candy stop.

He shouted after her: "If you think you can bluff me into taking any old bum job by pretending you've become the family hero ———"

She didn't hear the rest of it. Expressionless, chilly, she marched to the tedious trolley.

The second evening she said mildly, "Anything today?"

"There was not! I didn't look. Till you cut out this fool stuff of pretending to be the little breadwinner, and making me ridiculous before all my friends, I'm going to stay home and enjoy life. I had a lulu of a time today. I slept till eleven and played solitaire and—oh, honey, honey, quit it! It makes me sick to think of your working like this. You don't need to. I can borrow all we need—and something will turn up. Please, honey!"

For the first time, she was not touched by his wheedling. She silently prepared dinner, silently did the dishes—while he played the phonograph—and silently tramped out to work.

On the third evening, as she slowly took the pins out of her hat, she staggered and for a second held her hand over her eyes, while against the pencil blackness of her vision blue spotty suns revolved and tumbled. She was startled out of her trance by his scream.

"All right! All right! All right! If you're going to take every advantage you can, what can I do? You win! It means I'll never be able to hold up my head before decent folks again, but what's a little thing like that?" He was jamming his hat on, banging out of the flat.

He was not there when she returned from the candy shop. She had been asleep for ten minutes when he wakened her by stroking her forehead and crying: "I'm ashamed the way I talked. It just—it kind of got me to see you so tired. I didn't mean anything I said. I went out and hooked up with the Siever Repair Station. They were darn glad to get a man who's got some savvy about ignition. The shop is cram-jam full of work, and I've been at it all evening. Say, it wasn't so bad. I put one over on the foreman all right! I traced a short in the wiring that he's been hunting for two days! Kind of tickled me. And then you know my philosophy—be a sport. That's the idea! See how I mean?"

VIII

While Paul worked as a motor mechanic, Emily kept her position in the dentist's office, but dropped the candy shop. They had their evenings together. They were shy of the group with whom they had been so friendly. Paul made—and fully explained to Emily—the discovery: "Don't make any difference what folks think of what we're doing. We're not running our lives to suit them."

Within a few months Apthorpe deliveries were renewed, and the agent sent for Paul, gave him back his position. He immediately sold two cars and collected several commissions on delayed sales. He began to lunch again with McNew, Jason, Jenson and the other lights of the Black Bass Club, and three weeks after his return to magnificence he came into the flat shouting, "Harry Jason wants us to sit in on a poker game tonight!"

"But I thought—you said you were going to cut out poker."

"Well, gosh, got to show the world we're back on our feet!"

"But how will poker show it? Can't we go and not play? You know, dear, you really don't play—you have such bad luck."

"Now don't be a crab! Show a little speed! This'll be practically the first party we've gone to for months. I'm looking forward to it a lot."

"Do you really like Harry Jason, Paul?"

"No, come t' think it over, don't know's I do. But still, a fellow has to live up to———"

He halted as she went to the wardrobe. On her return from the dentist's she had changed to a negligee, but now she was taking down the baggy black skirt and cheerless white blouse which she wore to work.

Paul demanded: "What's the idea? You're not going to wear that behind-the-counter stuff to the party? By the way, I've been thinking—you better chuck the tooth-jerker job, now that things are booming."

"I really think I like to work."

"Yes, but it don't look nice. Folks might almost think I don't support you. Say, for tonight, why don't you put on that—what d' you call it—taffeta?"

"But I have to see someone after the party."

"Eh?"

"The candy shop is so busy till after eleven-thirty. Best time to talk to the manager is after that."

"What's the———"

"Why, if you're going back to being a good sport, of course I'm going back to the candy shop."

He was too angry to answer. He stalked beside her to the Jasons', while she sweetly discoursed on politics and dentistry. He went into the poker game with a splash. Emily said that she didn't care to play—would they forgive her if she just looked on? While Paul chattered she sat in a corner, across the table from him; sat silent, expressionless—in her shop blouse and black skirt.

He was vociferous but jumpy. He gloated, "Watch me rake 'em in tonight!"

But twice his twitching elbow knocked over his pile of chips—his steadily dwindling pile of chips. Half of it he lost in three plunges. Then he played close to his chest. He looked worried. He wasted nothing but antes. He came in only on sure things—which didn't always prove to be sure things. However desperately he tried to save them, he lost his first two dollars' worth of chips in twenty minutes. He pushed back his chair, looking doubtful.

"I think—I don't feel much like playing tonight, Harry."

Harry Jason bellowed in the manner of the professional good fellow: "Oh, rats! Come on! Luck's bound to change! Don't be a piker! Take another dollar's worth. Thought you were a good sport!"

Paul glanced at Emily in her corner, expressionless, bleak, in blouse and skirt marked with work. He spoke with a slowness unnatural to him.

"Nope, I've got something that's got that beat a mile, Harry. I'm not a good sport. I'm a rotten sport. I'm a tightwad. I'm a miser. I'm the pikingest, bummest, worst sport in this town, and I like it! I'm going to cut out poker. I"—he choked—"I'm a punk player. But—but, honest, I used to play one grand game of bridge! When—when I was in practice I could play alongside of anybody in Baltimore!"

A MATTER OF BUSINESS

Candee's sleeping porch faced the east. At sunrise every morning he startled awake and became a poet.

He yawned, pulled up the gray camping blanket which proved that he had gone hunting in Canada, poked both hands behind his neck, settled down with a wriggling motion, and was exceedingly melancholy and happy.

He resolved, seriously and all at once, to study music, to wear a rose down to business, to tell the truth in his advertisements, and to start a campaign for a municipal auditorium. He longed to be out of bed and go change the entire world immediately. But always, as sunrise blurred into russet, he plunged his arms under the blanket, sighed, "Funny what stuff a fellow will think of at six G.M.," yawned horribly, and was asleep. Two hours afterward, when he sat on the edge of the bed, rubbing his jaw in the hope that he could sneak out of shaving this morning, letting his feet ramble around independently in search of his slippers, he was not a poet. He was Mr. Candee of the Novelty Stationery Shop, Vernon.

He sold writing paper, Easter cards, bronze bookends, framed color prints. He was a salesman born. To him it was exhilaration to herd a hesitating customer; it was pride to see his clerks, Miss Cogerty and the new girl, imitate his courtesy, his quickness. He was conscious of beauty. Ten times a week he stopped to gloat over a print in which a hilltop and a flare of daisies expressed the indolence of August. But—and this was equally a part of him—he was delighted by "putting things over." He was as likely to speculate in a broken lot of china dogs as to select a stock of chaste brass knockers. It was he who had popularized Whistler in Vernon, and he who had brought out the "Oh My! Bathing Girls" pictures.

He was a soldier of fortune, was Candee; he fought under any flag which gave him the excuse. He was as much an adventurer as though he sat on a rampart wearing a steel corselet instead of sitting at a golden-oak desk wearing a blue-serge suit.

Every Sunday afternoon the Candees drove out to the golf club. They came home by a new route this Sunday.

"I feel powerful. Let's do some exploring," said Candee.

He turned the car off the Boulevard, down one of the nameless hilly roads which twist along the edge of every city. He came into a straggly country of market gardens, jungles of dead weeds, unpruned crabapple trees, and tall, thin houses which started as artificial-stone mansions and ended as unpainted frame shacks. In front of a tarpaper shanty there was a wild-grape arbor of thick vines draped upon secondhand scantlings and cracked pieces of molding. The yard had probably never been raked, but it displayed petunias in a tub salvaged from a patent washing machine. On a shelf beside the gate was a glass case with a sign:

ToYs FOR THEE CHILRUN.

Candee stopped the car.

In the case were half a dozen wooden dolls with pegged joints—an old-man doll with pointed hat, jutting black beard, and lumpy, out-thrust hands; a Pierrot with a prim wooden cockade; a princess fantastically tall and lean.

"Huh! Handmade! Arts-and-grafts stuff!" said Candee, righteously.

"That's so," said Mrs. Candee.

He drove on.

"Freak stuff. Abs'lutely grotesque. Not like anything I ever saw!"

"That's so," said Mrs. Candee.

He was silent. He irritably worked the air-choke, and when he found it was loose he said, "Damn!" As for Mrs. Candee, she said nothing at all. She merely looked like a wife.

He turned toward her argumentatively. "Strikes me those dolls were darn ugly. Some old nut of a hermit must have made 'em. They were—they were ugly! Eh?"

"That's so," said Mrs. Candee.

"Don't you think they were ugly?"

"Yes, I think that's so," said Mrs. Candee, as she settled down to meditate upon the new laundress who was coming tomorrow.

Next morning Candee rushed into his shop, omitted the report on his Sunday golf and the progress of his game which he usually gave to Miss Cogerty, and dashed at the shelf of toys. He had never thought about toys as he had about personal Christmas cards or diaries. His only specialty for children was expensive juveniles.

He glowered at the shelf. It was disordered. It was character-less. There were one rabbit of gray Canton flannel, two rabbits of papier-mâché, and nine tubercular rabbits of white fur. There were sixteen dolls which simpered and looked unintelligent. There were one train, one fire engine, and a device for hoisting thimblefuls of sand upon a trestle. Not that you did anything when you had hoisted it.

"Huh!" said Candee.

"Yes, Mr. Candee?" said Miss Cogerty.

"Looks like a side-street notions store. Looks like a racket shop. Looks like a—looks like——— Aah!" said Candee.

He stormed his desk like a battalion of marines. He was stern. "Got to take up that bum shipment with the Fressen Paper Company. I'll write 'em a letter that'll take their hides off. I won't type it. Make it stronger if I turn the old pen loose."

He vigorously cleared away a pile of fancy penwipers—stopping only to read the advertisement on an insurance blotter, to draw one or two pictures on an envelope, and to rub the enticing pale-blue back of a box of safety matches with a soft pencil till it looked silvery in a cross-light. He snatched his fountain pen out of his vest pocket. He looked at it unrelentingly. He sharpened the end of a match and scraped a clot of ink off the pen cap. He tried the ink supply by making a line of O's on his thumbnail. He straightened up, looked reprovingly at Miss Cogerty's back, slapped a sheet of paper on the desk—then stopped again and read his mail.

It did not take him more than an hour to begin to write the letter he was writing. In grim jet letters he scrawled:

FRESSEN COMPANY:
GENTLEMEN,—*I want you to thoroughly understand*—

Twenty minutes later he had added nothing to the letter but a curlicue on the tail of the "d" in "understand." He was drawing the picture of a wooden doll with a pointed hat and a flaring black beard. His eyes were abstracted and his lips moved furiously:

"Makes me sick. Not such a whale of a big shop, but it's distinctive. Not all this commonplace junk—souvenirs and bum valentines. And yet our toys—— Ordinary! Common! Hate to think what people must have been saying about 'em! But those wooden dolls out there in the country—they were ugly, just like Nelly said, but somehow they kind of stirred up the imagination."

He shook his head, rubbed his temples, looked up wearily. He saw that the morning rush had begun. He went out to the shop slowly, but as he crooned at Mrs. Harry McPherson, "I have some new lightweight English envelopes—crossbar lavender with a stunning purple lining," he was imperturbable. He went out to lunch with Harry Jason and told a really new flivver story. He did not cease his bustling again till four, when the shop was for a moment still. Then he leaned against the counter and brooded:

"Those wooden dolls remind me of—— Darn it! I don't know what they do remind me of! Like something—— Castles. Gypsies. Oh, rats! Brother Candee, I thought you'd grown up! Hey, Miss Cogerty, what trying do? Don't put those Honey Bunny books there!"

At home he hurried through dinner.

"Shall we play a little auction with the Darbins?" Mrs. Candee yawned.

"No. I—— Got to mull over some business plans. Think I'll take a drive by myself, unless you or the girls have to use the machine," ventured Candee.

"No. I think I might catch up on my sleep. Oh, Jimmy, the new laundress drinks just as much coffee as the last one did!"

"Yes?" said Candee, looking fixedly at a candle shade and meditating. "I don't know. Funny, all the wild crazy plans I used to have when I was a kid. Suppose those dolls remind me of that."

He dashed out from dinner, hastily started the car. He drove rapidly past the lakes, through dwindling lines of speculative houses, into a world of hazelnut brush and small boys with furtive dogs. His destination was the tarpaper shack in front of which he had seen the wooden dolls.

He stopped with a squawk of brakes, bustled up the path to the wild-grape arbor. In the dimness beneath it, squatting on his heels beside a bicycle, was a man all ivory and ebony, ghost white and outlandish black. His cheeks and veined forehead were pale, his beard was black and thin and square. Only his hands were ruddy. They were brick-red and thick, yet cunning was in them, and the fingers tapered to square ends. He was a medieval monk in overalls, a Hindu indecently without his turban. As Candee charged upon him he looked up and mourned:

"The chain, she rusty."

Now Candee was the friendliest soul in all the Boosters' Club. Squatting, he sympathized:

"Rusty, eh? Ole chain kind of rusty! Hard luck, I'll say. Ought to use graphite on it. That's it—graphite. 'Member when I was a kid——"

"I use graphite. All rusty before I get him," the ghost lamented. His was a deep voice, humorless and grave.

Candee was impressed. "Hard luck! How about boric acid? No, that isn't it—chloric acid. No, oxalic acid. That's it—oxalic! That'll take off the rust."

"Os-all-ic," murmured the ghost.

"Well, cheer up, old man. Someday you'll be driving your own boat."

"Oh! Say!"—the ghost was childishly proud—"I got a phonograph!"

"Have you? Slick!" Candee became cautious and inquisitive. He rose and, though he actually had not touched the bicycle, he dusted off his hands. Craftily: "Well, I guess you make pretty good money, at that. I was noticing——

"Reason I turned in, I noticed you had some toys out front. Thought I might get one for the kids. What do you charge?" He was resolving belligerently, "I won't pay more than a dollar per."

"I sharge fifty cent."

Candy felt cheated. He had been ready to battle for his rights and it was disconcerting to waste all his energy. The ghost rose, in sections, and ambled toward the glass case of dolls. He was tall, fantastically tall as his own tall emperors, and his blue-denim jacket was thick with garden soil. Beside him Candee was rosy and stubby and distressingly neat. He was also uneasy. Here was a person to whom he couldn't talk naturally.

"So you make dolls, eh? Didn't know there was a toy maker in Vernon."

"No, I am nod a toy maker. I am a sculptor." The ghost was profoundly sad. "But nod de kine you t'ink. I do not make chudges in plog hats to put on courthouses. I would lige to. I would make fine plog hats. But I am not recognize. I make epitaphs in de monooment works. Huh!" The ghost sounded human now, and full of guile. "I am de only man in dose monooment works dat know what 'R.I.P.' mean in de orizhinal Greek."

He leaned against the gate and chuckled. Candee recovered from his feeling of being trapped in a particularly chilly tomb. He crowed:

"I'll bet you are, at that. But you must have a good time making these dolls."

"You lak dem?"

"You bet! I certainly do. I———" His enthusiasm stumbled. In a slightly astonished tone, in a low voice, he marveled, "And I do, too, by golly!" Then: "You——— I guess you enjoy making ———"

"No, no! It iss not enjoyment. Dey are my art, de dolls. Dey are how I get even wit' de monooment works. I should wish I could make him for a living, but nobody want him. One year now— always dey stand by de gate, waiting, and nobody buy one. Oh, well, I can't help dat! I know what I do, even if nobody else don't. I try to make him primitive, like what a child would make if he was a fine craftsman like me. Dey are all dream dolls. And me, I make him right. See! Nobody can break him!"

He snatched the Gothic princess from the case and banged her on the fence.

Candee came out of a trance of embarrassed unreality and

shouted: "Sure are the real stuff. Now, uh, the—uh——— May I ask your name?"

"Emile Jumas my name."

Candee snapped his fingers. "Got it, by golly!"

"*Pardon?*"

"The Papa Jumas dolls! That's their name. Look here! Have you got any more of these in the house?"

"Maybe fifty." Jumas had been roused out of his ghostliness.

"Great! Could you make five or six a day, if you didn't do anything else and maybe had a boy to help you?"

"Oh yez. No. Well, maybe four."

"See here. I could——— I have a little place where I think maybe I could sell a few. Course you understand I don't know for sure. Taking a chance. But I think maybe I could. I'm J. T. Candee. Probably you know my stationery shop. I don't want to boast, but I will say there's no place in town that touches it for class. But I don't mean I could afford to pay you any fortune. But"—all his caution collapsed—"Jumas, I'm going to put you across!"

The two men shook hands a number of times and made sounds of enthusiasm, sounds like the rubbing of clothes on a washboard. But Jumas was stately in his invitation:

"Will you be so good and step in to have a leetle homemade wine?"

It was one room, his house, with a loft above, but it contained a harp, a double bed, a stove, a hen that was doubtful of strangers, a substantial Mamma Jumas, six children, and forty-two wooden dolls.

"Would you like to give up the monument works and stick to making these?" glowed Candee, as he handled the dolls.

Jumas mooned at him. "Oh, yez."

Ten minutes later, at the gate, Candee sputtered: "By golly! by golly! Certainly am pitching wild tonight. Not safe to be out alone. For first time in my life forgot to mention prices. Crazy as a kid— and I like it!" But he tried to sound managerial as he returned. "What do you think I ought to pay you apiece?"

Craftily Papa Jumas piped: "I t'ink you sell him for more than fifty cent. I t'ink maybe I ought to get fifty."

Then, while the proprietor of the Novelty Stationery Shop wrung spiritual hands and begged him to be careful, Candee the adventurer cried: "Do you know what I'm going to do? I'm going to sell 'em at three dollars, and I'm going to make every swell on the Boulevard buy one, and I'm going to make 'em pay their three bones, and I'm going to make 'em like it! Yes, sir! And you get two dollars apiece!"

It was not till he was on the sleeping porch, with the virile gray blanket patted down about his neck, that Candee groaned: "What have a let myself in for? And are they ugly or not?" He desired to go in, wake his wife, and ask her opinion. He lay and worried, and when he awoke at dawn and discovered that he hadn't really been tragically awake all night, he was rather indignant.

But he was exhilarated at breakfast and let Junior talk all through his oatmeal.

He came into the shop with a roar. "Miss Cogerty! Get the porter and have him take all those toys down to that racket shop on Jerusalem Alley that bought our candlestick remainders. Go down and get what you can for 'em. We're going to have———— Miss Cogerty, we're going to display in this shop a line of arts-and-crafts dolls that for artistic execution and delightful quaintness———— Say, that's good stuff for an ad. I'll put a ten-inch announcement in the *Courier*. I'll give this town one jolt. You wait!"

Candee did not forever retain his enthusiasm for Papa Jumas dolls. Nor did they revolutionize the nurseries of Vernon. To be exact, some people liked them and some people did not like them. Enough were sold to keep Jumas occupied, and not enough so that at the great annual crisis of the summer motor boat trip to Michigan, Candee could afford a nickel-plated spotlight as well as slip covers. There was a reasonable holiday sale through the autumn following, and always Candee liked to see them on the shelf at the back of the shop—the medieval dolls like cathedral grotesques, the Greek warrior Demetrios, and the modern dolls—the agitated policeman and the aviator whose arms were wings. Candee and Junior played explorer with them on the sleeping porch, and with them populated a castle made of chairs.

But in the spring he discovered Miss Arnold's batik lamp shades. Miss Arnold was young, Miss Arnold was pretty, and her lamp shades had many "talking points" for a salesman with enthusiasm. They were terra-cotta and crocus and leaf green; they had flowers, fruits, panels, fish, and whirligigs upon them, and a few original decorations which may have been nothing but spots. Candee knew that they were either artistic or insane; he was excited, and in the first week he sold forty of them and forgot the Papa Jumas dolls.

In late April a new road salesman came in from the Mammoth Doll Corporation. He took Candee out to lunch and was secretive and oozed hints about making a great deal of money. He admitted at last that the Mammoth people were going to put on the market a doll that "had everything else beat four ways from the ace." He produced a Skillyoolly doll. She was a simpering, star-eyed, fluffy, chiffon-clothed lady doll, and, though she was cheaply made, she was not cheaply priced.

"The Skillyoolly drive is going to be the peppiest campaign you ever saw. There's a double market—not only the kids, but all these Janes that like to stick a doll up on the piano, to make the room dressy when Bill comes calling. And it's got the snap, eh?"

"Why don't you———? The department stores can sell more of these than I can," Candee fenced.

"That's just what we don't want to do. There's several of these fluff dolls on the market—not any of them have the zip of our goods, of course. What we want is exclusive shops, that don't handle any other dolls whatever, so we won't have any inside competition, and so we can charge a class price."

"But i'm already handling some dolls———"

"If I can show you where you can triple your doll turnover, I guess we can take care of that, eh? For one thing, we're willing to make the most generous on-sale proposition you ever hit."

The salesman left with Candee samples of the Skillyoolly dolls, and a blank contract. He would be back in his territory next month, he indicated, and he hoped to close the deal. He gave Candee two cigars and crooned:

"Absolutely all we want is to have you handle the Skillyoolly exclusively and give us a chance to show what we can do. 'You tell 'em, pencil, you got the point!'"

Candee took the dolls home to his wife, and now she was not merely wifely and plump and compliant. She squealed.

"I think they're perfectly darling! So huggable—just sweet. I know you could sell thousands of them a year. You must take them. I always thought the Jumas dolls were hideous."

"They aren't so darn hideous. Just kind of different," Candee said, uncomfortably.

Next morning he had decided to take the Skillyoolly agency— and he was as lonely and unhappy about it as a boy who has determined to run away from home.

Papa Jumas came in that day and Candee tried to be jolly and superior.

"Ah there, old monsieur! Say, I may fix up an arrangement to switch your dolls from my place to the Toy and China Bazaar."

Jumas lamented: "De Bazaar iss a cheap place. I do not t'ink they lige my t'ings."

"Well, we'll see, we'll see. Excuse me now. Got to speak to Miss Cogerty about—about morocco cardcases—cardcases."

He consulted Miss Cogerty and the lovely Miss Arnold of the batik lamp shades about the Skillyoolly dolls. Both of them squealed ecstatically. Yet Candee scowled at a Skillyoolly standing on his desk and addressed her:

"Doll, you're a bunch of fluff. You may put it over these sentimental females for a while, but you're no good. You're a rotten fake, and to charge two plunks for you is the darndest nerve I ever heard of. And yet I might make a thousand a year clear out of you. A thousand a year. Buy quite a few cord tires, curse it!"

At five Miss Sorrell bought some correspondence cards.

Candeee was afraid of Miss Sorrell. She was the principal of a private school. He never remembered what she wore, but he had an impression that she was clad entirely in well-starched, four-ply line collars. She was not a person to whom you could sell things. She looked at you sarcastically and told you what she wanted. But the girls in her school were fervid customers, and, though he grumbled, "Here's that old grouch," he concentrated upon her across the showcase.

When she had ordered the correspondence cards and fished the copper address plate out of a relentless seal purse, Miss Sorrell blurted: "I want to tell you how very, very much I appreciate the

Papa Jumas dolls. They are the only toys in Vernon that have imagination and solidity."

"Folks don't care much for them, mostly. They think I ought to carry some of these fluffy dolls."

"Parents may not appreciate them, and I suppose they're so original that children take a little time getting used to them. But my nephew loves his Jumas dolls dearly; he takes them to bed with him. We are your debtors for having introduced them."

As she dotted out, Candee was vowing: "I'm not going to have any of those Skillyoolly hussies in my place! I'm——— I'll fight for the Jumas dolls! I'll make people like 'em, if it takes a leg. I don't care if I lose a thousand a year on them, or ten thousand, or ten thousand million tillion!"

It was too lofty to last. He reflected that he didn't like Miss Sorrell. She had a nerve to try to patronize him! He hastened to his desk. He made computations for half an hour. Candee was an irregular and temperamental cost accountant. If his general profit was sufficient he rarely tracked down the share produced by items. Now he found that, allowing for rent, overhead, and interest, his profit on Papa Jumas dolls in the last four months had been four dollars. He gasped:

"Probably could make 'em popular if I took time enough. But— four dollars! And losing a thousand a year by not handling Skillyoollys. I can't afford luxuries like that. I'm not in business for my health. I've got a wife and kids to look out for. Still, I'm making enough to keep fat and cheery on, entirely aside from the dolls. Family don't seem to be starving. I guess I can afford one luxury. I——— Oh, rats!"

He reached, in fact, a sure, clear, ringing resolution that he would stock Skillyoolly dolls; that he'd be hanged if he'd stock Skillyoolly dolls; and that he would give nine dollars and forty cents if he knew whether he was going to stock them or not.

After the girls had gone out that evening he hinted to his wife: "I don't really believe I want to give up the Jumas dolls. May cost me a little profit for a while, but I kind of feel obligated to the poor old Frenchie, and the really wise birds—you take this Miss Sorrell, for instance—they appreciate———"

"Then you can't handle the Skillyoolly dolls?"

"Don't use that word! Skillyoolly! Ugh! Sounds like an old maid tickling a baby!"

"Now that's all very well, to be so superior and all—and if you mean that I was an old maid when we were married————"

"Why, Nelly, such a thought nev' entered my head!"

"Well, how could I tell? You're so bound and determined to be arbitrary tonight. It's all very well to be charitable and to think about that Jumas—and I never did like him, horrid, skinny old man!—and about your dolls that you're so proud of, but I do think there's some folks a little nearer home that you got to show consideration for, and us going without things we need————"

"Now I guess you've got about as many clothes as anybody ————"

"See here, Jimmy Candee! I'm not complaining about myself. I like pretty clothes, but I never was one to demand things for myself, and you know it!"

"Yes, that's true. You're sensible————"

"Well, I try to be, anyway, and I detest these wives that simply drive their husbands like they were packhorses, but———— It's the girls. Not that they're bad off. But you're like all these other men. You think because a girl has a new dancing frock once a year that she's got everything in the world. And here's Mamie crying her eyes out because she hasn't got anything to wear to the Black Bass dance, and that horrible Jason girl will show up in silver brocade or something, and Mamie thinks Win Morgan won't even look at her. Not but what she can get along. I'm not going to let you work and slave for things to put on Mamie's back. But if you're going to waste a lot of money I certainly don't see why it should go to a perfect stranger—a horrid old Frenchman that digs graves, or whatever it is—when we could use it right here at home!"

"Well, of course, looking at it that way————" sighed Candee.

"Do you see?"

"Yes, but there's a principle involved. Don't know that I can make it clear to you, but I wouldn't feel as if I was doing my job honestly if I sold a lot of rubbish."

"Rubbish? Rubbish? If there's any rubbish it isn't those darling Skillyoolly dolls, but those wretched, angular Jumas things! But if you've made up your mind to be stubborn——— And of course I'm not supposed to know anything about business! I merely scrimp and save and economize and do the marketing!"

She flapped the pages of her magazine and ignored him. All evening she was patient. It is hard to endure patience, and Candee was shaken. He was fond of his wife. Her refusal to support his shaky desire to "do his job honestly" left him forlorn, outside the door of her comfortable affection.

"Oh, I suppose I better be sensible," he said to himself, seventy or eighty times.

He was taking the Skillyoolly contract out of his desk as a cyclone entered the shop, a cyclone in brown velvet, white hair, and the best hat in Vernon—Mrs. Gerard Randall. Candee went rejoicing to the battle. He was a salesman. He was an artist, a scientist, and the harder the problem the better. Mechanically handing out quires of notepaper to customers who took whatever he suggested bored Candee as it would bore an exhibition aviator to drive a tractor. But selling to Mrs. Randall was not a bore. She was the eternal dowager, the dictator of Vernon society, rich and penurious and overwhelming.

He beamed upon her. He treacherously looked mild. He seemed edified by her snort:

"I want a penholder for my desk that won't look like a beastly schoolroom pen."

"Then you want a quill pen in mauve or a sea-foam green." Mrs. Randall was going to buy a quill pen, or she was going to die— or he was.

"I certainly do not want a quill pen, either mauve or pea-green or sky-blue beige! Quill pens are an abomination, and they wiggle when you're writing, and they're disgustingly common."

"My pens don't wiggle. They have patent grips———"

"Nonsense!"

"Well, shall we look at some other kinds?"

He placidly laid out an atrocious penholder of mother-of-pearl and streaky brass, which had infested the shop for years.

"Horrible! Victorian! Certainly not!"

He displayed a nickel penholder stamped, "Souvenir of Vernon," a brittle, red wooden holder with a cork grip, and a holder of chased silver, very bulgy and writhing.

"They're terrible!" wailed Mrs. Randall.

She sounded defenseless. He flashed before her eyes the best quill in the shop, crisp, firm, tinted a faint rose.

"Well," she said, feebly. She held it, wobbled it, wrote a sentence in the agitated air. "But it wouldn't go with my desk set," she attempted.

He brought out a desk set of seal-brown enamel and in the bowl of shot he thrust the rose quill.

"How did you remember what my desk set was like?"

"Ah! Could one forget?" He did not look meek now; he looked insulting and cheerful.

"Oh, drat the man! I'll take it. But I don't want you to think for one moment that I'd stand being bullied this way if I weren't in a hurry."

He grinned. He resolved, "I'm going to make the ole dragon buy three Jumas dolls—no, six! Mrs. Randall, I know you're in a rush, but I want you to look at something that will interest you."

"I suppose you're going to tell me that 'we're finding this line very popular,' whatever it is. I don't want it."

"Quite the contrary. I want you to see these because they haven't gone well at all."

"Then why should I be interested?"

"Ah, Mrs. Randall, if Mrs. Randall were interested, everybody else would have to be."

"Stop being sarcastic, if you don't mind. That's my own province." She was glaring at him, but she was following him to the back of the shop.

He chirped: "I believe you buy your toys for the your grandchildren at the Bazaar. But I want to show you something they'll really like." He was holding up a Gothic princess, turning her lanky magnificence round and round. As Mrs. Randall made an "aah" sound in her throat, he protested. "Wait! You're wrong. They're not ugly; they're a new kind of beauty."

"Beauty! Arty! Tea-roomy!"

"Not at all. Children love 'em. I'm so dead sure of it that I want——— Let's see. You have three grandchildren. I want to send each of them two Papa Jumas dolls. I'll guarantee———— No. Wait! I'll guarantee the children won't care for them at first. Don't say anything about the dolls, but just leave 'em around the nursery and watch. Inside of two weeks you'll find the children so crazy about 'em they won't go to bed without 'em. I'll send 'em up to your daughter's house and when you get around to it you can decide whether you want to pay me or not."

"Humph! You are very eloquent. But I can't stand here all day. Ask one of your young women to wrap up four or five of these things and put them in my car. And put them on my bill. I can't be bothered with trying to remember to pay you. Good day!"

While he sat basking at his desk he remembered the words of the schoolmistress, Miss Sorrell, "Only toys in Vernon that have imagination and solidity."

"People like that, with brains, they're the kind. I'm not going to be a popcorn-and-lemonade seller. Skillyoolly dolls! Any ten-year-old boy could introduce those to a lot of sentimental females. Takes a real salesman to talk Jumas dolls. And———— If I could only get Nell to understand!"

Alternately triumphant and melancholy, he put on his hat, trying the effect in the little crooked mirror over the water cooler, and went out to the Boosters' Club weekly lunch.

Sometimes the Boosters' lunches were given over speeches; sometimes they were merry and noisy; and when they were noisy Candeee was the noisiest. But he was silent today. He sat at the long table beside Darbin, the ice-cream manufacturer, and when Darbin chuckled invitingly, "Well, you old Bolshevik, what's the latest junk you're robbing folks for?" Candee's answer was feeble.

"That's all right, now! 'S good stuff."

He looked down the line of the Boosters—men engaged in electrotyping and roofing, real estate and cigar making; certified accountants and teachers and city officials. He noted Oscar Sunderquist, the young surgeon.

He considered: "I suppose they're all going through the same thing—quick turnover on junk *versus* building up something permanent, and maybe taking a loss; anyway, taking a chance. Huh! Sounds so darn ridiculously easy when you put it that way. Of course a regular fellow would build up the longtime trade and kick out cheap stuff. Only—not so easy to chase away a thousand or ten thousand dollars when it comes right up and tags you. Oh, gee! I dunno! I wish you'd quit fussing like a schoolgirl, Brother Candee. I'm going to cut it out." By way of illustrating which he turned to his friend Darbin. "Frank, I'm worried. I want some advice. Will it bother you if I weep on your shoulder?"

"Go to it! Shoot! Anything I can do———"

He tried to make clear to Darbin how involved was a choice between Papa Jumas and the scent pots of the Skillyoolly. Darbin interrupted:

"Is that all that ails you? Cat's sake! What the deuce difference does it make which kind of dolls you handle? Of course you'll pick the kind that brings in the most money. I certainly wouldn't worry about the old Frenchman. I always did think those Jumas biznai were kind of freakish."

"Then you don't think it matters?"

"Why, certainly not! Jimmy, you're a good business man, some ways. You're a hustler. But you always were erratic. Business isn't any jazz-band dance. You got to look at these things in a practical way. Say, come on; the president's going to make a spiel. Kid him along and get him going."

"Don't feel much like kidding."

"I'll tell you what I think's the matter with you, Jimmy; your liver's on the bum."

"Maybe you're right," croaked Candee. He did not hear the president's announcement of the coming clam bake. He was muttering in an injured way: "Damn it! Damn it! Damn it!"

He was walking back to the shop.

He didn't want to go back; he didn't care whether Miss Cogerty was selling any of the *écrasé* sewing baskets or not. He was repeating Darbin's disgusted: "What difference does it make? Why all the fuss?"

"At most I'd lose a thousand a year. I wouldn't starve. This little decision—nobody cares a hang. I was a fool to speak to Nelly and Darbin. Now they'll be watching me. Well, I'm not going to be an erratic fool. Ten words of approval from a crank like that Sorrell woman is a pretty thin return for years of work. Yes, I'll be sensible."

He spent the later afternoon in furiously rearranging the table of vases and candlesticks. "Exercise, that's what I need, not all this grousing around," he said. But when he went home he had, without ever officially admitting it to himself that he was doing it, thrust a Jumas doll and a Skillyoolly into his pocket, and these, in the absence of his wife, he hid beneath his bed on the sleeping porch. With his wife he had a strenuous and entirely imaginary conversation:

"Why did I bring them home? Because I wanted to. I don't see any need of explaining my motives. I don't intend to argue about this in any way, shape, or form!" He looked at himself in the mirror, with admiration for the firmness, strength of character, iron will, and numerous other virtues revealed in his broad nose and square—also plump—chin. It is true that his wife came in and caught him at it, and that he pretended to be examining his bald spot. It is true that he listened mildly to her reminder that for two weeks now he hadn't rubbed any of the sulphur stuff on his head. But he marched downstairs—behind her—with an imperial tread. He had solved his worry! Somehow, he was going to work it all out.

Just how he was going to work it out he did not state. That detail might be left till after dinner.

He did not again think of the dolls hidden beneath his bed till he had dived under the blanket. Cursing a little, he crawled out and set them on the rail of the sleeping porch.

He awoke suddenly and sharply, at sunup. He heard a voice—surely not his own—snarling: "Nobody is going to help you. If you want to go on looking for a magic way out—go right on looking. You won't find it!"

He stared at the two dolls. The first sunlight was on the Skillyoolly object, and in that intolerant glare he saw that her fluffy dress was sewed on with cheap thread which would break at the first rough handling. Suddenly he was out of bed, pounding the unfortunate Skillyoolly on the rail, smashing her simpering face, wrenching apart her ill-jointed limbs, tearing her gay chiffon. He was dashing into the bedroom, waking his bewildered wife with:

"Nelly! Nelly! Get up! No, it's all right. But it's time for breakfast."

She foggily looked at her wristwatch on the bedside table, and complained, "Why, it isn't but six o'clock!"

"I know it, but we're going to do a stunt. D'you realize we haven't had breakfast just by ourselves and had chance to really talk since last summer? Come on! You fry an egg and I'll start the percolator. Come on!"

"Well," patiently, reaching for her dressing gown.

While Candee, his shrunken bathrobe flapping about his shins, excitedly put the percolator together and attached it to the base-board plug, leaving out nothing but the coffee, he chattered of the Boosters' Club.

As they sat down he crowed: "Nelly, we're going to throw some gas in the ole car and run down to Chicago and back, next week. How's that?"

"That would be very nice," agreed Mrs. Candee.

"And we're going to start reading aloud again, evenings, instead of all this doggone double solitaire."

"That would be fine."

"Oh, and by the way, I've finally made up my mind. I'm not going to mess up my store with that Skillyoolly stuff. Going to keep on with the Jumas dolls, but push 'em harder."

"Well, if you really think———"

"And, uh——— Gee! I certainly feel great this morning. Feel like a million dollars. What say we have another fried egg?"

"I think that might be nice," said Mrs. Candee, who had been married for nineteen years.

"Sure you don't mind about the Skillyoolly dolls?"

"Why, no, not if you know what you want. And that reminds me! How terrible of me to forget! When you ran over to the Jasons' last evening, the Skillyoolly salesman telephoned the house—he'd just come to town. He asked me if you were going to take the agency, and I told him no. Of course I've known all along that you weren't. But hasn't it been interesting, thinking it all out? I'm glad you've been firm."

"Well, when I've gone into a thing thoroughly I like to smash it right through. . . . Now you take Frank Darbin; makes me tired the way he's fussing and stewing, trying to find out whether he wants to buy a house in Rosebank or not. So you—you told the Skillyoolly salesman no? I just wonder——— Gee! I kind of hate to give up the chance of the Skillyoolly market! What do you think?"

"But it's all settled now."

"Then I suppose there's no use fussing——— I tell you; I mean a fellow wants to look at a business deal from all sides. See how I mean?"

"That's so," said Mrs. Candee, admiringly. As with a commanding step he went to the kitchen to procure another fried egg she sighed to herself, "Such a dear boy—and yet such a forceful man."

Candee ran in from the kitchen. In one hand was an egg, in the other the small frying pan. "Besides," he shouted, "how do we know the Skillyoollys would necessarily sell so darn well? You got to take everything like that into consideration, and then decide and stick to it. See how I mean?"

"That's so," said Mrs. Candee.

NUMBER SEVEN TO SAGAPOOSE

I

Mr. Rabbitt had a puckery mouth, a mild mustache, a scratched suitcase, a button of the League of Traveling Salesmen, and no other landmarks whatever. If you had studied him for days, ten hours a day, you would have remembered nothing but his button and suitcase and mustache and diffident mouth.

Number Seven crawls into Sagapoose at nine in the evening, and if you are taking the branch line to Mount Forest you wait till ten-sixteen.

Mr. Rabbitt emerged from Number Seven, looked up and down the greasy plank platform, shook his head as though he couldn't see any way of making ten-sixteen come earlier than sixteen minutes after ten, and crossed the road to the Depot Lunch. He sat on a high stool at a counter covered with white oilcloth, and said to the waiter, "Cuppacofee and a slab of apple, please." As he stirred the coffee he noted that the waiter—who was also head waiter, chef, check boy, cashier, and cabaret—was a hot-eyed youth with hair so curly that the rope-colored kinks must have hurt. He was ferociously cleaning the kerosene stove.

"Kind of a slow town, Sagapoose," said Mr. Rabbitt.

The youth looked surly, "Yes, it's———" He exploded, "It's doggone slow! It's fierce!"

"I suppose there's some fellows that do best in a small town.

They like it. That's fine. They're happy. Then again, seems like some that are built for the big burgs. I guess they ought to go there, and get into the scrimmage. Now you—I'd say you were the scrappy kind. You hate too easy a life."

The youth twanged the tines of a toasting fork: "Yep, that's me. But Ma and Aunt Bessie think I'm crazy to want to get away."

"Yes, I'd kind of figured it out that way, somehow. What do you want to do?"

"I want to be a doctor. By golly, if I could be a surgeon——— Fat chance! Me, going to medical college! Aah!"

"Well, that's how it goes." They looked at each other ruminatingly. The youth seemed to draw comfort from the glance of the older man, which accepted him not as a boy nor as a lunchroom waiter, but as a human being. He listened sharply while Mr. Rabbitt droned:

"Now me, if I wanted to be a surgeon, I believe I'd go and borrow books off some doctor, and study 'em here at night. Kind of got a hunch that if the doc saw I was in earnest, if he saw I'd been studying, and could answer the questions he put to me, maybe he might help me to go to medic school. Of course I'd don't know. Gosh, I'm no sawbones! I'm a drummer, and not much good at it. But that's how I'd figure it. I wonder if most of us don't have as much trouble getting a start on a thing as we do making good after we've started. I guess it's up to us to kick in and make the start. Well, good night, old man. Thanks for helping me kill time between trains."

Mr. Rabbitt went away. Mr. Rabbitt took the ten-sixteen. It was twenty-three years before Mr. Rabbitt again spoke to the youth with the curly hair.

The name of that youth was Max Dixon. He was the son of a widow. Next morning he edged into Doctor Elder's office and growled that he would like to borrow *Gray's Anatomy*. He was surprised that the doctor did not laugh at him, and he gained confidence. He read the book. He made drawings of muscles and arteries. One year later Doctor Elder lent him a hundred dollars and bade him go to the state university. Seventeen years after Mr. Rabbitt's yawning exit from the Depot Lunch, Dr. Max Dixon was the most original and creative of the younger surgeons in Chicago.

Not once in the seventeen years did he think of a man named Rabbitt.

In the Great War Doctor Dixon was commissioned a colonel, but he was kept in a laboratory in Paris, studying gas bacillus and experimenting with the Carrel-Dakin solution on wounds. Among the respectful men under him in that series of tiled rooms were an Italian general, a Russian prince, and the daughter of an Oregon professor—she the best man of all those eager men who in the quiet fought portentous battles. Colonel Dixon had time one day to stop and look up. He was pleased and bewildered to discover that his girl assistant was pretty. Then, for three months, he had no more time for loafing; but the very next opportunity that came, he glared at her, took her to dinner, proposed, and married her.

The Dixons returned to the United States. The doctor perceived that with his skills and his wife's graciousness he was likely to be the biggest surgeon in Chicago. It cannot be reported that he did not think of the money. He could look forward to two or three hundred thousand a year; to a dozen servants, and a fleet of motors. Just at this agreeable time, he was pestered by an office to become head of the experimental surgical department of the Stone Foundation Laboratory. There he could develop the brain surgery which he had always liked and never had time to master. He might, perhaps, revolutionize two or three kinds of operations, and benefit mankind for all time, but—the salary was only ten thousand a year, and Dixon did like limousines, and his wife knew how to wear clothes.

He was nervous and confused. He irritably put off the decision and ran down to see his mother. In the smoking compartment of a Pullman connecting with Number Seven for Sagapoose, he met a Plain Man. If he thought about it at all, Doctor Dixon would have said that he had never seen this person before. But he vigorously didn't think about it.

The Plain Man was mild and scraggly. He peered at Doctor Dixon. "Nice weather," said he.

"I suppose so," growled Dixon, absorbed in his secret struggle. He rested his feet on a chair and regarded his supremely polished toes. The Plain Man fussed. He did all the kinds of fussing known to Pullman smokers.

He washed his face, making a snapping noise with the patent brass handles of the bowl, pumping the soap machine and trying to get enough liquid soap on the back of his left hand. He examined his lack of shave in the long mirror. He stared at the matchbox holder, gave up trying to produce matches by staring, and found a broken match and a lone ticket stub in his lower left vest pocket. He read the words on the ticket stub and sighed. He curled in a corner of the long seat and looked over the accumulated literature, which included one paper from Akron, one from Grand Rapids, and one manicure-outfit catalogue. He pulled down the curtain, got the runners off their rail and, with the curtain maddeningly askew, got them back. All the while he was watching Doctor Dixon, and at last he hinted:

"What's your line, brother?"

Curtly, "I'm a surgeon!"

"Oh, I see. I'm in shoes. Rabbitt is my name, Joseph D. Rabbitt. Now, you take selling shoes; that's a useful occupation—getting feet comfortable. But a surgeon—why, he's a miracle worker! Think of having life and death and happiness in your hands!"

"Humph! There's a lot of other things a surgeon has in his hands, too—bills for his wife's bonnets, and begging letters, and—— A surgeon is a fool if he isn't practical."

"That's so. But I guess you pay the rent all right, and get your three squares!"

"I do!" rudely.

"Then, after that, of course, the thing a fellow looks out for is fun. If we don't get fun out of life, we're not sure of getting anything. But I should think—— Of course, I'm just a seat-pounder, riding around in trains and waiting in depots. I got a suspicion I don't know a whole lot. Yes, sir, I'm an old dub circulatin' around and askin' fool questions. But I should think a surgeon would have more fun out of doing good operations, and maybe finding new ways to save lives, than out of vittles and swallowtails and being patronized by gold-painted young pups. Gee! He might find a way that would save the life of a Shakespeare of a Lincoln! That's miracles!"

"I suppose so," mumbled Doctor Dixon.

He was not attentive to the Plain Man's further ramblings—because he was framing a telegram to the Stone Foundation accepting the chair in experimental surgery.

Mr. Rabbitt left the train at Moler's Crossing. He waved his hand in farewell, but Doctor Dixon was not conscious of his going.

"Fine young fellow," reflected Mr. Rabbitt, as he lugged his ancient suitcase across to the Mansion House. "I wish I were a big gun like that, one that had power, that molded folks' lives. Huh! Listen to me ravin'! . . . Evening, Mr. Doherty. Got a room for me?"

II

Jake Maxom was the boss of Sagapoose County, in those days. He is gone now, and the illicit interests work by methods subtler than bribery; they are on the defensive and seek to show the world a new-washed visage of indignant virtue. But in 1895 Jake Maxon was boss, and he had, this afternoon, to pick a candidate for state senator. It was not easy. A lot of cranks were threatening the one true party. As he rose on Number Seven to Sagapoose, Jake lounged in the smoking car and scowled and marvelously spat. Beside him was a traveling man so neat and patient and uninspired that he wasn't worth pumping for gossip

"Nice weather," the traveling man ventured.

"Yuh," admitted Jake.

"You're Mr. Maxom, of Buffalo Bend."

"Yuh."

"My name's Rabbitt. I'm with the Excelsior Shoe people. I remember hearing in the Bend how you helped the Methodist fund."

It was the only thing acknowledged as virtuous that Jake had done in twenty years. He saw that Mr. Rabbitt was a sensible and understanding man.

"They tell me that the wise guys all listen to you, in politics. That's fine. Must be great to have power and help folks you were brought up with."

Jake was suspicious. "Aw, you got to look out for Number One in politics."

"That's so. You have to win elections before you can do anything else. So I suppose you'll be picking Le Peters for next state senator."

"Peters? Who the deuce is he?"

"Don't you know? Leonidas Peters, that young lawyer at Hebron? Smart fellow, smart's a whip. Never spoke to him—he wouldn't know me from Adam's off ox. But I heard him win the ditching case for the Widow Preston."

"Oh, *him!* Why, he's one of these up-crick reformers!" The devil's manner of referring to holy water, right at home, at breakfast, with nobody around but Mrs. Devil and the family, was loving compared with the manner in which Jake pronounced the word "reformers." "I've read about this Peters. Why, he takes law cases free! He's one of these goats that if they were let into the party they'd bust it wide open with a lot of fool theories. Theories! Gaw! Him state senator? Why, frien', when he gets to be state senator, I'll be the Emperor of Terre Haute! Who the et cetera ever even thought of mentioning him for senator?"

"Don't suppose anybody ever has," Mr. Rabbitt apologized. "Kind of too bad. Of course, I don't know a thing about politics. I just circulate around and peddle shoes. But of course anybody can see that unless you nominate some fellow like Le Peters, your party will get the tar licked out of it this fall. Too bad."

"B-but———— Suppose we did have to put up some yellow reformer. Why would anybody pick a dark horse like Peters?"

"Folks like him, at Hebron. They trust him. They say he's got a swell education. But, gosh, just listen to a ringer like me advising Jake Maxom! Nerve! But if I was you I'd ask the Hebron committee man what the farmers think of Le Peters. You know—just kind of out of curiosity. Prob'ly you'd find I was wrong."

Mr. Rabbitt tittered and, as Jake Maxom frowned and ignored him, opened the *Shoe and Leather Gazette* and read the personal items. Jake thought and spat. He nodded heavily when Mr. Rabbitt chirped, "Well, here's where I leave you!"

At Sagapoose, Jake's first remark to his prize township leader was, "What do you know about a lawyer named Leonidas Peters, or some such fool name, up Hebron way? I don't mean politically. He's nobody. But I got a hunch he might be good timber, this year. We godda look virtuous. What's he like?"

The township leader was admiring: "Never thought of Peters. Nice idee. He'd be one grand spieler, if you could ever get his nose out of his books. Say, you're a swell picker, Jake."

"Well, I got my eyes open. I don't go to sleep standing up, like some of you fellows!"

Mr. Leonidas Peters was elected state senator.

As he was unknown in most of the district, it was a fight. But he was reelected with ease—though he had outrageously kicked out his kind, helpful, wise friend, Mr. Jake Maxom. When he was nominated for governor of the state, he ran ahead of the ticket; and later his selection as United States senator was popular even among the cautious oligarchs of Up-in-the-City. His acquaintanceship in the state was enormous; but it did not happen to include a traveling salesman named Joseph D. Rabbitt, and when Senator Peters went on to Washington, he said no farewells to Rabbitts of any hue.

It was in Senator Peter's third term at Washington, when he was more used to Turkish baths than to Hebron Creek, that the Amson Child Labor Bill was introduced. It was a bill not at all popular with certain sorts of manufacturers. The senator liked it, but he also liked the clever friends who never, never did anything in such bad form as lobbying when they gave him small agreeable dinners.

"Have to be sensible. Perhaps those children are just as well off working and getting money ahead as going to school," he worried.

In his haystack of mail was a letter on the smudgy stationery of the Mansion House, Moler's Crossing. The writer said, among other artless things that were amusing to the sophisticated senator:

```
    Boss, you're a great man. But when you die you'll
die just as dead as us small fry. Now me, I'm a
drummer, an old drummer, crick-jointed and dry be-
hind the ears, and one of these days I'll cash in.
But I figure the Mansion House isn't any nearer to
the cemetery than Massachusetts Avenue is. This is
a bum old tavern, Senator. They still dish up spin-
ach that looks like a lake jam-full of reeds—like
the lake you must have paddled in as a kid in
```

Hebron. Remember? You were a poor kid. You'd rather have gone to school ánd become a lawyer than work in factories. You liked to read. Well, Senator, I'm just rambling on; but as a fresh constituent I'd like to ask you, when you do make the last big jump, will you want to see a lot of pale dead little kids standing between you and St. Peter? Rats, here I am getting slushy as a wedding! And the nerve of me writing to man that's sat at dinner with Joffre and the Prince of Wales! Say, Senator, I made Hebron last week, on a jump here from Sagapoose. I saw the house they told me you were raised in. On the barn were some old blurred figures in paint. I wonder if maybe you didn't make them when you were a kid trying to get an education. Remember? Right on the north side of the barn they were, near the corn crib.

Yours respfy,

Joseph D. Rabbitt

The senator looked up at his secretary. "Here's a constit signing himself Joseph D. Rabbitt. Know who he is?"

"Never heard of him, sir."

"Well, I——— Say, bring me the report on the Amson Bill hearing. I think I'll run through it again."

"You told Senator Filbert———"

"I don't care a whoop what I told Filbert! I've been thinking, and I believe it's a good bill and ought to be reported out of committee."

"Any answer to this Rabbitt letter, sir?"

"Rabbitt, Rabbitt, what do you mean, Rabbitt?"

"The letter you were just reading."

"That? Oh, that. Just skimmed through it—don't exactly remember what was in it. Shoot him some Back Home stuff. Now bring me the Amson data."

The Amson Child Labor Bill was passed at that session of Congress. It would not have been passed without Senator Peter's support. It affected the lives of about three thousand children. It was for this service to this bill that Senator Peters received his well merited degree of LL.D. from Harrodale.

III

Mr. Rabbitt was elegantly sojourning at the Grancourt Hotel, Chicago. The Excelsior Shoe Company insisted that its representatives be known as staying at the most expensive hotels, and Mr. Rabbitt's suitcase, now whiskery with age, lay timorously on a chair done in amethyst velvet. But that did not mean that Mr. Rabbitt dined at the Grancourt.

Augustly strolling through Peacock Alley, Mr. Rabbitt stalked out of the hotel, hastily dropped his poise, and sneaked across the street to dinner at the Scranton Lunch.

He sat at a long marble-topped table beside a smallish, youngish woman, and as he gravely wolfed his breaded veal chop, coffee, and mince pie, Mr. Rabbitt studied her. She slowly messed at her corned-beef hash. Her eyes were stained. She reread a letter with the heading "Hotel Beau Temps." Mr. Rabbitt caught one line of the letter:

```
    . . . why you stand for him when I am waiting and
    crazy to show you a good time?
```

"Will you please pass the salt?" said Mr. Rabbitt to the young woman.

He tried to find something on which to use the salt, failed, looked foolish, and went on:

"Nice weather."

"Is it?"

"Come to think of it, it isn't. Sister, I'm an old drummer. I'm old enough so's I can't seem to keep from butting in. So———— Why don't you put your wedding ring back on? Or you might lose it."

She answered with a dreadful catch of breath.

"Not that I think wedding rings are necessarily sacred. Nothing is sacred unless you think it is. But, still, you'd hate to lose it just by carelessness, eh?"

"How————"

"Why, sister, that red streak round your finger is a dead give-away. Pretty bad, was he? Not much shakes of a husband? Cranky?"

"He was! He was beastly! He never appreciated anything I did! He'd come in and throw his overalls, with paint on them, right on my nice clean floor, and sit down to supper and never say one word. I couldn't stand it. I won't!"

"I know. Men. Not much good. Thick-skinned. Never been married, myself. Guess a woman would find it hard to live with me. I tell tough stories, and cuss and swear and shoot craps and chew tobacco. Oh, I'm an old he-one, a hairy old he-one. Yet if I was married, I figure that sometimes I might be meaning to be a lot nicer than the wife ever savvied. I know. Funny geezers, husbands. But now this fellow that got you to run away—he's nice, eh?"

"He's wonderful! He's handsome, and so rich—he wears a diamond as big as, as big as anything. And he's always so polite, and he appreciates my ideas!"

"That's so. Probably he's a good fellow. Probably easy to fool him. Probably doesn't know what a rotten hole the Beau Temps is. I guess he's kind of a simp!"

"He—is—not! He's the—he's the smartest man I ever met!"

"Funny, then, his being fooled into staying at a place like that. I don't understand it."

Mr. Rabbitt looked puzzled. So did the woman.

"Tell you, sister. I'd find out, before I went to him, how come a smart man like your new fellow could be fooled into wanting to take you to the Beau Temps. Just ask any cop about that place!"

"I don't care! I love him!"

"That's right. Fine thing, love. Sure. But just first, I mean, I'd wait and find how he got fooled about the place. Great joke on him! You'll have a fine chance to jolly him about it! So I'd—I'd just wait, and let him do some explaining."

"I can't. I haven't any more money."

"Well, maybe you'll find a job. Say, for instance, as chamber-maid in the Grancourt, right across the street. Be fun to work in a tony place like that!"

"Oh, it would! To see the swell people———"

"You bet. Elegant. No guests at the Grancourt but what are

millionaires! That's how it is. Well, good night. Say, uh——— If I was a pretty girl like you, and knew how crazy my husband was about me———"

"I won't go back to that hole, ever!"

"That's right. You're your own boss. I just mean——— Maybe he'd look different, if he was up here in Chicago. Before I tied up with my new fellow, I'd kind of let hubby have my address, and then if he loved me enough to come up here and be decent——— But you're right. Sure. Don't go back—unless you want to. Well, here I am butting in and giving advice. Nerve! Good night. If you sent your husband your address—just to see what happened—might be fun, eh?"

Mr. Rabbitt poked out of the lunchroom, across the street, into the Grancourt lobby. He noted that the door of the Gold Ballroom was closed and he caught a rustle of talk and music. He smiled on the captain of the bell boys.

"Big doings?" he hinted.

"Big is right. Swell dinner," said the captain, with a nice commingling of respect and authority. "Senator Peters, United States Senator, is a giving a dinner to Dr. Max Dixon—you know, the new head of this Stone Foundation. They say the senator is going to spring the idea of a government health department, and if he gets it through, he'll support the doc for first Secretary of Health. Oh, they're starting something in there tonight!"

"Well, by golly! I saw Senator Peters once, years ago, when he was just a kid lawyer. Like to see him again. And I sure would like to lay an eye on Doctor Dixon. I keep reading about him, but I never did see him. Hear he's a world-beater. Don't suppose there'd be some way I could sneak up in a balcony or something and just get a little peek at 'em, do you?"

"Afraid it's impossible, sir."

"Well, that's right. Folks like them—they're kind of royalty. Got to work in private. Good night."

As he entered his room, after writing his letters, Mr. Rabbitt sighed, "I'd like to have the influence of Dixon or Peters, just for one hour. Oh, I'm a fool, and I'm getting to be an old fool. Me—influence!"

He squared his suitcase on the velvet chair, took out his old-fashioned, red-edged cotton nightgown, fussily brushed his teeth, just so many times across, just so many times up and down, and opened the window nine inches, no more, no less. He lay in bed, an insignificant, work-marked, rather rustic figure in that magnificence of florid spread and cane-and-maple headboard.

"Old and foolish—and fussy," he reflected. "Yes, and selfish. Regular old bach. I ought to have given the world a son like Doc Dixon, and given him a start in medicine. I'm an old deuce of spades. And yet I've had a good time, wanderin' around and talking to different kinds of folks. People always been mighty nice to me. I wish I could have peeked at Dixon. That'd be something to tell the boys on the road about. But——— Had a good time———"

He was asleep, making a small, mild, rhythmic bumble.

One hundred feet straight below him, in the Gold Room, the Honorable Leonidas Peters was concluding, "So we see here to-night, gentlemen, the beginning of a movement which may save a million lives a year! Can history since time began show such a victory?" (Tremendous applause.)

Mr. Rabbitt stirred in his sleep as he dreamed that he had sold the biggest bill of shoes the Excelsior people had seen in six months.

One hundred feet straight above him, in the maids' quarters, a woman who had that evening found work as chambermaid tore up a sheet headed "Hotel Beau Temps," and began a letter to her husband. It was a grudging, illiterate letter, yet through its gray there sifted a tremor of dawn.

A fugitive from advertising, Anthony Di Renzo teaches professional writing and American business history at Ithaca College. His essays and satires, which have appeared in such journals as *Syracuse Scholar*, *Il Caffé*, and *River Styx*, often depict the clash between American commercialism and Italian-American culture. His critical study, *American Gargoyles: Flannery O'Connor and the Medieval Grotesque* (Southern Illinois University Press, 1993), was named a *Choice* Academic Book of the Year and was nominated for an MLA Prize for First Scholarly Book. *At the Round Earth's Imagined Corners*, his novel-in-progress, is both a roast of Lee Iacocca and an elegy to the Northside, Syracuse's Little Italy.